I0652799

THE BEGINNING & THE END

Selena Jones

Mint in Box Press

This novel is a work of fiction. Any references to real people, events, establishments, organizations, or locales are intended only to give the fiction a sense of authenticity and are used fictitiously. All other names, characters, and places, and all incidents portrayed in this book are the product of the author's imagination.

THE BEGINNING AND THE END. Copyright © 2014 by Selena Jones. All rights reserved. Printed in the United States of America. No part of this book may be used or reproduced in any manner without written permission except in the case of brief quotations embodied in critical articles and reviews.

For more information: Visit www.selenawrotethis.com

Book Layout and Cover Design by Ana Maria Jappe

ISBN-13: 978-0615999241
ISBN-10: 0615999247

First Mint in Box Press edition: October 2014

For Dana.
You put up with me,
and I don't know what that says about you
but thank you and please don't stop.

1

"Please," he said.

"You are weak. Your body is overrun with disease. Let me take you to the hospital."

A sigh, filled with exhaustion. "Do you work for the hospital?"

"No. I am not a doctor. But there are others—"

"I want no one else. Please."

Iliana slipped onto the satin cushions beside her client and covered his hand with hers. With the fingertips of her other hand she swept the damp tendrils of hair from his eyes. She kissed his forehead, her painted lips leaving a ring of red.

"Let me help you," she urged. His fever burned her lips. Even as she offered help she was not sure the doctors could save him.

His body trembled in her arms. He pressed some folded bills into her hand, payment for the services he was about to receive. "Just love me."

Iliana slipped the money into a hidden pocket in her dress and complied with her client's wishes. She pressed him back onto the cushions and stroked his hair. His bloodshot eyes drifted shut as her fingertips danced down toward his temples. He sighed again. His left hand caressed a velvet pillow, drawing nonsense pictures across its surface.

She trailed her hands down his right arm and then lifted it. One by one Iliana touched his heated fingers to her lips and a shiver passed from his body to hers. He was impatient. His skin smelled of fear and sickness, of sweat and moist earth warmed by the sun.

"Would you like a prayer?"

"You are my God."

It was never Iliana's intention to assume that role so she did not offer him a prayer.

His arm lay open before her, the many scars and healing scabs like a garden of wounds planted in his flesh. Iliana slashed the crook of his elbow with her metal thumb. The blood spurted in a crimson fountain that spilled down his arm. Iliana removed the blood-drawing tool and set it aside, then bowed her head to meet the wound. His arteries trembled with the passage of his blood, quickened by her touch.

She closed her eyes and joined him on a trip into his past. She experienced skinned knees and first kisses, the unexpected promotion at a hated job, the anguish of losing his wife as his newborn daughter, slick and mottled purple, screamed in his arms. Events and faces and names streamed by up to this, his last conscious memory, and there the flight stalled. She experienced his mounting panic, his last epic battle against mortality as a growing ache in her heart. And when his fever began to flush her cheeks Iliana released his arm.

She sat back and watched the movement of his chest slow, become shallow, cease completely. Withdrawing a crisp, white handkerchief from her bodice Iliana patted her mouth. The cloth came back with an imprint of her lips in a telling brownish-red. She pulled her logbook from her bodice and made an entry, then and scowled to realize that she was still behind. But the night was still young.

After notifying maintenance of the body she went out into the streets, where the endless hum of thousands of lost souls yearning for benediction buoyed her strength for the long night ahead.

It was the end of the month and Iliana had a quota to fill before sunrise.

2 The walls inside the bar were dark red and peppered with octagons of beveled glass. The space was tunnel-like and solid with bodies. Their dark clothing swallowed the light. Their voices blended into one indistinct chant, rising and falling as the swells of interest turned and returned, now multiplied, now diminished. And beneath it all surged a powerful tension, the tension of promises yet unfilled.

Iliana swept into this atmosphere, her body filled with such grace that she seemed to float across the ruddy brown tiled floor. She ensnared all eyes that looked upon her but she ignored those men already claimed by her colleagues. Her eyes roamed the crowd, searching for a solitary man, a potential client. And she didn't have to look long. He sat at the bar. The wood before him glittered with empty glasses and he gripped his head with both hands as if afraid it might fall off. Illness seeped from his hunched form, assaulting her nostrils, pungent as mold. Once seen, she knew she couldn't leave him like that.

The din of a hundred voices muffled her footsteps and when she reached out and pressed the man's shoulder he shied away from the contact with his entire body. When he turned to see who had touched him his torso lurched sideways and he slipped from his padded black barstool and came to rest, arms and legs akimbo, on the tile.

Some who had seen this graceless fall chuckled but Iliana did not smile. Instead she caught the eye of the bartender to draw him over and inquired as to how long the man had been there.

"Every night for the past three weeks. He comes in, sits on that same stool and drinks till sunrise."

"Has he been with any escorts?" Iliana asked, though she

already knew the answer. The state he was in, she couldn't believe any of her peers would take him and not heal him.

"Not one. He practically hisses like an angry cat if anyone gets too close to him."

"Where is he staying?"

The bartender didn't know. Iliana knelt beside the man, careful not to let her dress pool on the filthy floor, and touched his forehead. At the moment of contact she knew he was more than ill as death swept through her like a fever. He needed help. And perhaps he would be so grateful to be well again that he would make up the remainder of her quota.

She stood and called out, "Will anyone volunteer to help me carry this man back to my cell?"

In a moment three young men were bearing the body through the streets of frenzied partiers to the center of the city and the Palace Nyssa. They garnered little attention from the tourists, who were too busy indulging their desires to notice anything else. But once the group passed within the black iron gates of the Palace they drew the eyes of curious Natives. Iliana nodded politely at those she knew, other escorts trussed in the ornate costumes of their trade, but she stopped for no one. The grave procession climbed the stone steps and passed through the main Palace doors, which had been hewn from two enormous blocks of wood and carved inside and out with the serene faces of cherubs and seraphim.

The foyer of the Palace glowed from the light of hundreds of candles that reflected in gilded mirrors and walls papered with golden scrollwork. Iliana led her troupe to the elevators through the crowd of clients awaiting their escorts. She watched her reflection in the mirrored doors as she waited, stoic. Her eyes never wavered to meet the questioning glances.

The elevator arrived. They boarded it, her helpers backing up against the plush walls to avoid crowding Iliana. Only after she pressed the button for the twenty-ninth floor did she finally acknowledge the onlookers with a radiant smile. Then with a rattle and a clang the doors slid shut.

3 In Cole's dream he lay immobile in darkness. He could not defend himself against the two rabid, toothy creatures that grasped his wrists and fed off of him. Little teeth like needles pricked him over and over, pausing just long enough for him to heal before beginning the assault once more.

It was dark when he opened his eyes, the kind of darkness that was a precursor to madness, cloying as honey. The muggy air entered and left his lungs in gentle waves, slow and steady, lapping against his panic, eroding it.

He lay still for a moment in that tomblike darkness, wondering where he was, if he had been struck blind, if God had finally punished him for his many sins. But his vision returned like an unwilling accomplice when the faintest bit of sunrise slipped in through the high, tiny windows and revealed the soft shadows of an unfamiliar room that appeared to be empty save for him.

Cole's lips formed the phrase, "Thank God," but he did not believe that this change in scenery was a miracle. He had lost his faith in the miraculous.

Cole cleared his throat and absorbed his surroundings. He sat in a square-shaped pit filled with a thick layer of colorful velvet and satin pillows, situated in the center of the room. Indistinguishable forms of dark furniture dotted the walls between thick, stone pillars with ornate tops and enormous square bases. A black chandelier, the candles snuffed, dangled from the vaulted ceiling where someone had painted a portrait of a reclining woman. Translucent fabric swathed her body and a devious smile lifted the corners of her mouth. Her heavy-lidded eyes seemed to mock him.

While Cole tried to discern exactly which damaged parts of

him she seemed to be mocking he heard a voice.

"Hello, Father."

Cole jumped at the sound and rotated on his knees as his fingers moved automatically into his pants pocket but clutched only the lining.

"Why'd you call me Father?" he asked, lifting his gaze in the direction of the voice.

A woman with the carriage of a queen sat before him on a divan the same blue-black color of her dress. The streaks of sunlight had not yet reached her but her skin seemed luminescent. Her dark hair was pulled back from her glowing face and twisted atop her head. Her eyes regarded him with humor. One of her glowing hands stroked the arm of the divan as if it were a favored pet.

She looked like living, breathing sin and Cole steeled himself against her. She seemed to know what he was and he recognized her as well. She was an escort, and by the opulence of their surroundings, a well-paid one. Cole wondered whether disclosure of this situation would destroy his chances of ever returning to his position within the Church. And then he wondered if he even cared.

"I called you Father," she began in a voice so soft it commanded silence, "because I found these in your pocket."

She lifted one hand and his eyes followed the string of uneven white pearls dangling there: his prayer beads, the different names for the One True God spinning on silver discs between the pearls. Then she raised her other hand, the hand that had been stroking the couch, and Cole saw that it held his red collar that identified him as a Priest of the Ceremonial Church. The three gold lines on one end of the collar further marked him as a high-ranking member of the Church Congress.

He asked himself for the hundredth time since his arrival in Adara Vega why he had brought that with him. And was that why she had brought him back to her room? Had she recognized the symbol of his status? Had he been kidnapped? Cole felt the panic once again rising to the surface, tempered by righteous anger that she would dare to act against a Church Leader.

"Give them back," Cole demanded through clenched teeth.

"Anyone else would leave all remembrances of home at home. Only a priest would bring something on vacation that might allow him to talk himself out of whatever it is he's worried he'll do. Only a priest would carry his guilt around with him like a security blanket, a favorite toy. What do you think, Father…"

"Cole," he answered without thinking.

"Cole. Father Cole."

"Why did you bring me here? What do you want from me?"

She ignored his indignation. Rolling each bead of his necklace between finger and thumb in a semblance of prayer, she said, "Oh, I've already taken all I want from you. My name is Iliana, by the way… And you should thank me."

"Why?" he sneered as his eyes searched the room for an exit. But the farthest walls remained obscured by shadows and drapery.

He turned back to her. The light touched her now and he watched as her lips curled into a smile of the same sort as the woman painted on the ceiling. "How are you feeling, Father Cole?"

He realized then that he was not sick. His body felt healthy and rested and hungry, a combination not often experienced during his recent binge. But instead of showing gratitude toward this creature that had obviously helped him, he became incensed.

"What have you done to me?"

"I cleaned you out."

"You are a demon," he spat, scooting away from her on the floor until his hand brushed the cold, polished stone on the other side of the pit. "The One True God will protect me!"

"Yes, because demons make a habit of saving lives. Besides, how will your god protect you when you wear your protection in your pocket? It is not like a Congress member to hide the symbol of his status."

"What do you know about it?"

She stood and walked around the rim of the pit to where he cowered. Her antique-looking dress with its full skirt and enormous bustle challenged the silence with its white noise as she moved. "You have no idea how many men I have seen, men just like you, gone mad for lack of freedom, suffocating beneath their own decisions. This is why we escorts exist, why so many people come here each year. To escape—"

"You don't know me…"

"Tell me then, why did you come here? You can be riddled with self-doubt just as effectively in another city… a city with fewer temptations."

She waited for him to answer. At first he was not about to comply but when the silence became uncomfortable and it appeared that she would wait all day for his answer he finally said, "In another city I would have to wear my collar."

"And here you have anonymity. Here you are just one more lost soul among the sinners scavenging for meaning."

"Something like that," he agreed, though she hadn't quite summed up his entire existence. She couldn't have understood what he had seen, what had made him leave, and he couldn't tell her. Still, he didn't feel she had the right to distill his complicated emotions into one callous sentence. "Let me go."

Iliana smiled then and her face lit up with an innocence so convincing he found himself wanting to believe it. "You are not a prisoner. Go," she said, gesturing toward a corner of the room still dark with night.

Cole clambered to his feet, anger and shame making his movements jerky and imprecise. "Where am I?"

"You are in the center of the city, the Final Circle, in the Palace Nyssa. Twenty-ninth floor dormitories." Iliana backed away from him, her hands pressed together before her in feigned modesty.

"The Final Circle," he muttered, "The center of Hell. How fitting."

"Your mythology, not mine."

Cole turned, stumbled over the pillows, threw open the door and ran from the woman and her wickedness as fast as he was able. As he stood in the elevator he reached into his pocket for his beads. Finding the pocket empty, he began to sweat. He had left his collar and prayer beads behind.

4 Iliana hadn't been asleep for long before a soothing voice eased her into wakefulness. "Good morning, sister. Or rather, good afternoon. I trust you slept well. Though not as well as I did, I'm sure."

She opened her eyes and then shut them once more as the harsh afternoon sunlight struck her full in the face like a celestial spotlight. The day was old already. She slid to the foot of her bed and lowered herself onto the floor, to a place where the sun had not yet reached, before she opened her eyes again.

Iliana looked up into the angular brown face of her older brother smiling down at her with manufactured benevolence. His thick black eyebrows were peaked in interest. Over his shoulder her bedroom door stood open and sunlight painted the walls in the ante-room.

"I heard you spent all night with the same man, you naughty girl." Adam placed his grinning face directly in front of hers. His breath smelled bitter, like strong coffee.

Iliana grasped his perfectly dimpled cheeks and pushed his face away. He sat on the floor beside her and swept his hair from his eyes. He kept it long in front and short in back just for that purpose. It made the clients swoon, men and women alike. Iliana just rolled her eyes. She was used to his practiced gestures just as he, no doubt, was used to hers.

She wiped at her face with a lazy hand and began to slip the pins from her hair and rub the spots where they had bothered her skull all night. Each tendril of her night-colored hair spilled down her shoulders like a dark waterfall and pooled into the hollow of her lap.

"Who told you?"

He plopped down beside her on the floor and though his body was strong and angular, grace infused his every movement. He spoke with an easy excitement, like a lazy thunderstorm. While they were alone he could drop the games and formalities of speech invented to attract clientele and become his true self, the self that Iliana both loved and lamented.

"Everyone saw you carrying him in last night like a funeral procession. And then just after the sun rose the guards saw him run out of here as if the devil himself were chasing him. What did I tell you about scaring the clients?"

"I didn't scare him."

"But you know you're not allowed to spend the entire night with one client unless it's pre-approved and he pays up front. I checked the books. You only had one scheduled appointment."

"And?"

"What could you possibly do to him that would take all night?"

"I cleaned him out." She placed the last hairpin on the floor beside her and began to massage her scalp and comb through her hair with her fingers.

"What'd you get for it?"

She shrugged, "Nothing. He ran away before I could even mention payment."

"So you did scare him then."

Iliana smiled to think of the priest's obvious terror. "I may have, but I didn't mean to."

"What do you mean?"

"He was a member of the Church Congress. High-ranking, too."

Adam's face lit up as it always did at the idea of intrigue. "You didn't ask him for money but you heard his life story?"

"Not quite. He had prayer beads and a red collar in his pocket. They... fell out at some point during the cleansing process."

"Of course they did. How many bars did he have?"

"Three. And one looked new."

"Wow. Two steps away from Father Demon—"

"Father Deven, you mean."

"I said what I meant. So he was two steps from the big

boss… Even I've never had one that high. What was his name?"

"Father Cole."

"Cole? I've never heard of him."

"Neither have I," Iliana admitted.

Adam rose and brushed off the seat of his black leather pants. "I must be off so you're on your own."

"What does that mean?"

"Governor Drake was asking about you because your totals were down. I told him you just forgot to turn in your paperwork."

"How kind of you." Iliana began to construct an excuse for her poor performance. She stood and placed her hairpins in a silver dish on top of her dressing table then met her gaze in the mirror that hung above it. Exhaustion shone in her dark blue eyes but was not evident elsewhere on her face. She sighed and bit her bottom lip, which was still stained a dull rose color from last night's lipstick.

"Don't get snippy. I was just trying to help. Drake should be here any minute," He tousled Iliana's hair. "So try to look presentable."

"How were your totals?"

He grinned and leaned up against the open doorway. "Above average, as usual. The people love me."

Iliana plucked a pillow from her disheveled bed and threw it at him but he was too quick. The door to her cell closed and the pillow hit the wall instead. With the promise of a visit from the Governor looming over her head her actions with the priest seemed ill-advised. She should have cleaned him out and then put him back on the street so that she could get through as many clients as possible. At least then she could honestly say that she tried.

She was not frightened of punishment. She had not done enough yet to lose her status as the darling of the Palace. But her totals for the last few months had been abnormally low and the Governor would likely scold her, which was quite inconvenient.

She had not even time enough to think of an excuse before the door in the outer cell opened once more and she heard the Governor's voice call out, "Hello, Iliana?"

"In here," answered Iliana as she took her place behind a tri-fold screen painted with a tranquil desert sunrise and began to shed her wrinkled clothing from the night before.

Governor Drake opened her bedroom door without knocking. The many medals given to him by the Church glittered on his chest like little stars in the streaming sunlight. He had combed his thick, silver hair straight back from his face to the top of his stiff collar, where it became unruly and curled into little ringlets. A thin layer of vivid blue paint covered all of his wrinkled features from his hairline to just beneath his chin. The paint had little effect on Iliana. Because she knew it was there she could see two faces looking out at her: one was the smooth face of a handsome, youthful man and the other was the Governor's true face, that of a wrinkled old man who, once upon a time, may have turned heads, but not anymore. Not without help.

With the paint applied, clients could be bewitched into seeing an old man as a handsome gallant, an old woman as a youthful seductress. The magic in the paint was what kept her people working long after age stole their beauty. This deception was a necessary evil if they wanted to keep up with the ever-increasing taxes imposed upon them by the Church.

Despite the paint Iliana recognized the Governor for what he was, an old man growing older by the second and terrified of death, of leaving his people with nothing to cling to. The Governor had fought for them against the Church, making both friends and enemies in the process, but mostly the latter. And once he was dead and no longer there to fight for them, he feared the Church would swoop in and annihilate the entire race, finish the job they had begun hundreds of years ago. He wanted a legacy. He wanted an empire like the ones his people had before the Colonists came and stole their land and their lives, but the likelihood of that faded a little more with each passing day.

Governor Drake sank down onto the foot of her bed, shaking his head so that some strands of flyaway hair waved before his face like silver ribbons in the sunlight. His features were pinched toward the center of his face the way they always were when he was deep in thought. Iliana thought he looked like a piece of old, wrinkled fruit and stifled a smile.

"Iliana, what are you doing?" he panted. He was out of breath as if he had climbed the stairs all the way to her cell.

"What do you mean?"

"Your totals are down. You haven't logged many clients this month and then last night you bring one here who doesn't leave until morning... What am I to think?"

Iliana wrapped herself in a black satin robe and came out from behind the screen. She sat beside Drake on the bed and met his stern gaze with ease to show him that she didn't have anything to hide.

"That was unintentional. I expected him to wake up shortly after I cleaned him out. He was supposed to pay and leave but he didn't wake up until sunrise and I couldn't just leave him in my room alone."

"I hope you charged him for the night then?"

"He was just so upset..." She looked down at her hands and spun the delicate silver rings she was wearing around and around her fingers.

"You didn't charge him?"

"I didn't get a chance to—"

"Iliana," he began and she knew a lecture was to follow. She worked hard not to roll her eyes at the words she had heard countless times. "You are smart. You know what men need and you give it to them. You have been among the top earners ever since you came out as an escort but these last few months have been rather disappointing. And right now we cannot afford to be disappointing. The eyes of the Church are watching us, searching for weaknesses."

"But surely one person—"

"One person can ruin us all!" His voice trembled with suppressed emotion and Iliana wondered what had him so upset. He was usually a stoic man but today he seemed like an exposed nerve, jumpy and unsure. When he withdrew a handkerchief from his breast pocket and pressed it to his glistening forehead his hand shook. The blue paint did not smear.

"This is all that the Church left us. This is what we are to do if we are to survive. You are special to me but if I let you get away with not carrying your weight it will cause derision among your peers. We can't afford that."

"I understand," she lied. Governor Drake was exaggerating, of course, but she enjoyed the personal attention he gave her. And she knew that it was his protection that kept her where she was, privileged above the others. She was not related to him by birth but when she was a child he had taken a special interest in her. Iliana had been told that it had something to do with her mother, who was dead and therefore unavailable for comment.

"Do you really understand?" he asked. He touched her arm. His hand was warm.

"Yes," she said and looked away, surprised by the unexpected feeling of guilt that swept through her. Drake had been so kind over the years that she didn't like to disappoint him.

"I am not trying to punish you but I do expect better from you in the coming weeks. I need your cooperation. We all need to work together to survive. Maybe someday soon things will be different, but for now—"

"Different? When?" Iliana's mind jumped to a time where she would not have to work all night every night, to a time when they would not be under the Church's thumb, when she could leave the prison of Adara Vega and see the world.

The Governor blanched beneath the blue paint and shook his head. "Never mind, Iliana. Just the wishes of an old man who is tired of seeing his people suffer. I want things to be better for you."

"Oh," she said, deflated.

She stood and walked the few steps to her dressing table, where various bottles of perfume and cosmetics huddled in groups like regiments of soldiers awaiting their orders. She wondered what character she would play that night.

"I have to go now," said Governor Drake. As he stood both of his knees popped and Iliana saw him wince. "The Council is having a meeting this evening and I must prepare."

"What about?" she asked, but her interest flagged when she noticed the priest's prayer beads lying coiled among the bottle-soldiers like a snake. She had wondered where they were.

The Governor noted her distraction and so told her, "We are strategizing to remove ourselves from the Church's rule with the help of a secret weapon."

Those last words brought Iliana back to reality with a shudder and filled her mind with bloody, menacing shadows. She blinked to clear the thoughts from her face. "What? Secret weapon?"

He chuckled and squeezed her shoulder. "I'm joking, of course. We are just going to discuss the Festival of Semiveh, the births we will have. You know, your name is on the list this year."

She sneered and wrinkled her nose. "I do not want to have a child now. Perhaps next time."

"We shall see," he said. As he walked to the outer door he added, "Make me proud tonight, Iliana."

But the words fell on deaf ears, for Iliana was already searching the floor around her dressing table for the priest's scarlet collar. It was time to collect what she was owed from the wayward priest, whether he liked it or not.

5 The day was restless. Within the gleaming city a ripple of anticipation made the few people who braved the uncertain weather short-tempered. Beyond the fortified city walls the desert lay wrapped in the steel gray arms of a sudden storm. Every now and then a purple bolt of lightning seared the air and thunder invaded the city. Even with the coming storm the heat pressed against the skin, insistent, extracting sweat.

Cole was drunk again. He leaned against the balcony railing and glared at the people strolling beneath him, at the facades of the buildings across the street, the dimpled stone and corners blunted by the desert climate, but he could find God in none of these things. The world that met his eyes was too fake, too harsh, the people too stiff and uncertain and devoid of life, of humanity.

He wanted to call out to the people, to clasp hands and speak words of benediction and prayer over them. He wanted to listen to their confessions, to hear voices lifted in song, to give absolution. But he was not among souls who craved repentance, at least not until they returned, guilty and sated, to their lives, their homes and their churches.

And then, out of the trickle of meandering bodies below him, a random face lifted, a stranger's eyes met his eyes and the world dissolved around him. And when it reassembled Cole was reliving memories, searching for meaning out of the sad, painful images. That single face in the street transformed into the face of one of the young Natives he had seen in the dungeon below the Church's capitol building. They were the first Natives Cole had ever seen.

A floor to ceiling chain fence had penned in a group of about 25 Natives. They were criminals, Father Serrano had said, captured during attacks on Colonists in the outer circles of Adara Vega and brought here in secret.

Some cried without noise, some raged and all were filthy and implored Cole with those empty, bejeweled eyes of theirs. One young man in particular had strode up to the fence and stared at Cole with blatant resentment. Pure hatred had passed out of the Native's faded blue eyes and pierced Cole's heart, drowning out Father Serrano's voice as he explained the course of the experiment, something about extracting the secret to health and long life.

Father Serrano and the others involved in this experiment had been so proud, yapping at Cole and each other like a bunch of overexcited puppies. But Cole had felt only disgust, for himself and for his Church. And as he had stood in the elevator to return to the surface world Cole felt like he was returning to a fiction.

He had gone immediately to see his adoptive father. Father Tanaka was third in command of the Congress, a place Cole had been groomed to take over since childhood.

In that darkened room Cole had sat beside his father's bed and clasped the old man's soft, dry hand. Father Tanaka had been asleep, but startled at the contact and squeezed back with what strength he could muster.

"Cole?" His once proud voice was little more than a sigh and Cole winced to hear him sound so weak. The old man's face and body had withered but his eyes were still strong as they locked onto Cole's face and drew a confession out of him, as they had on so many other occasions.

"Father, I am confused."

"That is our lot in life, as they say. I suspect you will spend many more years in that state." Then he chuckled, but it was little more than a cough.

"They showed me the experiment," said Cole and he remembered the sound of Father Tanaka's breath catching. When next he spoke Cole knew that he was choosing his words with care, all the time studying his face. Tanaka appeared to be searching for something but Cole couldn't guess what it was.

"And what is your impression?"

Cole had hesitated for only a moment before admitting, "It feels wrong." Tanaka had smiled then, which gave Cole the courage to continue his blasphemous speech. "They may not have eternal souls and they may be vessels of sin and vice, but should we be using them this way? Doesn't that make us just as evil?"

"Have you ever been to Adara Vega, my child?" Tanaka asked.

Cole dropped his father's hand and sat up straight. "Of course not! I'm not a saint but I've never done that."

"Then perhaps it's time for you to see for yourself."

"What?"

"They have imagined big things for you but you do not have to be the person they desire you to be. You do not have to believe everything they tell you. Be your own man, my son, and you cannot go astray." Father Tanaka had closed his eyes and coughed. Without looking at Cole again he said, "I am tired now. But will you return this evening and read to me?"

"Of course, father." Cole had left then, his head more full of clouds than before.

Cole had never made it back to read because just a few hours later Father Tanaka was dead and Cole was asked to take his place as the Church's third in command. He heard himself accepting the position but he felt numb, weighed down by his grief.

The numbness and the confusion still enveloped him as his memory shifted and the landscape shimmered. The faces in the street below him became the faces of his congregation on the morning of his breakdown, the morning they had announced Father Tanaka's death and Cole's promotion.

He remembered Father Deven speaking in a stern voice. He remembered looking out into the crowd and seeing the sleepy eyes, the nodding heads and children passing notes. And deeper still he saw the greed with which Father Piotr eyed the collection plate, how the husbands and wives sat leaning away from each other. Anger, resentment, malice and greed flowed freely between members of the congregation. And beneath it all he heard the hollowness of Father Deven's sermon.

What he had seen in the dungeon and what his father had said to him had rendered Cole incapable of seeing his fellow priests as men of God. They were empty vessels. It showed in Father Deven's desperation to hold the crowd's interest and led him to dwell on the surface texture of his parables rather than delving into them to provide illumination and inspiration. The room was ripe with the stilted fruit of spiritual dryness. God was not there.

Cole remembered Father Piotr raising his arms and the congregation stood as one like good little sheep, but when everyone else sat down, Cole remained standing. He had felt the eyes of everyone in the church searching his face like a roomful of inquisitors. He knew he must have looked crazy because Father Deven was at his side in a moment to guide him from the altar and into his plush office. Cole had started to sweat beneath his robes and imagined he was melting from the inside for his blasphemous thoughts. But even in the office of a priest there was no God, only statues and books and cold plaster walls.

He barely recalled what Father Deven had said then, something about working too hard and taking a sabbatical, because Cole was too horrified of what Father Deven looked like to pay much attention to the actual words. There was nothing grotesque about him, but neither was there anything saint-like. He was a man. Nothing more. That revelation had overpowered his senses and he crumpled like the most fragile piece of tissue paper in the hand of a merciless, absent God.

The panic of the memory sent him stumbling back into his hotel room, where the crimson walls worried his thoughts. The hulking, black furniture rested against the walls like the shadows of the personal demons that had followed him on this sabbatical. Three bottles of bitter red wine waited for him on the dresser. He uncorked one, filled a heavy hotel room glass and swirled the liquid beneath his nose. It smelled as cheap as it tasted.

"Blessed be," he murmured to no one and tipped the glass to his greedy mouth. It was early afternoon and already the buzz was wearing off. He needed more.

It was that woman's fault. Iliana. That woman who had taken it upon herself to heal his body though his soul remained a stinking pit. She had grace; he gave her that at least. Her body moved with fluid grace and her voice brushed his skin like velvet. She was like a wide river, calm on the surface but with deep, raging currents that you couldn't fight against, only relax and sink into with resignation.

But he had to fight. She had taken him, taken his blood without his permission and though he could not find any marks on his flesh he could feel them on his soul. They were tiny pinpricks of impurity tarnishing what he had worked so hard to keep wholesome. In one night she had proven that his belief system was correct: the Natives were evil. They tainted everything they touched.

But then he thought of his father. His father had encouraged him to come here, had spoken near blasphemy in encouraging him to think on his own with regards to the Natives. And it was his father's hints that something existed beyond the teachings of the Church that kept him from fleeing the city. Down to his soul he felt that his father was right. There was more to life than what he had come to believe. He just didn't understand what part the Natives played.

With that last thought he poured himself another glass and carried it and the bottle to the bed and sat. Out in the street the thrumming music continued. The vague murmur of voices reached his ears through the open balcony door. He sipped the wine at first but as the first drops of rain splattered against the balcony he set aside the glass and glued his lips to the bottle, his only friend, his new salvation.

6 During the day the storm had crept over the city's walls, blanketing Adara Vega in premature night. Only then was Iliana ready to leave the Palace. Cole's prayer beads and collar rattled in her otherwise empty black velvet bag as it brushed against her hip. She didn't know where the priest was staying but she was confident that she would be able to find him. Being Adam's sister had its perks. He had connections and so did she.

Beneath the ceiling of bruised and swollen clouds the music that always filled the courtyard of the Palace felt too loud, too insistent, like the constant grumbling of a caged animal. The rhythm thrummed within her chest where the cavity swelled to make room for its alien heartbeat.

Iliana approached the gatekeeper, a Native named Mario who was too short to become an escort but whose powerful body made him an excellent soldier. He was one of Adam's friends, which made the task at hand much easier.

"Good evening, Mario. How are you?"

He did not smile, but gave a slight nod. "Good evening, Iliana."

"How long have you been on watch?"

"Since just before sunrise."

"Did you see a man dressed in black tearing out of here as though the devil himself were chasing him?" She tried to feign only the vaguest interest in his answer. The gatekeepers were the eyes of the Council and after Drake's warning she didn't want her search for the man to be misconstrued.

"I did," Mario said, his bright blue eyes suddenly curious.

He offered nothing else, forcing Iliana to ask, "And?"

"It was just after I came on. I called after him to stop but he didn't. I considered chasing him. I thought that perhaps he was a thief but there was no one else to watch my post."

"And in which direction did he go?" she asked, exasperated. She was hoping to narrow down her search and Mario was being impossible. The streets to the right and left of the gates contained hotels and hostels. The street running straight out from the gates was made up of bars and clubs and other businesses renowned for all-night debauchery.

If Father Cole had run straight then he was probably already out of the Final Circle and beyond her reach. Palace Escorts were pampered but imprisoned, forbidden to leave the Final Circle. Circles Two through Six were populated by the street escorts and those Colonists who could not afford to pay large sums for their mental vacations. The caliber of the people and the city descended the farther out you went. Circle Seven was a haven of piracy and murder, dangerous for Natives and Colonists alike. It was the largest, most stubborn blemish on the beauty of Adara Vega. Iliana had never been there. It was the one place she hoped to never have to go.

Mario's lips twitched in a smile and she realized that he was just teasing her. "Why are you looking for him?" he asked.

"I need to return something he left in my cell. Now are you going to tell me where he went or not?"

"He went right."

"Thank you." As Iliana turned to follow Cole's trail she swore that Adam's attitude was rubbing off on his friends and it was not a good thing.

The first bolt of lightning flashed. It was a welcome sign. The desert storms were sudden and violent and almost always caused a flood of clientele into the center of the city, which was on higher ground than the other circles. More clients meant more money, which meant Iliana might meet her quota this month.

Iliana was well-known among the hotel concierges and all were eager to help her out, though none of them had seen Cole. She flirted her way through the questions, touching when touch was required, leaning in just enough, promising great rewards with her eyes if only they would answer her questions.

"I'm so sorry, love. I don't know his last name. But he stands this tall. He has brown hair, brown eyes... Wait they all have brown hair and brown eyes, don't they? How silly of me. So you haven't seen him? Thank you. You've been a dear."

And then in the seventh hotel she checked, the clerk finally said, "Yes, he's here. Room 46."

The hotel was small and directly across the dusty avenue from the bar where Iliana had first rescued Cole. Thick chips of crimson paint flaked from the walls when she passed by as though the mere disturbance of the air currents was too much for them. The hallways were too short, the elevator too small and creaking, and the carpet too soiled for Iliana's taste. The décor was fitting for a man who came here only to punish himself.

She reached a white door with angular black numbers above the painted-over peephole reading "46". She knocked three times.

7 Two bottles of wine later Cole grew tired of his own company. He switched on the battered radio in his room. There was only one station and the Church ran it but it was better than silence and the sound of his own shuffling feet wearing a path in the carpet.

The last notes of a song faded and then a deep, soothing voice said, "And now a word from our sponsors."

"Wonderful," Cole muttered. He sank onto the bed and glared at the radio. His hands felt empty. He needed another drink but he couldn't make himself move to open the final bottle. It took him a moment to recognize the familiar voice issuing from the radio as his own.

"Mankind is weak; let us give you strength. Mankind is divided from within; let us mend you. Mankind is devoid of spirit; let us fill you."

Cole's memory of recording these ads had a dreamlike quality. He could no longer imagine himself as that man anymore, a man full of passion for his beliefs and eager to spread the word, a man in love with his God.

"There are those wish to lead you away from the path of righteousness with temptations of pleasure and excess. Do not pay them notice for they will crumble to dust and fade away. Come to the Universal Truth. We will show you the way."

The announcer explained, "The previous announcement was paid for by the Friends of the Church of Universal Truth."

Cole rolled his eyes. He had been so sure then of his way and it showed in the tone of his voice, compassionate yet commanding. Now he was a shell, a shadow, the antithesis of his former self. He was nothing.

In the pause between commercials a soft sound from the hallway disturbed Cole's drunken reverie: a rustling, like the sound of the desert wind stripping sand from the dunes, followed by three taps on the door. As he dragged his body off of the bed and shuffled towards the door the air became host to a voice once more. But this time the voice was feminine and full of promise, a sultry invitation to an awakening.

"Are you lonely, unhappy, terminally ill?"

"Yes," Cole answered.

"…Do you pass through life only a spectator to your own automatic actions?"

"Yes," he mumbled again.

"…Within the walls of Adara Vega you will find serenity. Let us heal you, empower you, nurture you…"

"Snack on you."

"…Let us show you the path of transcendence, of desire, of love. Come to Adara Vega. We will show you the way."

Cole opened the door. "Speak of the devil," he said.

Iliana did not smile as he looked her up and down with sluggish eyes. She looked statuesque in a scarlet gown and black gloves. Half of her black hair tumbled over her shoulders while the rest fell in curls to frame her face. He took it all in then sighed and tried to close the door. But she would have none of that and strolled past him into the room.

Iliana's critical eyes scanned the room and Cole followed her gaze with his own. The red walls and black furniture seemed an attempt to imitate the life that thrived outside. But the room was cramped and the scent of old cigars lingered in the air. It was like a womb, giving birth to dark thoughts and darker urges.

"I don't like it," she declared before turning and finally setting her gaze on Cole.

He agreed completely but only said, "Get out," as he stood in the doorway and held onto the door for support.

A smile spread across her lips. It traveled outward and lit upon every feature of her face as a ripple changes the surface of still water; it even touched her exquisite eyes, which were like a cloudless winter sky and fringed by long, dark lashes. She truly was a devil come to pay its respects in the guise of an angel.

"I brought you a gift. Would you like it?"

"Get. Out." He opened the door even wider and glowered at her, willing her out of the room and out of his life.

From her handbag Iliana withdrew his prayer beads and collar and placed them on the dresser beside the unopened bottle of wine. Then she walked over to the radio and switched it off. Silence surged in to fill the tiny room to overflowing.

"You shouldn't listen to the radio. You do know your Church puts hidden messages beneath the music, don't you?" she asked.

Cole scowled. He couldn't remember having heard anything about that but then again maybe it was a secret only known to those at the top. And he would soon be one of them. But then how would she know about it? No, she had to be wrong. She was a liar by nature and trade, which made anything she said suspect.

Iliana shrugged and walked out onto the balcony. She leaned over the railing, appearing to be unfazed by Cole's disapproving frown. The rain had slowed to a drizzle and the breeze rustled her hair.

"I was just about to leave. So if you would go…"

Iliana whipped around with that smile still lifting the corners of her mouth. "Are you returning to your Church so soon? Have you reconciled your differences?" Her eyes flicked to the two empty wine bottles lying perpendicular to each other on the bed like a defective cross, then back to Cole's bloodshot eyes. "Evidence suggests otherwise."

"Just…" He sighed, unable to finish his thought. His head was beginning to ache from trying to form the right words.

"I had another reason to see you. I came to collect my fee."

Cole felt his face flush like a boiler ready to explode. "Your fee?" He spoke so softly that Iliana had to come back into the room to hear him. "I am not going to pay you for violating me against my will."

"I didn't violate you. You needed it."

"There is nothing I would ever need from you." He snorted and wiped at the hair that was plastered to his forehead. The air was far too humid for his taste. He wished he had some ice. And he wished Iliana would go away. But she didn't move. She just stood there and looked at him with the same pity with which one looks at the terminally ill.

"You were dying," she said. Her voice as casual as if she were discussing the weather. "You were poisoning yourself and had I not intervened you would have died within days, maybe hours, maybe even the next time you picked up a drink."

Cole stumbled to the bed and sat. He put his head in his hands and refused to look up again. He jumped at the loud click when Iliana closed the door and knew that she was waiting for him to speak. But his disobedient tongue was mute. He could only wonder why he hadn't died, why God had seen fit to save him through this woman, this unholy creature.

Iliana did not come any closer. Her voice remained impartial. "So you see. You needed it. Now, if you would pay me for my services I will leave you to kill yourself in peace and this time I promise not to intervene."

Seconds passed in silence. Cole felt her gaze like a heavy blanket draped over his shoulders. His mind whirled with questions that had no answers. Was this part of God's plan? Was there a reason he had gone to that bar that night? Was he meant to return to the Church or was God rejecting him by giving him this evil woman as his savior?

"Is this some kind of joke?" he asked into his hands. "Is this some kind of joke?" There was no response and so he looked up to see Iliana standing there, staring at him.

"Are you playing with me?" he demanded.

"I am not interested in your spiritual crises. You came to this city of your own accord. You went to that bar of your own accord. You drank yourself into oblivion of your own accord—"

"But I did not ask you to snack on me!" Cole stood as the anger rose. At his sides his fists clenched and unclenched as he tried to restrain himself. He had never wanted to hit someone as much as he wanted to now and that thought alone sobered him.

Now Iliana stepped toward him, undaunted by his righteous anger and he felt the force of her pride as if it were a physical thing brushing up against him, pushing him back. "I did not snack on you. I cleaned you out."

"A sin is a sin."

"You left the Church for a reason and yet you still cling to its teachings. You are like a man combing the desert in search of an oasis while ignoring the water in his own canteen. There is something wrong with a religion that alienates its parishioners so much that they feel the need to turn against the dogma and sin just as hard as they had prayed before—"

"Shut up," Cole whispered. He covered his eyes with the sweaty heels of his hands and gripped his scalp with his fingers. His palms smelled of wine, of Communion. He didn't want to hear this, to think about it. He wanted only to be left alone with his misery because his spiritual dilemma was different, special. It had to be.

"Let me guess... your red collar identifies you as a Ceremonial priest, and the gold bars upon it mean that you are a man of some status within the Church. But remember that you are still just that: a man. So here is your life at a glance: you pray and then you sin because that is what your people do. And then, tired of sinning if no one is going to make a big deal about it, you return to the Church. You give a detailed account of your debaucheries to some man in a cabinet and he mumbles some words, tells you to mumble some words and you are cleared of all charges—"

"Shut up!" he hissed through clenched teeth. He wanted to strike her down but something in her words kept his arms at his sides. She spoke the truth.

"...Washed clean and made whole once more until the next time you feel the call of life."

"Stop it!" he cried. "You have no right to say such things. You are a blasphemer, a heretic!" Though the hypocrisy she spoke of was part of his crisis, but this woman, this creature, should not be allowed to harass or berate him about it. She wasn't allowed to say those things because she was not a part of it; she couldn't know what he had lost.

"I am no more a heretic than you. By your own beliefs you damned yourself by coming here. And though you will return and make amends with your Church, both you and your God will know what you've done, what you will do before you leave."

"How do you know what I will do?"

"Your spirit will not be satisfied with drink alone. It is in your nature to want more."

"What do you know of my nature?"

"More than you."

They stared at each other for a moment. The argument had had a sobering effect on Cole; his anger had used the wine for fuel and now he felt clear-headed. He was still angry but no longer felt as if he might explode.

"Look, Father, it is not my job to rob my clients of their delusions and I do not exist just to damn your eternal soul. You were in trouble and I helped you. My motivation ran no deeper than that."

How is that possible? He wanted to ask. Instead he leveled his eyes at her and said, "Get out." Her eyes were full of life, curiosity even. Even after his rudeness he could tell that she felt no malice toward him, and that softened his anger further, drained him.

"Get out."

"Not until I am paid." Iliana's gaze was as steady as his.

He sighed and reached into his back pocket for his wallet. He thumbed it open, pulled out all of the bills and tossed them at her. "Now go." Cole turned his back on her and moved to the bed, where he sprawled on his stomach and buried his face in a pillow.

8 Iliana did not move. She could only stare at Cole's back in amazement. The bills fluttered around her like bits of ash and fell to the floor, so bright they looked obscene in the morbid red and black room. When the steady hiss of Cole's breathing became lost beneath the sound of the gusting wind outside, Iliana left. The money remained where Cole had thrown it. Iliana would not stoop to pick it up.

Outside it began to rain. This storm was going to be bad. To avoid the showers she ducked into a nearby bar. It was just past sunset and the place was still empty but she needed a way to kill some time. Iliana met the bartender's gaze and he nodded in the direction of a solitary man who sat at a table in the back corner.

Iliana immediately tucked herself into the booth across from him. He looked up from his beer and his expression traveled from exhaustion to interest in a matter of moments. She couldn't ascertain his age but that wasn't surprising. All of the Colonists looked alike, with brown hair, brown eyes and dusky skin, and so sometimes it was difficult to guess their ages.

"Hello," he said and extended his hand, "I'm Robert. What's your name?"

"Iliana," she said and smiled as she returned the handshake. His grip was firm but she felt the smallest tremor running through his muscles. He was nervous.

"What are you doing here? I thought that your kind didn't venture out during the day." His voice was suggestive. After her time with Cole, Iliana found Robert's entire attitude, the attitudes of most of her clients, grating, and she had to rein in her emotions in order to play the role that they expected of her. Until now she hadn't realized how weary she had grown of herself.

"I was looking for you," she managed to say without sounding ridiculous. Robert's smile widened, which meant he had taken the bait. "Where are you from?"

"Afet's Wall."

Iliana snapped to attention and before she could stop herself she asked, "Have you heard of a preacher named Father Cole?"

Robert thought for a moment then asked, "Do you mean Father Cole of the Congress?"

"I don't know. Perhaps."

"If that's who you mean, then yes. I'm not into the Ceremonial Church myself, they're too strict for my taste, but I have heard of him. He hasn't been around too long but he's supposed to be some sort of genius. People travel a long way just to hear him preach."

"Interesting," said Iliana. She couldn't imagine the broken man she had saved from self-destruction could be the same man. It didn't seem possible.

"Why do you ask? Have you heard of him here?"

Iliana reined in her wandering thoughts and leveled her eyes at Robert. She was making a mistake. He was as plain and boring as the rest of the Colonists but he was a potential client and she would never meet her quota without giving him her undivided attention.

"I have heard of him in passing," she admitted in an off-hand way. Then she lowered her voice until it was almost a purr. "So, Robert, how long have you been in Adara Vega?"

"I just got here today," he answered. He seemed happy that the conversation had turned back in his direction, as the Colonists always were.

"And have you ever been with an escort?"

"No."

Iliana stifled the urge to stand up and walk away. She was not in the mood for an initiation but this early in the evening she didn't have much of a choice. She took solace in the fact that he wouldn't last long since it was his first time.

"Then I will be your first," she said, the tone in her voice leaving no room for disagreement. His smile widened.

One down and countless more to go.

9 "We cannot use her if she refuses to cooperate," Sigrid brushed her voluminous hair back from her face, hair spun of the finest silver that clung to her damp temples like cobwebs. She was the only elder member of the Council to go without the blue paint on a regular basis. She didn't need it, either. She was a handsome woman who would have been striking if she ever smiled. She was one birth cycle younger than Drake and was always cold toward him, as if jealous that he had become the Governor instead of her.

"You say you have spoken with Iliana, Governor Drake?" she asked.

"Yes. I spoke with her this morning." Governor Drake did not hide his irritation at the Council's lack of cooperation. He leveled his eyes at each Council member in turn, twelve in all, and gave each of them a chance to turn away. None did.

"And was she amiable?"

"Absolutely." The indignation in his voice ricocheted off of the high ceiling before reaching the Council's ears. Painted on the plaster above, plump cherubs, their rosy cheeks faded to pallor over time, watched the proceedings as if awaiting a summons to action.

Drake continued, "She understands her duty and even as I left this morning she was preparing for work."

"But you said she is already hesitant to bear a child this term?"

"Of course she is nervous. It is only natural. Besides, we will not be asking her to bear a child, will we?"

A few members smiled at Drake but Sigrid did not join them. "We have no time. If we do not act now then we will have to wait a hundred years before we have another chance and by then we will most likely all be dead. Do you want that to happen, Governor?"

"Of course not."

"Then perhaps we should choose someone else, someone older, who can handle the burden of—"

"Enough!" Governor Drake slammed his fist down on the table. "We have been planning this for Iliana since her birth. No one else is capable of carrying such a burden, I assure you. Must I remind you that we have gone through too many young women experimenting with the process? Jade died, Alana died, Montrice went mad and ran into the desert and we have to assume that she died as well. Finally, Gabriella was too far-gone to save. She died but not before giving birth to Iliana.

"That girl has the connection built-in, so to cast her aside in favor of someone else would be an error that we will never get another chance to rectify. Is this clear?"

"You can be confident of your choice because of your bond with her. Give us a chance to speak with her, to question her. Let us make up our own minds as to whether or not she is the right subject for the Transformation."

Governor Drake sank back into his plush chair and wiped his forehead with his handkerchief. Then he smiled, a gesture calculated to diminish the tension. But the tension was stubborn. It remained.

"Fine. I will set up an interview if that's what it will take to convince you. Just give me time."

"Of course, Governor. And Iliana will be left alone until then," one of the younger members said.

"Good," he said, "This meeting is over. Tomorrow I'm leaving to meet one last time with the Church Congress of Elders." He paused for effect and was not disappointed. Several of the members rewarded his statement with sharp inhalations. Governor Drake was the only Native authorized to leave the city and though many envied him for it, none of them would have chosen to take his place. And he would not have given it up.

"I will be gone for at least three days, maybe longer. I'm going

39

to plead our case yet again, though I do not expect miracles. So, the plan will remain in place. We only have 29 days left."

The Council members nodded and, mumbling, filed out of the three arched doorways and into the hall. As Governor Drake watched them leave he noticed Adam weaving through the bodies, trying to gain entrance to the room.

"Hello Adam," the Governor said once the Council was gone.

Adam eased himself into one of the recently vacated chairs. "So, what happened? I heard you yelling."

Governor Drake chuckled. "Sometimes they can be so frustrating that I lose my temper."

"And…"

"And everything is fine. Iliana will be our savior."

Adam smiled. "That's great. Except I still don't see why it couldn't be me. You know I'm willing and you wouldn't have to lie to me."

"Don't be ridiculous. The books are clear that only a woman can grow life within her body and so only a woman will be able to bestow life upon her charges after the Transformation. A man could kill but he would be sterile and therefore useless."

"Fine. So when do I get to reveal our plan?" he asked, as eager as a child with a secret he's dying to tell.

"Not yet. The sooner we tell her, the longer she has to think about it and the more possible it is for her to form attachments to the Colonists. She cannot be allowed to do that."

"So we wait?"

"So we wait."

"I hate waiting."

"Keep yourself busy. Have you heard anything else about the newest murder?" Drake asked. For the weeks leading up to the Festival of Semiveh the number of altercations between Colonists and Natives always increased. Just a few days into the month and already there had been 26 murders and three times as many non-fatal injuries.

"Not much. I was almost jumped when I started asking questions. Just a few Church kids here for a three-day holiday.

They lured an escort into their hotel room, tortured him and killed him. It was a pretty nasty scene, from what I heard."

Drake tried and failed not to envision the body of the murdered Native. He had seen it so many times that the images sometimes even haunted his dreams. "They know something is coming. It's making them restless. What about your informant? What does he say?"

"I'm seeing him tomorrow. Hopefully he'll give us more to go on."

"Hopefully," Drake repeated.

Adam leaned back in the chair and stared at the ceiling, unsmiling. Governor Drake pressed his lips to the steeple of his fingers. He called for strength and let his eyes follow the murky gray sunlight up toward the windows, where a stormy sky hovered, holding everything beneath it to account.

10

Ignoring Iliana's presence, Cole had tumbled into the dense, indecipherable visions of drunken sleep. He had slept through the first few hours of night and now, as he focused his bleary eyes at the hotel room walls, he was overwhelmed. His body felt fevered, sore and ill. The balcony and the street below were sodden. For the moment the rain had stopped but the turgid clouds overhead told him that the storm was not over yet.

He dressed in a clean white shirt and grabbed his coat. Down to his fingernails he was filled with the desire to escape the visceral power of the blood-colored room. He felt disjointed. His fevered mind imagined that the heavy black furniture crowded him, threw out little barbs to catch onto his flesh and keep him still, restrained, uncomfortable. Plus, he was out of wine.

He spilled out of his hotel room into a world of noise and night where the ever-present music bounded off of the clouds and scraped against his eardrums. With the bills that the woman, that creature, had neglected to take stuffed back into his wallet he went in search of the oblivion she had stolen from him. The usually dusty street was awash with mud that sucked at his shoes.

The wind picked up again. Flyers ripped from brick walls pranced down the street and tangled around the legs of pedestrians. One of them slapped Cole's cheek as he exited his hotel. Without looking at it he brushed it aside and while he turned and walked into the wind toward the outer edge of the Final Circle the flyer, white with red letters, fluttered in the opposite direction, flew up, sank and was lost among the partiers.

Cole didn't know where he was going or what he was going to do once he got there. His head was filled with the conflicting voices of Fathers Tanaka and Deven: one encouraging him to explore and create his own belief system out of his observations, the other voice condemning his every thought, every action, his very existence. At that moment he wanted only to find a drink and drown those voices, to push them down into the deep well of forgotten things. And then that woman's words, adding to the chorus of voices, drowning out the others. He heard her mocking voice repeat over and over again that he was going to die, and worse, that he was going to sin.

If he was ready to die, why had God seen fit to give him to that woman? She had saved him but by any twist of logic could she be called his savior? It was wrong. She was wrong. And he wanted more than anything to argue with her again, to make her understand that his situation was unique, different.

Around him the streets became less crowded, the businesses and hotels seedier. Dilapidated buildings fringed the muddy road and Cole found himself stumbling into a shadowy doorway to get his thoughts under control. The scent of rain could not wash away the smell of sweat and urine and booze that wafted from a nearby alley. He heard voices, laughter, a sigh of the kind that only comes after sexual fulfillment. All of this filled him with disgust, disgust with people, with himself, with everything. The Colonists were not the chosen ones and God was not anywhere, especially here.

"It's all just a big, fat joke," he muttered to no one. But his heart did not echo his lips. Just like in Church he spoke lies that nobody heard or even cared to listen to. He laughed at himself and the futility of his beliefs. He needed a drink.

Cole kept walking, the voices in the alleyway fading behind him. His fevered eyes searched the buildings for signs of peace but the bars he passed were crammed with so many patrons they spilled out onto the street. As he walked on the bars became clubs whose pounding music competed with the music that still poured out of the overhead speakers and punctuated the storm. He didn't want to go into those places so he turned his back on them and began walking in the opposite direction.

Up ahead, the glittering tower of the Palace glowed like the head of a monster with a thousand golden eyes. The original Cathedral that formed the bottom levels of the Palace had giant stone arches and buttresses that curved into the body and resembled legs. This behemoth appeared to be poised to scuttle about, feasting on the unsuspecting souls in the courtyard and the streets.

Against his will his mind imagined that woman, high up there in her luxurious cell, tormenting some poor soul into the greatest sin. His eyes fell from the tower to the faces of the people around him. He searched their glazed eyes for a sign, a sign that it was not over, a sign that the Church was right, that he could return to the life he had known before. But he found no solace there. He could not reconcile his mind to such all or nothing mentality. There had to be a middle ground.

He was searching faces when he saw her.

She passed him on the street, so close he couldn't imagine that she hadn't seen him. Anger boiled inside him, making his face flame until his cheeks almost steamed in the frigid desert night. Like a man not in control of his own body Cole turned once more and followed her. He didn't know what he would say when he caught up to her but he had to talk to her again.

She had changed since she had been in his room and it was not an improvement. Before she had been unreal, elegant, and only the knowledge of what she was had branded her as evil. Now she looked like what she was: walking death. Tight, shiny leather pants trapped the various shades of neon signs on her thighs and hips and a sleeveless corset of the same material cinched her waist, the black thong that laced down the back slapped against her thighs as she walked. Her black ponytail swung back and forth like a metronome that kept time with her spike-heeled footsteps.

Cole followed her to a club bathed in blue light with the uninspired name of "Blue". A line of people started at the door and continued around the corner of the building. She ignored the line. With one black-gloved hand she patted the enormous Native doorman on the shoulder. He grinned at her and stepped aside and she entered. Cole jogged up to the entrance but the doorman stopped him with a hand on his chest.

"Get in line," he said. His voice was high but gruff, the only voice that could be heard above the strange blend of music from within and without.

Cole pointed into the club. His ears became attuned to the different rhythm of music coming from that darkness and his mind went toward it without thought, searched for the woman, as if she had left an invisible trail for him to follow. "That woman who just went in…"

The doorman folded his arms across his chest and asked, "What woman?"

"Iliana," Cole finally spurted out, forcing himself to speak her name, to give her an identity. He had been trying to make her vanish, to deface the memory of her, to pretend that she didn't exist. Now all that work was for nothing. She had a name. She existed. Cole cleared his throat.

"I'm here to see Iliana." He could feel the people in the long line at his back getting restless but he didn't care. Cole's only worry was that the doorman might send him to the back of the line, where he wouldn't be able to see when Iliana left.

"You're her man? Go ahead then." And with that the man stepped aside and allowed Cole to enter. Cole was on the verge of disputing this because he didn't want anyone to think he was Iliana's "man", but instead he bit his tongue and went inside.

If the outside of the club imitated a mock blue daylight then the inside of the club aspired to be a moonless night. Invisible speakers filled the small room with music so loud it strained the walls that held it. Here there were no strobe lights, no velvet couches or other such pretensions, and the patrons seemed not to care. Tables were crowded with male and female escorts clad in outfits that matched Iliana's, some of them striking lurid poses, spreading their legs to straddle seated patrons. Others clung to the arms of their chosen partners for the night like grinning diseases.

As he passed one escort she opened her voracious mouth to lick the neck of a man in leather who was tied to a chair. The man had a black gag in his mouth and as her tongue touched his skin his eyes rolled upwards and his entire body seemed to quiver with anticipation. Cole turned away from them.

Lust and laughter and music surrounded him and he could only think of how much he needed a drink, a shot of liquid courage for the confrontation ahead. And then he would find Iliana and then… What? He told himself it didn't matter. The words would come to him when he needed them. He only knew he had to confront her.

From behind the crowded bar the bartender, a pale Native with spiky hair the color of a flaming orange sunset watched him with curious green eyes. Her gaze felt invasive, like the way a scientist might look at a dissected animal and Cole pointed to something on the shelf behind the bar to get her eyes off of him. She turned around and took down a black bottle with a label stained brown and unreadable. He didn't care what the beverage was, save that it was wet. The bartender placed a shot glass before him and filled it with the contents of the nameless bottle. The stuff was black and thicker than syrup. It filled the glass slowly as if it were easing into itself.

While the bartender poured Cole noticed that her fingers were tattooed with delicate scrollwork in black and gray. His eyes followed the lines and a pattern emerged that grew larger and simpler as it traveled up her arm. The sequence of geometric designs mesmerized him, soothed him. He wanted to see more. He wanted to see where the pattern ended. He wanted those delicate hands to touch him. He wanted…

She finished pouring the drink and took her hand away and the spell shattered. Cole blinked hard, disoriented and confused at the desire that coursed through him unbidden, seeking an outlet. He looked up at the bartender and she smiled. She knew exactly what that pattern did. She had shown it on purpose. She looked at him as though waiting for him to speak, to take the bait. Instead Cole turned from her and swallowed his errant curiosity. And though every instinct fought him he didn't ask to see her arms again.

He placed a few bills on the counter and lifted the glass. In the dimness the liquid within was impenetrable. As he tipped the drink it sucked at the walls of the glass, staining them a translucent rust color. He closed his eyes. He drank. It tasted like anise. When he swallowed he could feel it sliding down his throat in one gelatinous mass. He gagged, swallowed several times to clear his mouth of the taste, but it had coated his tongue and teeth and now all he could taste, all he could smell, was that bitter, spicy liquid.

Completely unsatisfied but not willing to risk another encounter with the bartender, Cole left the bar to wander between tables, searching for Iliana and her client. He told himself that he wanted to pay her, to stop her from hurting anyone else. But the sad truth was that he really just wanted to see her. When he could not find her right away he began to feel foolish. What could he say that she hadn't heard a million times before? Why did her opinion matter to him anyway?

Cole paused in his search to lean against the railing that surrounded the open dance floor. He rubbed at his face with both hands and grasped the railing in anger and futility. From there he looked over the rest of the room, the parts of it that writhed with bodies, and then the shadowy space on the other side of the room.

And there she was, perched on a man's lap, her gloves removed and her long fingers working into his hair. The man was thin and dressed in black, his pointed features softened by a languorous smile. The man leaned forward and pulled Iliana close to him and beneath the waterfall of her hair Cole could see him nuzzling her pale throat. Iliana's face was turned toward the wall, and as Cole watched them their movements grew slow, dreamlike. When the sensation did not pass immediately he realized that he was drunk. This realization came over him in slow motion, in much the same way as Iliana now took the man's hand and pulled him out of his chair. With their hands intertwined she led him onto the dance floor.

The music stopped, the muted lights flickered and in those moments of silence Cole could feel each of Iliana's spike-heeled footsteps echo in his chest. When everything started up again they were only a few paces from Cole, already moving to the new music. Moments later a woman's voice sliced open the heavy beats. The music intensified, demanded to be heard. And Cole listened. Cole watched.

Iliana formed a circle around her client's head with her thin arms. Her long fingernails, painted black and white, played with the hair at the nape of his neck. The man held onto her hips in a familiar way but his arms were stiff and his knees were locked. She molded her body against his, her hips swaying, her body crashing like a wave against the rock of his posture. But as Cole watched she wore him down and he began to move, to bend his knees a little and to sway with her.

Cole became aware of a hissing sound behind the music. The sound came from his right and grew louder until it drowned out everything else. Like a sleepwalker he turned his head and as he did time and space became fluid and the entire club wrapped itself around him, the patrons bumping against his cheeks, chairs and tables pressing against his eyes. When the world unwound and became flat once more he noticed a little machine pumping smoke onto the dance floor, a cheap way of making mystery where none existed. He turned again.

Iliana and her client stood knee-deep in hungry smoke that clawed its way up their bodies. For Cole the other patrons disappeared and he saw only Iliana enacting her seduction without fear. The man had pulled her close once more and they moved together, seamless, shameless. Though his back was to Cole, Cole could see how the man's arms were stroking the lace-up back of Iliana's corset, petting her like an animal. Iliana's pale face nuzzled the flesh at the junction of his neck and shoulder. One hand eased the collar of his shirt away while the other twined in his hair and pulled his head just to the side, opening him.

In response Cole opened his mouth. He wanted to cry out. But when he tried the scent of anise choked him, brought tears to his eyes. He gripped the cold metal railing with both hands until his arms shook, unable to walk to them and push them apart, unable to call out a warning to the man. And as Iliana's lips parted, with the utmost care and deliberateness, her gaze lifted from where she had been pondering the man's throat and focused on Cole. In that moment her sparkling eyes seemed malicious, evil. Cole stopped hearing the music. Time turned to syrup once again and oozed around him through tufts of counterfeit clouds.

Iliana used her thumb, tipped with some silver implement, to break open the man's skin. One breath passed. Iliana opened her mouth and the darkness within seemed deep and impenetrable, and just when Cole thought she would swallow the world, she closed her mouth on the man's throat. Her lips tensed as she began to drink from the wound, but her body never stopped moving to the music that Cole could feel now as a pounding that shook his entire body. Her eyes never left Cole's and they seemed to smile at his disbelief and disgust.

Cole was terrified. He was entranced. He held onto the railing for his life even as he sank into the brilliance of her eyes. And he couldn't even fight to get free. He felt the man's life passing between Iliana's lips. He felt their pulses, at first distinct but becoming one, and his heart sped up to match their frantic rhythm. He felt Iliana's hands in the man's hair, the man's hands clutching at her back, her waist, tangling in her ponytail. He felt pressure building in the man's chest, hot and insistent, and he held his breath lest it escape. Then Iliana blinked and the connection broke.

Cole let go of the railing and staggered backward until he hit a wall. He tasted blood. He lifted a hand to his mouth and pressed it with numb fingers. His fingers came back covered in a dark liquid. He had bitten the tip of his tongue. When he looked up again the place on the dance floor where she had taken her victim was filled with strange, dark forms that convulsed in time with the new song. He cursed, apologized out of habit, and fled the club.

His head felt stuffed to bursting with clouds but the dream was over. And it hadn't even been his dream. Once more that woman had forced herself upon him and he felt defiled. When he was outside he spat on the ground to try to get rid of the taste of his blood and looked around. The line to get inside had not diminished despite the drizzle that made the already dilapidated buildings look soggy and broken. The large doorman grinned at him in collusion and Cole gagged. He turned and spat again and started back to his hotel. His tongue throbbed.

He didn't know what to make of what had just happened. He didn't know why Iliana could affect him when nothing had moved him for such a long time. He didn't know why he craved that feeling but at the same time he hated her for it, for giving him another sin to add to his mounting collection. He grimaced and kept on walking, hoping that the movement would clear his head. And at first it worked. Then as he passed an alley he felt someone slip out of the shadows and fall into step with him, just a few paces behind. He ignored it, hoping it would go away. His tongue would not stop bleeding and the throbbing had become almost unbearable, like a second heartbeat in his mouth. He spat again.

"Don't waste it," a soft voice said.

Cole stopped and sighed. His shoulders sagged. He tried to walk on, to tell himself to ignore her but in the end he turned around. Iliana's face was a mask of innocence, the glistening red lipstick on her pouting lips mocking the blood that had just passed between them. Her eyes were wide, not with surprise, but with secret knowledge, as if she had read his mind and what she saw there intrigued her. Cole felt the alcoholic dizziness hovering close, waiting to spring on him and finish him off.

"Why were you following me?" she asked.

"What did you do to me?" he growled in return. He kept his voice low because he didn't want a scene. Iliana just laughed at him.

"What I did, I did for Father Matteo, not for you."

"Father…" he said, trying to wrap his mind around the meaning of her words.

She raised an eyebrow at him. "Yes, 'Father'. And, unlike you, he likes it when I call him Father. The heresy turns him on."

Cole reeled back in disgust. Her indecency knew no bound-aries and for that she frightened him. To convert a man of God into a heathen required great power. Just standing close to her he felt power like heat coming off of her in waves, like pure electricity buzzing in his mind. He shook his head and said, "And you did it in public? That's brazen, but expected I suppose. Isn't it against the law?"

"Only if someone tells on me…" she slid up to him and placed an open palm on his chest. She wore gloves once more and against his white shirt her hand looked like a shiny, black insect. "You won't tell on me, will you?" she pouted.

Cole stared at her and felt the drunken illusions closing in. Iliana's eyes caught the colored lights of the signs and swallowed them, her voice drowned out all other noise until all he could hear was her suggestive whisper. He could feel himself slipping back into that frightening dreamlike state and he wondered again what he had drank. He needed to move but he could not. He wanted to scream but he was mute. He wanted to run away from her but he was paralyzed. Only Iliana's eyes remained bright and clear as the rest of the world dimmed.

"God…" he whispered. The street beneath him felt like it was made of pillows and in this unsteady state it wavered beneath his feet. He stumbled.

"Why are you doing this to me?" he whimpered. Then his voice cracked and he fell to his knees into the soft cushion of the street. He felt judgmental eyes picking at his flesh but had nowhere to hide.

He heard a voice say, "Father Cole?" but he could not answer. He searched for God in the unwavering eyes of a woman, a woman who could have been anyone, and he saw nothing but those deep blue orbs staring back at him, able to reach into him and read the sins written upon his soul. But he could not confess because God was not there either.

11

"Is he dead?"

"I don't know. He looks dead. Can Colonists be that color?"

"Dead Colonists... Wait... I think he just took a breath..."

"..."

"So he's not dead."

"You sound disappointed."

"Shut up."

"Look, we have to get him out of the street. He could drown in that puddle if he moves."

"I don't think he's going to move any time soon."

"Come on, help me search his pockets. Maybe there's... a key."

"Got it."

"Let's take him to his hotel."

"Can we rob him?"

"No. Get his legs."

"I hate this job. If anyone but Iliana had asked us..."

"I know, I know. Let's just get this over with."

Cole's world was a place of extremes. His back, one side of his face, pulsated with heat. His stomach, the other side of his face, was damp and somewhat sticky. And the voices around him hailed from somewhere else entirely. He couldn't concentrate. It made no sense. He blacked out again.

12 Cole knew peace, unalterable and unending. Then he opened his eyes. It took him an excruciating moment of constant blinking to recognize the angular shapes of the hotel room furniture. And perched on the dresser, hovering like a vulture would hover over a newfound carcass, was a Native. He was clad in black leather pants, a dark blue shirt and a black leather trench coat. His dark eyes laughed at Cole's bleary shock but his lips remained taut in a steady, sadistic half-grin.

Cole scowled at the stranger in silence for one minute, which stretched into two. Still the man sat and stared and did not move or speak. He seemed more a statue than a man: a creepy, leering statue, a demon in a man-suit.

"Get out of my room." Cole's voice came out as harsh as the sunlight that cut a sliver of light across his bed. Still nothing. No movement, speech, breath.

The longer Cole sat there, locked in a staring contest with the stranger, the longer he was awake and upright, the worse he felt. His swollen tongue throbbed in his mouth. Half of his face felt sunburned, half of it stiff. When he wiped at his cheek little clods of mud flaked off onto his hand. The room lurched around him. He was going to be sick.

Cole risked soiling the sheets long enough to tell the stranger, "You'd better be gone when I get back." Affecting an air of control he crawled off the bed, side-stepping a puddle of cold vomit as he walked into the bathroom.

He felt terrible and he knew that it would only get worse. A small part of him had expected that evil woman to clean him out again, to help him. But she hadn't. She had let him lay there in the mud and refuse and rain, and it was humiliating. Instead of focusing him, anger only made the nausea worse. His body felt like it was turning itself inside out in order to expel the toxins from his system.

When he finally dragged his eyes open and looked blearily into the toilet, he saw tiny rivulets of bright red shot through the yellow bile. He stood, wiped the string of spit from his lower lip and splashed water on his face. One quick glance in the mirror showed him that he looked as bad as he felt, which was slightly better than a day-old corpse lying in the sun. How much of her healing had he now undone?

Back in the bedroom the Native continued his game. Though he had threatened violence Cole knew he hadn't the strength for it. He sighed in resignation, folded his arms over his chest and leaned against the wall for support.

"You win. What do you want?" Cole asked.

Those seemed to be the magic words. The man's smile widened as he hopped off the dresser and then leaned against it, mocking Cole's use of the wall, but Cole didn't move because the wall was the only thing keeping him upright.

"You almost made me angry. Instead of the warning I meant to give you I came this close to just killing you." The man held up forefinger and thumb with an inch of air in between. "It would serve you right but to spare the strained relations between our people I will control myself."

Cole swallowed. He did not doubt the stranger's ability to kill him, especially in his current state. The Native smiled again, as if pleased by Cole's acceptance.

Cole took a deep breath to quell the nausea, swallowed hard and said, "Thank you so much for sparing my life. I'll try to remember your mercy before the One True God casts you into Hell. Of course, my memory is quite short so unless we both die within the next week or so your chances at salvation don't look so good…"

The stranger laughed. "And you have a direct line to the Holy Father, don't you, Father Cole? What are you… Second? Third in line? How many people have to die before you can seize control of the Church Congress?"

Cole's breath caught. He spoke slowly, "How do you know who I am?"

"I have my sources."

"Did Father Deven send you?" Cole asked.

The Native tossed his head back and laughed even harder, as if Cole had just told the most hilarious joke he had ever heard. At the moment Cole felt as if he was the joke. "Not quite. I don't think your illustrious father would employ one of us to collect one of his wayward priests. We have ways of being very..." The Native paused and licked his lips before continuing, "distracting."

Now that he knew that this man had not been sent by the Church Cole relaxed, but only a little. "Then what do you want?"

The Native pushed away from the dresser and came forward, his every movement as menacing as they had been sensual only a moment before. "You will leave Iliana alone. I am here to collect your debt to her. Feel free to stay in the city if you must, though I'd advise you to move into one of the outer circles to avoid any potential misunderstandings."

"You're kicking me out of the city? You're kidding me."

"I'm not kicking you out. I'm giving you a chance to leave."

"This is ridiculous," Cole muttered. For lack of a better way to vent the rising heat within him he turned around and punched the closest wall. The plaster cracked beneath the blow. His knuckles came back dusted with white powder and spotted with blood. He didn't feel any better and ruled out violence against inanimate objects as a way to deal with anger in the future.

"Ridiculous or not, it is the only way to avoid an unfortunate accident."

"An accident."

"Think of it more as retribution. You people keep coming to the city in the guise of tourists and killing us while we attempt to survive on the only living you have left available to us. Maybe we should fight back. Maybe we could make an example of you, hang you outside the city walls on a tall pole, your guts steaming, a tempting snack for scavengers and maggots—"

"How about this instead," said Cole, "You tell Iliana to stay away from me. I never asked her for anything. She cleaned me out on her own. And as for my debt to her? I tried to pay her once but she didn't take my money. I'm not going to try again. I'm not leaving the city or the Final Circle and I certainly hope that I will never see her again."

The Native clucked his tongue in a condescending manner and moved toward the door. Cole stepped aside to let him through. "Your choice," he said as he left.

Cole closed the door, then stared at it and seethed. But the door with its chipped red paint did not give him any satisfaction. His hand still throbbed, bringing his mind back into focus. The disorientation had ended and now he was clear on what had happened and the simple truth only made him angrier. That woman had left him in the street. She had left him there to die and then had second thoughts and sent someone to carry him back to his room. Then she sent a henchman to threaten him.

Despite this certainty there was another part of him that remained determined to point out the fallacy in his logic. He had railed at her for helping once and now he was angry with her for not helping him again. He was waffling and he knew it but blaming her was easy. Calling her sinful, thinking of her as nothing more than a temptation to be avoided was the easiest way to talk himself out of the need he felt even now to seek her out and talk to her. He welcomed the anger that burned him from within. Anything was better than complacent disillusionment.

Cole moved to the balcony to get some fresh air. His room reeked of vomit and stale sweat and other unpleasant bodily fluids. Last night's storm had passed, leaving behind a blue sky disfigured by rigid lines of white clouds. He looked to the sky, to his palms, shiny with perspiration, to the gaudy false fronts of the bars and clubs across the street. He needed guidance but nothing stirred within him. Nothing changed. He was struck by no divine inspiration.

He sighed, swearing that he hadn't expected anything, and looked down at the half-empty street. A few people milled around, indecisive in their motivations now that daylight was upon them. And then there was Iliana, standing beneath his balcony and looking up at him. The people in the street moved around her like drones while she, the queen, ignored them.

Time stopped, the world slowed and Cole was swallowed by her deep blue eyes, by the concern on her face. Iliana wore a white, corseted dress that reached her ankles. She looked like an angel. No, he told himself, she looked like a fallen angel. Was this the sign he had asked for?

At first she stood still, frozen as if in a tableaux. But then she smiled up at him and Cole suddenly knew what he had to do: confront her, stop her, help her. And maybe, somewhere in the process of helping her, he would find himself, find his own salvation. The woman with the hypnotizing eyes and the blaspheming tongue would be his test. Pass or fail, it didn't seem to matter as long as he made the attempt.

13

Iliana watched Cole watching her. He looked a little green but at least he was alive. She had asked the city clean-up crew to retrieve him and take him back to his hotel and her purpose beneath his balcony was to make sure they had done as they promised. Nothing more. She held her breath until a minute later when he finally turned and retreated back into his room.

Then she sighed. Their acquaintance was over. She wished him luck with his disillusionment but whether she wanted him to decide one way or another she couldn't say. Her eyes swept down from the empty balcony just in time to see Adam exit the hotel's front doors. His face was stern, like a man with a mission.

At once she forgot the confused priest and became curious to know what Adam had been doing there. Adam loved only fine things so he usually spent his time in the nicest hotels, seducing only the wealthiest, most beautiful people. And even though this was nowhere near a slum, here he seemed out of place. They both did.

"How are you, big brother?" she asked as she fell into step beside him. Alone their beauty was like a ripple in a pool of standing water. Together they were a wave, washing over everyone they passed, the people unable to do anything but stare until they were gone, leaving in their wake a vague sense of discontent, of something gone amiss. For this reason they seldom spoke to each other in public and preferred to work alone.

"Iliana, what a surprise," he smiled and said in a way that insinuated her appearance was not much of a surprise, nor was it welcome. He put his arm around her waist. In his dark jacket beside her white dress he looked like her evil twin, her shadow.

"What are you doing here, Adam? Are you following me?" She had no reason to be suspicious and yet she was. They shared a mother, which meant they shared other things. She knew when he was troubled or happy. She also knew when he was lying.

"Working. Just working."

"You never work this part of the city."

"I'm trying to pick up some of the slack you left by being below quota." He paused to let the remark sting, which it did, though her face showed nothing. When she didn't give him the satisfaction of a response he continued, "Times are hard. You have to take work where you can get it, even if that means lowering one's standards."

And there it was. They rarely had occasion to be dishonest with each other but he was lying. There was a pinch in his voice that gave it away. Something was going on that Iliana wasn't supposed to know, which, of course, made her want to know what it was.

"Times aren't that bad," she countered, hoping for an answer with specifics.

"You can't even imagine." His face suddenly became vague, his fake smile collapsed and he looked down the street toward the palace as if toward some invisible goal. It made Iliana nervous. She stopped walking and pulled away from him. Adam turned to her but his face remained serious.

She said, "If things are that bad, then I must get to work. I wouldn't want people to think I am the reason our city is in such a sorry state."

Adam's face paled as she spoke. When she turned for her triumphant exit he grasped her arm and eased her back to his side. "You have to be careful now," he said.

"Why?"

"Have you given any more thought to what the Governor asked of you?"

"How do you know what we talked about?"

"I spoke to him. He is worried, you know. He doesn't have many years left and he probably won't be here for the next Festival. He just wants to have everything set."

"Set for what?" Against her better judgment she felt herself getting pulled into this intrigue and she hated it. She just wanted be left alone, to live as she chose, without borders and double standards. At the same time she knew it wasn't going to happen, at least not in her lifetime. But Adam had had a way of drawing her in, of making her want to know more, want to learn other people's secrets. He would make a great Governor someday if he ever learned to stifle his impulses. He was like a fire, flaring whenever a new idea crossed his path, and hanging about the Council as he so often did, he always had plenty of kindling.

"You'll see," was all Adam said. He had found his newest bundle of firewood and was smoldering from the inside out. She figured that he was not supposed to tell her anything about it.

Iliana rolled her eyes. "You always do this. Why do you have to hint at things when you know you're just going to end up telling me anyway? Why don't you just tell me now and be done with it?"

Adam grinned his famous, disarming grin and loped away from her but not toward the Palace. Iliana sighed, knowing that she was destined to remain unsatisfied where Adam was concerned. If she wanted to know something he withheld the information. If she didn't want anything to do with it he usually offered it to her on a golden platter. It had always been that way. He relished the power of knowledge.

Sometimes it seemed like her lot in life was to be disappointed in everyone and everything around her. She told herself she wasn't interested in Adam and walked into the nearest bar, hoping to lose her curiosity in the warmth of a client's body.

14

Adam strode through the hallway but his footsteps made no noise. Between the stone archways sunlight shone in, broken by the shadows of the thriving trees in the courtyard. This was a place of reflection, meditation. Someday Adam wanted to come here and make use of the space but it would have to wait until the restrictions on his people were lifted. As things stood he had broken several rules as soon as he set foot into this compound but since he had done so several times in the past he walked without fear.

He reached his destination without encountering another soul and stepped inside with catlike silence. The room was small and plain. It contained only a bed with a brown wool blanket, a bookcase full of religious texts and a large wooden relief of the three stages of man: the angry, the angelic, and the mortal caught somewhere in between, which was to this particular sect of the Church the ultimate truth. The room also contained a desk where Yourian, a cleric, sat and read. He was young, barely 20, and clad in a thin, white wool robe. His left hand scratched at his torso as he read.

Adam shut the door. The coming together of door and jamb broke through the silence like a thunderclap and Yourian jumped. His head shot up and swiveled in Adam's direction. Adam leaned back against the door and smiled. He knew he was beautiful when he smiled and so he made a point of doing it often.

"What are you doing here?" Yourian asked. His hands trembled as he removed his wire-framed reading glasses. He was pale for a Colonist and the dark circles beneath his eyes made him look ill or chronically exhausted but his voice was strong.

"I came to see you, Yourian," Adam replied. He dragged out each sound of the boy's name as though savoring the feel of them on his tongue. Yourian squirmed in his seat. Adam enjoyed watching him squirm.

"You aren't allowed to be here."

Adam stalked the young cleric, each footstep sounding off against the stone floor and ticking off the seconds. With the door closed and no window for a breeze, the air grew dense and hot almost immediately. Yourian began to sweat and Adam could smell it, salty and thick. It smelled sharp, like fear.

"Kick me out," Adam teased.

Yourian's fingers twitched against the back of the chair, the corner of the desk. "I'll scream for help. These grounds are guarded. They won't let you hurt me."

"If you scream I'll break your neck." Adam's voice was low, threatening, yet his smile stayed. He imagined himself as a cat toying with a cornered mouse, the consummate predator.

"Please!" Yourian said as he fell to his knees. Nervous sweat darkened the robe around his neck, beneath his arms. His brown hair clung in damp strings to his forehead. "Please don't kill me."

Adam glided toward Yourian, took a position behind him and pulled him to his feet by his throat. Beneath his palm Yourian's pulse raced, his throat quivered as he swallowed, his lips mouthed the words of the Prayer of the One True God.

Adam licked the young man's neck above the pounding vein. His sweat was bitter and bland at the same time, like watered down beer. Yourian's diet was far too healthy for Adam's taste but fear added enough spice to make it worthwhile.

Yourian shuddered. "Please," he whimpered.

Adam wrenched Yourian's head to the side and sliced at the exposed flesh with his metal-tipped thumb. Yourian's back arched away from him but Adam held him in place as he placed his mouth over the wound and drank. The blood was almost tasteless.

After a time Yourian stopped struggling. He even relaxed into Adam's arms and sighed as if he were being kissed instead of having his life drained away. It seemed the embrace lasted only a few moments before Adam felt Yourian's heart stutter. He could take no more.

Adam withdrew his lips with great care to keep the blood from gushing out of the wound and carried the young man's sagging body to the bed, where he laid Yourian down on top of the blankets. Adam then sat at the desk and waited and watched Yourian's rake-thin chest rise and fall with hypnotic slowness. Then, bored of that, he looked over what Yourian had been reading: an essay entitled, "The Impossibility of the Existence of a Native Soul." Adam snorted and looked away.

"You weren't supposed to come today," Yourian said. His words were languid, his voice nearly a whisper. "Not that I'm complaining. I like it better like this, as a surprise."

"I couldn't wait," Adam replied, and Yourian gave him the response he wanted, a genuine smile. Adam knew that Yourian loved him in his way. He also knew how to use that love to his advantage and he quickly doused any fire of fantasy with a splash of the truth.

"Time is running out. I need to know if you have heard anything else about the Church and its plan. We have to be prepared for what is coming or we will all die."

Yourian gave him a lazy shrug and reached into a pocket in his robe, retrieving a small metal tin. He twisted off the lid and the pungent aroma of medicinal herbs spread rapidly in the heated air. He dipped two fingers into the tin and spread the translucent green salve inside over the tiny wound on his throat. It would be healed within a day.

"I wish you would trust me," Yourian said. He sat up. "I've told you everything I know so far. They hold a group of your people captive in Afet's Wall and they have been experimenting on them. There is talk that they have created a virus that can kill you and that they may attack during the Festival of Semiveh."

"They might? They may? Our deal is not based on hearsay and speculation. The Festival is a three-day event. If you can't tell me anything more specific after all this time then you might as well start paying for my services—"

"I've tried, I've listened."

"I think you want us to die. You want me to die."

"No! I'm just a cleric. They don't tell me important things."

"You don't care."

"But I do!" Yourian wailed, "I need you." His eyes were fe-ver-bright, revealing his arousal. Adam was not flattered. Smiles and fawning adoration were commonplace in his line of work.

"Yourian. We are going to die. I am going to die if you do not help me."

"I am trying," Yourian cried. His face crumpled and his eyes filled and then overflowed with tears.

But Adam was a predator. He did not know how to console this ridiculous man before him so he only said, "Try harder."

He cracked open the door and peeked outside. A quick glance told him the hallway was deserted and he stepped out, leaving the door hanging open behind him.

15 Night again: hungry and alive and full of devils. And yet people laughed. Laughed at the mist that shrouded the buildings and tickled their faces. Laughed at the money they threw away in bars and clubs and gambling halls. Laughed as they sinned over and over again.

The morning would be harsh, as it always was. Sunlight would reveal the wasteful excesses of the evening hours, haggard faces smeared with make-up, crumpled bodies, broken souls. Some would flee the city in fear of what they might do come sunset. Others would embrace the guilt and laugh once more.

Cole pulled his guilt close to himself like a shroud to hide him from the eyes of strangers and walked the streets of the Final Circle, the center of things. For the first time since his arrival in Adara Vega he was sober. And having never seen the city at night through lucid eyes he could now see some of its appeal.

Before this night his drunken eyes, tinted by self-loathing, had seen only the chipped paint and crumbling concrete, the bodies of insects darkening the intermittent streetlights, the dust of the desert and beneath that, the loneliness and pain, the conflicting emotions of ecstasy and guilt that fueled these people to wander, to pray, and to sin some more.

But now he saw deeper. It wasn't that those things weren't there anymore, but they became background to what he finally saw was the real city. Here in the Final Circle the buildings felt ancient and alive. The bars and clubs here had been converted from churches or schools and much of the original architecture remained. Carved wooden doors stood open, their faces dulled by layers of varnish. Stone gargoyles snarled at passersby. And inside those bars the walls were faded frescoes of religious figures, the windows made of stained-glass and showing the deeds of now nameless saints admonished and blessed by a stern-looking God. The doorways were arched and the bars sat upon raised platforms, the altars of the new gods of pleasure and excess. Cole had grown to know them well.

His feet drew him closer to the Palace Nyssa. He had never seen it up close at night and had been too sick during the day to venture out. The great golden tower of the Palace was always visible, even from miles away and far beyond the city walls.

But before that the Palace had been a modest church, like so many of the buildings in the area. According to the history books Adara Vega was one of the first towns to have been erected out of the desert when the Colonists arrived. It had been built by a sect of the Church that practiced asceticism. When they arrived they immediately eschewed the abundant wealth and control the Church wielded and had taken to the desert to practice their faith, abstaining from all worldly pleasures in order to bring their souls into harmony with the Divine. Their church stood alone in the desert so that those who wished only to pray and lead simple lives would have a place of peace, yet close enough to the Capitol City of Afet's Wall to enable easy contact with the head of the Church.

But terrible things had happened to the once devout people of this city. One day it had been a haven and the next day it was a ghost town. Everyone in the city had disappeared. There were no bodies. And though people had investigated there were no explanations. Instead of trying to reclaim the city the Colonists abandoned it and the Natives moved in, developing the land, expanding the outer walls further into the desert, rebuilding and restructuring the original church until all traces of the ascetics were buried beneath golden accents and carved stone.

It was an architectural marvel, with arches of stone and iron, engravings, relief sculptures, countless gargoyles and enormous, amber stained glass windows that yawned like the mouths of demons in the façade. The monstrous tower glowed day and night, a homing beacon for lost souls.

People now gossiped that the Palace itself had become a monster, a place to lose oneself forever, soul and all. Cole had believed them of course, because it was all he had known. But he found he couldn't practice such blind faith any longer, and this was the source of his current dilemma.

He had to know why. And if a priest began to question the workings of his God then it was only a matter of time before his congregation did as well. Unchecked curiosity was the disease that could devastate the Church. The curiosity that led him here disproved all of his excuses.

That woman had saved him and he must know why and for what purpose. If she had saved him out of the kindness of her heart then she had to have some goodness on some level. And if she was good she might have a soul. And if she had a soul then he could not let the Church continue its experiments. He had to talk to her to determine if she was an instrument of God or the devil. He had to know.

Cole forced his legs to walk around the building toward the massive front gate. Electric lanterns swung in lazy circles from the top of the iron perimeter fence, a boundary of light dividing within from without. His fingers trailed along the iron bars of the fence, warm from the light that flooded over them even though he could see his breath in the cloudless night.

As he walked he watched the people in the courtyard putting on airs, changing partners, laughing. Their movements were calculated, almost choreographed. Iliana had moved the same way, with a grace so complete he couldn't believe it was spontaneous. The people, Natives and Colonists alike, strolled in waves, meeting other waves, exchanging pleasantries that bubbled up like foam on their lips and then backing away again, only to collide with another group, swaying with the rhythms of polite conversation.

Cole was absorbed by their movements and didn't notice the guard at the gate until he reached out and caught Cole's shoulder.

"Pardon me, sir, but you can't enter the Palace grounds without an escort." The guard let go of Cole's arm with a gentle push.

Cole looked over to see a man of the same height and build as himself, but towheaded and with eyes the color of jade set in a pale, smooth face. Cole blinked hard. He had never gotten used to the brilliant eye colors all of the Natives seemed to have, another aspect the Church had used as an example of their evil. Those eyes were too beautiful, too tempting to be holy.

"But," Cole protested, "I'm meeting someone." It wasn't exactly a lie but that little sin deepened his resolve to find the truth.

"And who is that?"

"Iliana." He averted his eyes when he spoke her name. It felt like blasphemy on his tongue. Again he felt her taking up space in his head, swelling to life in a mind that had tried a million times to smash her out of existence.

"It's all right, I'll escort him to Iliana's cell," said another voice, high and bright as sunlight.

Cole turned to see a woman who appeared to be much younger than himself take his arm. Her skin was dark and in the glowing yellow lights from the palace she looked as if she were carved of obsidian glass. Her black eyes were wide and honest, her lips curled into a smile. Cole couldn't tell if it was genuine or all a part of the act.

As Cole let her lead him into the Palace yard he heard the guard call out, "And you tell Iliana that from now on she needs to be down here to escort her own clients."

"Thank you," Cole said to the woman. Her thick black hair was plaited close to her head with streamers of gold and green woven in with the strands. Such ornamentation was an indulgence most Colonists couldn't have attempted without outright scandal but this woman wore it well.

"You're welcome," she answered. Her voice was like music, an operetta sung only for him. "Iliana is already entertaining one of her regular clients. Does she know you're coming?"

Cole almost backed out then but the feeling passed. If he left now he knew he would never have the nerve to return and he would likely end up jumping off a tall building just to end this infuriating doubt. It was not an attractive future. Better to learn what he could and then decide whether or not to do himself in.

"She knows," he said.

"Of course she does," the woman answered. He felt the heat of her gaze searching his face but he couldn't meet her eyes. Cole could tell she didn't believe him but she said nothing else as they wove between groups of escorts flirting with their clients.

The woman led him up the steps and into the foyer of the Palace, and there Cole paused. The first time he had passed through these doors he had been running hard and beyond caring about his surroundings. Though this was now a place of sin and perversity Cole was still standing in the remains of an ancient church and he was determined to savor it.

The floor was made of gray slate smoothed by centuries of foot traffic. On both sides of the great main doors sat alcoves filled with shelves of little white candles, all lit to warm the stilted air between doors. Cole let the nameless woman lead him through the second set of doors, carved with smiling angels whose wings were spread and brushed with gold and glittered in the candlelight. They crossed that second threshold and Cole had to remind himself to breathe.

Beneath the gilded edges and decoration some bits of the original church remained. The ceiling, though partially blackened by centuries of candle smoke, was still indigo with gold pinprick spots like stars dotting the vaulted sky. Along the walls were clear frescoes depicting scenes from nature, trees and streams and tranquil pastures. What looked like a stone altar now stood at the entrance, buried beneath piles of paper. Two people, a man and a woman dressed in impeccable black suits, bustled about behind it, making notes, exchanging money with satisfied customers. And above what would have been the pulpit, had the place not become a lounge, still stood the formal statue of the three stages of man that adorned every Church.

Cole didn't know what to make of these sights and his guide didn't give him any time to process the information as she steered him away from the lounge, past the desk with the couple who weren't paying them any attention and over to the elevators. His reflection in the mirrored doors disturbed him and he had to look away. He didn't like the image of himself standing arm in arm with a Native but he couldn't muster the rudeness required to pull away.

What would his father think if he could see him this way, he wondered? Would he be pleased?

His reverie was interrupted when the woman asked, "Do you know which floor Iliana is on?"

"Twenty-nine," he said. The endless ride from her cell to the ground floor on that panicked morning would not let him forget.

"Just wanted to make sure," she said. She let go of his arm, stood on tiptoe to kiss him on the cheek and left him there. Cole was too shocked to respond before she disappeared into the crowd.

When the elevator doors opened a few men and one woman tottered out, their faces flushed and exuberant. As they went to the reception desk Cole shook his head at their soft laughter and entered the elevator. With sweating fingers he pressed the button for Iliana's floor and when the elevator began to rise his stomach plunged into his feet. He wiped his moist palms on his trousers and licked his lips. He watched the little light count off the floors without seeing it. His mind raced in circles, thinking the simple question, "Why?" over and over again. He couldn't answer. He only knew that he had to do it.

When the doors finally opened on an empty, opulent hallway Cole suffered a moment of panic. What was he doing there? What was he thinking, approaching her like this? He told himself that it was a necessary evil, swallowed his panic, and forced himself to step into the hallway, turn right and walk across the mosaic tile floor to the door he knew led into Iliana's cell.

He paused just outside when he heard a sigh and a man's voice, followed by Iliana's small laugh. The client was still inside. He went in anyway out of morbid curiosity, telling himself that he only wanted to watch her work on a client, weave her lies, steal a man's soul.

Iliana and her client lay in the pit of cushions, so involved in each other that they paid the door no attention. With the fitful candlelight as a shield Cole crept into the room and hid behind a thick tapestry that smelled of damp wool. It scratched his face as he peered out from behind it to watch the scene with undeniable interest.

"Do you ever get to leave this place?" the client asked. He was younger than Cole and of a slighter build, with a full beard and shaggy brown hair. His clothes were rumpled as if he had slept in them but he reclined against the cushions like an indifferent prince giving audience to his subjects. For all that he could have been Cole's brother. But then most of the Colonists looked alike: skin somewhat tan to medium brown, hair brown, eyes hazel to brown. Very plain, very monotonous. No wonder people came here, if only to add some color to their lives.

Iliana looked breathtaking as usual and sat with her body inclined suggestively towards her client. Her face glowed in the soft candlelight and her lips glistened. She licked them before she spoke.

"I can leave the Palace, of course, but not the Final Circle, and never the city."

"Why?" the man pouted. Though his back was to Cole, Cole could hear the pout in his voice and immediately disliked him. What a stupid and obvious question. They were the last of their kind. Outside there existed a thousand souls who would kill a Native as soon as look at one. But within these walls the Church offered protection, limited though it was. It wasn't safe for them outside of the city.

Iliana offered no answers, only laughed. "That's just the way it is."

"Have you ever been anywhere else?" he asked.

Iliana rolled up one of his sleeves with nimble fingers. She was slow and deliberate about it, making sure to touch his bare skin often, and Cole saw the man relax beneath her touch. The care with which she handled his sleeve, the reverence with which she looked at the exposed flesh, it seemed so focused and intimate that Cole almost felt guilty for witnessing it.

As she worked she said, "I have never left this city. But you have. Tell me where you're from, George."

The way she said the man's name caused Cole to shiver

71

with unwelcome desire. He fought it and then caught himself reaching for the prayer beads he normally kept in his pocket. They weren't there. He hadn't touched them since Iliana returned them, so instead he clenched his hands into fists at his sides.

The man sighed and let his head fall back onto the cushions. Now Iliana hovered over him, a smile thinning her lips, her fingers still idling in the crook of his elbow. Her long fingernails made tiny indentations in the smooth, tan flesh.

"I was born in Franklin," George said.

"What was that like?" She continued to stroke his forearm and Cole couldn't take his eyes off of her. Where he had expected to see polite, professional interest, Cole saw instead what he thought was genuine longing on her face. She wanted to hear him speak, to know what was out there. Against his better judgment he felt himself warming towards her. She appeared so innocent and yet here she was about to drain a man of his life, his money and his purity.

"It was boring." The man spoke in the eerie monotone of a sleepwalker. "That's why I left. Now I explore the new territories, looking for places to set up colonies."

"You must have seen such wonders… I can't even imagine…" Iliana's voice had become soft, hypnotic. It washed over Cole in warm waves of sound even though he was standing at the other end of the room. Cole blinked hard to clear his head. It didn't help.

"This one time…" the man began, his voice excited once more, shaking off the tranquility that Iliana's presence caused. Iliana silenced him with a finger against his lips.

"Be still. Just think," she said. She opened the flesh in the crook of his elbow with her metal-tipped thumb and blood welled black in the half-light. Then she bowed to his outstretched arm, opened her mouth and drank.

Once again, even though he was only a spectator, Cole swooned and had to hold onto the wall to keep from falling over. His feet shuffled a bit on the marble floor and he drew back behind the tapestry in case they happened to look up. For several minutes he listened to the man's deep, almost obscene moans and the occasional rustle of Iliana's dress against the cushions. His heart pounded in his chest hard enough to shatter bone. To still his spinning head he closed his eyes and forced his lungs to take deep, even breaths. His body grew tight and he felt the frenzied fire of need ripping through his body, radiating from the same place where Iliana drank from her client.

Cole fought the overwhelming, sinful urge to look again until he heard the man clear his throat. He came back to himself only with the greatest effort, stood up straight and ran a hand through his hair, now damp with sweat. Only then did he hazard a peek around the edge of the tapestry.

Iliana helped her client to stand on unsteady legs then led him to the edge of the cushions and held into his arms until he had his footing. From his back pocket he withdrew a wallet and folded a couple of bills into Iliana's palm.

"Thank you," he said and leaned in to kiss her. At the last minute she turned her head so that his lips only brushed her glowing cheek. And then he left.

From where Cole hid, a statue of an angel with outstretched wings obscured his view of the door but he heard it open and close. Still, Cole just stood there, not knowing what to do now that he was alone with her. He heard her skirt slide across the stone, her heels tick against the floor. She sighed and in the empty room the sound echoed. Then she spoke in a clear, loud voice that reverberated off the walls.

"He tells me to stay away, and yet he hunts me down and spies on me. To maim, to kill, to persecute… Certainly not to apologize, for why would one as high as he stoop to my level to apologize. I mean nothing to him."

Cole stepped out from his hiding place with a bowed head, his face flushed like a child who had been caught stealing which, in a way, he had. But upon seeing the mocking smile that turned one corner of her painted mouth, Cole's anger flared.

She was not afraid of him or his God. She was not even chastised by his presence. He took a deep breath before he spoke and reminded himself that she had saved his life. And he had come to her this time with the possibility of saving something infinitely more precious, his soul, and if she had one, maybe even hers.

Cole scowled. "Please, don't start. I haven't come to hurt you or persecute you or even lecture you. I've come to offer you a deal."

"I knew you didn't want to apologize," she mused. Then, "Let me guess. You want to save my soul in exchange for my services. You're not the first man of God to want to atone for his sins that way, nor will you be the last—"

"I cannot offer you that deal because I am not interested in your services and I do not know if you even have a soul to save." His scowl deepened but he was determined that she not misunderstand his intentions. Cole held his breath as Iliana crossed to her velvet divan and sat. Her bare arms glowed against the dark material.

She finally met his eyes and asked, "And what does your Church have to say on that matter?"

Cole spoke without thinking, reciting a rhetoric he had learned by heart and repeated innumerable times over the years. "The Church teaches that you are not human, so therefore, like any other animal or tree or living thing, you have no souls."

"If we are soulless then why did we help you when you came to our land? Why did we cure you of the blood disease? Why did we help you survive?"

Cole didn't know the answer to that one. "Self-interest," he offered, but that excuse sounded pathetic even to his own ears.

Iliana frowned. He had upset her and was surprised to find that he felt bad about it. But watching her regain her composure was fascinating. Her brow smoothed, her lips became straight and the hardness in her eyes faded. Only her voice continued to reflect her anger.

"If that is the case," she said, "then what could you possibly want from me?"

It was a valid question but Cole could only tell her half of the answer. He couldn't tell her about the prisoners in the Capitol City. Not yet. Not until he knew whether the lives of the Natives were worth turning against the Church and everything he had ever known. "I want to know more about your people. I need to understand why you saved me—"

"Because you would have died," she said and rolled her eyes as if they had already run this point into the ground.

"But that's just it!" he exclaimed, "If you are supposed to be soulless and evil, as the Church teaches, then why do you care if I live or die? I'm a stranger. I mean nothing to you. So why save me?"

Iliana narrowed her eyes. "What would your fellow men of God think of this bargain you are offering?"

"Some would be appalled but most would probably call me my father's son and laugh it off, certain that it is only a passing curiosity."

"And is it?"

Cole answered with as much honesty as he was able to at that moment. "I don't know."

Iliana paused, searched his face, and apparently found what she was looking for because she suddenly said, "I will see you, but under these conditions: you must pay me for my time and my time is valuable. You will not drink liquor anymore. You cannot berate me or call me false no matter what I tell you. You must listen to what I say and see what I show you without covering your ears or your eyes. If you question me we can discuss it, but respectfully. If at any time I feel threatened by you or your dogma, the deal is off."

Cole nodded, relieved by her willingness to participate in this insanity. He had plenty of money. His life at home had been one of thrift and the Church paid well enough for him to have amassed a healthy savings. They stared at each other for a few moments in silence. Cole wasn't sure what to say now that their clandestine pact had been made.

Iliana stood and moved toward the door. She was the most beautiful, graceful creature he had ever seen. She was walking temptation for a man given to excesses like himself. Before taking his vow as a priest his life had consisted of drinking and women but when he became a priest he gave it all up. What had he gotten himself into?

"Well then, I must bid you goodnight for the evening," Iliana said and walked away.

This sudden change caught Cole off guard. He stammered, "Oh, so... um..."

"I have to go out. I cannot just sit and talk, like you. Thanks to your Church, I still have a quota to fulfill." She reached the door and turned back to look at where Cole was still standing in the middle of the room, feeling for all the world like his entire life had just passed him by and left him holding the bill.

"So, when..."

"Tomorrow. I'll come to your room just after sunrise. Can you find your own way out?"

Cole nodded and Iliana swept out of the room. Cole gave her a head start before he left because he didn't want to ride in the elevator with her and the uncomfortable silence. No one paid him any attention on his way out. It was only after he left the Palace grounds that he thought of the stranger's warning to stay away from Iliana.

Cole tucked his head into his collar and hurried away from the Palace. He didn't want to be discovered before he had gained the knowledge for which he was risking his soul.

16

Governor Drake appeared confident but he was not stupid. After so many centuries as Governor he knew better than to expect miracles but neither would he stoop to grovel. So even though the 75 members of the Church government, known as the Congress of Elders, sat in their boxes above him and all around him and glared at him with blatant disgust, he stood before them with pride. Numerous medals, presented to him by the Church for being an ambassador of the Church Congress to his people, glimmered on the breast of his jacket. He had tied his hair back into a ponytail to keep it neat. He had almost forgone the blue paint for this visit but then thought that they might view his age as a weakness, so at the last moment he had slathered it on.

The walls in the vaulted chamber shifted and seemed to breathe as paintings accented by the stolen gold of centuries of thievery came alive around him in the light from the two glass chandeliers.

Powerful lights also shone at even intervals along the first row of boxes, making the Governor's shadow appear grotesque as it stretched across a painting of the One True God smiting down a flock of naked, cowering people. The men and women being destroyed all had smears of crimson around their mouths. The message was clear: Governor Drake and his people were nothing more than demons to the Colonists. He knew the honors bestowed upon him meant nothing, that they were mere trinkets meant to placate him. In their collective eyes he was evil, he was a monster. But even though he already knew the outcome of this meeting he still held the tiniest hope that they would relent and he wouldn't have to show the Church just how monstrous they could be.

"Governor Drake," said Father Deven, the High Priest and voice of the Church, from his perch four rows above the floor, on a dais above the other members of the Congress. Father Deven wore bright yellow robes with red trim. His face, by contrast, was a web of suntanned wrinkles and a network of white hairs that swept back from his temples. His features were gentle and trustworthy like a grandfather, a wise man, a holy man. But the Governor knew it was a façade. By report Father Deven indulged in a Native's arms as often as any of his people, the difference was that he was above reproach.

To Father Deven's left sat the second-in-command, Father Piotr. Father Piotr was the foil to Father Deven's brightness. He wore a wide, black hat and shawl draped over his head and a black robe with red trim. The scowl of disapproval on his mocha-colored face matched those of the rest of the Congress. The seat to Father Deven's right, once occupied by Father Tanaka, sat vacant.

"How nice to see you again," Deven said without conviction. His was the rich, comforting voice of the Church. Every ideal the Church held, every conclusion they reached, every decision they made was communicated to the public through him. If he suddenly declared that the Church would begin sacrificing virgins there would be plenty of eager souls lining up outside the Capitol City to offer their daughters to the cause. Father Deven had the last word in every affair and, staring up at him, Governor Drake knew that a decision had already been made, and that his request for an audience had been accepted only so that he could hear the verdict in person.

Governor Drake nodded and answered with as much respect as he could muster for a man he had no respect for, "Nice to see you, as well, Father. I notice that Father Tanaka is not present. Will he be joining us?"

"Father Tanaka has gone to rest with the Lord," answered Father Deven.

"I am sorry to hear that. My condolences," said Governor Drake and he meant it. Even though he never defended the Natives out loud, at times Governor Drake swore that he had seen a flash of compassion in the old man's eyes. It made Drake believe that the Natives had, if not an ally among the Elders, at least a sympathizer.

Drake added, "Will one of the Elders be replacing him?"

"Yes. Father Tanaka's son, Cole, will be joining us once he returns from his sabbatical. He is an honorable man dedicated to his faith. Father Tanaka himself supervised his religious education."

"I see," said Drake. He wondered if something of the old man had rubbed off on his son, but now was not the time to think of such things. One man could not hope to stand against the entire Congress anyhow. Governor Drake was on his own. He pushed such matters out of his mind and cleared his throat to begin his practiced speech but Father Deven raised his hand. In that moment he looked like a benevolent lord about to grant favors to those who serve beneath him. But the moment passed and hard reality snapped into place.

"Governor, we are already aware of your plight so let's not waste any time with your impeccable oration and get right to the point."

Governor Drake held his breath. As many times as the Church had denied his requests, the waiting still made him anxious. The eyes of the Congress still pierced his stoic armor and their communal hatred of him still squeezed his chest like a thousand angry hands until his heartbeats resonated all the way to his fingertips.

Father Deven spoke down to the Governor. "Governor Drake, let me begin by saying that the Church has always maintained a solemn respect for your people and your culture. But as members of a nation living within the protective arms of the Church of Universal Truth, you must be subject to all of its laws and regulations. Therefore, we do not understand your insistence on bringing this issue to us again and again. Your kind cannot be permitted to leave Adara Vega. This would put our people in too great a danger…"

"Not if you would stop teaching your children that we are evil—" Governor Drake offered but he was ignored as Father Deven continued without pause.

"The land we gave you is suitable for your needs. You have even expanded over the centuries into territory that does not belong to you and yet we have not asked you to stop."

"You stuck us in the middle of a desert in a cursed city where none of your people wanted to live. It was necessity, not compassion that placed us there."

"That is not the point, Governor. You have land. You have space. We have not retaliated for your infractions. We have allowed you to grow, to prosper on your own."

The anger rose, burned Governor Drake's cheeks and the back of his neck, and he had to speak lest his head explode from the force of the pent-up emotions, even though he knew it was futile. "You have suffered our existence only because of our reproductive inferiority. We can produce children every 100 years, so your people flourish while ours die out and you do not have to blame yourselves for our diminishing numbers. But you are to blame," he turned to speak to the entire Congress. "You insist on perpetuating the lie that we are less than you. You encourage your people to treat us like animals, to injure and kill us."

"And it is your insistence on continuing the 'tradition' of sharing blood that keeps you where you are."

"You didn't mind it so much when we shared with you for free. Once we took back our sacred rituals for fear of them being abused that your people stooped to tyranny."

"The punishment fits the crime."

"Our crime was in trusting you and now we have no choice. As the Festival of Semiveh approaches the unrest grows. There have been 26 skirmishes in the past month alone in the outer circle. My people were attacked, in some cases tortured, in all cases murdered. Does your Church condone such behavior?"

Father Deven was unflappable. "Without our protection it would have been worse."

"Protection? Who will protect us from you? You preach hateful propaganda to your people while turning a blind eye as they exploit us for their pleasure. Meanwhile you keep raising our taxes and continue to pick us off one by one. Soon we will have nothing left to give."

"The taxes you pay for your safety and the safety of the Church's people while they are within your city's walls. The price of sin is not cheap. If you continue to prey upon our people with lies and vanities then we will continue to tax you—"

"You have left us no other choice!" Drake exploded, then chastised himself for letting his emotions get the best of him. When Father Deven smiled Drake knew that he had given them what they wanted. He had shown his weakness and they fed upon it, puffed themselves up with it until they looked like a bunch of bloated swine gorging on the leftovers of a rich meal. Drake was ashamed but he met the priest's gloating smile with proud eyes.

Father Deven offered a gentle admonishment, like a father to his dull-witted son, "Please do not displace the blame for your present situation. You know as well as I how you got there. The One True God punishes the wicked and so will we, as His messengers here. This conversation is over. Your audience is deaf. And please do not bring this issue before us again."

Drake bowed, turned and strode from the room without another word. Once the massive doors creaked shut behind him he stood in the hallway and took a few deep breaths to calm his racing pulse, to cool his anger, but the heat continued to burn his cheeks beneath the paint. He didn't acknowledge the emotionless armed guards that stood on either side of the door, waiting to escort him back to his vehicle and out of the city.

He had given the Colonists every opportunity to back down, to cease their misguided condemnation of his people. But they continued to insist upon their righteousness. The time had come and once the war began there would be no stopping it. Not until they were all dead, one way or the other.

17

Father Deven leaned back in his chair and folded his hands in his lap, unruffled by the heated exchange.

"Well, that was spirited," he said with a chuckle and the Congress laughed along with him. "Now, to real business. Father Serrano, please give us an update on your experiments."

Father Serrano stood and inclined his head in deference toward Father Deven, then to the rest of the Congress. He lifted his logbook and his hands shook as if from palsy and his fingers left little sweat stains on the paper. Father Deven noticed his nervousness and forgave him for it. This was only Father Serrano's second time speaking to the entire Congress. The first time he had been detailing his experiments, which had been well-received. This time he had less-than-positive news and he wasn't in agreement over how Father Deven wanted to proceed.

"Father Deven, esteemed Congress," he paused, took a deep breath and continued in a voice that shook as much as his hands, "My experiments have not gone as planned. I have not been able to isolate the variable that allows the Natives to live such extended lives. It is not in their blood, nor is it in the drinking of the blood of others. Thank you, by the way, to those brave men and women who sacrificed a little of themselves to further my research, but it was fruitless.

"The immunity from all illnesses and their ability to cure us of our diseases appears to be in their tissue. Given our current technological limitations I have found no way to isolate and extract it."

"So what does this mean?" Father Piotr asked.

"This means I cannot continue my experiments. We must make alternate plans."

The Congress members began to titter in their seats. Father Deven noted that some of the Elders appeared delighted while other appeared nervous. He noticed disappointment that twisted Father Serrano's face. Prior to this meeting Father Serrano had argued in private for the lives of at least a few Natives so that he could continue his research along other routes, a request which Father Deven had denied. There was only one possible future now. The game was over and the Natives had lost.

All eyes in the great hall turned toward Father Deven, expectant. The hall filled with sharp inhalations as they held their breath as if they were one organism. They all knew what the answer had to be, for the new power and the former power could not coexist in peace if one refused to submit to the other.

"It shall be done," Father Deven announced. "You have tested the virus, I assume."

"Of course," croaked Father Serrano.

"Good."

"And the original timeframe?" asked Father Piotr.

"It remains. Notify our people in the city that we will release the virus in Adara Vega on the second day of the Native Festival. All of our followers must vacate the city three days before the Festival begins or they will be considered enemies of the Church."

"If it be the will of God," chanted the Congress as one.

"It is," said Father Deven. Then he smiled. "Let's take a break now and return in, say, two hours?"

Over the sound of shuffling papers and tramping feet of the Congress members leaving the great hall, Deven turned to Father Piotr and asked, "Have you heard from Father Cole? Has he returned from his sabbatical?"

"I have heard nothing, Father."

"Give him a few more days. If he has not returned by then send someone to go and collect him from Adara Vega. His sabbatical is officially over. He should be here to witness this historic moment."

"Of course," replied Father Piotr.

18 A quiet voice commanded Cole into wakefulness. "Forgive me, Father, for I have sinned."

The world to which Cole awoke was harsh and full of confusion. For a moment he thought he had fallen asleep in the confessional. Then he became aware of the heaviness of the quilt covering his sweating body, the coarse sheet against his face and the warmth of the sun on his cheek that could not have sought him out in the dark, curtained cell of the confessional.

"What?" he asked with an arid mouth and a vacant throat. For the first time since his arrival in this city he had fallen asleep sober and now he was thrown by the lack of nausea and the absence of spins.

The voice repeated itself, only softer. "Forgive me, Father, for I have sinned."

Cole opened his weary eyes to see Iliana sitting on the bed beside him. He blinked. She was still there.

"What are you doing here?" he asked before he remembered their agreement. He groaned and cleared his throat and, not for the first time, doubted his choices.

"How quickly we forget. I am here for our first meeting," she said, then grinned and added, "And because I have sinned."

Cole sat up in irritation and scratched his bare chest. "Stop saying that." He slid to the opposite side of the bed, plucked an undershirt off of the floor, sniffed at it, shrugged and then put it on. He did the same thing with the trousers, except he slid them on without standing up. It felt wrong to be half-naked in front of Iliana, as if she could see through his skin and into the shadows of his soul. And for all he knew she could, in fact, see through his skin. Believing it to be an expression of devoutness, he had deliberately kept himself ignorant of Native culture. The irony was not lost on him that now that knowledge might be the only thing that could heal his faith.

"But I have, I have sinned." She continued to smile as if she enjoyed his irritation. "It has been... Well, a lifetime since my last confession..."

Cole turned on her, "Why do you insist on tormenting me? I thought we had a truce."

Iliana stood and smoothed the front of her dark blue gown, the same one she had worn the night before. Cole doubted she had slept at all but only a hint of weariness around her eyes gave her away. Her curls had fallen somewhat, drawn down by the weight of her hair, otherwise she looked much the same as she had at the start of the night.

"Do you want to learn the truth or not?" she asked.

"Of course."

"Then the first thing you must do is lighten up."

"How dare you—" Cole started but Iliana ignored him.

"You must approach the truth with an open mind. You're not going to like a lot of it and anger will only cloud your understanding."

"Fine," he agreed with a grudging sigh. "I am open."

"Just the way I like them. Let's get some breakfast. But first you have to change into fresh clothes. You're a mess. I will not be seen with you looking like that." Cole hesitated, so she added, "I promise not to watch." And she turned her back on him.

Cole saw the wisdom of her request and changed into the only clothes left hanging in the closet. They were wrinkled but at least they were clean. Everything else was dirty since he hadn't much cared about laundry during his binge.

In the bathroom he splashed some water on his face and combed his unruly hair. When he returned Iliana was still looking through the glass doors onto the balcony.

"You can turn around now," he said.

She turned and looked him up and down. "That's a little better."

They left the hotel room, Iliana leading the way and Cole following behind like a lost puppy.

19 In an overpriced café, over tiny cups of bitter black tea and eggs and toast growing cold, Cole spent several minutes avoiding Iliana's gaze. She could tell that he was too nervous to eat but didn't know how to start the conversation.

Iliana sipped her tea and said nothing. He was, after all, paying for her time. If he wanted to spend that time contemplating his breakfast then that was his choice, though she doubted it would achieve the desired results. Theirs was a tense silence, a threshold on which they paused before their inevitable ideological confrontation. But after several more minutes passed and Cole still said nothing she finally broke the silence for him.

"Why did you come here?"

Cole winced and admitted, "You already guessed it. I am having a spiritual crisis and I came here to sort it out."

"And near-death experiences are helpful?"

"Not one bit."

"They never are."

He suddenly blurted, "I'm sorry, but I can't believe I'm doing this. I can't believe I'm sitting in a café with a woman I would have crossed the street to avoid only a few weeks ago. Only a few weeks ago I wouldn't have referred to you as a woman, either."

Iliana felt like she'd been slapped. Even though she had suspected that he was one of those Colonists who believed the lies his people told him it was still a shock to hear the words spoken out loud. She glanced out of the window at the haggard bodies lumbering home after the night's excesses.

"Then what could you hope to learn from a sub-woman like me?" Iliana asked.

"I didn't mean it like that," Cole said, scowling. "I just…" His voice trailed off, because he knew there were no excuses. He took a swig of his tea to wet his throat and pursed his lips at the bitterness. "I don't know. I don't know what to expect from you. I just want to understand. I want to know what you've been taught about life, about the Church… I suppose I want justification for everything."

"Why do you think you deserve such justification?"

The question took Cole back to his church on the morning of his breakdown. He shuddered. "I was in the Church, during Ceremony. And I looked out into the congregation and I saw… boredom, lust, envy. The interior of the cathedral, instead of being a testament to the power and the glory of the One True God, suddenly seemed just a gaudy testament to the tyrannical power of the Church."

"You had never felt this way before?"

"Never."

"What had changed?"

He hesitated, as if considering a revelation then licked his lips and whispered, "I saw something that…" His voice trailed off as his eyes focused on something outside.

Iliana followed his gaze and saw her brother in the street. Adam's eyes met hers and he came toward the café. Cole shot to his feet and backed away from the table.

"What are you doing?" she asked.

"Hiding. I can't let him see me with you." That was all the explanation he offered before he hid behind the dusty lace curtain that separated the café and the dark back rooms set aside for private meetings. Iliana was irritated by his behavior and stared at Cole with open disdain until Adam came in and blocked her view.

"Hello, sister. How are you this morning?" he asked and slid into the seat across from her.

Iliana's lips spread into a wide, fake smile and her eyes flicked to Cole's hiding place. He was watching them through the holes of the lace and shifting his weight from foot to foot like a nervous child.

She looked back at Adam's grinning face and lied, "How could I be anything but wonderful?"

"Did someone just leave in a hurry?" Adam dipped his finger into Cole's tea and then licked it. Though they were usually relaxed in front of each other Iliana felt that his nonchalance was a bit forced.

"Just the way I like it," he said and then drank the remainder of the tea in one gulp, infusing the gesture with the sensuality that always hovered near the surface of his chameleon personality. Iliana felt the appreciative eyes of the other patrons and employees trained on them and realized that it was always a show. Adam never stopped performing. So neither would she.

Iliana straightened her spine, affected her most regal and blasé attitude and leveled her eyes at Adam. "It doesn't matter now, does it? You drank his tea."

Adam leaned back against the seat. He did not look like other men would in that position, lazy and sloppy. Instead he looked a little worn out from a long but pleasant night.

"How did you do last night?"

"My night isn't over yet," she countered, suspicious. Once again she had found her brother in a section of the city he wouldn't deign to spit on before. And once again their rapport felt different. It was almost like being with another client but instead of tempting the client into her confidence and her room, she had to protect herself from being drawn into Adam's secret conspiracy.

"Fair enough," Adam said, "Then how are you doing up till now?"

"Why are you suddenly so interested in my business?" Iliana narrowed her eyes and frowned.

"What is that supposed to mean?" His pretend pout died an early death when something caught his eye. Adam smiled the smile of a predator, all teeth and wicked eyes, and licked his lips. Iliana turned to see one of the servers, a curly-haired Colonist of about 20, almost fall over himself beneath Adam's suggestive gaze. When the boy noticed Iliana watching as well he blushed and moved into the back room.

"I have to ask once more, are you following me?" Iliana glanced again at Cole's hiding place. He glared at her as if offended that she was entertaining her brother instead of him. Though she was eager to find out why Cole felt he had to hide, his cowardice annoyed her so she didn't mind letting him sweat a little.

"Everyone has their secrets," he said. "Your client seems to be taking a long time. Are you sure he's still here?"

"Maybe he's just waiting for you to leave so he can have his seat back."

Adam's eyes went wide. He leaned forward over the table and whispered, "Who is he? Someone important and well known? Is that why you're meeting him during the day, so no one will see him?"

"Everyone has their secrets."

"I understand, little sister." He stood, then bent down and kissed Iliana's forehead. His lips were warm and dry and when Iliana looked up at him he grinned like someone who knew a secret he shouldn't and who reveled in the knowing. "Enjoy your day."

Iliana watched him amble down the road until his body shimmered from the heat and the dust that made the air appear to dance. He walked in the direction of the Palace and Iliana wondered if it was to rest for the night ahead. When she turned her attention back to the table Cole crept out from behind the curtain, keeping one eye trained on the street as he took his seat again. After a few moments he relaxed.

"Why did you hide from my brother?"

"Your brother?" Cole asked. He appeared to be surprised by the revelation. "Is he always overprotective?" He frowned as a different server brought him a new cup of steaming tea and went off with the empty.

Iliana was loath to speak ill of her relations in front of a practical stranger, and a stranger who despised her for that matter. "He watches out for me. What did you do to make him dislike you?"

"He was in my room yesterday when I woke up. He just sat there and stared at me. He is a disturbed man."

Iliana said nothing right away. And when she finally did speak she chose her words with care to keep Cole from hearing the suspicion in her voice. "I can't disagree with you. What did he want?"

"He told me to stay away from you. I figured you sent him to scare me."

"And so you came looking for me? He didn't scare you that much, I see."

"He did at first. But some things are more important than fear."

Iliana sipped her tea to hide the panic she felt streak across her face like a dark bird, there then gone in an instant. Adam had followed her and then lied to her about it. But she set that plot aside and focused on Cole's problems. He had paid her to listen, to teach him, and the least she could do was be mentally present during their meetings.

"I did not send him. I don't know why he was there. He is not my keeper."

"Okay," he said. He blinked at her for a moment as if he wanted to ask something, then looked away and dropped the subject.

The silence returned. Cole sipped his bitter tea and studied the scarred and dented table in front of him. Iliana stared at the whorl of plain brown hair at the crown of his head.

After some time had passed she said, "This is your time, so if you want to sit in silence we can but it might be more beneficial to you if we actually had a conversation."

Cole once again adopted a defeated posture, the shape almost identical to the one that Adam had made look so appealing only a few minutes before. "I want you to help me understand. If you saved me just because I was dying, then you cannot be all bad."

"All bad?" If Iliana had had any doubts whether or not Cole saw her as an equal he had just proven to her that he did not. Despite the fact that he was willing to sit and converse with her he still saw her as a lesser creature, an animal, even.

Cole seemed ignorant of the truth he had just given away

and continued. "So now I have to ask. Why do you drink blood? Can you not eat real food?"

Iliana rolled her eyes, snatched the cold toast from his plate and took a bite. With a full mouth she said, "Well, we just debunked that myth. What's next?"

"Why do you drink blood then, if you don't have to?"

The cold smile started small and blossomed even though she didn't find the question humorous. "So tell me, Father, what does your Church say on the subject?"

"They prefer not to have anything to say about it. I was taught that it was a heathen practice that you refused to give up and that's why you could never join the Church." He looked down at his hands and then added, "Some people said that you had come to thrive on the blood of your victims, like demons."

"How deliciously simple."

"But is it true?"

She paused. She could reveal everything now and be done with this game. But there was a shadow behind Cole's eyes that told her that that tactic would do more harm than good. "You aren't ready to know this. Ask something else."

He sighed but did not argue. "Fine. Where did you come from?"

"We came from here, which is more than I can say for you. So now you tell me, where were you taught that you came from? I know what we were taught about your origins and I would like to compare notes."

"We came here seeking refuge," Cole responded, reciting with mechanical ease the information he had been taught his entire life. "We fled persecution on our home world and came here seeking refuge, a new home and a place to practice our beliefs without fear of reprisal."

Iliana let his words swell in the air between them and said nothing. She waited for the hypocrisy to finally materialize in his head and she didn't have to wait long. Realization brightened his face as slowly as a sunrise, and with realization came humility. He turned his gaze to his teacup and didn't look up even when Iliana cleared her throat.

"How foolish," he mumbled. Cole placed his elbows on the sticky table and rested his head in his hands. "What have I been teaching all these years?"

To her surprise, Iliana felt somewhat guilty for cracking open Cole's tiny, constructed view of the world. Instinct and habit told her to make some glib comment and walk away. But since Cole had paid for her company and for her knowledge she didn't know how to react.

In an attempt to comfort him she said, "You cannot blame yourself for believing the lies of those in power. They lie to get what they want."

Cole looked up at her. "That couldn't be it. I must have misunderstood something along the way. But it sounds so ludicrous now. How many times have I repeated those exact words without hearing the hypocrisy in them? This is the story I've taught to so many people. I just spoke by rote what I thought I was told from the beginning of my life."

So this was not remorse she was witnessing, it was emphatic denial. "Let me share what we were taught about your people," she said.

"Your Church wanted to incorporate us into its vast political system and we resisted, which was a new experience for them. All the other times it encountered resistance it just made itself known in the community, quietly spread its dogma and infiltrated people's minds. And then when a leader died the Church would approach the next in line. By that time the Church had become such an ingrained part of people's lives that it made sense to join up, to bow down, to give in.

"But the old ways didn't work against an enemy who lives almost ten times longer that you. And they could not infiltrate a people who were so physically different. There was no way to bribe its way into the hearts and lives of people when it was selling the same thing it was the last time, and the time before that. Dead people forget. The living don't."

"I don't believe you—"

Iliana's sympathy died in an instant. To keep herself from smacking him she smacked the table before her with an open palm and everyone in the café turned in her direction. Cole jumped, startled by the sudden outburst. Iliana continued to glare at Cole with unsympathetic eyes until the rest of the café had gone back to its business.

"You are weak." She opened her hand, palm up, on the table in front of him. "You asked for the truth and then flinch when it stares you in the face. You leave your Church but still make excuses for its lies. If this is the way you choose to interpret what I say then you are not ready for what I have to show you. Now just pay me for my time so that I can be on my way."

Cole blinked at her for a moment before rage contorted his features. He glowered at her and anger lent a spark of life to his flat brown eyes. "How dare you trivialize what I am going through," he said through clenched teeth.

Iliana smiled and withdrew her open hand. "I like you better full of anger than full of denial. The Church lied to you but it isn't the end of the world."

"But…" stammered Cole, unable to defend himself in the face of her absolute certainty but still trying.

"Think on it. I promise you that after a while it will become clear. But I must go now." She stood and put out her hand again for payment. Cole reached into his wallet, shuffled about some bills and placed a few in her palm. She glanced at them for a moment before folding them and placing them in her handbag. "Thank you."

"What now?" Cole asked, looking more lost than ever.

"I will come to you tomorrow in the early evening." Cole nodded in silence. "Good. Until then."

She strode out of the café without looking back at him.

20 Once Iliana was gone Cole finished his bitter tea, now lukewarm, and studied the scratched-up table. The longer he looked the more a vague pattern began to emerge out of the nonsense. He felt like he should recognize it but he couldn't. It seemed each person who had sat here added one more line to this never-ending testament to life, which only made him feel small and insignificant.

Cole's eyes crossed, so he blinked hard and rubbed them and then looked at the table again. This time there was no pattern. The marks were a meaningless mess, just like his life.

Cole paid the bill and went out into the stagnant heat, his hands in his pockets and nowhere to go. The day stretched out sober before him and his throat itched for a drink. His newfound sobriety left him with nothing to do in a city where the major attractions were to drink and to be drunk from. He wiped the hair from his forehead then shoved his hand back into his pocket, where the palm prickled with sweat within moments.

The few people out at this early hour paid him no attention. In this place everyone was a stranger. There weren't many Natives among the stragglers. Just tourists, either heading back to their hotels with lewd grins spread on pallid faces, or passing by with the determined strides of those set to begin their debauchery early. They would have a while to wait if they sought escorts. The Natives who dealt in that trade rarely left the Palace grounds before midday.

Without purpose he shuffled down the street, his feet kicking up small clouds of orange dust that fell straight back down to the ground with no breeze to disperse them. All streets in the city were made of earth packed hard by centuries of foot traffic.

The Natives never allowed vehicles to pass through the city gates. Visitors to the city left their vehicles in huge, dusty lots just outside the city walls so that at all times, in all directions, long arms of gleaming metal cars radiated outward from the city.

It was charming, Cole thought, but you could only travel so far on foot and it was already too hot to be outdoors. He turned to head back to his hotel room and barricade himself in against the heat and fell into step behind three young women.

The one in the middle dragged her feet and the two on either side of her struggled to keep her upright. The middle girl's head hung forward onto her chest and bobbed like a broken doll with every laborious step.

Concerned, Cole caught up to them. "Is she okay? Do you need any help?"

The trio paused and the closest girl turned to stare at him. Her face was half-hidden behind hair dyed the color of red clay. Her light brown eyes were heavy-lidded and glassy. Cole realized before she spoke that she was under the influence of something, but whether it was pharmaceutical or the afterglow of donating to an escort, he couldn't tell.

She spoke in a voice as flat as the desert landscape, "She asked to see a priest."

Cole felt a sudden flash of adrenaline just before a feeling of inadequacy rose up and snuffed it like wet fingers pinching out a candle flame. He looked again at the pathetic girl dangling between her two friends. Crimson gore stained the front of her pale blue shirt, streaking down from her throat where a long, clean cut still oozed blood. She did not have long to live but Cole did not feel confident enough in his faith to hear her confession.

He looked up for help and his eyes picked out the pointed spire of a nearby church, or at least what used to be a church. Without asking he plucked the nearly comatose girl from the arms of her friends. Her bare arms and legs were clammy in spite of the heat.

He said to her friends, "Follow me. Let's get her out of the sun." The girls complied. Cole hurried toward the church, praying that it would be tended.

He reached the church first and entered it. The customary oil lamp stood vigil beside the door, as it would all day, and dispelled the shadows in the windowless entry. He glanced at the girl in his arms. Her eyes were two white moons eclipsed by her eyelids. Her face was pale in the dim light. Her lips were bloodless.

"Hello?" Cole called out and ventured farther into the church. He heard the girls come in behind him. The creaking door invited a gust of sweltering wind into the cool confines of the church.

"Hello? I need help."

As the last echo of his cry died out, a serene and smiling man appeared through a small door to the left of the altar. "Can I help you?" he asked, but then he saw the girl in Cole's arms and ran toward them. Cole laid the girl's body on the stone floor and stepped back.

The priest reached them and knelt at her side. As he attended the dying girl something about him struck Cole as familiar. But Cole hadn't been inside this church before, and he couldn't remember seeing any priests since his arrival in Adara Vega. Unable to place him, Cole set his suspicions aside and turned his thoughts back to the girl.

The priest moved aside her thick mane of hair and examined the gaping wound in her throat. He placed two fingers on the other side of her neck to feel her pulse and said, "She's dying."

Cole closed his eyes. The air of the church cooled his burning cheeks.

"What happened to her?" the priest asked. His hands moved across her body, searching for something. He felt inside her pockets, opened her curled fingers. Her friends exchanged glances that were nowhere near as concerned as they should have been.

The redhead turned away and stared at nothing. The one with the scraggly, dyed black hair and shadowed eyes elbowed her friend. The redhead sighed, turned toward the priest and spoke in that same haunting monotone as before.

"She wanted a priest so we brought her here." She shrugged in a non-committal way. "That's all."

The priest snapped at her, "Don't be an idiot. Before that. How did she get like this?"

The redhead had become absorbed in the feeling of the wall against her back and she had closed her eyes and started rocking back and forth against it. Cole looked at the other girl, whose eyes remained wide and fixed on her friend's body. Her lips trembled. Her speech was halting as if she had a weak grasp on reality. Each word was a struggle.

"She wanted an escort. We all did. But we went first... Her guy was mean, weird. She paid him and... and he grabbed her and said something about us... being a plague... or something. Then he cut her and ran away. And she just kept bleeding..." her voice trailed off and was swallowed by the dense silence of the church.

The girl on the floor whimpered, sounding more like a wounded kitten than a girl, and the priest leaned over her. He lowered his ear to her mouth and Cole could see her lips moving but her voice was too weak to carry.

A minute passed. The dark-haired girl took a tentative step forward and held her breath. Cole felt foolish and impotent so he stayed back and watched as the priest sat back on his knees and the girl stopped breathing. The final breath left her lungs in an extended, rasping sigh. The church was still.

The dark-haired girl knelt in slow motion beside her friend and reached out to touch her ankle. She closed her glassy eyes as if comforted by that small contact.

Cole cleared his throat and asked, "What did she tell you?" The three of them jumped and turned to look at him as if they had forgotten that he was there. The girls stared at him, recognition lighting on their faces with great reluctance.

The priest touched the dead girl's forehead. "She said that her name was Ann. She has been sick for some time now." When none of them responded he added, "She was dying already when you brought her to Adara Vega. She wanted an escort to lead her out of this life."

"This is murder," Cole mused out loud, allowing his distaste for the Natives to darken his voice.

The priest said, "In this instance, yes, I would say it was."

"Does this happen often?" Cole asked.

"More so now than in the past. But this is unusual. People come here to die every day but when one steps willingly into death's embrace you cannot call it murder."

Without waiting for Cole's retort he stood and helped the dark haired girl to her feet. Then he led her to her friend and both of them looked up at him with the wonderment of children seeing something for the first time.

He spoke to them in a soft, non-threatening voice. "We will take care of your friend, I promise you. Is there anyone we can contact regarding her passing?"

The redhead handed over a silver, cylindrical purse. She seemed too shocked to speak. The priest was not at all ruffled by their reactions.

"Thank you, ladies. Now please go, and may God be with you always. Remember your friend as she was and if you need to speak with anyone you can find me here every day. My name is Father Matteo."

As Father Matteo ushered the confused girls toward the door Cole realized how he knew this priest. Cole felt again the satin rippling of time almost as he had the night he had followed Iliana into the club, where he had watched her take her client, Father Matteo, on the dance floor. Nausea gripped him and wanted to say something snide or cruel, something important, but nothing came.

Father Matteo returned and, seeing Cole still standing there, sized him up. Then he asked, "Are you one of her friends?"

"No," replied Cole.

Father Matteo smiled an easy smile and relaxed his shoulders. "Good, because I'm not that great at consoling the bereaved. Would you mind lending me a hand?" He moved to the girl's arms and grasped her wrists. "Just get her feet and help me carry her into the other room."

Cole did as he was asked. He had seen death before and it always unsettled him. But this time he wasn't as bothered by the feel of the dead girl's clammy skin as he was by the apathy with which Father Matteo treated the situation.

They hefted her through a low stone passageway just wide enough to accommodate them. They passed several rooms devoid of personality, empty rooms and rooms half-full of draped furniture, paintings covered by thin sheets, and dusty statues. Cole imagined that these rooms has once housed classrooms full of eager children, special places for quiet meditation, cells for priests to occupy while in tenure here. He focused on this imagined past to keep his mind off the bony ankles he carried in his hands and the heretic walking in front of him. The hallway ended at a perpendicular corridor but their strange processional turned right into a room just before that junction.

This room was unlike any of the others, in that the floor and walls sported pale blue, ceramic tile. The electric lights bounced harshly off of the four flat metal tables that stood against the walls. Following Father Matteo's lead, Cole hoisted the girl onto one of those tables. The metal was cold and smooth and lifeless and he felt a pang of guilt for having to leave the girl in such a sterile place.

His eyes must have lingered a moment too long because Father Matteo said, "She'll be fine. Don't worry. We have people who will take care of her." Cole looked up to see Father Matteo standing in the doorway with his arm extended in the direction of the hallway in an invitation to leave. Cole turned his back on the girl.

As they walked back toward the chapel Father Matteo asked, "So, did you know the girl at all?"

Cole shook his head. He felt that it was wrong for her to be tended to by a hypocrite priest willing to partake of the same vice that took her life. But he couldn't say so.

Father Matteo seemed tickled by Cole's reaction to the situation and didn't bother to try to disguise it. "This is your first time here, Mr. ..."

"Father Cole. I'm from the Northern Arm of the Church of Universal Truth."

Cole could have been wrong but he thought he saw Father Matteo flinch before he recovered and asked, "Oh really? Which branch?"

"Ceremonial. My Church is in Afet's Wall."

"Ah. So you're the illustrious Father Cole. I've heard of you. They say you're the model of priestly behavior. And yet you're here…"

"My father passed away recently. I'm on sabbatical." Cole didn't like what Father Matteo was insinuating and wanted to set the record straight.

The slight lift in Father Matteo's eyebrows was the only thing that gave away his surprise at the news. But he recovered his manners and said, "Father Tanaka was a decent man. I am sorry for your loss."

"Thank you."

"Have they named his replacement yet?"

"Yes," Cole said. "Me."

They had reached the empty chapel by this time and Father Matteo extended his hand, more a formality than a gesture of warmth. All of a sudden he seemed preoccupied and nervous. "Well, thank you for your help in this matter, Father. Please let me know if I can offer you any assistance."

Cole wasn't given a chance to respond before Father Matteo closed his office door. As the unique silence that can only be found in churches and mausoleums settled over him Cole realized that this was the first time he had been in a church since his breakdown. The thought saddened him.

As a child he had taken as much comfort from the physical edifices of the great cathedrals as he had from quiet communion with God and from the stories and fables he had heard there. But now when he looked at the stained glass, the gray stone floor, the altars, benches and statues, he saw wood and stone and glass, lifeless and meaningless. He saw vanity and futility.

Cole stepped toward the front of the church, climbed the pulpit steps and stood behind the unadorned wooden altar. The basic tools of a priest's trade were the same in every city: a golden chalice, a bell, a censer, a book of prayers. Some branches added candles or herbs or statues or stones or any number of implements dictated by the supplemental holy books of each sect. Here, however, there sat only the basic tools in a specific order atop this altar in preparation for the evening rituals.

He hesitated before touching them, as if expecting to receive a shock for his lack of faith. Instead he was rewarded with a coating of dust on his fingertips. His touch left bright prints in the layer of dust surrounding the golden chalice. A similar layer of fine, gray dirt covered the rest of the items as well and he wondered how long it had been since they had been used.

He raised his eyes to take in the whole church. Bright colors filled the empty spaces, content just to dance unmolested in the air and paint the morose stone walls, floor and vaulted ceiling with their lurid colors. Directly in front of him, at the back of the church, the wall from floor to ceiling was painted in great detail with the standard representation of man: a three-faced, six-armed image depicting man's rise and fall. One angelic face looked upward between lifted arms to catch the grace of God as it fell from the sky to bless the righteous. In contrast, one face was turned downward, scowling at the ground it stood upon, the hands clenched into fists at the ends of arms straight as temple pillars. The face in the middle showed no emotion, for it was caught somewhere between these two extremes, and this was where humanity resided. In this limbo peace was a myth, for man waged a constant internal battled as good and evil vied for his attention.

The arms of this middle man stretched out toward the congregation, beckoning for understanding. Those strong arms offered solace for those who chose to fight against man's most primal urges. This was the face of the Church. Cole knew how well its painted eyes lied. The Church offered comfort and denial in a simple, easy-to-swallow daily sermon. It didn't solve problems; it buried them beneath an avalanche of irrelevant dogma and ritual. Cole almost wished he could go back to that place of blind faith, of simple belief and obedience. Almost.

"You're still here."

Cole turned to see Father Matteo standing in the open doorway of his office. He did not look especially pleased to see Cole. Cole blushed and stepped out from behind the altar. He hadn't even heard the door open.

"Sorry," he muttered, feeling like a scolded child even though no scolding had been given.

"No problem," Father Matteo said. He approached the nearest bench and set a stack of tattered prayer books upon it. "Feeling homesick?"

Cole couldn't handle Father Matteo's glib demeanor. He acted so unconcerned and Cole couldn't stand that he seemed not to care that his actions at night made a hypocrite out of the preacher he played during the day.

He wanted to call him out but all he could manage was, "Not really. Just checking everything out."

"You an inspector?" Panic flickered across Father Matteo's face, only to be replaced after a moment by that easy smile. "Of course you're not. No inspectors ever come here. The Church wouldn't dare send them."

"Why is that?" Cole asked as he sat beside the prayer books on the first bench and tried to look nonchalant.

"There's too much temptation here. The Church wouldn't risk losing its most devout members among the sinning hordes, now would it?"

"So why are you here?" Cole asked, seeing his opportunity to delve into the psyche of a man who could be two things at once in a profession that demanded strict one-dimensionality.

Father Matteo smiled down at Cole and at that moment he seemed so much older, so much wiser, and Cole hated him for it. "Are you implying that I am not one of the Church's more devout members?"

Cole matched Father Matteo's steady gaze with one of his own and tried to keep the blame out of his eyes.

Father Matteo's smile widened. "You'd be right."

Cole jumped up to attack. "Then how can you get up in front of a congregation and preach? How can you be a mouthpiece for a system of beliefs you don't believe? It's hypocrisy."

Father Matteo didn't flinch at Cole's accusations. It was as if he had expected them from the moment Cole walked through the door with the dying girl in his arms.

"Hypocrisy is a strong word." He walked to the altar and

began rearranging the implements there.

Cole followed him with his eyes. "It's the right word."

"Perhaps. But let me ask you a question, do you believe in God?"

Without hesitation Cole answered, "Yes."

"Good. So do I. Now, do you believe that the Church is the only one, true vessel through which the people are informed of the will of God?"

Hesitation, then a slow, painful, "No." Cole's shoulders fell. He sank back onto the bench and placed his head in his hands in defeat.

"Me neither. Here we find ourselves of a like mind, which means that if I am a hypocrite then so are you and, I suspect, many more priests on this world and all of the others."

"You're wrong. I feel guilty for my sinful thoughts and that's part of the reason I stepped away from my position and came here to work it out. You stay and play the part of a priest when you're nothing more than a disingenuous actor getting paid very well for his performance."

Father Matteo scowled at Cole and slipped around the altar until he stood in the center of the raised dais. Then he spoke in a voice Cole imagined he used during sermons, a voice powerful enough to fill minds with disturbing images of hellfire and damnation. "Look at this church. It is beautiful. It looks devout. In my costume I look quite the priest. The instruments are right, as are the statues and the paintings. But when do you think the last real ceremony was conducted here?"

Cole shrugged, not seeing the point.

"I have not been attended by a congregation in over 13 years."

Cole said nothing. There was nothing to say.

"You see," Father Matteo said, "There are three kinds of people who come to Adara Vega. The largest group consists of those people who come to get away. They save up for a long time to come here and buy an escort. Even once in a lifetime is a special occasion. These are the tourists and they do not need the Church.

"Then there are the people who come here to work with us in the bars and shops. They do not believe the Natives are evil, so they do not need the Church.

"The final group consists of those who are ill, and it is larger than you might think. Some of them come here to be cured. And some of them come here to die."

"To die?"

"Like that girl you carried in. She had a disease that was sucking away her life bit by bit, day by day. Who would want to live like that? So instead of a slow, painful, humiliating death she chose the momentary sting and then the sweet, undulating pleasure that an escort can provide. I can assure you that it would be a much more pleasant way to die. And it is this last group that sometimes comes to me for guidance. I can only assure them that the One True God loves them and takes pity on them and forgives them for their sins."

"But buying time in the arms of a Native is a sin and if it kills them they have no time to ask for forgiveness. The rules are clear on that."

Father Matteo threw up his hands in frustration at Cole's lack of comprehension. "Don't you get it? These people need understanding, not damnation. They need forgiveness. And I am not going to deny them just because some strangers wrote in a book somewhere thousands of years ago what is and is not sinful. Sin is as subjective as opinions on popular music and it is erroneous for anyone to try to generalize such definitions."

"So is that why you let her take you? Because, subjectively, you do not see it as a sin?"

Father Matteo blinked at Cole in confusion. But as understanding dawned on him his eyes widened and he opened his mouth without words, struck mute for the first time in their conversation. And before Father Matteo could recover and defend himself Cole spoke once more and his bitter accusation strained the air between them.

"I saw you. You let her take you. In public."

"Is it less of a sin if it's done in private?"

"No, but that's not the point. How can you go so completely against the teachings of the Church and still call yourself 'Father'."

"This is where we differ." Father Matteo sat on the dais and leaned forward with his elbows on his knees. "I am of the belief that the Church has outgrown its own dogma. Or perhaps the people have outgrown the Church. Either way, its descriptions of sin are quite subjective, based on what those in power deem to be sinful at any given time." Father Matteo narrowed his eyes as if just speaking of the Church and its disagreeable teachings left a bitter taste on his tongue.

"And don't think that those in power are pure and holy. They are above reproach because of their status but they are not without sin. You could not name one of them who has not employed a Native for some purpose or another. They take their pleasure as often as other men and women. The only difference is that they have the luxury of anonymity."

Cole stood up in defiance even though the logic of the argument coupled with what he had seen stole some of the heat from his anger. "You don't know what you're talking about."

"Don't I? I live here. I see things. I hear things. Your leaders are sinners just like the rest. They are, after all, just men and man by his nature sins for many reasons."

"Stop it," Cole said. He shook his head as if to dodge the words Father Matteo flung like knives to cut away the protective garments of Cole's faith. He wanted support from somewhere, from anywhere. He wanted the saints and martyrs to come down from their windows, to climb off their marble pillars and beat Father Matteo into submission for his blasphemy. But nothing moved. The church remained so silent, the air so still in the afternoon heat that Cole heard nothing but the twin sounds of their breathing, Cole's rushing in and out of him like a man struggling to catch his breath after a race, and Father Matteo's, slow and steady.

Cole swallowed hard and started to say something but Father Matteo cut him off by holding up his hand. Cole flinched when Father Matteo placed that hand on Cole's shoulder and squeezed it, as a father might do to allay his child's irrational fears. When he spoke it was with authority and Cole dared not respond. It would make no difference even if he had.

"You cannot defend the Elders because they are indefensible. You have seen the truth and you have heard it and I hope that it will inform your conscience during your time on the Congress. Do with this information what you will but know this always: you do not need the Church to talk to God. There are many conduits that can be accessed by the individual: nature, the stars, dreams and visions. Iliana is but another of those conduits."

He let go of Cole's shoulder and went back to his office. "Now, if you'll excuse me, I have some business to attend to. I have to contact the girl's family and let them know her fate."

"What are you going to tell them?"

"Oh don't worry. I will report the crime to the authorities. But I'm going to tell the family that she was ill and came here to die. They do not need to know the specifics. It would only make the loss harder to bear."

"So now you're protecting the Natives." Cole didn't mean to sound so accusatory but he couldn't help it. He just wanted to understand.

"I can see that this is an argument I can't win because you refuse to see the bigger picture. I have work to do. Good day."

The door closed, punctuating a conversation Cole couldn't believe had just happened. He stood there for a moment with a scowl wrinkling his brow and his eyes trained on the closed office door. When he was certain Father Matteo would not return he left the church. He lit no candle. He said no prayer. He just left.

21

"She's up to something."

Governor Drake looked up from his work as Adam came in. Had it been during business hours one of the two guards on duty would have come in to request an audience on behalf of the visitor. But the night was over and the guards had left at sunrise so Drake had the entire floor to himself.

"Who is up to something?"

"Iliana." Adam shut the door, strode across the burgundy rug and sat in one of the leather chairs in front of Drake's enormous desk.

Governor Drake set down his pen and leaned back in his chair. "What makes you say that?"

"I just had a rather hostile conversation with her in a less than impressive café. She was alone but there was a plate of food and an extra cup of tea on the table. She said she was waiting for a client to show up but he didn't come while I was there. She seemed evasive. She's doing something we wouldn't approve of. I can feel it."

"But you have no proof. Besides, there are few things that I disapprove of. As long as she remains in the city we have nothing to fear. We will find her when the time comes and she will undergo the Transformation—"

"Do you think she might try to leave?"

Drake shook his head and chuckled. Adam had a wide impulsive streak so Drake thought he had better give the boy something to do before he spilled vital information about their plans out of sheer boredom.

"Adam, I am relieving you of your duties as an escort from

now until the Festival of Semiveh. I want you to focus on Iliana's comings and goings, her clients and her life outside of her clients. Monitor how she spends her time and report back to me."

Adam grinned, his eyes full of mischief. "Must I forsake all clients?"

Drake chuckled. "Of course not. Take clients as you please but you need not be concerned about your quota."

"Sounds like fun." Adam stood and moved to the door but Drake stopped him.

"Adam, wait," Drake said. When Adam turned around he added, "Please don't drop any hints. She's a smart girl. If you say anything she'll be able to figure it out and then she'll probably try to run. She must remain ignorant of our plan until everything is set. By then I am sure she will agree with us that we have no other options. Do you understand?"

"Of course." Adam left the office, shutting the door behind him.

Drake rubbed at his face with both hands to wake the tired flesh. He loathed lying to Iliana but more than that he loathed seeing his people killed off by the self-righteous, bigoted Colonists. The Colonists had infected this place like a disease then mutated over the centuries until they seemed like a part of this world. But they were deadlier than any virus and though they had bestowed many honors on Governor Drake for his cooperation, he knew that the honors were false. The many medals were nothing more than smoke crafted into a shape, just as they no doubt knew that his cooperation was grudging at best.

As the time of the Festival of Semiveh drew closer, Drake found himself more and more often retreating to the haven of youthful memories. He had once been as impulsive and impetuous as Adam. But unlike Adam, Drake had always known (even in those early years when the Colonists were still like children in their land) that you should never underestimate them for they were too full of fear to be trusted.

For a time they had tried to live in cooperation but their fear and greed had betrayed them. Drake had once hoped that the Church would bring about its own downfall, for it seemed that the stifling of one fear always led to the emergence of another. But the time for hopes and wishful thinking was over. If Drake did not act now, or if the Transformation did not go as planned, his people would not live to see the next Festival.

A knock on the door startled Drake from his thoughts. He cleared his throat and did his best to banish the worry from his face.

"Come in," he called out and stood up as the 12 members of the Upper Council filed into the room and stared at him with matching taut lips and concerned eyes.

Once the door closed behind the final member Drake began his prepared speech. "My friends, our days of peace are near an end. When the Festival of Semiveh comes, the war will begin."

"What did the Church say to our demands?" Sigrid stepped up to Drake's desk and rested her fingertips on the polished top. At that moment everything about her was intimidating. Her hair was pulled back from her face so tightly that her eyes were frozen in permanent surprise and her thin face was all angles and shadows. But Drake had known her intimately at one time and so her show of fierceness was lost on him. He met her fiery gaze with his own.

"They told me not to bother them with our problems anymore. They have no interest in our border disputes and see nothing wrong with the murder of our people."

"So they gave away nothing of their plan?" asked Nero. He was the oldest Council member, at almost 1,100 years old, and he knew more than the rest what they had lost when the Colonists came.

"They said nothing. But even so, we are learning about the Church's plan through our allies in their organization. The details are still unclear but we know that they are planning to release some sort of virus during the Festival. They want us gone. And somehow they have found a way to wipe us out completely."

"So what do we do now?" Sigrid asked.

"We wait. Adam is keeping an eye on Iliana as well as exploiting his connections for information about the Church's plot. No one is to bother him. I have released him from his quota and all of his energy will be focused on these tasks. Is this clear?"

The Council nodded almost as one.

"Good. The priests are working on a new translation of the old texts to see if there was something we missed before. We cannot risk the same thing that happened to Gabriella happening to Iliana." The Council met him with austere silence.

"Iliana's level of participation remains to be seen. You haven't forgotten your promise to let us meet with her, have you?" Sigrid asked.

"Of course I remember. I will give you the time and place once everything is set. That is all for now. I ask only that you keep me apprised of anything you might see or hear that could affect our plans. Good day."

The Council members filed out in the same somber air with which they had entered. Drake turned to look out his wide window and sighed at the empty street that met his gaze. His office was on the second level on the back side of the Palace and on most days he enjoyed the privacy the location afforded him. People seldom loitered in the shadows behind the Palace because all of the excitement took place out front. Sometimes he went hours without seeing anyone. The ramshackle buildings behind the Palace were the personal dwellings of either Colonists or those Natives who could not be escorts. The buildings were quiet since at night the people worked in bars or clubs and during the day the workers slept. Drake had chosen this office because he liked the peace. He had seen enough excitement in his lifetime.

But now as he looked out at the near-empty streets and dark windows, the absence of life agitated him. He had the sudden impression that he was the last of his kind, that the city he viewed through his window was a post-apocalyptic one: a world where the war had been fought and his side had lost. The sensation ran through him like a cold river and tried to sweep all hope of victory from him.

He needed reassurance. He moved to the bookcase on the right hand wall and reached behind it, where a small button sat flush against the ornate wallpaper. Drake pushed it and the bookcase popped out to reveal a secret room.

Here, under glass, were hidden scrolls so old that to handle them was to risk their destruction. Here were treasures of gold and wood and paper, treasures of the written word and those from Native artisans from the time before the Colonizers, at least what they were able to rescue as city after city was demolished and looted in the name of the Church.

Drake passed over these items and made for an item on the bottom shelf along the back wall. This was the most sacred of their treasures. He lifted a purple velvet cloth to reveal a box. It was just as Drake remembered it, dark and sticky with a substance he knew only too well. The Transformation bled the subject and from what he had seen in the aftermath of Gabriella's unsuccessful conversion it was not a pleasant experience. The top of the box was carved with the Natives' ancient symbols for protection, strength, and growth. Drake did not presume to know what was in the box or how it worked. He knew only that it was magic in its purest form and just a touch could drive you mad.

As if aware of his presence the power rippled across his skin. He reached out to touch the box and stopped halfway, as if his hand had encountered an invisible barrier. He tried to will his fingers to stop trembling but after a few moments his nerves won out and he withdrew his hand. He covered up the box that had caused him so much heartache and promised to cause him so much more, and left the room.

Drake pressed the bookcase back into place and stumbled to his chair and collapsed into it. Hands still trembling, he dabbed at his moist forehead with his handkerchief and focused on slowing down his relentless heartbeat.

Through his window Drake watched the people coming home from their shifts, unknowing and therefore safe in their ignorance. He watched the crowd until the street was filled with light, one hand gripping his handkerchief and the other gripping one arm of the chair hard enough to crack the wood.

22 Iliana backed away from the peephole and popped the little bit of ragged wall back into place. After leaving Cole at the café she had gone back to the Palace to sleep for the day. It had been a long night, made even longer by Cole's crises. But when she entered the Palace Adam stood at the front desk flirting with one of the receptionists. She was a buxom girl of Iliana's age who, though beautiful, with waist-length blonde hair and skin the color of cinnamon, had the personality of a wet rag and could never be an escort.

Curious, Iliana lingered in the doorway and overheard him tell the girl that he was on his way to meet with the Governor. When Adam went to the elevators, Iliana made for the stairwell and beat Adam to the second floor by moments.

Just adjacent to the stairwell was a closet, and Iliana hid herself there. The elevator chimed Adam's arrival just after the closet door closed. As she eased the worn chink of wall from the peephole she tried to keep her heart from hammering, her breath from trembling in her lungs.

She and Adam had carved through the wall when Iliana was only a child and eager for knowledge of the world around her. They had used it to spy on the High Council's private meetings and through the years had learned a great many things they should never have known. Iliana and Adam had spied on several meetings involving the punishment of Colonists and Natives alike and a score of meetings involving the increasing tyranny of the Church. They had been the invisible judges of their elders and used to plot ways to wrest their lives from the Church's rule. All of their imagined scenarios ended in all-out war and though

Iliana blanched at the thought, Adam was thrilled by idea of commanding armies and inspiring his people to bloody victory over their oppressors.

Only she and Adam knew about the hole so she wasn't worried about being discovered. She doubted Adam would remember it considering he now had much greater access to the Council and the Governor in person. So she listened, her eye pressed up to the hole, her deliberate breaths hitting the wall and returning to warm her chin, her nose. She watched the well-groomed hair on the back of Adam's head and then the nervous fidgeting of the Council members.

And after everyone left and her mind reeled from the revelations, Drake opened that secret room behind his bookcase and the energy hit her. Her mind filled with images of women screaming and covered in blood, of Colonists being torn apart by invisible hands and she felt the weight of death upon her shoulders. Iliana reeled backwards but the energy followed her. She closed her eyes and took several deep breaths but she could taste it, so she shut her lips tight to keep it out.

All at once the air in the closet tasted like blood. She suddenly wanted, needed, to find a client and drain him within an inch of his life and just the thought seemed to soothe her racing mind, dispel the bloody images.

A moment later, just as quickly as it had begun, the magic was gone. Iliana lay on the floor of the closet, regaining her breath, wondering what had happened. And what was hidden in that room?

She crouched beside the peephole again but the bookcase was back in place and Drake was back at his desk, staring out the window. The show was over for now.

But at least she had her answers, or some of them anyway. She knew what was happening, why Adam and Drake had been so strange around her lately. She did not wonder why the rumor of the Church's plan was not made public; the Church would try to crush them in a moment if they found out how much the Natives knew.

So the people prepared for the sacred Festival of Semiveh

without knowing that it could be a massacre. And Iliana waited with them for the coming of some strange fate she knew nothing about. Governor Drake always told her that he had promised her mother he would care for her but desperate times call for desperate measures and if the Church was to lay waste to the city 19 days from now, then the Governor was desperate. Desperate enough to sacrifice his fake daughter to save his people.

Iliana leaned against the wall, feeling as cold and heavy as a pillar of marble. She didn't know what this Transformation entailed but if the High Priests had to make a new translation of the "old texts" she didn't think she would enjoy it. And according to Drake it had killed her mother. She didn't want this. She tried to reign in her overactive imagination but her mind revolted, instead conjuring a thousand horrific ways to die until she had worked herself into a frenzy. In the darkness the arms of the coats around her seemed to come alive and grasp at her with hollow sleeves. The darkness itself seemed to hold some sinister presence, threatening, close and getting closer, and she had to get out of there.

She stuck her head out of the door and looked up and down the hallway, then snuck away to the left and back into the stairwell. Adam and the Council members were long gone and she hadn't heard Drake leave his office so she knew she was safe for now. She had to think. She had to figure out what the Council wanted to do to her and then find a way to get out of it.

23 The prayers ended, the meeting adjourned and the clerics filed out of the chapel in excited clusters, chattering to each other like children on holiday. "A change is coming," Adam heard them say more than once as they passed by his hiding place. He wondered how many of them were smiling as they contemplated the destruction of the Natives and felt his cheeks burn with suppressed anger. He gripped the doorframe until his fingertips throbbed with his heartbeat to keep himself from lashing out at them as they went by.

Yourian, as usual, was last to leave. Adam watched from his hiding place in a dark and unused classroom as Yourian juggled a stack of books and crumpled papers and hugged them to his chest. His face was flushed with a different kind of excitement than on the faces of the others.

As Yourian passed by Adam reached his arm into the hallway, gripped the shoulder of Yourian's robe, and yanked him into the darkened room. Yourian was too surprised to cry out though he did drop all of his books, which slapped against the tile floor and came to rest in a haphazard pile.

Adam could feel Yourian's heart as it battered his rib cage from the inside. The pace only increased as he shut the door and the thin sliver of light from the hallway slimmed and disappeared completely and darkness swallowed them. Yourian was terrified. The fear stank because it was not coupled this time with expectation.

Adam lit a match and in the light from the sputtering flame watched recognition smooth the panicked creases from Yourian's face. The young cleric's heart slowed, his breathing stilled and he composed himself. Yourian grinned in relief but Adam did not give him the satisfaction of a kind look, instead he just narrowed his eyes and frowned.

Yourian said nothing as Adam let the match burn out on his fingers then tossed it aside. It made a soft click as it struck the tile floor a few feet away.

When the darkness enveloped them once more Adam moved across the room and Yourian finally found his voice. He could tell from Yourian's body language that he was blind in the darkness but Adam could see the smallest of physical ticks. "We had a meeting with a messenger from the Church Elders. She told us a lot of what was going to happen—"

"Why did you not scream when I pulled you in here?" Adam asked, his voice soft, yet threatening. He felt Yourian flinch and he smiled.

"What?"

"You didn't cry out. Are you used to being pulled into dark rooms by strangers? One of your brothers, perhaps?"

Yourian was quick to give assurance. "Of course I'm not used to this. I was just too surprised to make any noise. You just frightened me, that's all. I promise."

Adam strode across the floor until he was standing right beside the cleric, not touching him, just hovering. He spoke into Yourian's ear. "Are you forming an army to kill us all in our beds on the final night of the Festival?"

Yourian jumped and cleared his throat. "The Church has decreed that three days before the Festival begins all Colonists are supposed to evacuate the city. Anyone who misses that deadline will not be allowed to leave."

"Why?" Adam could feel Yourian's shudder of anticipation so he made sure not to touch him in any way just to prolong the torture.

"They consider anyone who does not leave the city by the deadline to be a Native sympathizer, which means that they have given their souls to evil and do not deserve to live. To make sure of it they are going to barricade the exits as soon as the deadline passes: no one in or out."

"So what then?"

Yourian took a deep breath and expelled it in a rush of words. "They are going to release the virus on the second day of the Festival. Within 12 hours all the Natives will be dead. It's supposed to be harmless to us but we're all supposed to leave just in case. Once it has run its course they are going to come in and finish off anyone still alive, including any Colonists who refused to leave the city."

Adam's controlled voice did not belie the turmoil he felt inside at this news. He had known about this plan for quite some time but now he had the details. It was going to happen. A war he could comprehend but how does one go about combating a virus? "How will they release this virus? Is it airborne? Blood borne? What time on the second day?"

"I don't know," Yourian whined. "I stayed afterward to ask but the priest wouldn't tell me anything specific. He only hinted that this was a long time coming. They've been planning this for decades, maybe longer."

"So why now? What has changed? Why during Semiveh?"

"For most of the Festival you will all be gathered in and around the Palace. Waiting until you are all convened in one place will make it easier for them. They see it as the only way of containing the experiment."

A moment passed. Adam lifted his hand, prepared to slash it across Yourian's throat, open him, drain him and leave him. But then he heard Yourian catch his breath. This was what he expected, what he had been waiting for. So Adam changed his mind.

Without warning he pulled away. And when he spoke his voice was cold. "That's good, Yourian. But it is not enough."

Without another word Adam opened the door, checked outside to make sure the hallway was empty, then left. Before the door closed once more he swore he heard Yourian let out a cry of frustration and Adam allowed himself a smile.

24 Iliana tamed her unruly curls from where the desert wind had whipped them into a tangle and smoothed her black dress around the swell of her hips. Her outfit was conservative for an escort, the fabric was neither velvet nor satin and her dress bore no ornamentation. She wanted to appear as serious as she felt when she told Cole that she had to break their contract. As much as she wanted to help him through his crisis, self-preservation took priority. She needed to find out what Drake and the Council were up to before it was too late.

Once she was satisfied with her appearance she knocked on Cole's door. It was early in the day so she expected him to be in. She had spent the night concocting a way to discover the secrets of the Transformation without being found and she had finally decided on a course of action. The plan required that she start immediately but she had promised Cole that she would come for him and she didn't like going back on her word.

The security chain slid back and the door opened. There stood Cole, smiling and looking healthier than he had since Iliana met him. He had combed his wavy hair back from his face and his clothes were clean and straight. His dark brown eyes held none of the sick shine from the day before and his face had regained a more natural color, which was a great improvement from the greenish-yellow tint from before.

"Good morning," he said and stepped back for her to enter. She cast a wary glance at Cole as she passed him. The bed was unmade but at least the trash was gone and the breeze that blew in through the open balcony door seemed to have abated the pungent odor of sweat and booze that had permeated the room during her previous visits.

"You know," she said, turning around to face him, "They say that when your enemy is suddenly kind to you it usually means that he is planning your destruction. You don't, by chance, have a knife behind your back, do you?"

Cole shut the door. "Not at all. I just thought that since you are willing to give me your time, I might try being civil to you."

Iliana stiffened at this unexpected kindness. She didn't want Cole to be cruel again but she had no warmth to offer in return. A lifetime of playing at friendship had left her struggling to be genuine, especially since she had come to break their truce. "You are paying for my help," she said, "You do not have to be kind to me."

As soon as the words left her mouth she wished them back but the damage was done. They struck Cole like a slap in the face. He blinked hard and looked away, embarrassed.

Iliana touched his arm to try to salvage what she could of the situation. Cole pulled away. It was better to be frank, so she began, "I understand that you are trying to work through your doubts and I know that we had an agreement…" she paused and watched Cole's face fall as he realized what she was about to say before the words even left her mouth. But she couldn't stop them from coming. "But I must break our contract…"

"If it's the money, then I'll pay you more. The money means nothing to me. I just need to understand," he said, his voice tight. Iliana usually detested desperation but this time it didn't bother her. She knew that she was abandoning him on the threshold between knowledge and understanding, resentment and madness, but she didn't know any other way. She needed to focus. Cole was a distraction.

Iliana clenched her jaw to keep herself in check and said, "Something has come up that requires my immediate attention and…"

"What?" he asked.

Iliana blinked, surprised that he would ask. "Pardon me?"

"What has come up? You're just making up an excuse because you think I'm a lost cause, aren't you?"

"No," Iliana said, "That's not it at all."

"Then tell me why you can't be the one to help me."

Iliana paused. Cole's face seemed heavy and lined and full of disappointment. She didn't want to be the cause of that disappointment so she decided to be as honest as she was able. She sighed, "I am not making excuses, but neither am I being completely honest with you."

"I'm listening."

"I recently discovered that the Council has plans for me but I don't know what they are. I need to find out. That is why I cannot help you."

"Let me help you, then," he said and Iliana's head snapped up. She studied Cole's face and found him earnest.

"Why?"

"Because you are helping me. I'll admit my aim is selfish, though, because if I can help you solve your problem then you can get back to helping me with mine."

"Why not just find another escort to suit your needs?"

"I like you. You're honest and direct and you don't just tell me what you think I want to hear. And you don't pressure me to donate."

"We only drink from a client if they ask. No reputable escort would ever pressure you to donate."

Cole smiled. "I'd rather not take any chances. So what can I do to help you?"

But Iliana wasn't yet convinced, "Are you sure that this is what you want to do? Don't you hate us? Wouldn't helping me be some kind of sin in the eyes of your god?"

"See, our time together has already changed me. I want to help a Native. I'm concerned about a Native. And an escort, no less."

"What would your Father say about this?" she muttered. She said it with as much sarcasm as she could muster, but Cole surprised her with an answer.

"Father Deven would likely cast me out of the Church without another thought. But my real father? He would say that I was finally doing the right thing."

Iliana looked into Cole's plain brown eyes and saw something there that gave her the courage to ask for help.

"To find the information I need to retrieve something out of... an office in the Palace."

Cole seemed to sense her hesitation and asked, "Whose office?"

He was more astute than Iliana gave him credit for. She was caught, so she bit her lip and said, "Governor Drake's Office."

"You're joking, right?"

"Unfortunately, no."

"Your brother has threatened death if I so much as look at you, but you want me to break into the Governor's office? Are you trying to get me killed?"

"You don't have to go. I can do this alone."

"No, I will go. I don't think it's wise and I will caution you against it but I promised to help you and so I will. But why can't you just ask for the information? You are the Governor's daughter, aren't you?"

Iliana opened her mouth but nothing came out. How did he know this? "Not exactly... But how do you know anything about that?"

Cole shrugged. "I've been here for a while and people talk. And now it's time for you to talk. Tell me what we're doing."

Iliana started to talk, and once she did she was surprised at how easily the truth rolled off of her tongue. "I need information that no one will give to me. My fate is not my own and I need to know what they have planned. But there is something else."

"What?"

"There is something in his office that affects me in a strange way and I need to know what it is. I cannot just ask because in this cause I have no allies among the Natives."

"What about your brother?"

"He is a part of it."

"How do you know this thing won't affect me, as well, and we both won't be discovered?"

"I don't."

He hesitated, but only for a second, before he said, "Okay,

let's go," and Iliana marveled at how relieved she was that she didn't have to do this alone.

As Cole moved past her Iliana wondered if she was making a mistake but she would not second-guess herself now. She followed Cole out and shut the door behind her, feeling like she was shutting the door on her old self and her old life. She only hoped the next one would be better.

25 No one paid attention to Iliana and Cole when they entered the palace grounds even though it was after hours. Every time the Church increased taxes the working hours for the Native escorts became longer and longer. They did not speak in the elevator, since they shared the car with several other escorts. The others acknowledged Iliana with nods and appraised Cole in silence. Iliana's appearance gave nothing away, but behind her impenetrable façade she wondered what the others were thinking about her. And she loathed the way they looked at Cole, like he was a side of beef for sale, a jewel in a shop window. Cole kept his eyes on his feet and she felt his nerves, taut as the strings on a guitar, as if they were her own.

Though he had grown used to Iliana's company and no longer recoiled when she touched him, she knew that this situation unnerved him. He didn't hide his discomfort very well so Iliana took his hand and squeezed it to remind him to relax. His fingers were hot and damp.

When the last person got out Cole still clung to her hand as if she were the last dry patch of land in the middle of a tempest. By the time they reached the 29th floor a strange claustrophobia had settled over them like a mist, surrounding them on all sides, restless in that cramped silence.

They exited the elevator and Cole turned toward Iliana's cell but she pulled him in the other direction. "Not that way. We need to take the stairs"

"I thought we were on the top floor already."

"We're going back down to the second floor. We couldn't get off the elevator there because only the Councils' offices are on the second floor and there's no reason for us to go there during the day. Most of the time the offices are empty from around midday until just after sunset."

Iliana opened an unmarked door on the left of the elevator and let Cole enter first. The staircase hugged the square walls of the stairwell, which was lit from above by a crystal chandelier. Cole looked down the center of the stairs where the steps descended into darkness and then scooted back against the wall, his eyes wide. A dim sconce hung on the wall beside him, casting a pool of light for a few feet in either direction.

"Are you afraid of heights?" Iliana whispered, smiling.

"No, but spirals do not always agree with me."

"Then I would suggest you not look down. Let's go."

Cole started down. He gripped the lacquered wooden handrail with one hand and trailed his other hand across the wallpaper. The pattern was in relief, white on gold. Iliana noticed that he made a point of not looking down the center of the stairwell again.

"This is the fanciest stairwell I have ever seen," he muttered. Even so, the echo of his voice lingered for a while. Iliana didn't answer. So he just kept climbing down, down, down until they reached a landing with yet another unremarkable, unmarked wooden door.

"This is it," she said. She tugged on the gold handle, peeked into the hallway, then grabbed Cole's hand and led him out of the stairwell and just to the left into an alcove with double doors.

She opened her dark blue satin handbag, withdrew an iron key and twisted it in the lock. Her hands shook as she withdrew the key so she gripped the doorknobs to keep Cole from seeing just how nervous she was. After checking once more to be certain that no one was in the hallway, she opened the door.

Iliana stepped inside but Cole hesitated. She didn't blame him but if he was going to second guess himself there were a hundred less incriminating places he could have done it than where they were now.

Iliana whispered, "Come inside and close the door."

26 Cole obeyed and shut the door but stayed near the exit. He didn't trust the ease with which they had accomplished their task. He worried that any wrong move might raise an alarm and get them caught but Iliana didn't seem to share his concerns. She stood in the center of Drake's office, her eyes closed, swaying on her feet and oblivious to Cole's presence.

Drake's office resembled a more tasteful and expensive version of Cole's hotel room. The walls were papered in burgundy with gold flecks, the carpet was burgundy, and the desk was carved out of red wood and polished to a high gloss. Full, well-organized bookcases sat against the walls on both sides of the desk, and those were ultimately what shook him out of his paralysis and propelled him forward.

"Where are you going?" asked Iliana, her eyes opening. Her voice sounded languid, as if she were drunk.

"I want to look at the books. Are you feeling okay?"

She shook her head. "I told you there was something in here that affects me. Can't you feel it?"

"No. What does it feel like?"

"Energy. Power. It's cold. The air is humming against my skin. I never noticed it before but now I can't *not* notice it."

"I don't feel anything," Cole admitted and turned his attention to the books. Some were bound in cloth and some in animal hide, and the spines had handwritten titles: *Sun Changes, Moon Changes, Crop Cycles, A Record of Births: Vol.12,* and *A Record of Deaths.*

"These are amazing," he whispered as Iliana came up beside him. He pulled out the enormous volume titled *A Record of*

Births and opened it to a random page. It appeared to be a ledger containing the ages and names of mothers, how many children were born to them in the past and the names of the children born that term. He flipped to a different page and the dates were exactly one hundred years later. Another page, another one hundred years. The fathers were listed in appendices at the end of the book as if they were unimportant, just a means to an end. It put an image in his head of the Natives as cattle being bred just to get a viable child. He shuddered when he pictured Iliana being used in such a way and put the book back where he had found it.

"Why are there only records of births every one hundred years?" he asked as he studied the other titles.

"Because we can only give birth every one hundred years." Cole stopped perusing the titles and looked over his shoulder at her, expecting to see a smile, but her face was serious. She wasn't joking.

"I don't know why but I always assumed that that was a myth," he muttered. He was in awe of the ancient origins of the Natives and felt himself shrinking right there in that room until his life seemed like a grain of sand compared to a desert filled with centuries of experience. And when he was gone, all of this would still be standing, Iliana would still be alive and beautiful while he would be nothing more than an entry in a logbook, a headstone in the ground.

"So how old are you?" Cole asked, hoping that he hadn't been bemoaning his life to a woman who had seen a millennium change. Somehow that would make his confessions even more embarrassing.

"I was conceived at the last Festival of Semiveh, so I am almost 100 years old. I don't think I've ever asked this question, but how old are you?"

"Thirty-seven," Cole said, realizing how insignificant that number was in comparison. Though he had not been for a very long time, she made him feel like a child, a feeling that intensified with every new thing he learned. Iliana's very existence forced him to confront the fact that he knew very little of life, of people, of nature.

Iliana watched him process this information with a gentle smile on her face. "If it makes you feel any better, since my people can live to be about one thousand years old and yours can live to be about one hundred, in your world I'm the equivalent of a ten year old."

"Not like any ten year old I've ever seen." He meant it as a compliment and was glad when her smile widened. "So what is the Festival of Semiveh?"

"It is a fertility festival."

"I saw the flyers in the street but I didn't understand why it's such a big deal. Now it makes sense. So who is Semiveh?"

"According to the myths, she was the mother of us all, the first woman to bear children and the reason we are fertile only once every one hundred years."

"I don't understand."

"She did not want us to have to go through that pain too often."

"So how does it work? Do you get married? Do you even believe in marriage?"

In response she reached across him and plucked a book from the shelf and placed it in his hands. "This is the book we learn from as children. Please keep in mind that by the time this was written, about one hundred fifty years after your people had arrived, Adara Vega had become our prison. So we were a little bitter."

The book was bound in stiff orange fabric and entitled *The Story of the Outlanders*. As he opened the first page Iliana said, "If you have questions after you read this, as I am sure you will, then we can discuss it."

Cole started to read and the room fell away.

"Here begins the cataloguing of the stories of the Outlanders, as transcribed by Governor Brand in this year Thirty-seven Sixty-nine.

"The visitors came to us when their world became unlivable. They claimed to have created a unifying vision for their people that ended all war and suffering and resulted in worldwide peace. With no war, and technological advances allowing for longer life spans,

the planet became overcrowded. Our visitors are one of several different groups sent from their home planet tasked to find livable space elsewhere…"

Cole sank onto the corner of Governor Drake's desk. There was no denying it now, no more room for misunderstanding. His people had lied. His Church had lied.

He felt a breath on his neck and looked up. Iliana had moved very close to him, far closer than she had ever been. But she wasn't reading over his shoulder. Her eyes were glazed and trained on his throat and her full, red lips were parted just enough to seem like an invitation. Her breath came in staccato gasps.

"Iliana?" he asked.

Iliana shook her head and scowled as if trying to snap herself out of a trance. A moment later she focused her eyes on him and then reeled backwards as if she had just realized how close she was. She turned her back on him and moved to the side of the bookcase.

"Are you okay?" he asked.

"No. I am not," she answered as she felt along the edge of the bookcase. Tiny beads of sweat sparkled in her hairline and there was the tiniest crease between her eyebrows. She was not her usual, unflappable self.

"What are you looking for?" he asked.

"I'm not sure. A button. Or a latch of some kind…" A moment later the entire bookcase popped away from the wall. "Got it," she said. Then she pulled the bookcase out a little further and stumbled backwards.

Cole set the book on Drake's desk and rushed to steady her. She grasped his arm hard enough to bruise and leaned into him and she was heavier than he thought she'd be. "What's happening, Iliana?"

Her head lolled against his shoulder as if it was too heavy to lift. "I don't know," she whispered, "You still don't feel it?"

"No. What does it feel like?"

"My head is full of voices."

"What are the voices saying?"

Iliana turned her gaze up to meet him and for a moment Cole saw something cold and alien reflected in her eyes. A shiver ran through him as she licked her lips. "They are hungry."

Cole's breath caught in his throat as thought and judgment and resistance dissolved in her bottomless eyes and he couldn't even make himself care. He wanted to close the distance between them. He wanted to give her everything she wanted and more. All she had to do was ask.

"Cole," she mouthed and her voice echoed in his mind.

"You're not supposed to be in here," said a voice and Cole jumped and whipped around. Iliana came with him because he was still holding her up, but the spell was broken, at least for Cole.

"Hello, Jacob," Iliana purred and pulled away from Cole.

"Who is this?" Cole asked.

"Jacob is a custodian. He has been here for almost as long as I've been alive. Almost."

Jacob stepped towards them, smiling with obvious glee and revealing tobacco-stained teeth. When they were face to face she stood a full half-foot taller than him. She brushed his wrinkled cheek with her fingertips. The old man sighed and Cole's stomach turned.

When Iliana spoke next her voice was cold, seductive, though the words were anything but sweet. Cole did not recognize the voice at all. It wasn't hers. "Your skin is like paper left out in the sun and the rain until the pages folded in on themselves. It is so delicate, so easily torn…"

Cole's eyes flicked to the bookcase and wondered if that was the cause of her strange metamorphosis. It was only open a fraction. It wouldn't take much to close it, to cut off the flow of energy.

"Don't play games," Jacob admonished.

"But I love to play games," she said.

Cole couldn't take it anymore. He inched closer to the bookcase and pretended to lean on it, instead shoving it with his body weight. It slid back into place and latched without a sound.

At once Iliana's shoulders slumped forward as if she had been a puppet on a string and the puppet master suddenly disappeared.

"Cole?" she asked and her voice was once again her own. She turned and Cole saw fear in her fevered eyes. They were in danger. Cole said a silent prayer of thanks that she seemed to be all right, followed by another prayer that they both be delivered from this situation without harm to anyone. He was too nervous to chastise himself for the heresy of praying for the safety of a Native escort.

"I am here," Cole said.

"But you are not allowed to be here," Jacob said.

With her eyes Iliana told Cole to follow her lead and Cole nodded. Then she blinked. And in an instant she was someone else and the change was so sudden that it startled him. She had adopted a new façade, that of a bored courtesan.

"It's good to see you again, Jacob," she said as she turned back toward the old custodian.

"What are you doing in the Governor's office with a client? You know better than this, Iliana."

"My client wished to be taken in a forbidden place." She rounded Jacob so that he stood in between the men.

"Is that so?" Jacob asked. He turned to glance at Cole but didn't look for long. His grin widened as he turned back to Iliana, his voice eager. "Still," he said, "it's not allowed, and since I am the custodian I could get into trouble if anyone finds out. I should turn you in. But maybe we can make a deal…"

Cole opened his mouth to speak but then closed it a moment later without saying anything. He didn't want to get them both into bigger trouble than they already were. He didn't want Iliana to get blackmailed into doing something she didn't want to do but it was clear that she felt she had no other choice.

Iliana led Jacob into the nearest corner, blocking him from escape with her body. She took her sharp silver implement from her purse and placed it over her thumb. One quick motion against his tissue paper skin and the blood welled. Iliana bowed her head and began to drink.

27 Cole felt like a third wheel. He watched the old man's face grimace as Iliana opened him, then bliss smoothed out his features like dough rolled out on a board. Despite himself, despite his disgust at the act he was bearing witness to yet again, Cole fought to squash the jealous part of him that wished that she were drinking from him instead.

As Jacob clung to Iliana's hips with twitching hands Cole averted his eyes and sat on the edge of the Governor's desk, knocking the book he had been reading onto the floor. He looked up but they hadn't reacted to the noise. Jacob's arms went limp and fell to his sides and still Iliana took more. Before he could second guess himself Cole plucked the book off of the floor and tucked it into the waistband of his pants at the small of his back and pulled his shirt out to cover it. He figured he might as well get something out of this clandestine visit.

When Cole straightened back up Iliana's arms tensed as Jacob's legs gave out and she had to hold him up. And then it hit him. Cole felt again the wicked longing that had swept through him the other time he'd witnessed her take a client. He swore he did not want to exploit Iliana for her services but his rebellious body responded to the sensations nonetheless.

He felt pressure on his neck like a phantom leech drawing the life out of him. He stumbled to the bookcase and leaned against it as his head began to buzz and the dizziness threatened to topple him. The air in the room became hot, almost unbreathable. His stomach tightened, his muscles clenched and he tottered on his feet.

He wondered what it would feel like if he ever allowed

himself the indiscretion of her services but the thought faded as a new wave of sensation passed through him until he could no longer think, he could only exist. He felt the flow of blood through his veins, through the old man's body and into Iliana's mouth, the triple heartbeat that shattered the air and beat inside his head.

Just as Cole closed his eyes to try to block it out, it ended. The phantom pressure on this throat weakened and the air that met his lungs was suddenly crisp and cold. He dragged his eyes open in time to see Iliana release her client. The old man slid down the wall and came to rest on the floor like a life-size doll. His head lolled onto his chest and his arms hung useless at his sides.

Iliana turned as Cole pushed away from the bookcase and stood on legs as steady as pillars of loose sand. Iliana's eyes were fever-bright, her skin flushed and alive. Cole wanted nothing more than to be disgusted by the sight of her like this but to his surprise it had the opposite effect on him. He backed away from her and turned his attention toward Jacob to avoid confronting those visceral feelings. The old man's wrinkled skin was pallid and it seemed to take ages for him to exhale and then draw the next shuddering breath .

"Are you ready to leave, Cole?" Iliana asked. Without waiting for his reply she took his arm and led him out of the office as if nothing had happened. Her body radiated heat like a miniature sun. Cole did not pull away but he tried to keep some distance between their bodies, hoping she wouldn't notice how much her time with Jacob had affected him.

"Did you kill him?" Cole asked as they entered the stairwell. Fear and desire had tightened his throat and made his voice a mere whisper.

"Don't be a fool," she snapped. "We have rules regarding the taking of a life. It is a private experience and afterward the body is treated with reverence and respect. We do not just kill without discretion and leave the body behind."

But Cole remained leery. "Are you sure?" He thought about the girl in the Church and the way her friends say she was killed.

He opened his mouth to mention her then shut it again when he saw Iliana's scowl. Now was not the time to tell Iliana about his visit with Father Matteo.

"Yes, I'm sure."

"Because he looked terrible."

Iliana finally met his gaze and offered Cole a smile and the fever faded from her eyes like a veil had been thrown off. "I admit I took a little more than I should have. But he'll be fine. He's used to it, trust me."

"I do trust you," he said, and the words felt like a revelation.

"And I am glad for that, at least. But let me get you away from here. I need to rest."

Cole was unconvinced. But she strode past him on the stairs and started to descend. For the first time she had let the mask slip and he had spent enough time counseling people in crisis that he could tell something was wrong. He felt something coming off of her, a tightly restrained panic. He wanted to ask, to talk to her but the stern set of her jaw prevented him from saying anything else.

She did not look at him again, not even when she released his arm outside the palace gate and told him she would come for him the following day. As he watched her walk back across the courtyard and disappear into the palace he wondered what it was that had her so shaken.

28 "I wouldn't lie about this, Adam," Jacob said. He licked his lips and his ferret-like eyes, still somewhat glazed from his donation, darted all over the courtyard like small rodents seeking escape.

Jacob had been waiting on the front steps of the Palace Nyssa when Adam returned after a long night of work. Once upon a time the old man had haunted all of Adam's comings and goings but in the past decade or so Adam had seen little of him. Now he had come to tell Adam of Iliana's crime and Adam could not contain the fury that welled within him.

"You saw her yourself?" Adam asked from between clenched teeth. He didn't want to believe that his sister, the hope of their people, would be so rash as to bring the enemy right into their midst. Adam shook his head and asked, "And she had a key?"

"There was no sign that she had broken in."

Together Adam and Iliana had stolen and copied the keys to most of the doors in the palace, but not for this. This was wrong. He didn't even care that she would tell on them both when he brought her to Governor Drake to be punished.

And then he hesitated. Was this punishment necessary? On one hand her actions flirted with the edge of unforgivable. On the other hand she was his sister, his friend, his companion and he didn't want to hurt her. If he dragged her before Drake their easy relationship would end. They would become enemies.

"I caught her in Governor Drake's office with a man. I told her she couldn't be in there and she said that her client wanted to be taken in a forbidden place."

"That's no excuse."

"But he was too tense. She hadn't taken him yet."

Something clicked in Adam's head. He narrowed his eyes and asked, "What did he look like?"

"Tall with brown hair and eyes. Probably in his forties. Quite plain."

The light in Adam's eyes dimmed. "That could be anyone. You people all look the same. It's amazing you can even tell one another apart," he grumbled.

"She called him Cole."

If he gave himself time to cool off he could have turned a blind eye to Iliana's trespassing but this pushed him over the edge. Adam let the blood boil into his face, relishing the feel of it percolating through his limbs. When he spoke again his voice was dark with anger.

"Where did she go?"

"I don't know. I passed out after she drank from me."

"She drank from you?" Adam asked, disgusted that this pitiful excuse for a man had used Iliana's situation to his advantage. No matter how wrong she might have been she was still his sister and she was better than that. Jacob nodded and a goofy grin spread across his face. Adam grasped the front of Jacob's shirt and threw the old man up against the wall as hard as he could. Jacob's eyes squeezed shut as his head smacked hard against the stone.

Adam breathed into his face. "Watch Drake's office but be inconspicuous if you can manage it. If she comes in again send someone to find me immediately. But do not blackmail her into taking you again or I will kill you myself. Do you understand?"

Jacob nodded as well as he could, his dark eyes full of tears. Adam let him go and stormed into the palace. The crowd parted as he passed.

29

"Are the pairings acceptable to all parties?"

"Yes."

"Good," said Governor Drake. He had kept the Council in discussion since just before sunset pairing up acceptable couples for the Festival and he was glad it was over. They always tried to pair men and women who liked one another but that wasn't always possible. Had Iliana not been chosen for the Transformation she would have been one of the unlucky few who would be forced to couple with a near stranger. Iliana had few people she could call friend beside her brother. Some of that was due to her position in the Palace hierarchy but the rest was due to her aloof nature.

Governor Drake stood and announced, "The matches have been made. You all have your lists. Please go out into the city and notify your people of their partners for the Festival. Good luck."

As they prepared to leave Adam burst into the room. The door slammed against the wall with a dissonant crack and all heads turned in his direction. Sigrid opened her mouth to fling angry words at Adam but Governor Drake beat her to it, his voice swelling to fill the room and leaving no space for competition.

"I do not appreciate this interruption."

Adam shut the door and announced, "Iliana was in your office this afternoon."

For a moment no one spoke and the violent music from outside flowed into the windows and filled the silence until the very walls seemed to thrum with a foreign heartbeat.

Then to refute any doubts Adam added, "Jacob caught her," and that stopped any potential questions from the Council. No one would doubt Jacob's word.

And then the final bombshell. "She had a client with her."

Expressions of outrage filled the room as everyone tried to voice their fury at once but Sigrid spoke loudest. "Governor Drake, I demand that you bring her before us and force her to explain herself. The fact that she trespassed is bad enough. But to bring a Colonist into the seat of our power, so close to our greatest treasures…" Sigrid's handsome face crumpled for a moment.

But even adrift in that sea of rage she found her voice once again to demand, "That girl must be punished!"

The other members of the Council knocked on the table in a show of support and the hollow sound echoed in the room until Governor Drake raised his hand to quiet them. He looked at Adam's furious face as he waited for silence.

When he once more had control of the room he cleared his throat and asked, "Do you know who she was with?"

"His name is Cole. He is the same man who spent the entire night in her cell several days ago. I told him to stay away from her but—"

"Adam," Governor Drake interrupted with a sigh, "When will you understand that with their kind the more you insist a thing is not to be done the more certain it becomes that they will do it? Your warning probably only reignited his interest in her."

"Unlikely. When I spoke to him I got the impression that he didn't care if he ever saw her again. He hates us, I'm sure of it."

"So you think Iliana sought him out?"

Adam's silence confirmed the statement and Sigrid jumped up once more. "Drake, this is ridiculous. How can you put the lives of your people in the hands of a rebellious girl who cannot follow even the simplest of rules? She knows that she is not to see the same client two days in a row. She knows that she cannot befriend them."

Governor Drake cut her off. "I will not condemn her until she has had a chance to explain herself." He reminded himself how much was at stake and tried to be considerate of his colleagues' fear, but at the same time he was frustrated by their lack of faith in him and his decisions. He turned to Adam, who was exchanging angry glances with Sigrid, and cleared his throat to get his son's attention.

"Do you know where Iliana is?"

Adam shook his head. "No, but I can find her."

"Good. And when you do just tell her that I wish to discuss the Festival. Do not hint that she may be in trouble because she might run and hide and I do not want to have to hunt her down."

Adam gave a curt bow and left the room. Once he was gone someone muttered, "Those two will be the death of us all." Some of the council members nodded in agreement. Governor Drake leveled his eyes at the member who had spoken and stared hard until he looked away.

Then Governor Drake cleared his throat and swallowed his emotions: the fear, the anger and the disappointment. And when he spoke next his voice was smooth as glass.

"You have your assignments. We will meet tomorrow at sunset. I hope any concerns you have can wait until then. Thank you."

30

"I grew up as a ward of the Church. Father Tanaka took me in and raised me after my parents died on a missionary expedition."

"That name sounds familiar…" Iliana tapped her fingers on the table in front of her and sipped her coffee.

"He was the Church's third in command. He advised Father Deven on several issues."

"Like the Natives?"

Cole hesitated, thinking of the group beneath the Church Capitol and the face of Father Serrano, puffed up and proud of his accomplishments, twisted though they were.

"No," he finally said. "There are other men for that task."

"So was he kind, this Father Tanaka?"

"Very. He raised me under close Church supervision so that I could grow up to stand with him beside Father Deven. He passed away last month."

Iliana touched his hand, "I am sorry," she said. Her hand was soft and cool and her touch drew Cole out of his memories and back into the moment.

"Don't be. He had been ill for a long time. His death was a blessing. But it meant that it was my turn. Father Deven called me up to take my father's place."

"You have powerful friends."

"I know. It was a dark shadow to grow beneath. I had my share of blunders, of course, but they all seemed to think I fared well and they rewarded me with my own Church."

"Wait. What kinds of blunders could you have made?"

Cole answered without feeling, though whether he truly felt nothing or if the emotion had just been bled out of him over the years he couldn't have said. "Foolish adolescent things. Sex mostly, which is a sin, but forgivable. In fact all things are forgivable if you only ask with honesty in your heart. So I asked and so I was forgiven."

"By whom?"

"By God, of course."

Iliana laughed. "You mean by some man in a cabinet pretending to have a closer personal relationship to God than anyone else."

"The priest is a conduit, a pathway, nothing more. The forgiveness is divine no matter which medium delivers it. But I can understand why, if you believe your simplified man in a cabinet theory, you can't understand our beliefs."

"I understand them. I just don't accept them. We don't need a conduit. We are each a part of God."

"What God is this?"

She sat up straighter, arranged her face into a disapproving scowl and adopted the tone of voice that Cole had once used to condemn her. It was just another mask, another role to play. "Ours is the God of blood and flesh. The God of hunger. The God of nature, creation and destruction, life and death. Our God is present within us at all times."

Cole chuckled as she relaxed back into her seat. "Sounds angry and unforgiving."

"That's not it at all. We have the freedom to mess things up just like anyone, but we believe that those mistakes are a part of us and of God. The difference is that we lack the spiritual rules you use to stifle your people."

Cole shook his head as if trying to dislodge the information she placed in his mind but it was too late. It had already taken root and it grew with each passing breath. "I don't understand," he said. "If everything you do is correct then why hasn't your society deteriorated into chaos? With no boundaries or no restrictions you should be barbarous. But you're not. You're…"

"Civilized?"

"In a manner of speaking, yes."

"Religion does not have the market cornered on civility.

Each of us makes a decision to follow the norm. We govern by what feels correct in our souls."

"Even murder?"

She shrugged. "We don't condone it but there are always exceptions, as I'm sure there are in your culture."

Cole sat dumbfounded across from Iliana and stared at the polished wooden table, at the pale water spots, bright marks in the varnish, at the cold and congealing remnants of his breakfast. The noise of the restaurant faded into silence as his world tunneled down to this moment. Cole heard only his own breathing, his heartbeat. He was afraid to move, afraid to blink, lest this moment of peace be shattered. He had the answer now and he clung to it, afraid to lose the light of realization but also afraid to move forward.

This felt so familiar he could be sitting across from any member of the Church discussing dogma. They had more in common with the Natives than Cole ever realized but with one major difference.

The Natives trusted their people to lead good lives and allowed for some deviation from the norm. The Church did not trust its own people to be righteous, hence the strict regulations, the commandments, the rigorous penance required for breaking the rules. Asking the Church to relinquish control was akin to asking it to slit its own throat. But as Cole sat there the idea grew and spread in the fertile soil of his first blasphemous thoughts until he could almost smell the fragrance of the bloom, the sickly-sweet smell of heresy. His eyes watered.

"Cole?" Iliana's vivid blue eyes burned holes through him like a cigarette burning through paper. He felt that if she continued there would be nothing left of him but a wisp of ash hovering on invisible currents of air. He looked away.

"Cole, are you all right?" She touched his arm and Cole flinched. She must have felt it because her face closed up in an instant. It was like watching a flower bloom in reverse and he regretted the involuntary movement but didn't know how to take it back.

In an attempt to salvage the conversation Cole smiled and

muttered, "You're turning me into a heretic. You should be proud."

"You are what you are. You wanted to know and you sought me out. How you choose to process the information I give you is your own problem—"

"Iliana," Cole cut her off and she looked up at him. He covered her hand with his. "I'm trying to say thank you."

Iliana smiled but her eyes remained dark. So Cole changed the subject. He had read the book pilfered from Drake's office until late into the night and his mind was full of disorganized questions. So he just picked a topic at random and ran with it.

"Why did your people let our scientists experiment on them? I read in that book from the governor's office that we treated you like animals to be studied."

"We allowed it at that time because your people were dying of a blood disease and no medicine they had brought with them could combat it. They needed our help. And we were curious about you, too. So we viewed it as an exchange: we taught you about us and you did likewise. It was a simple sharing of information."

"We teach our children that we had to beg you for the cure to the disease, that we had to capture and torture you to get you to reveal the secret."

"All lies. When we realized that you would all die, we offered up our own bodies as living filters to cleanse your blood. It was this act of charity that brought such swift damnation upon our heads."

Cole thought of the dungeon beneath the Church's Capitol building, of the experiments no doubt still being performed there. Against all odds he found himself more willing to believe the Native children's book than the teachings of his own people.

"Wait," said Iliana. "You wouldn't have had time to read much of the book before Jacob discovered us. How did you know what we thought of the experiments?"

Cole blushed. "While you were busy with Jacob I hid the book beneath my shirt and carried it out." Iliana's already pale face became ashen and her eyes widened. Cole saw fear flicker across her features.

"I have to go back," she said. "I have to go back and return the book and get out without being discovered. I hope that no one noticed it was missing. It was a horrible idea to go there in the first place. I don't know what I was thinking. I—"

"Iliana," Cole cut her off and her wandering gaze settled back on his face. "I will go with you. I will help you."

"I can't ask you to do that."

"You're not asking. I'm volunteering."

Iliana bit her bottom lip as she mulled over his proposal, as if he would have given her a chance to say no. But eventually she said, "Fine."

Cole stood, pulled out his wallet to pay for breakfast and said, "I'm ready."

"Oh no," Iliana said, her voice almost a whisper. She touched Cole's arm and eased him back into his seat. "Tomorrow, just after midday, meet me at the Palace gate. Wear a coat with the collar turned up and don't tell anyone you're coming to meet me."

"I don't know who I would tell."

She stood then, picked up her bag and her wrap and turned away. Cole was surprised to find he didn't want her to go. So he stood as well and asked, "Why do you have to go? We could talk some more if you want. I'll pay for your time."

Iliana answered, "I can't," before walking out the door.

Cole looked down at his half-eaten breakfast and pushed the plate away, no longer hungry. The truth had quenched his hunger better than any food and like a junkie he craved more.

Still, there was a part of him that missed the Church after this extended sabbatical. There was a certain peace only meditation could provide but ever since his Father's death he had lacked focus for such a task. The teachings of the Church were no longer an option, for he could now make out the pinprick holes in the fabric of his faith as clearly as if they were huge tears. But even though his faith in the Church was compromised, his faith in God remained strong.

He left a few crumpled white bills on the table and left, wondering where to go. The hotel room would never do. There was nothing soothing about those throbbing red walls. He couldn't sit on one of the benches that lined the streets, for even though the afternoon traffic on this main thoroughfare was sparse, in a few hours it would be too hot. And he couldn't go back to Father Matteo's Church, not after their last conversation.

He wandered down the street, moving away from the Palace and into a part of the city he had never visited before. Most of the shops and clubs he passed had closed doors and dark windows. Through the doorways of the few open businesses were men and women huddled over cups of coffee or something stronger, wrestling with the demons awakened the night before. He heard random, undecipherable utterances like a sea of sound. Cole couldn't stand to be in a place like that, surrounded by lost souls drowning in their confusion. So he moved on.

Above those buildings loomed the enormous stone wall that separated the Final Circle from the Second Circle, pale yellow beneath centuries of vandalism. Cole was too far away still to make out the exact words or pictures tattooed there but he imagined them to be lewd and risqué and wondered why no one had covered them up. They didn't seem to fit into the world of the Palace escorts as he had come to know it. But maybe they fit here, farther away with the rest of the city. That graffiti was the only sign that the rest of the world even existed, a world he would have to return to sooner or later.

That thought stopped him. He didn't want to think about going back, about what might happen to his mind should he resume his post, about whether or not he could continue to preach. He knew he couldn't run away forever but he was in no hurry to return. Not now that he had met Iliana.

Cole's wanderings brought him to a dead-end. And at the very end of the street stood a modest chapel. He approached it with caution, half expecting Father Matteo to walk out at any moment and accost him. But the street remained empty. The oil lamp burning bright in a front window told him the chapel was open and occupied so he went inside, hoping to find the peace he needed.

31 "Help me." A whisper in an alleyway in the pale morning light. Such a plea could not be ignored.

Adam turned and peered into the shadows, and a shape coalesced out of the darkness. Even he had to admit that she was beautiful for a Colonist, with eyes the color of molten gold and skin that almost matched the bronze tones of his own. Her long, dark brown hair was pulled back into a thick braid that trailed down her back, opening her face. Adam's fingers ached to touch her. He was supposed to be looking for Iliana but perhaps a short break was in order to clear his mind and relax him.

"Please," the woman whispered again, "I need you."

Her dress was simple and brown, her face clean and young. The way she held herself suggested money and Adam was happy to take it from her. He looked right and left. The street was empty so soon after dawn and shimmered already in the heat that promised to be oppressive come midday. He could do this, he could take this client and return to his duty soon enough. He was owed this small pleasure.

Adam slipped into the alleyway, his movements sensuous, his eyes locked upon the eyes of his client, drawing her out, drawing her toward him. She wavered on her feet but stood her ground, a nervous smile twitching the corners of her mouth. Adam sniffed the air for any sign of illness and smelled nothing but the refuse, urine and dirt of the alley underscored by a faint, flowery perfume. She was clean. This would be pleasant.

"What would you like?" he asked, close enough now to feel her muscles trembling beneath the skin.

"Your kiss."

Adam moved behind her as his hand stole into his pocket and palmed the sharp metal thumb so that he could break her skin. Then with deft fingers he moved the heavy braid aside and she tensed.

He whispered into her ear, "Do not be afraid," and kissed her neck, just a brush of lips against her skin. She shivered and tensed anyway in anticipation of the pain, the rush.

He placed the tip of the thumb against her throat and she gasped. Goosebumps raced across her skin and a film of sweat glistened beneath his hands. As he pressed the thumb harder the sound of footsteps made him look up just in time to see a fist flying toward his head.

Before he could duck the punch connected with his right eye and Adam stumbled backward, releasing the woman and bringing both hands to his face. They came back bloody. His cheek throbbed already just below his eye and promised later agony.

"What is wrong with you?" Adam yelled and staggered backwards.

"You seduce our women. You pollute our souls," said the man who had delivered the punch. He stood a head taller than Adam and was wider, darker and full of rage.

"I do nothing that is not requested. She asked for it." Already the numbness in his cheek had become pain. But the pain faded beneath the fury that welled within him, a storm that could not be diverted. And on the heels of rage came the excitement, the exhilaration of a fight, surging like electricity to his fingertips.

"A decoy," said another voice and Adam turned around toward the back of the alley to see two more men coming toward him. One was his size and the other was even larger than the first. It was the smaller one who spoke.

"A decoy for your savage hearts."

Adam turned back to the woman and she looked away as if ashamed. He doubted she was in any state to join the fight, which made it three against one. Those were odds he could handle.

"I was doing my job," Adam said.

"The work of a demon," said the first man.

"Come on then," Adam said with a smile, his arms open wide in invitation, "Let me show you what a demon can do."

They all attacked at once. Fists, feet, teeth flew at Adam in a maelstrom of flesh. Adam dodged the first blow but caught the next on the chin. His head snapped back with such force his neck cracked and his vision swam with pastel colors. And then a foot sunk into his stomach and Adam went down. His fingers curled into the dirt of the alley and as the first man grabbed a handful of Adam's hair and yanked his head upright, Adam flung the dirt in his face. The man screamed and staggered away, wiping his face with both hands, but his friends grabbed Adam by the arms and yanked him up.

"You should learn not to fight back," the smaller one said. For punctuation he punched Adam in the face twice in rapid succession. The world swam but Adam held onto consciousness. He knew if he passed out that would be the end of him.

"Yeah," the man holding Adam's arms said, "The others didn't fight back. By the end they were even begging to die."

Adam kicked backwards into his captor's groin. And then before he could respond Adam whipped around, jammed his metal thumb deep into the man's throat, and then ripped it to the right, leaving a jagged hole that spurted blood. The man went down, spraying Adam with his blood on the way.

Covered in gore, Adam turned to face the other two men, now pale and shaking. The larger man's eyes were fiery red and irritated and he blinked hard, still trying to get rid of the sand.

"You killed him," the smaller one said.

"Of course," replied Adam.

"You'll pay."

"I'm sure I will."

As both men charged Adam pulled a knife from a hidden sheath at his waist. While his left hand slashed out with the knife and plunged it deep into the big man's soft belly, his right hand threw a punch that knocked the smaller man to the ground.

The large man moaned. In response Adam withdrew the

knife and slashed it across his throat. Once again he was splashed with gore. Adam then turned to the other man, who was coughing and sputtering on the ground, came up behind him and twisted his head hard to the right, breaking his neck.

As the last body toppled to the ground silence settled over the alley. The battle had only taken a few minutes and Adam felt unsatisfied. The anger and adrenaline still scalded him from within just as it had at the start. He needed release. And as he thought this the sound of someone crying pierced the haze.

Adam turned to see the temptress who had first lured him into the alley. She was hysterical. Her hand covered her mouth but did little to stifle the sobs that shook her entire body and echoed off the buildings. She had done this. She had led him here.

Instinct took over. Adam strode toward her. When she turned to run he grabbed her hair and yanked her back toward him. She yelped as she slammed into Adam's body. Adam put his arm around her, trapping her arms.

"Please, please, please..." she muttered over and over again, like a prayer. Her body trembled against him. Beneath the perfume he now smelled fear, strong as wine and coursing through her veins.

"How many of us have you hurt?" he demanded. They were too organized for this to have been a one-time thing. They knew what they were doing. They had done this before.

"Please, not me—"

"How many?"

"Six," she admitted.

"Six." Six of his people dead at the hands of these fanatics. Six of his people tortured and killed. Six lives lost to the battle.

"But it wasn't just us."

"Were you acting for the Church?"

She hesitated for only a moment before answering but it was enough for Adam to know that she was about to lie. "No. On our own. Please forgive me. Forgive us." The idea almost made Adam smile. That a member of the Church would beg for his forgiveness was amusing sacrilege

"You'll find no forgiveness here," he said. He wrenched her head to the side, opened her throat with his metal thumb and locked his mouth onto the wound.

Her memories bobbed to the surface like oil rising in water but he didn't want to know about her loves and her happy moments. He didn't want to know about her life. Instead he thought of the worst things he could: the mutilated bodies of his people he had seen firsthand, violent rape, the increasing numbers of lifeless Native children whose bodies were left to rot in the sun after each Festival.

She began to scream as his thoughts infested her brain and overpowered her memories. The more she screamed the more disgusting his thoughts became. Torture, fingernails pulled off, eyeballs plucked out, electrocution, the acrid, sweet smell of burning, rotting flesh. And that is how she died, in Adam's wicked embrace, her mind overflowing with repulsive thoughts.

Adam dropped her and staggered to the nearest wall for support. His head swam. The harder he blinked the worse it seemed to be. He glanced down at his shirt, sticky with drying blood and other fluids, and his body responded with violence, emptying his stomach onto the dirt, heaving until his face prickled from the strain. He felt worn out, used up, broken as he stumbled into the main street. Fever burned his brain just as the heat burned his skin.

Adam had never killed anyone in anger before, though he had killed in self-defense. He had hurt Colonists, sometimes hurt them badly, but he hadn't killed in a very long time. The woman had posed no immediate threat to him. He didn't have to kill her. But he did kill her, and the anger still ached within his chest, screaming for release.

32 Wayward grains of sand scraped beneath Cole's tread as he entered the Church. The vestibule walls had been painted to reflect the tones of the desert so the place seemed like a mirage rising out of the dust to tantalize Cole with visions of the one thing he needed, solace. An alcove to Cole's right held prayer candles and cones of incense that he passed by without another glance.

The simple space gained substance as he made his way down a center aisle flanked by hard wooden benches. Tapestries depicting man's foibles and ultimate redemption adorned the walls and an altar sat at the front of the Church. There were no other decorations, even the windows were made of plain glass so the sunlight that lit the chapel was bright and unyielding instead of multi-colored and muted.

The chapel was empty save an elderly man in a plain white robe sitting in the front pew. Cole tried to make as little noise as possible, noting that the priest appeared to be in deep prayer. Instead he headed toward a rectangle of sunlight streaming in through an open door at the front of the church and when he reached it he knew that he had found what he had been looking for.

A large courtyard garden was situated in the center of a square created by four long buildings that Cole assumed were dormitories. It was the green, living heart of the compound. The space was full of lush trees, new grass and flowers, bordered on all sides by neat paths of gravel the color of the desert sand. He was surprised to see nature thriving in this arid climate where little seemed to grow and his senses gorged themselves on the idyllic scene.

Cole took a few tentative steps into the garden and closed his eyes. If he stood still he could hear the diminutive voices of priests that floated out of the rooms and into the courtyard. Their words formed a web of soft incantations that almost drowned out the ever-present cacophony of the city.

When he had first arrived the music had been like a balm to his frazzled nerves because it had kept his mind too full of heavy beats to ponder his heretical thoughts. Since meeting Iliana more often than not he just ignored the music. He hadn't realized how much he had missed this sort of serenity until that moment. He felt safe.

Someone tapped Cole on the shoulder and he whipped around to see the old priest who had been praying. He was paler than most Colonists and his skin looked like old leather. Wisps of white hair ringed his shiny head like windblown clouds.

"Young man," he said, "Have you come to pray?"

Cole judged him to be at least 80 years old but despite the weight of his years on his wizened face he wore a hopeful smile. His pale, caramel-colored eyes were opaque and his bottom lip quivered after he spoke as if there was something more he wanted to say but couldn't.

"Yes," Cole said, "I've come to pray."

Cole held out his hand and the old man grabbed it and shook it with such excitement that Cole thought of Father Matteo's words, 'I haven't conducted a full service in over 13 years.' Cole had the feeling it had been even longer for this man.

"Wonderful, wonderful. It's nice to see a young person take responsibility for his soul in the hereafter. What did you say your name was?"

Cole smiled. "I didn't. But my name's Cole."

"Cole…" the old man repeated in a daze. He appeared to be combing his memory for a way to place the name. When it seemed the man might stand there all day staring into space Cole decided to help him along.

"It's Father Cole. I have a church in Afet's Wall." At the mention of the Capitol City the man's face became bright, then darkened at once.

"Father Cole. Tanaka was your father. I am sorry for your loss. He was a very spiritual man."

"Thank you."

"Is there any truth to the rumors that you will be taking his place?"

Cole sighed and gave the only answer he could, though at that moment he wanted anything but to return to his position in the Church. "When my sabbatical ends I will return and take my father's place if that is what Father Deven commands."

"As it should be," the old man said, though his smile was not as bright as before. Cole had the feeling that he wanted to say something else but restrained himself.

"And what is your name, Father?" Cole asked to get the conversation flowing once more.

The old man chuckled. "Oh, there are no Fathers here. We are all brothers. The Brotherhood of New Life. My name is Brother Jerome. I suppose I'm like a prefect here."

Brother Jerome gestured to the courtyard and the dormitories beyond. "Sixteen of us live and work here. Seven others have homes elsewhere in the city but choose to spend their days here in prayer. We have several spare rooms if you need a place to stay. We're not quite a destination for the tourists anymore."

"Thank you, but I already have a place to stay."

Brother Jerome nodded. "Of course. Please feel free to use our space as you need. Our doors are always open. But if you will please excuse me it is time for our services." He gestured to the courtyard, where several men in white robes exited the closest dormitory and came toward the chapel. Cole stood aside to let the men pass.

"You may join us if you like," Brother Jerome offered.

"No, thank you, brother. At the moment I would prefer to pray alone. Perhaps some other time."

"As you wish."

Everyone else was seated when a lone man came out of the dormitories and tore across the garden. His robe was a little too large for him and several times it twined around his legs and tripped him up. But he eventually made it through the door, only a little behind the others.

"You're late, Brother Yourian," Brother Jerome said as he

clapped the young man on the back. Yourian's curious eyes glanced in Cole's direction for a moment before he tucked his head and sped into the chapel like a dog that had misbehaved and was trying to become invisible.

Brother Jerome nodded to Cole and turned away. Cole wandered to a sandstone bench beneath a tree and sat down, leaned back against the fat trunk and closed his eyes. His mind whirled with thoughts he hadn't felt capable of entertaining until now.

His Church had fabricated a history so the people would sanction the oppression of the Natives. It took a Native, someone on the outside, to show him how duplicitous that false history was. From what he had read the Church was like an abused child that became an abusive father.

But was the Natives' version of the story even true? If the lesson book was correct and the Church had become an all-encompassing humanitarian force then why become so cruel when faced with a different race of people? The precedent had been set for a peaceful coexistence with anyone they might encounter.

Part of him thought that it didn't make any sense. But the rest of him argued that it made perfect sense if Iliana was right and the Natives fought being absorbed into the Church's all-encompassing conglomerate of faith. Add to that any jealousy and bitterness that the Natives inspired out of the Church's followers. The Natives lived longer and looked different. They were colorful while the Colonists were drab. Cole remembered the first pair of blue eyes he had ever encountered. They had been startling, beautiful and amazing. And they had burned through him out of a filthy face twisted with anger. The Natives beneath the Capitol had been the first he had seen in person and up-close.

The Church's condemnation of the Natives' long lives was based on fear. Perhaps those in control of the Church feared that their followers might see something akin to divinity in the long lives of the Natives and quit their faith. The "sin" of eternal life, or at least what seemed to be eternal, was just too much for the overwrought devout to understand. So the Church behaved like a jealous ex-lover, cruel when you're together but nasty when you leave. It started to demonize the Natives to keep people from exploring the mysteries of their long lives. The Native practice of drinking blood made it that much easier.

But if the Natives were evil why did the Church continue to accept their money? For as long as he knew his people had been aware of what the Natives could do. He plotted a rough timeline in his head and instinct told him that he was right. The Church had corralled the Natives into this small plot of land, Adara Vega, and then taxed them without mercy, hoping that they would submit. Instead this tactic forced the Natives to lure in more of the Church's members to make up the money to pay the taxes. Cole thought that if the Church really disagreed with what the Natives did it would refuse any money earned through sin. But it did not, and so the Church grew fatter and richer year by year on the blood of its followers.

As the pieces fell into place Cole felt a startling tranquility settle over him. For several minutes he relaxed into it. His mind stopped its incessant whirling and it felt good.

Then a violent crack whipped through the courtyard, ending Cole's moment of peace. He opened his eyes, irritated at the interruption and looked toward the open door of the chapel. Through it he saw Brother Jerome, still as a statue, his mouth agape as he stared at something in the back of the chapel.

He heard someone scream but the words were unintelligible from that distance, so he stood up and jogged toward the open door. As he got closer the words became clear.

"...and you think you're better than us? You are nothing but a mote in the eye of destiny. Without us you would all have perished within a decade and still you persist in this mockery of civility, of honor and piety."

Cole reached the door just in time to hear Iliana's brother, Adam, growling in a voice like thunder, "You are the monsters. I curse you and your god."

Adam then spat on the floor and wiped his mouth with the back of one filthy hand. He looked like walking death. His hair was matted with blood and each footprint left a dark stain on the floor. And though one eye was almost swollen shut and his cheek was cut open Cole doubted that much of the blood was his.

Adam took another step forward, determined, brimming with animosity that made the hair on Cole's arms stand up. His eyes bounced from face to face like a ball until he locked his gaze on the three-faced statue of God behind the altar.

"Your God is a God of lies and deception. Your God is a God of pain and retribution." He turned to the closest brothers and rained bloody spittle on them with every word. "You would kill your children if your God asked you to. But what kind of God demands such blind faith?" The brothers just blinked at him in silence and Adam laughed like a wild animal.

"The kind of God who sees his creations as a game."

Adam started walking toward the altar and those who were content to have him stay at the rear of the church stiffened and looked toward Brother Jerome as if for the signal to attack.

"You've taken everything we have," Adam screamed. "And now you want to wipe us out."

Brother Jerome found his voice and spoke in a voice that was both soft and stern. "You need to leave this place. You defile it with your continued presence here."

"I defile it? Me?" Adam let go a laugh like a gunshot and then spat on the floor again. When he looked back up his eyes found Cole standing in the doorway. Adam's nostrils flared and his mouth twisted. He took another step.

"You," he said, pointing at Cole. "I warned you what would happen… I warned you."

"You need to leave now," Cole said, surprised at the lack of fear in his voice. Now that he had Adam's attention he had to draw him out of the chapel. He couldn't let Adam hurt these men even though he doubted that he could take on the raging madman alone. Still, Cole stepped up beside Brother Jerome and said, "You heard the Brother. Leave this place and touch nothing and no one on your way out."

"Why not? Because I will defile it?" With something akin to a smirk on his ruined face Adam touched the back of the nearest bench with one finger. "Will your God smite me? No, because I defile nothing.

"You defile our land, our city. You pollute our lives and our minds with your ridiculous dogma. You vomit lies and hatred. You poison your people against us and attack us without provocation. No, sirs, I believe that you are the defilers. You are wicked and you will die a thousand deaths—"

Adam's voice broke. He leveled his eyes at Cole and paused and in the silence Adam's eyes issued a challenge. Cole's body tightened in anticipation of the attack just as Adam charged the altar. Brother Jerome cried out and stepped back as Adam leaped through the air. Cole put out his arms out to defend himself. Out of the corner of his eye he saw three of the brothers vacating their pews but they were not fast enough to keep Adam from slamming into him. Together they tumbled against the altar, then the wall. Implements rolled off of the altar and clattered to floor.

Cole hit the floor so hard he lost his breath but Adam recovered with ease. He pressed Cole's face to the side and held him there with one hand while the other hand went to his throat. Cole stiffened when he felt the sharp bite of metal against his skin.

"You were warned," Adam hissed and pressed harder. Cole tried to pry Adam's hands off of him but as he was still lying on his back he was at a disadvantage. He felt the sudden pop as his skin gave way. Should he pray? Should he ask God for forgiveness before his life ended? It seemed he had all the time in the world as his mind struggled to find the words to make amends with God and came up empty. The blood tickled as it flowed down his neck. He realized that he had nothing to say.

Suddenly Adam was lifted off of him and Cole coughed and sat up in time to see the brothers dragging Adam away from the altar. One of the brothers punched Adam in the face and blood spurted from his nose and all over the floor, the new blood was too bright against the dried brown gore that already covered him head to foot.

"Please," Brother Jerome said, "Not here. Not now. We are unharmed." He gestured to Cole to prove his point but no one was listening.

Adam's attack was the perfect excuse to act on years of stifled anger and frustration. Cole pulled himself to his feet using the wall for support. He felt light-headed. He touched his throat.

The wound oozed blood but it was superficial.

He watched the men drag Adam out of a door on the other side of the chapel. Adam struggled as he went but he was outnumbered and already weary from whatever he had endured earlier. He continued to preach his blasphemy, his voice the only part of him they could not subdue.

"You think you've won? You think you've beaten us? You have no idea what you're up against."

Then came the dull sound of flesh slapping flesh as the men began to beat him. The words stopped but in between those noises Cole swore he could hear laughter, slow and eerie. It was Adam, laughing even as they pummeled his body.

At the door, watching it all through wide eyes stood the latecomer, Yourian. His pallid face was pinched in horror. He wrung his bony hands and looked as if he was going to be sick. But even though he didn't join in, neither did he turn away.

Brother Jerome approached Cole, "I am so sorry for this, Father. Are you all right?" He eyed Cole's throat for a moment and said, "The bleeding has already stopped, thanks be to the Lord. I suppose you were lucky that my brothers intervened when they did." He looked toward the door, where the sounds of the beating could still be heard. "But I am sorry that you had to witness this, Father. They are young. They get carried away sometimes."

"Can you stop them?" Cole wasn't sure what made him ask. Even though he had been attacked he didn't want the men to kill Adam. For the first time in his life he understood both sides of the conflict. He understood why Adam, why all of the Natives, were so full of rage. But instead of feeling open-minded and well informed he just felt divided.

"Not now. I have been able to keep the hostility at bay for a long time but they grow frustrated with the situation here, surrounded by temptation but unable to partake."

Cole understood that problem as well. He shifted his gaze from Brother Jerome's pleading face to the scene outside. "What will be done with him?" he asked, concerned for Adam's safety despite his great dislike of the man.

"From the looks of him nothing that hasn't happened before."

In the alley Adam screamed, "You can't stop me!" The phrase was punctuated by two dull thumps. And then, "Is that all you've got? Can't your righteous hands do more than that?" Cole cringed as he listened to Adam egg them on but he was at a loss for what to do. He felt like he should intervene but he was outnumbered and unwilling to get hurt on Adam's behalf.

"Are they going to kill him?" he asked, letting a little of his concern color his voice.

"Of course not," he said in a rush. "We are not monsters." When Cole didn't say anything right away Brother Jerome added, "Don't worry about him. Their kind is resilient. Not that it will help them."

Cole was unable to get the sounds of Adam and the brothers out of his ears. He looked deep into Brother Jerome's rheumy eyes and saw a conflicted soul. "What?" Cole asked, confused.

"You mean you haven't heard?" Brother Jerome asked. He placed his face so close to Cole's that Cole could smell the old man's breath, hot and stale.

Cole stopped breathing through his nose. "Heard what?"

"As a priest in Afet's Wall I would have thought you'd be the first to know, being so close to the Capitol and all—"

"I told you that I've been on sabbatical. What is it?"

"By noon, three days before the Native's Festival of Semiveh, all of God's people must leave the city."

"Why?"

"The Church is going to destroy the Natives and reclaim the city."

Cole studied the old man in shock but Brother Jerome's face remained earnest. He wasn't joking and he seemed unconvinced that this was the correct course of action.

"You don't agree with their decision," Cole said. A statement, not a question.

"No, I do not. I think it is unnecessary bloodshed. But it is not up to me."

"How are they…" Cole began, trying to wrap his mind

around the idea of his Church committing genocide. He thought of Iliana, innocent and alluring and more helpful to his people than a thousand misguided preachers. He knew that he couldn't let her die. He knew that he didn't want any of the Natives to die. Suddenly his memories collided with this new knowledge and he understood: the Natives beneath the Capitol were not there to be studied as Father Serrano had claimed. They were test subjects for something violent and fatal.

"A virus. They've been planning this for a long time, you know."

Cole's mind reeled. Unable to bend the Natives to its will through merciless taxation the Church would just kill them all, wipe them out in one broad sweep then come in later and clean up the mess.

Cole's claustrophobia returned in an instant and he had to get out of the chapel. The walls began to converge on him and he couldn't just stand there and let himself be crushed.

"Thank you for your hospitality, Brother. Perhaps I will see you again." The words felt false on his tongue but he had nothing else to say. He eased himself out of Brother Jerome's grasp and walked away, each step punctuated by the slap of flesh against flesh as the brothers outside continued their sport. Cole felt guilty for leaving Adam to their mercy but the feeling faded beneath the harsh glare of sunlight.

33

"You're here."

Iliana couldn't hide her surprise. She knew they were tempting fate by returning to Drake's office so soon but she couldn't risk anyone discovering that the book was missing.

"Of course I'm here," Cole whispered back, his mouth hidden behind the stiff collar of his overcoat.

"Do you have the book?"

"Of course."

Without wasting time on further conversation she took his arm and led him into the compound. She strode across the empty courtyard, trying to look both nonchalant and determined to dissuade unwanted conversation. To that aim she wore a dark red velvet cloak with a large hood that obscured her field of vision. It was something she didn't often wear and hoped that if someone happened to glance into the courtyard they would not recognize her.

The hallway for the elevator was empty. Iliana tapped a finger against her lips to signal to Cole to be silent and he nodded. It was too quiet for conversation. On the elevator Iliana pressed the button for the fifth floor because she didn't want the elevator bell to signal their arrival on the floor of Drake's office just in case someone was in the hallway. Cole didn't question her precautions and she was thankful for his prudence.

The elevator reached its destination and the doors swished open, accompanied by a "ding" that was far louder than she remembered. Iliana preceded Cole into the hallway.

Iliana steered him into the stairwell and began to descend. Fear lent her speed and she already walked fast, even in her high-heeled shoes, so she reached the landing first and peeked into the hallway. When Cole caught up with her and she told him, "I've already looked and no one is nearby. Are you ready?"

"Yes," he said.

"Thank you for doing this with me." She touched his arm. He didn't pull away and Iliana let out a little sigh of relief. He stood to lose so much more than she did if they were discovered this time. She wanted him to understand how much she appreciated his help but didn't know how to put those thoughts into words.

"My pleasure." Cole smiled, seeming to understand the unspoken sentiment behind her words. She nodded in acknowledgement but kept her crimson lips drawn in a straight line as she pulled him into the hallway.

They approached Governor Drake's door and Iliana whispered, "Keep watch until I am able to unlock the door." Cole did as she asked without question as she fished the key out of her bodice and made quick work of the lock. Cole followed Iliana inside and shut the door behind him.

34

"What is it?" Adam yelled before he was fully awake. Several hard knocks on his cell door had startled him out of a dark and dreamless sleep and he scowled, then winced, then groaned as he remembered his encounters of the day before. Whoever was banging on his door was going to get the brunt of his frustration at being awakened before his time.

He rolled over and sat up. Every part of his body ached as if he were still being pummeled. His face throbbed in time with his heart and one of his eyes seemed to be swollen shut. He could have checked since the mirror was across from his bed, but he turned away from it. It was far too early to deal with the horror his face had become.

The knocking started again and Adam sighed. "Well, that was ill-advised," he muttered to himself, then called out in a hoarse voice, "Come in already before you splinter the door."

He heard the outer cell door open and pulled his blanket forward to cover himself. He always slept unclothed despite the fact that there were no locks on the cell doors. He found bedclothes to be stifling, especially when one's entire body seemed to be a giant bruise.

A moment later Jacob rounded the corner, his withered face flushed with excitement and his hands wringing before him. And then he saw Adam and he stopped, his eyes wide and his jaw slack.

"This had better be good," Adam said. His lips felt numb and swollen and his words came out slurred.

"What happened?"

"That is none of your business. Why did you wake me?"

"I was hiding in the closet beside Drake's office like you told me to and I heard someone come in. It was Iliana. And she brought that man with her."

Rage boiled throughout his limbs and mindless of his pain and his nudity Adam stood. As he reached for his pants he started issuing orders. "Wake Governor Drake now and apprise him of the situation. Then come and wait outside of Drake's office for further orders."

Jacob turned and left as quickly as his age would allow. Once he was gone Adam's energy flagged and his multitude of injuries caught up with him. With more care than he had taken with his pants he guided his shirt over his bruised and scratched arms, then buttoned it with stiff, aching fingers.

He couldn't believe that his sister had done this again. He couldn't believe that the hope of their people rested on the shoulders of someone who repeatedly flouted their laws. His first reaction was to lash out and strike her down, but that was soon tempered by his affection for her. She was still his sister, however asinine her recent actions. He hoped that Drake could talk some sense into her or at the very least punish her and make her behave.

He smoothed his hair with both hands but did not even glance at the mirror before he left his cell, a purpose in his limping stride and darkness in his heart.

35 "Give me the book," Iliana said. Cole handed it to her without a word. She tried to ignore it but already she could feel the effects of the power in the secret room. Already it was calling to her, seducing her. They had to hurry. But as she moved to the bookcase and slid the book back into place she heard a voice in her head, whispering, imploring her. *Stay. Look behind the bookcase. Learn about the fate they have planned for you.*

Iliana paused, her fingers lingering on the worn leather of the book as if afraid to let go. The voice slid through her and captured her mind. It was right, of course. She should stay. She should learn what the Transformation entailed. She needed to know.

Instead of walking out and never looking back Iliana moved to the side of the bookcase, located the button and pressed it.

"What are you doing?" Cole asked but she didn't answer. She felt him come closer. "Iliana, don't we need to go? Is it that power again? Are you feeling something?"

"I have to know what's going to happen to me," she said without looking at him. As soon as the wall popped open a wave of power washed through her and she staggered backward. Cole caught her and helped her to stand up again. *He is warm. He smells like blood.* Those thoughts were not her own. Iliana stepped away from him and moved forward into the secret room.

"Aren't you nervous about someone coming in?" Cole asked, entering the room behind her.

No, Iliana thought. She was not nervous about being discovered because at that moment she didn't care. She took in the room in a glance. It was tiny and lined with metal shelves that stretched from floor to ceiling. A lot of the shelves were empty. Some contained books and papers and scrolls under dusty glass and others held artifacts of gold or wood, but these were of no interest to her. She headed straight for the back of the room, the bottom shelf, the source of the power that tingled through her limbs.

"Please help me," Iliana muttered, the plea was directed at the voice in her head. It no longer whispered but she couldn't make out much of what it was saying. So she opened her mind to it and the words filled her head once more.

Look for the birthing. The Transformation. Your mother.

Cole sighed and asked, "So, what is it I am helping you to do?"

Iliana turned and looked at him as if surprised he was still there. *You're so hungry and he looks delicious.* And then she saw the smallest pinprick scab on the side of his neck. There was blood just on the other side. He had been taken.

"Iliana?" he asked.

The power surged within her and filled her head with jealousy. "What is that?" she spat out, pointing to his neck. "You decided to donate to another escort? I was not good enough?"

Cole blinked hard and his hand flew to his throat. "It's nothing," he said and looked away.

But the voices in her head would not be put off. *He lied to you. Take him. Take him now.* "Was it good?" she asked at their insistence, "Did you enjoy it as much as you do when you watch me take a client?"

Cole sighed but did not seem ashamed. "Your brother attacked me today. He tried to rip my throat open but I got away."

Iliana shook her head to dislodge the whispers and for a moment it worked, the power lessened, reality felt real once more. "I'm so sorry," she said and this time the words were her own. "Why didn't you tell me?"

"What purpose would it serve?"

"I am sorry," she whispered. On the heels of her guilt the whispers started up again. *Just ask for a taste. Finish what your brother started.*

Cole smiled but it didn't touch his eyes. "No, I don't like him, but I can't blame him for being angry. I just happened to be there and he needed a focus for his anger. Now let's do what we came to do and get out of here."

Iliana nodded, amazed at his stoicism but unable to applaud him for it. She was afraid that if she opened her mouth she might latch it onto his throat. She had never craved blood before now and it would be so easy to take him. But before the power could manipulate her tongue into speaking lies she blurted out, "I need to find any information related to my mother. I need specific information regarding the Festival and any rituals having to do with it."

"Any idea where those might be?"

She pulled her gaze away from Cole's throat and glanced at the bottom shelf. There she saw something covered with a purple velvet cloth that seemed to shimmer in the half-light of the room. This was the source of the power and it seemed to know that she had seen it. The air surrounding the cloth began to pulse in time with her heart. She felt the steady beats in her lips, her ears, her fingertips.

Look.

Iliana looked to the right of the cloth and saw a stack of books in better condition than most of the others in the room. Their spines were blank, giving nothing away as to their contents. "There they are," she said and the voice echoed the words in her mind.

Cole came forward and gathered up the documents. "We won't be able to see anything in here. We might as well take them to Drake's desk. Come on."

Iliana forced herself to turn her back on the box and followed Cole out of the room. As soon as she stepped into Drake's office the air felt lighter and her head was not as muddled as before. In the interest of regaining more of her faculties she pushed the bookcase back into place before joining Cole at Drake's desk. The air became cool and fresh; the voice was a whisper, unintelligible. Iliana didn't fool herself into thinking that whatever was speaking to her was finished with her for good so she wanted to make good use of the time she had.

Cole opened the top book and started to turn the pages.

"Why are you doing this, Iliana? Why the sudden interest in family?"

Iliana hissed, "The Church is going to kill us all."

Cole paused, looked away and said, "I know. When you brother attacked me I was in a chapel. The prefect there told me about a plan to destroy you and reclaim Adara Vega. They told me to leave the city three days before the Festival to avoid being killed along with everyone else."

Iliana felt her face flushing with anger that she could not subdue. "And you said nothing until now?"

"I just found out and I admit I was hoping they were wrong. Besides, it's not like you've given me much of a chance to talk tonight."

Iliana looked away, closed up again like a flower after the first winter frost. Cole had angered her, of course but the damage had been done. She regretted getting him involved in her life, if only to save herself the frustration of having to consider someone else's feelings. The voice became audible in her mind once more, suggesting a bloody solution to her dilemma, and she was horrified to find that a part of her didn't disagree.

But Cole surprised her. Instead of backing down, instead of arguing, he touched her shoulder. And then he spoke with such humility that she could no longer hold his unfortunate omission against him.

"I want to help you," he said. "Whatever it is you're looking for, I want to help."

Iliana met his earnest eyes, her emotions guarded. "Thank you. Just find the information I need."

She could not apologize but Cole seemed to understand. They looked in silence through some of the nameless books and paperwork but after a time the voice began to insist upon her attention. So more to silence the voice than any other reason she began to talk about what she had heard.

"I overheard a Council meeting. Drake said that I was integral to the Festival of Semiveh and that it was vital for me to be a part of it. I don't know why I'm more important than anyone else but Drake was very interested in keeping tabs on me. He said something about translating some 'old texts' and keeping me ignorant of their plan. And he mentioned my mother. They want me for something."

"You mean you don't get a choice?" Cole asked.

"No. Every 100 years all of the women ages 100 to 500 must bear a child. It is the only time we are fertile. It is part of the reason our numbers dwindle while yours continue to swell."

"So that means you are slated to have a child?"

"Yes, though I don't think that's what they have in mind for me. And even if that's all it is I don't want to have a child this term."

"The responsibility alone..." Cole sympathized. He didn't often regret never taking a wife, having children, and now was not one of those times when he did.

"There is no responsibility. The mother and father are paired together on the first day of the Festival. The second day is the day of conception. On the third day we celebrate a Festival gone well. 112 days later there is a child.

"There is very little family involvement. The child is taken away soon after birth to live with tutors and the other children in a special school. At the age of 14 they are released into the world. We always know our mothers and fathers but there is not usually close bond. The quota requires strict discipline and family can get in the way." She paused and thought of Governor Drake and Adam.

"Except for the Governor, of course," she added, "Adam is his son and he wants everyone to know it."

"So that makes the Governor your father?" he asked, surprised.

Iliana shook her head. "My brother and I share a mother, but not a father. Our mother's name was Gabriella. She died after I was born. I do not know my father's identity. I always imagined that their union was not sanctioned by the Council and so the name of my father died with my mother."

"How terrible."

"Not really. We do not know any other way. A child is a burden when you have a quota to fill. Things were probably
168

much different before your Church decided to tax us to death."

"I would tell you I'm sorry if it would change anything," Cole said and the voice in Iliana's head hissed.

"It changes nothing, but thank you."

They looked for a time in silence, nothing but the crisp sound of pages turning breaking the monotony. Finally Cole announced, "I'm not finding anything," and sat back and rubbed at his eyes with both hands. "We've been in here for a long time. We should go before someone comes in."

Iliana was about to agree when she saw her mother's name scrawled at the bottom of a page and her own name written beside it. Her heart began to pump and she felt light-headed. Before her mother's name was a number and a letter noting which appendix would contain her father's name. With trembling hands she turned to the correct page.

A lock of hair fell into her face and she whipped it behind her ear. Her fingers ran down the page until she found the correct letter denoting her father's place. But the small box across from that code had, instead of a person's name, a small notation written in a different script than the rest of the book, "See *On Transformations*, pp: 113-115".

"What?" Iliana asked the book.

"Did you find something?" Cole asked and Iliana jumped at the sound of his voice.

There were so many names listed for other Natives, some she recognized and some she didn't. But she had no father. And why her? Why hide her father's name and no one else's? "I need to find another book," she said and consulted the list again, "*On Transformations.*"

"Oh, I know I just passed that one." He flipped open a few of the books to the title pages until he found the one she wanted and handed it to her.

Iliana hesitated before she took the book from him, as if she were afraid of what it might contain. It was thin, bound in black animal hide, and twice the size of her hand. No designs embellished the cover or the spine. She took a deep breath and opened it to the first page. It said something about the Festival of Semiveh and made a vague mention of a change. There were a lot of words that took up space but said nothing specific. The voice in Iliana's head urged, hurry. She flipped to the pages the appendix had indicated, passing other women's names in the process. She had to fight the desire to stop and read each one.

The title of the chapter was her mother's name, "Gabriella." Iliana sank into a nearby chair and began to read. Cole stood over her shoulder and read along with her, every now and then uttering some senseless noise as the tale unfolded.

36 Gabriella, like Iliana, had been the darling of the Palace Nyssa. According to the book she had even been the one-time occupant of Iliana's cell. She was paired with several different men during the Festivals but for some reason did not produce a child until the age of 500 when she coupled with Governor Drake, who had just become the head of the Native Council. Adam was born out of that union.

At the age of 600 she volunteered for the Transformation. It did not take, however, and she lost her mind and died. There was a brief mention in the book about this having happened before but not how many times before. Iliana assumed that the other names in the book were the tales of the other women lost to the cause. Still, Gabriella's case was different because before she died she gave birth to Iliana. Even though Gabriella was lost to them the Council was pleased at least that she had had a child. The book did not state whether Gabriella was with child before or after the Transformation, nor did it mention the name of her father.

While pregnant, Gabriella was confined to her cell. Her windows were barred and all furniture was taken away. The Council worried that she might hurt herself and the child, and rightly so. Gabriella was deranged, screaming and crying one moment and lucid the next, only to come back again in a never-ending arc of madness, swinging wider each day.

Iliana's birth took three agonizing days and Gabriella remained awake the entire time, screaming and crying while strapped to a table. Once she delivered Iliana she was whisked away to another room. Then she died. The book didn't say how.

Cole tried to read between the cryptic lines to see the truth underneath but the scant details the book provided left too much to the imagination. Iliana sat back and rubbed her face with both hands and Cole squeezed her shoulders to reassure her that they would find what they were looking for.

"But what did they do to her?" she asked, glaring at the book as if by sheer willpower she could force it to reveal its secrets.

"Nothing compared to what will be done to you," Adam said as he entered the room. Iliana and Cole jumped apart like guilty children caught playing with a forbidden object. Adam glared at them both with open hostility.

As Adam walked closer Cole heard Iliana gasp and her body stiffened. Even Cole was shocked to see him upright, looking the way he did. Adam was a mess, one eye was swollen shut and his bottom lip was split open and crusted over. His left cheek sported a mottled purple contusion and a scabbed over gash marred his right cheekbone. The cuts had been tended to but he still looked haggard. And he didn't move with the same grace Cole had seen before, which made Cole wonder what other injuries were hidden beneath that long-sleeved black shirt. But the hatred that flashed in Adam's good eye was enough to make what little guilt Cole still harbored for leaving him at the mercy of the brothers disappear.

"Adam," Iliana began but then stopped when he turned his fury on her. They had been caught and no amount of sweet-talk could save them now. Cole stifled the urge to step in front of Iliana to protect her.

"Iliana, how could you do this to me, to your people?" Adam growled.

"I needed answers no one would give. No one will tell me what's going on."

"Come with me now," Adam said, each word enunciated with care over swollen lips. He stepped forward, grabbed Iliana's arm and yanked her to her feet. The book she had been holding fell to the floor with a loud slap.

Cole moved to pick it up and Adam screamed, "Don't you put your filthy hands on that again! How dare you contaminate these sacred documents."

"I was trying to help her," Cole said, feeling his anger rise. Iliana had asked for his help this time and there was no way he would have refused. "Perhaps if you would not scheme so much behind her back she wouldn't need me."

Adam threw a punch with his free right hand and Cole turned just enough to miss the full force of it. It still connected with his jaw and the momentum caused him to fall backwards over Drake's desk, sending the haphazard stack of books toppling to the floor. Cole climbed to his feet and prepared himself to fight but Iliana stopped him with a word. "Don't."

He listened. He stopped. Adam grinned, that mocking smile made more wicked set against those deep bruises.

"You lead the way, Father." The venom in Adam's voice made Cole shiver. He got the impression that if he went along with Adam he would not be long for this world.

"Adam, please…" Iliana said.

"Don't speak any of your lies to me," he hissed, "You screwed up, Iliana." And then to Cole, "Go."

Cole walked toward the door and when he got there Adam said, "Stop," and Cole stopped. He stepped aside to allow Adam to go first, and as they passed by Iliana looked up at him. He saw no fear in her blue eyes, only anger that they had not learned more and frustration that they had been caught. That realization freed him from most of his concern for her, certain that she could handle whatever they threw at her. But he remained terrified for himself.

Before lowering her head in a very convincing representation of shame she mouthed one word, "Run." Cole set his mouth in a stern line and followed them out.

In the hallway stood Jacob, the old man who had caught them the first time. He sneered at Iliana, who didn't look surprised at all. Cole glanced at Iliana and she responded with the barest of nods. So when Jacob came forward to claim Cole's arm Cole took a deep breath, dodged the old man's grasp and ran for the stairs. Adam, too afraid to let go of Iliana to give chase, reached out with one hand, which Cole evaded.

He threw open the door and, fueled by adrenaline and fear,

practically flew down the stairs. He stumbled once and slid down half a flight for his trouble and when he reached the bottom his lungs burned, his breath was ragged and his body was trembling, screaming at him to stop. But he wasn't safe yet. He had to get out of the palace compound.

He took a deep breath, one as deep as his aching lungs would allow, and opened the door. Nothing. Cool, dry, late afternoon air wafted in through the crack, easing his torment. His body threatened to collapse but he steeled himself against this desire and stepped outside. The air cooled his overheated face but beneath his heavy coat, where the breeze could not touch, his shirt clung to his back.

Cole eased the door shut and forced himself to walk as if nothing was wrong. The stairwell had taken him to the right side of the building. The palace wall he walked along had no other doors or windows and the façade was pockmarked beige stone. He felt as if he were standing in the shadow of an alien monolith, which only increased his desire to get away as fast as possible. He scanned the line of the black fence and cursed under his breath. The fence had no other break, which meant he had to walk across the almost empty courtyard and go out the way he had come in. He flipped up his collar, hunched down in his coat and started toward the gate.

Halfway there a laughing male escort fell into step behind him. "Hey there. Where do you think you're going without an escort?" The young man had dark skin and laughing, honey-colored eyes. He was as tall as Cole but lithe and he seemed to be in constant motion, his limbs swinging as though his joints were held together by bits of loose wire.

Cole swallowed hard, looked the escort straight in the eyes and said, "I'm going home now. Good evening." He started to walk away but the man followed him

"Where is your escort?" he asked in a tone that suggested he might volunteer should Cole answer to his taste.

Cole hesitated. To utter Iliana's name would only complicate matters and could lead to being captured. He shuddered to think of what would happen to him if he ever saw Adam again.

He considered running but then thought better of it. The gate was over one hundred feet away and though the evening was very young there were a few escorts milling about in the courtyard. One of them would likely tackle him before he reached the gate.

So instead Cole summoned all of the acting talent he could and said, "You know, I can't recall her name right now."

He complemented the lie with a drunken giggle of the sort he had heard others make after being taken by an escort. It felt false but sounded believable, to his relief. All the while Cole kept walking toward the exit. And as they passed beneath the lanterns he widened his eyes as much as possible to make his eyes water. He hoped that the flush that still burned his cheeks and the sweat drying on his forehead would be sufficient to make him look like he had recently donated.

"To which floor did she take you? Where was her cell?"

Cole shrugged and pointed in the general direction of the stairwell. "She did it over there. Someone came over afterward and they started talking so I left. Not very professional if you ask me."

"Indeed," the man said. He scowled, irritated by Cole's mistreatment, but when they reached the main gate his easy smile returned.

"Here we are, sir. Have a pleasant evening and I promise that your escort will be reprimanded for her crude behavior."

Cole had to struggle to keep the relief from his face. He thanked the man and stepped outside the gate.

Through the bars he watched the man confer with another male escort who was as pale as a full moon with features accented by eye makeup, rouge and lipstick. After a moment they both headed in the direction Cole had indicated. Cole exhaled. He had gotten out. He was free.

He started back to his hotel to pack. He had to change hotels just in case Adam sent someone after him. Somehow he hoped he would be able to reach Iliana and let her know of his move, though he didn't know how he would accomplish this.

At the thought of Iliana he paused, turned toward the Palace and looked at the tower's top floor. He found himself saying a little prayer for her safety, a prayer that Adam and the Governor would treat her with kindness. He even allowed himself a chuckle at the blasphemy.

As he turned and started walking again he continued to pray for her wellbeing but he was certain that the worst was yet to come.

37 They entered Governor Drake's cell without knocking. Adam had dismissed Jacob after Cole escaped. He didn't need Jacob's help anymore and was eager to be rid of the old man.

Governor Drake sat in his antechamber in a large, comfortable-looking armchair. He had been dragged out of bed to oversee this inquisition. His shirt was untucked, his hair was loose and the strands had separated and curled around his face like fine silver wire. Without the blue paint, without the ghost of a younger face to hide the real one, he looked so much older. His eyes were bloodshot and the look in them was far from pleased.

Iliana entered the room of her own accord, not as frightened of punishment as she was angered by Adam's treatment of her, like she was some second-class citizen instead of his own sister. And she was furious at Drake for lying to her, for not including her in the planning of her own future.

"What happened to you?" Drake asked Adam.

"Nothing. A scuffle, that's all."

"Against twenty men?"

"Something like that," Adam muttered. "But we aren't here to talk about that. We're here because she broke the law by allowing a Colonist to see our most sacred space. And now she has done it a second time. She must be punished for this indiscretion."

Drake's eyes leapt to Iliana's face and when Adam finished speaking Drake asked, "Is this true?" His hoarse voice cracked, from exhaustion or anger she couldn't tell.

Iliana swallowed hard and said, "Yes, it's true, but I have reasons." She paused then and looked at Adam, whose hand still bruised her arm. Her voice narrowed to a sharpness that could cut. "Let go of me, brother. I am not going to try to run like some criminal."

Adam looked to Governor Drake for approval and Drake nodded. Adam released her and moved to stand just behind Drake's chair, at his right shoulder. Neither man asked Iliana to sit and she understood that she was on trial and so she did not ask if she could. Besides, she felt that her words would have more impact if she remained standing.

"If only you had answered my questions. I asked about my place in the festival and you said nothing. Then I overhear you and your Council planning my future without considering what I might want." She saw confusion then understanding spread across Adam's face as he realized that the only way she could have overheard was through the peephole they had carved into Drake's office wall. She had given herself away but there was no time for regret.

She continued, "I heard you mention the Transformation. And then I have to find out on my own that that is what killed my mother, not childbirth. How could you have kept this from me? I do not appreciate being a pawn in your game of revenge against the Church and I will not tolerate any more of your lies."

"We are all pawns, Iliana." Drake sighed, his shoulders bowed beneath the collective weariness of his people.

"I understand that we do what we must to survive. Fine. But why must I play a part in your schemes that I do not even understand? Unless you tell me everything tonight I will refuse to do what you ask and if you try to make me I will leave the city."

Drake hit the wooden arm of the chair with his fist, an explosive sound in the silence. Iliana flinched. His voice was raspy and his face became red as a desert sunset. "You do not have a choice. I do not have a choice. How can you be so selfish to think that your petty life is more important than everyone else's?"

Iliana rolled her eyes. She had heard it all before and she was not interested in his propaganda. "But—" she started but Drake cut her off.

"Since you were listening at keyholes I suppose you overheard that they are planning to kill us all." Drake seemed to have calmed down but his voice remained tight. "Do you understand? This is going to happen during the Festival. I cannot just sit back and watch my people die."

"I know. I heard."

"Then you know what's at stake."

"Why don't you evacuate the city?"

Drake closed his eyes and shook his head and when he again opened his eyes it was as if a great mantle of sorrow had been thrown over him. "And where are we supposed to go, Iliana?

"Should I lead my people into the desert? Should we live as nomads and become rabid and wraithlike while we wait for the Colonists to sweep in and pick us off one by one? No. And the mountains are just as arid as the desert. No life grows there. So no, we cannot evacuate the city. It would be tantamount to suicide."

Iliana remained stubborn. "Fine. We cannot leave. But why have I been singled out for the Transformation? Ask me to take up arms against our enemy and I will go to war for you. I'll even lead the battle. But I will not submit to this, whatever it is."

Just as quickly as it had come the anger seemed to dissipate. Drake became morose and returned to his chair. "We are all important."

"I heard you talking about me," she said. His apparent weakness gave her the strength to stay her course. "I heard you tell the Council that I had to participate, that it was vital. Why?" She paused as Drake looked up at her and then, once she caught his haunted eyes, landed the final blow. "Was it because of what you did to my mother? To all those other women?"

At the mention of Gabriella, Drake stiffened. Adam folded his arms across his chest and leaned back against the wall, a tiny smile playing at the corner of his mouth as if he were watching a play being enacted just for him. Iliana got the feeling that he was amused by her anger. She wanted to smack him across his bruised cheek but she promised herself that there would be time for that later.

"What do you know?" Drake asked.

Before her eyes Drake seemed to fall in upon himself and

for the first time that day Iliana's anger ebbed a little. But she couldn't stop now, not out of pity, not while she held him in her palm, and the questions exploded from her mouth before she thought to put them in any sort of order.

"What did you do to her? What is the Transformation? How is all of this connected to the Festival of Semiveh? Are you planning to do the same to me? Who is my father and why isn't he in the book like everyone else's?"

"Which book?"

"One of the books in the secret room in your office. It just referred to another book, On Transformations, and that said nothing specific. What is the Transformation? And what is in that box that speaks in my head?"

Adam's head snapped up. "The box?" he asked. "It speaks to you?"

"Adam, please," said Drake. Then to Iliana, "What does it say?"

"Answer my questions first."

"Iliana, please sit down." He gestured to the plush chair opposite his and waited for her to be settled before beginning. Adam did not look pleased about Drake's seeming change of heart but Iliana glared at him until he looked away. It was a small victory but a victory nonetheless.

Drake took a deep breath and began to speak, and with each word Iliana swore she could see him aging before her eyes. "Despite our current culture of solitude, despite the fact that we are raised to be isolated beings, it wasn't always this way. I loved your mother. I loved her before we were paired to produce Adam and I loved her for the 100 years that followed. When she volunteered for the Transformation I admit that I tried to talk her out of it. No one who had ever undergone the Transformation had survived. But she felt it was her duty to her people and I could not dissuade her."

"What is the Transformation?"

"Please, Iliana, this is difficult. Just let me finish before you ask questions."

Iliana pouted and sat back in her chair. "The rituals can only be performed during the Festival of Semiveh. Once again we had no luck and Gabriella went mad. But she didn't die right away like the others. She screamed and hallucinated that dark shapes were stalking her, invading her body and changing her. She carried on conversations with the wind. She wouldn't let anyone touch her and didn't recognize anyone.

"Still, she was alive, which was more than we had hoped for. The Council tried to persuade me to father another child on her before midnight on the second day of the festival. But seeing her there, screaming, naked and strapped to a table like some science experiment, I couldn't do it. When I left the room I told them it was done but somehow they knew I hadn't touched her. I just couldn't stand the way she looked at me, like she didn't even know me, like I was food.

"The next thing I heard, Gabriella was with child and confined to her cell, your cell. It hurt me to know that she was carrying a child that was not mine and everyone knew. So I never went to see her again. Not that she noticed.

"Your birth was difficult and took a very long time. As soon as you were out they swept in and took you away. They didn't even let her recover before they loaded her onto a truck, drugged her and left her far out in the desert to die.

"I didn't know what had happened until they brought you to me, wrapped up in a blanket. You were so small and silent, like you already knew everything and were just waiting for the words to explain. At first I hated the sight of you, the child that should have been mine. But then you smiled at me and I knew I had to take care of you.

"So there you have it," he said, deflated. It was as if the story itself had kept him fat and lively and now with it expelled in so many words he just collapsed, a hollow shell of a man.

Iliana stifled the urge to apologize for making him relive what was obviously an awful memory. She had done nothing wrong. She deserved to know.

"So what is the Transformation? What does it do?"

"It is an ancient ceremony. I don't understand it all even though I've presided over it several times. The old texts are unclear about the process, except to say that when we need it, it will help us. 'In our time of greatest need the Transformed one will save us.'"

"And what does that have to do with the box?"

"The box contains the magic but that is all I know. No one has ever witnessed the actual Transformation so I don't know how it is accomplished. But tell me, now that I have shared, what does the box say to you?"

"I can feel the power radiating from that secret room in your office. I never noticed it until you opened the bookcase and then it felt like there were hands in my head. And I was hungry. And there was a voice that egged me on, told me to dig deeper and discover more about the Transformation."

Drake made a non-committal noise and Iliana asked, "Do you hear it, too?"

"I feel power coming off of that box," Drake answered without answering. "And it is always the strongest in the days leading up to the Festival."

Iliana took a deep breath and asked the real question. Now that she knew what had happened to her mother she needed to know if Governor Drake had the same fate planned for her. She wasn't sure what he would say but she prepared herself to run if he said, 'yes'.

"Am I to be the Transformed one this time?"

A pause filled the room with tension but then Governor Drake laughed and the gesture was so unexpected that Iliana felt the doubts slip out of the brimming pool of her dark thoughts like a waterfall.

"The Transformed one must volunteer for the process, Iliana. I confess that I originally entertained thoughts of asking you to be the one but I abandoned that idea right away. I couldn't stand it if I lost you.

"And to be honest, the reason I pushed you to bear a child this term is a selfish one. I want to see my Gabriella's bloodline live on. You look so much like her, act so much like her, so beautiful and headstrong and opinionated. Even though I am not your father by blood I have always cared for you like a father and that means more to me than you know."

Drake glanced back at Adam, and as if on cue Adam stepped

forward and placed a hand on the old man's shoulder. For a moment they were the picture of familial bliss.

"You two are the living proof of my Gabriella. And I want it to see it live on because I may not be around for the next chance."

"So what of the Transformation, then?"

"It will not happen. It does not work. Something is getting lost in the translation from the old texts and so to continue to subject my people to it would be cruel. We are harming ourselves by sacrificing our own."

"And the box?"

"I am keeping it safe until such time as we can devise a way to destroy the magic inside it without destroying ourselves."

"I see," she said, even though she didn't. She suddenly felt foolish for bringing such harsh accusations against an old man. The bitterness of distrust lingered but she assumed it was just the aftertaste of deceit.

"Can you forgive me for being so evasive now that you know the pain I've held onto for so long?"

"I think so." She paused and then added, "I have to think." Iliana's head spun with this new information and barely left her enough mental capacity to speak. "I am going to retire for the evening. Goodnight."

"Wait!" Governor Drake said as she stood and started to walk out. "You're forgetting why you were brought here in the first place."

Iliana stopped in mid-stride and turned back to face them. At Drake's shoulder Adam was grinning again and Iliana threw him a stern look. Nothing had changed. She was still in trouble. She just hoped Drake would be lenient with her after his emotional revelation.

Governor Drake asked, "Why did you take a Colonist into my office? If it had been only you I could try to look past the indiscretion but you have broken our laws. What do you have to say for yourself?"

And so Iliana sat down and began her story, Cole's story, and she painted him as their greatest ally against the Church. Adam and Drake listened in patient silence as Iliana told them of her meetings with Cole, of his many epiphanies, of his views on the Church and the Natives.

"He wants to learn about us," she finished. "He came to me with questions and instead of just telling him things he might not believe, I showed him proof, books and records of the past that he could understand, things he could touch and experience.

"And he does understand. He will return to Afet's Wall and take his place beside Father Deven and share with them everything he's learned about us. He'll teach them that we are their equals and not to be feared or mistreated. He will be third in command on the Church Congress and he intends to petition for our freedom. He could help us."

When she finished she watched them both in silence. In Adam's eyes she saw the disgust he felt towards her and her relationship with Cole. Adam had always viewed the Colonists as something beneath him and she knew that the fact that she was helping Cole instead of using him sickened the puritan in him.

Governor Drake, however, appeared thoughtful. After a few moments passed in silence and Iliana began to worry for Cole's safety, Drake said, "You could be right." A long pause, and then, "But are you sure he is not a spy?"

"Positive. When I cleaned him out that first night I saw his memories. There is no deceit there, just confusion."

"And he does not want your services?"

"He has never mentioned it. In fact he seems set against our friendship taking that sort of turn. To make sure I meet my quota he pays for my company and my conversation, that is all."

Drake considered for a moment, then said, "All right, Iliana. Because I trust you and your judgment I will believe you. You may continue to see this priest and teach him but do not enter my office again, with or without him, under any circumstances. Conduct your lessons elsewhere, is that clear?"

"Yes, sir." Iliana smiled, pleased that she had gotten away with it and even more pleased by the sudden fury that turned Adam's face a deep scarlet. But Adam remained silent. It wasn't his decision.

"Perhaps he could help us after all," Drake said. "But only

if he returns to Afet's Wall as soon as possible. Is that what he plans to do?"

"I think so," Iliana lied, suddenly unsure. Though she knew that Cole would leave eventually she hadn't thought about when. He was no use to them if he broke all ties to the Church and stayed here. Even so she did not relish the thought of letting him go.

"Very well, Iliana." Unsure if she was dismissed, Iliana did not move from her seat. Governor Drake smiled, "I think there could be a place for you in the Council someday. You have a shrewd mind."

Once again his intentions were unclear and so she said, "Thank you."

He eyed her for a moment more, then said, "Since you seem to find the idea of bearing a child so distasteful and the Transformation cannot happen, I will speak to the Council of Elders and ask them to consider you for a position. You will have to pass an interview first, of course."

"An interview? And if I pass?" she asked, incredulous. The proposition seemed too good to be true so she was afraid to believe it.

"You will be a part of the Council that helps protect our people. I assume this would be more to your taste."

"Yes, it would."

"Good. I will inform the Council of your interest and once the interview has been scheduled I will contact you with regards to the date and the time."

"Thank you so much," Iliana said. She walked around the desk and kissed Governor Drake's forehead. He smelled of lavender soap and there was a thin rim of blue paint at his hairline where he had neglected to wash it off. The sight of it gave her pause as she realized that these might be the last years she had left with the man who had always treated her like a daughter. She didn't want to spend them arguing.

She stood, grinned at Adam one last time because she still had a lifetime to argue with him, then left. She felt as if she were bouncing down the hallway to the elevator, eager to share this news with Cole.

38 "Are you mad?" Adam hissed between clenched teeth. The tension in his resonant voice told Drake that Adam was trying hard to keep himself in check. He wanted to scream and Drake couldn't blame him. The punishment did not fit the crime but Drake was more interested in placating Iliana instead of angering her.

Governor Drake wiped at his face with both hands as if trying to dislodge the weariness that had set in but it would not be moved.

"I am not mad. I just do not see the point in keeping her upset. She is impulsive and she may just do what she threatens to do. She may try to run."

"She's bluffing." Adam snorted.

"But I can't take that risk. This changes nothing in our plan. She will not return to my office and she will not touch the papers in the secret room, so that at least those are safe.

"As for this priest, she trusts him and believes that he can help us. I see no harm in allowing such a hope if it makes her happy, no matter how foolish it is. I think we would all prefer to end this without violence. We are fast approaching the point of no return so I am willing to try anything."

"I thought you didn't want her forming attachments to the Colonists." Adam sat in the chair Iliana had just vacated, every movement precise and studied, adopting his courtly manners to hide the frustration he felt with the situation. But the deep scowl gave away how furious he was with both Drake and Iliana.

"I did say that, but the attachment has already been formed. It would do no good to restrict their communication now. She would question the motive and harass us and we could not hold out against her will for too long."

"You mean you could not hold out against her." Adam said, his voice thick with contempt.

Drake sighed, folded his hands on top of his desk and leveled his gaze at his son, making every effort to keep his face diplomatic and impassive. "Adam, you understand what is at stake because you have been involved since the beginning. Iliana does not have all of the information and so cannot grasp the situation. You need to be patient with her."

"But to bring a Colonist into your office..." Adam began but Drake cut him off.

"If we start a war with the Church none of this will matter."

"But he has seen our books. He knows the history we've kept contrary to the lies the Church has fed their people. He cannot be allowed to leave the city."

"Once again, if it comes to war then it will not matter what he knows so don't trouble yourself. Besides, perhaps he can take this alternate history, the true history of our people, back to his Church. Perhaps he can teach them."

"You're a fool," said Adam, unwilling to let it rest.

"Watch your tongue, Adam. I said do not trouble yourself. I am the Governor here and this was my decision to make, not yours. Continue to keep an eye on Iliana but do not interfere again. Come to me with any concerns you might have. And in two days' time, at midday, come to the meeting hall and bring whomever you've chosen as your commanders. I will be unveiling the plan in its entirety to the Council."

Adam watched Drake with fierce animosity for a moment then jumped up from his seat. As he strode out of the room Drake called after him, "Everything will proceed as planned. If all goes well Iliana will be our savior. We have desperation on our side, if nothing else."

Adam opened the door to leave and then turned around at the last moment. "If you think so. But you're making a big mistake by not keeping her under your thumb. Iliana will continue to do as she pleases if she senses that we are still keeping things from her. She can tell when I'm lying and so it's safe to assume she knows when you are, as well."

"We shall see," Drake said. Adam walked out and shut the door behind him. Drake stood up, his knees cracking in unison, and moved into his cell. There, in a locked drawer in a small writing desk, were the latest translations of the old texts. He had just received them that afternoon and had already spent hours studying them.

Drake unlocked the drawer and fanned the pages out across his desk and stared at them. They described the process of the Transformation and he had held onto the slimmest hope that perhaps something had been lost, that something had been missing and maybe this time they would catch it. But even though this was a new translation Drake was disheartened to find that it was not dissimilar to the version they had used for Gabriella's Transformation.

He reread the pages again, going over all of the parts he already knew by heart. He had lied to Iliana about not knowing the process. He knew the gory details all too well and he hoped for all their sakes that Adam was wrong and that she couldn't see the hidden truth behind his words.

The Transformation would take place as planned. Now he wanted only to be prepared for the thing that Iliana might become when it was over. The details of the change, the blood that would be shed, made his stomach turn, but he swallowed his doubts and continued forward because he had no other choice.

39 Cole could feel her presence the moment she entered the room. He sat at the bar sipping a glass of white wine and suddenly felt like someone had placed a warm hand on the back of his neck. This was how Iliana felt to him now, like warmth and safety even though she could promise him neither warmth nor safety. He imagined that, as his connection to the world of the Natives, he could have done much worse.

When he turned to see her he struggled to keep the relief from his face and failed. It had only been a day and a half and yet she looked different to him. She stood in the doorway, physically slight, but her presence filled the empty space. Her eyes found him at once and he recognized within them the same relief he felt at seeing her alive and well. One corner of her mouth twisted up into a smile and pulled the rest of her lips along. She was dazzling. He smiled back.

Iliana swept across the floor and embraced him and Cole returned the gesture, so relieved that she was all right that he didn't even care who saw them. Her hair smelled of the tiny white flowers that grew in the courtyard of his church back home and he knew that he would never be able to walk through that courtyard and smell that cloying fragrance without thinking of her.

"You made it," she whispered into his shoulder. She felt small in his arms, small but powerful.

Cole let her go and stepped back, aware of just how close they were standing and how natural such closeness felt. "I'm glad you're okay."

Iliana smiled at his shyness and the warmth in that gesture seeped into his skin, filled him up. She linked her arm with his and said, "Walk with me and I will tell you what happened."

Cole left some money on the bar to pay for his drink and Iliana narrowed her eyes at him. "Drinking again?" The tone was so disapproving that Cole had to laugh.

"Only a sip, I promise." When she continued to scowl at him he added, "Don't worry, I'm not going back into that darkness again. I don't need to run away anymore."

Iliana's smile returned and he allowed her to lead him out into the night. They walked for a while in silence, just enjoying each other's presence, until they were far from the crowds and the clubs. Cole recognized the street just as they reached the small chapel where the incident with Adam had taken place. Cole said nothing of the attack. Adam was fine so Iliana didn't need to know that Cole had watched the whole thing and done nothing to stop it.

Iliana sat on a bench just outside the front door of the chapel and pulled Cole down beside her. Before his body even touched the bench she said, "They think you'll be able to help us." Excitement strained her voice. "They let me go because they want you to help us."

Cole leaned back against the wall and closed his eyes. In his head he had replayed the scene a thousand times, had pictured himself standing before his congregation and preaching his new knowledge. He had pictured their faces transforming from anger, to disillusionment, to enlightenment. From there he had imagined teaching his peers. The word would spread until the Church could do nothing except absorb this new system of beliefs, allowing the Natives to roam free in their own land for the first time in almost a millennium. It was his dream. But it would take time.

He looked into Iliana's eager eyes and felt daunted by the hope he saw there. "But what can I do to help you now?"

"One man can stand against them. You need to go to the head of your Church, Father Deven himself, and convince him."

"That's impossible," Cole said. "You're asking too much of an institution that has resisted change for longer than I know. The Church will not abandon its doctrines just because some peon priest thinks it's a good idea. These things take time…"

"We have no time, Cole. Governor Drake confirmed that they are going to try to kill us all during the Festival of Semiveh. That means that before the Festival begins you have to go back and teach them."

"But…"

"Cole, please. I can't just sit here and wait to die."

Her voice was flat, matter-of-fact, and he knew that if he did nothing that's exactly what would happen. He shook his head against the sudden pressure of the realization, as if he could dislodge it from his head. But the weight of a few thousand lives had just been dropped onto his shoulders and he could not throw off the mantle of that responsibility.

Iliana touched his hand and he sighed. He was the face of their salvation. He, who, up until a short time ago, had been a wreck of a priest. But he could not look into those hopeful eyes and disappoint her. He owed her for saving his life and he would give his to return the favor.

"I will try."

"Thank you," she whispered and hugged him again. Once more he returned the gesture but the pleasure had faded. Now his body felt numb and heavy beneath the weight of her expectations. Now that he needed to think his mind blanked and he couldn't for the life of him think of an acceptable way to approach the Church and ask them to spare the Natives. He had been raised with the knowledge that when the Church decided it wanted to do something you got out of the way or it ran you over. It was not a democracy, it was tyranny, and that meant no disagreement, no falling out of line, no anything that could be seen as going against the grain. But when he thought of Iliana dead and gone it pained him. He had to help her.

With his mind reeling, Cole let Iliana go, and as he did he realized that they were not alone. A familiar face watched them from a few paces away. Cole hadn't even heard anyone approach.

"Father Piotr?" Cole asked and paused halfway out of Iliana's embrace. The old guilt stirred in his mind like a sleeping beast, feral and angry at being held at bay for so long. It was an innocent embrace but he felt as if he had been caught engaging in a much more scandalous activity.

He told himself he had nothing to feel guilty for, cleared his throat and asked, "Father Piotr, what are you doing here?"

Father Piotr glared at Cole and Iliana, not bothering to hide his disgust at Father Cole's choice of companions. His large, dark brown eyes flicked back and forth between the two of them like twin beacons of righteousness. Anger twisted his face, deepening the furrows in his skin. Father Piotr had a soft, almost feminine jaw line, full lips now drawn into a severe line and angry eyes. His full face sat atop a wiry frame draped in black robes and was topped off by his slicked-back brown hair.

Father Piotr was a gawky man who moved like a stick that had sprouted limbs. He had quite a good mind, which Cole believed was squandered on the Church and its stifling doctrines. Before his epiphany, Cole had considered Father Piotr something of a role-model.

When Cole thought the Father had sneered long enough in silence he said in a voice he normally reserved for sermons, a voice he knew Father Piotr would respond to, "Father, I asked you a question."

Like a man awakened by a nightmare his accusing gaze flicked to Cole. "Father, it is good to see you again, but I refuse to speak in front of that."

Anger flared through Cole's chest and must have showed in his face because Father Piotr took the smallest step backwards.

"You will tell me what you have come to tell me or you will leave without saying another word. I doubt the Congress would be kind if you had to tell them you had failed in your task."

Father Piotr stepped back. He couldn't have looked more surprised if Cole had slapped him. But he swallowed hard and with one quick, unhappy glance at Iliana, he began. "Father Deven sent me to fetch you. We need you back at home. Your congregation needs you."

"Why?" Cole asked, suspicious. "My leave of absence has not ended."

"Father Deven says that you've rested long enough. He demands that you return. We will leave in the morning."

Cole pulled away from Iliana, placed his elbows on his knees and hung his head. He took shallow, even breaths and tried to form the words his tongue rebelled against. He could feel the tension in Iliana's body, sitting so still beside him, her muscles taut and ready to fly as if she was afraid that if she moved, if she spoke, if she even breathed Father Piotr would turn his palpable disgust in her direction.

Cole said, "I can't go back with you, Father."

Father Piotr's shock was immediate, followed by a narrowing of his features in anger. "You don't have a choice. Father Deven needs you and so you will come back now."

Cole shook his head. He wanted to be able to wipe away Father Piotr's anger, to erase it all, but without an open mind that was impossible. All of a sudden he knew how he could lessen it.

"I cannot come back now," he said. And then before Father Piotr could respond he added, "But I will return in a few days."

Instead of diffusing the situation, Father Piotr narrowed his eyes even further until they were mere slits in his dusky skin, and switched his gaze back to Iliana. Cole felt her stiffen once more at his side and fought the urge to take her hand.

"Why won't you come now, Father? It is because of her?" Disdain made his voice dark. Cole responded in order to take the focus from Iliana, the lies blooming on his tongue like flowers in a garden. He knew the fact that he lied with ease should have bothered him but it didn't.

"She is not what you think and she is not the reason I need to stay. I have been working with Brother Jerome of this chapel," he gestured to the building behind him, "And Father Matteo, a priest from a nearby church. The projects we have been working on are nearing completion and until they are finished I will not leave the city."

Father Piotr paused, flicked his eyes to Iliana and back to Cole, and said, "Fine." It was clear from the stiffness of his spine to his guarded eyes that the Father didn't believe what Cole had said but he did not argue. "Just make sure that you are out of the city 3 days before the Festival."

"Why?" Iliana blurted out and both men turned to stare

at her. Cole, in surprise that she would speak in front of Father Piotr, and the Father that she would dare to speak at all.

"I owe you no explanations," Father Piotr hissed and then turned toward Cole. "So I have your word that you will leave the city at least three days before it begins? It is very important."

Cole blinked hard as realization dawned on him. Father Piotr was lying. The Church didn't need him. There were probably a hundred priests who would be more than happy to take over Cole's church, to replace him at Father Deven's side. They didn't need him back. Father Deven just wanted to take back control.

"You have my word," said Cole, softening the edge in her voice. "I will leave in six days." Father Piotr relaxed as if now that he had Cole's assurance all would be well. He even smiled, a simple, short gesture that never reached his eyes.

"Good then. I'll report back to Father Deven of your wise decision. He was worried that you had strayed but I find that you are much the same. All indiscretions can be forgiven when you return." He gestured to Iliana but did not look at her again, as if he were afraid she could bewitch him with her eyes.

"Goodnight, Father Cole. May you have a safe journey home." He turned and left them alone once more.

Cole said nothing right away for there was nothing to say. It had been foolish, he knew, to hope that the rumors were false, that his Church did not have designs of genocide, but he had hoped anyway. And now he knew the game. Brother Jerome's timetable had been confirmed.

"Three days before the Festival..." he said.

"You have to go," Iliana finished for him.

"But what am I supposed to do?" Cole asked, overwhelmed by the prospect of having the fate of a nation on his shoulders. He found himself wishing for a drink and just the imagined taste of wine on his tongue calmed him. But he would soon face a governing entity that killed first and asked questions later, one that punished dissonance without mercy. He could not afford to be drunk when he did so.

"I know I have to go," he admitted with reluctance. He looked up at Iliana and the concern that etched her face with fine lines buoyed his faith a little. He did not want to deepen those lines with his worries, namely that if he went before the Church Congress and pled for the Natives' lives there was a good chance that they'd throw him into prison, or worse, execute him, and then carry out their genocide as planned. Instead he pushed such thoughts away. They were of no use.

"But I need to know more. I need concrete information to take to them. Like why do you drink blood? How is it that your bodies can cure our diseases? What does a man feel, think, when he dies? Have you seen what lies on the other side? How do you live so long? How do you ease pain and bring pleasure through your kiss, and how are you able to share that feeling with me without even touching me?"

The last question seemed to shock her out of her melancholy. "What feeling?"

"What I felt in the club when I saw you with Father Matteo. I felt what you did, what he did. And then with that client in your cell, and with Jacob… How did you do that?"

Iliana sat for a moment and stared at Cole in silence. She seemed to be searching for something in his face, a gauge of his honesty perhaps, and must have found it for she answered, "I do not know. I wasn't aware I was doing anything. But I do have answers for the other questions."

"Teach me all you can. You have six days to turn me into an expert."

Iliana smiled but it looked forced. "I will do my best. Come." She stood and smoothed the front of her dress. "Let's go back to your hotel room. I don't feel safe discussing such private issues out here."

Cole stood and offered her his arm. He led her to his new hotel room, wondering just how he had gotten involved in all of this and whether or not it was worth his life. Then he looked at Iliana, her face awash in bright neon lights, and he knew the answer. Yes, it was.

40 "So, where would you like to start?" Iliana asked as soon as they were comfortable in Cole's room. Iliana sat at the table while Cole sat on the bed with his back up against the headboard. He had opened the window when they came in and an occasional wind lifted the dingy, threadbare curtain like a flag and then let it fall.

This new room was not as disturbing as the last one. The bed was old and sagged in the middle and the wooden table and chairs were scarred with age, but the walls were covered in fresh white paint and at least this room did not smell of old sweat and recent illness.

"I guess we can start from the beginning," Cole answered with a nervous smile.

"And that would be?"

"Tell me more about the blood. You promised to once. You showed me that you can eat food, so if blood is not the only thing you can ingest, then why would you drink it?"

"Are you ready to hear the truth?"

"That's why I'm here."

"Just checking. So, here is our history as it is taught to us, the Natives."

She rose from her seat and began to pace at the foot of the bed as she spoke. The movement soothed her, acting like a metronome for the pace of her thoughts. "In the beginning bloodletting was a sacred ritual. We shared blood at the forming of any contract or bond, between men and women, between friends, between business partners. When we shared blood with each other we saw hidden motivations, the truth or the deceit behind another's words. With such a precaution it was almost impossible to lie to each other and get away with it."

"Sounds ideal."

"It can be. But your people arrived and threw off the balance. We cultivated a positive relationship with the first Colonists. We helped them to survive in our world and they tried to learn our ways and live beside us in peace. When the original peace treaty was negotiated between the two groups they wanted our signature on paper and we wanted their blood as a sign of good faith. The leader of that particular colony offered his blood and our Governor at that time drank from him. It was, for both parties, an enlightening experience."

"I can imagine."

"No, you can't," she answered. "When we drink from each other we get flashes, emotions, impressions. When we drink from you we get entire memories, whole images played out in our minds. We have even been known to dredge up things from a person's past that have been long buried. It is this crumbling of the imaginary wall between the real and the forgotten that causes the euphoria in the client. Some people can experience it and go on, feeling fuller for the experience. Some people become fixated, either on their past or on their escort or both. They become addicts."

Iliana sat beside him on the bed and Cole stared straight ahead at the empty air in front of him. "It makes sense," he said. "Humanity is vain and led astray with an idle promise and you opened a new pathway to them. It's no wonder they want more."

Iliana nodded. "It wasn't so bad at first. You shared blood and technology and we shared the secrets of the land. Your people thought that they were seeing God through us, which was a delusion we were happy to entertain. But as the years went on more and more of your people came here and began to make use of our services. Whereas before the ritual had occurred only between leaders or people in powerful positions, now it was regular people with no information to trade, just a yearning to feel what others had felt.

"We stopped sharing the blood ritual with your people

because we felt it was being abused. That's when the problems started. We tried to explain that it was a sacred act and not to be entered into on a whim, or used to take pleasure. And in response the Church named us evil and pulled their people out of our cities."

"Harsh."

"Very. But we were fine with that because we were used to being alone. We did not need your friendship or your patronage to survive. And your people did leave us alone for a time.

"But when the blood disease started they returned to us for help. Of course we saved those we could and the disease disappeared, but our ability to filter the tainted blood through our bodies became fuel for their righteous fires. And once the crisis had passed and we once again withdrew our services the Church turned on us, condemned our ways, condemned our very existence.

"It took time to cultivate the ignorance in future generations but to us the time passed in a rush. By the time we realized what was happening many of us had already died. There was a battle that killed many of your people but we were still outnumbered. We had lost."

When Cole said nothing, Iliana added, "So that is the real reason why we drink blood. Not because we need to and not because we enjoy it, but because you forced us to use what was in our nature to survive. Had we kept our secret, as we should have, most of your people would have died from the plague and we would not be in this situation. We created addicts out of ignorance and now we must feed off of you to pay your Church for the privilege to exist on our own land."

Iliana stopped talking and looked at Cole. For his part, Cole could only sit and stare in awe of the secret past that had shaped his entire system of beliefs.

"Cole?" she asked as she sat beside him on the bed and touched his knee. The muscles of his leg were taut beneath her hand. Cole continued to stare at his hands. "Are you okay?"

He closed his eyes and shook his head. "I never even thought to question it..." he left the thought unfinished and raced on to the next. "It's amazing how different the stories are and yet… I just should have asked. I should have pressed for more information."

"Repetition of a litany can brainwash even the most cunning of minds."

"Are you saying I'm smart?" Cole asked, looking up at Iliana and grinning.

She laughed, took his hand, and pulled him to his feet. "You are smart because you asked for the truth instead of settling for a quick and easy balm for your wounds, or drinking yourself into oblivion.

"Come on. Let's go for a walk. I can feel sunrise coming and I want to watch it."

"Can you really feel the sunrise coming?"

She smiled back at him. "No. But for some reason my clients like to hear me say that."

41 They left Cole's hotel and turned against the pedestrian traffic, moving away from the shadow of the Palace. In his weeks since arriving in Adara Vega he had finally become accustomed to the way that life here began at sunset and ended just after dawn. Several of the escorts walked arm in arm with their final clients of the night. And though they had worked all night long very few of them looked tired. Compared to them the Colonists looked ragged, with their wrinkled clothes and shadowy eyes, their various odors of sweat and booze. For members of a theocracy they looked anything but devout.

At the next intersection Iliana linked her arm with his and led him off to the right, down a less crowded avenue. Cole settled in beside her, content just not to be alone anymore as the sky brightened over the rooftops of the houses in front of them.

Cole had come to love the desert sunrises, the way each day began with such drama, making you feel as though the whole world was waking just for you. Maybe all sunrises were like that but somehow he doubted it. In Afet's Wall the drama would have been underscored by the sound of passing traffic, motor noise and shouting, church bells and choral music. Here, though the music still pumped out of speakers all around the city, it was almost as if the still, cool air of the morning swallowed most of the unnatural sounds to make the streets silent. Here the sunrise signaled his bedtime and so he had taken to staying awake just long enough to savor it as if there would not be another.

They stopped when they had the slightest view of the mountains between the walls of two low houses. Each exhalation hung in the air before them as if afraid to let go of the night and then dissipated. Cole and Iliana stood close and watched the colors change over the mountains. The sky above them was a clear and glorious orange and Cole felt as if he could see for miles in every direction. He had the sudden desire to scale the buildings, to get to the rooftops and take advantage of the sight. But he didn't move. His wondering eyes soaked up the beauty that the world had to offer.

Cole glanced at Iliana out of the corner of his eye. She seemed oblivious to him and continued to stare at the changing sky. He saw the lines of black that rimmed her eyes, the flecks of mascara on her cheeks. He could see the places where her lipstick had rubbed off, leaving behind nothing but a crimson stain on her lips. In those moments, when her defenses were down and her mind was occupied, Cole felt close to her, closer than to anyone in his entire life. He found peace in her imperfections, small though they were, and smiled to himself. Content, he turned back to the sunrise.

As the street brightened and the sun illuminated the shadows of the alleys, Cole became aware of a man standing in a doorway a few buildings away, watching them. The man was too far away for Cole to make out his features but he could feel the weight of eyes watching him and assumed that the sensation came from the direction of the stranger.

Iliana closed her eyes as the sun crested over the tops of the houses and highlighted the contours of her face in gold. Cole hated to interrupt but he was gripped by the sudden notion that they should not stay where they were.

He cleared his throat and muttered, "Iliana, I think we should move on."

She smiled, her eyes still closed, "Why? Will you burn up in the sunlight?" When he didn't answer she opened her eyes and looked up at him. "What's wrong?"

Cole gestured with his eyes to the figure in the doorway. Iliana glanced in that direction and said in a flat voice, "Let's go."

She turned on her heel, took Cole's arm and started back towards Cole's hotel. Cole had just enough time to see the stranger start after them before he turned. His heart began to pound. The man was too short to be Adam. What if it was someone else from the Church sent to fetch him back? Though he swore he was not ashamed, neither did he want to be discovered walking arm in arm with a Native by another one of his colleagues. Not yet, at least. It took all of his willpower not to look back.

"Ignore him," Iliana said. "In a few minutes we will be back at your hotel and we can lock the door and he can't come in after us."

"Iliana!" the man cried from behind them and Cole felt Iliana's fingers tighten on his arm.

He thought the voice sounded familiar and he was about to stop when Iliana said, "Please. Just keep walking."

"Do you know who it is?"

"You know what I said about addicts?"

"Yes," Cole answered, aware that their lives were now in danger. In his line of work he had been around enough drug addicts to know what they were like when in the throes of withdrawal. While the fever was upon them you just tried to stay out of their way. Iliana didn't answer. She just sped up.

"Iliana, who is it?"

She sighed and mumbled, "Father Matteo."

"Iliana, wait!" Father Matteo cried again and the echo of it chased them down the street like an angry dog.

"Shouldn't we at least say something?" Cole asked. He didn't want to stop but Father Matteo sounded so pitiful that he couldn't help but feel sorry for the man.

Iliana's voice became hard. "I would rather not."

"Iliana, please!" Father Matteo screamed and then wailed like a demented animal.

"This is torture," Cole said. "He sounds terrible."

"Why are you so concerned about a stranger?"

"He's not a stranger," Cole admitted.

"What?"

Out of the corner of his eye Cole could see Father Matteo getting closer. In a rush he said, "I spoke with Father Matteo after our first morning in the café."

"You were checking up on me?"

"Of course not. After you left me last time I came upon

a group of young girls and one of them had been attacked by and escort. She was bleeding out. I carried her into the nearest church, which happened to belong to Father Matteo. I helped him move the body after she passed."

"Did you confront him?"

"I did."

"Did you discuss me?"

"Yes."

Iliana stepped away from him and when he reached for her she put up her hand.

"Iliana," Father Matteo called out. He was close. They had stalled for too long. They could not avoid a confrontation.

"I'm sorry," Cole said. "I didn't mean to keep anything from you."

Iliana studied Cole's face for a moment, as if searching for something. Suddenly she said, "I understand. You were confused. But I wish you would have told me." The tranquility from watching the sunrise had fled from her face. Her eyes were sad, like sharp, bright sapphires beneath a deep scowl. "I will not be held accountable for what follows."

"What do you mean?" Cole asked, taken aback by the defeated look on Iliana's face.

"You want to talk to him? You want to see what it does to people? Just remember, the reason I haven't been able to see him lately is because I've been with you so he is not very pleased with either of us."

"I won't let anything happen."

"And what will you do to stop it?" she asked, incredulous. She stepped in very close to Cole so that he could feel her breath on his chin. "You will do nothing but stay out of the way. The last time I was with him was that night in the club. I usually meet with him every other day."

She stepped back just as Father Matteo reached them. Iliana's smile was brilliant. All traces of disdain of fear were gone, replaced by the calculated pleasantries of her profession.

"Hello, Father. How nice to see you."

While Iliana's true emotions remained buried behind her

rigid professional mask Cole remained at her side, unsure of himself. He felt nothing but animosity radiating from Father Matteo's skin and knew that no matter what Iliana ordered him to do, if Father Matteo attacked Iliana, Cole would step in. The priest smelled like sour incense and looked like he hadn't slept in weeks. His black hair hung in greasy strands before his face and when Cole looked there was hatred in those sunken eyes, deep hatred and longing, a dangerous combination.

They stood in silence for so long that the tension began to build between them. Cole was about to throw himself in front of Iliana to protect her when Father Matteo spoke, his voice hoarse from screaming. "Iliana?"

"Yes Father," she answered. And with those words the hatred faded from his eyes and his entire frame slumped as if his fury had been the only thing holding him up.

"Why did you leave me? Why haven't you come?" His voice had lost its power, too, becoming whiny and unsure.

"I am sorry you feel I have neglected you, Father. Truth is, I have neglected most of my clients—"

And there it was, that temper that had died down, flared once more. "Don't speak to me of other clients. You know I hate to hear about the others."

Iliana blinked hard. For a moment the smile faltered and Cole could see the tiniest cracks in her otherwise professional mask. "Of course, Father."

Without warning Father Matteo turned his attention to Cole and narrowed his bloodshot eyes. "Why are you doing this? You come here and you chastise me for being with her and now you steal her from me?" Blind rage returned in full force and Father Matteo's voice was choked with it. "Why can't you find your own escort? Why does it have to be Iliana?"

Cole sounded calm but he could feel his own temperature rising. "I didn't steal her. I hired her to help me. Besides, she does not belong to you any more than she does to me."

"Liar! She is mine!" Father Matteo screamed and leapt at Cole, reaching for his face. Cole grabbed the man's wrists and pried Father Matteo's claw-like fingers off of his head. Father

Matteo's face was wild, his lips curled up into a snarl and his breath smelled like stale beer.

"You're just using her!" he snarled as they struggled.

"No, you are," Cole countered. He pushed as hard as he could and let go of Father Matteo's wrists.

Father Matteo fell backward onto the dusty street and clambered back to his feet just as Iliana hissed, "Enough, both of you." They both stopped and looked at her. Cole could tell that she was not angry. Somehow this display had damaged her and now she seemed like nothing more than a sad and broken doll standing between them.

Iliana approached Cole. She closed the distance between them with a strong hand on his chest and leaned into him until her lips brushed against his ear. Her breath on his skin sent shivers all the way to his toes and for a moment he imagined letting her mouth close upon his throat. For a moment, only a moment, he imagined giving in. But that thought passed as his gaze touched upon Father Matteo standing a few paces away and watching them with forlorn eyes. He never wanted to end up like that.

"I will do this now," she said. "But ask nothing more of me." She turned from him and Cole felt as if he had been slapped across the cheek. He didn't understand, couldn't comprehend her anger. He had no quick response, no questions, just surprise.

She approached the broken man before them and wiped the sweaty, matted hair from his eyes and kissed his forehead. From that light touch alone Father Matteo stopped shaking. Such a small touch and he seemed imbued with tranquility.

"Come, Father," she said in a soothing voice. "Come with me and I will give you what you need."

Father Matteo's eyes welled with tears as Iliana took his hand and led him into a nearby alley. Cole looked down the street and once he was sure that they were alone he followed them.

The city was full of such places, little nooks and niches where Natives could take their clients. Where else could one go for a quick rendezvous but into the shadows of buildings and garbage bins? The Church had banned all public displays of affection between the Natives and the Colonists, thinking that if people couldn't see it then they wouldn't want it. Instead the resulting hurried trysts and secret lovers only served to ignite passions and increase profits.

The dirt in the alley was moist along the edges where it crept up the sides of the buildings, as if it were trying to climb out of itself and overtake civilization. The city clean-up crew had already passed through and so there was no trash, just the stale scent of spilled alcohol and the faintest trace of mildew. The sun could not reach the alley so it remained shrouded in the pre-dawn gloom.

Iliana and Father Matteo stopped a few paces ahead. They did not speak. Cole halted, feeling suddenly self-conscious about witnessing such a private encounter. Before it had been different. Before he had held nothing but contempt for Iliana and her clients and so it had seemed a necessary evil to witness the act, almost an act of contrition. But now that he had a relationship with her it felt wrong, dirty.

His heart began to pound as Iliana turned to face Father Matteo. Then she glanced over his shoulder at Cole and the animosity he saw in her eyes made him flinch. And before he could blink, Iliana slashed her metal thumbnail across Father Matteo's throat with such violence that his blood spattered her face and dress. After one long, last look at Cole she placed her mouth against the wound and began to drink.

Father Matteo moaned and his arms curled around Iliana's waist. From where Cole stood they looked like lovers squeezing the last drop of pleasure from the final moments of dawn. Cole could see neither of their faces and he wasn't sure he wanted to.

He held his breath, expecting at any moment to feel the psychic runoff from the pair before him. He waited, excited but afraid to admit it to himself. A minute passed. Then another. Then another. And still Cole felt nothing but the cool morning air against his face. His heart slowed and his palms dried as he realized that it was not going to happen this time. The power was there, the air prickled with it, but he was locked out. And he was surprised by the magnitude of his disappointment.

Time crawled in the alley. Another minute passed. And another. Without even realizing how much he had craved that feeling again the disappointment passed, replaced by frustration that she would not let him share this.

Feeling defeated and foolish, Cole backed away. Their intimacy unnerved him. When he moved his foot scuffed against the dirt, an echoing sound in the morning stillness, and Iliana raised her eyes to meet his. Cole froze.

He felt as if he had plunged into a warm, salty sea. The world around him became fluid and full of enticing currents and he swayed a little farther from reality with every labored breath he could force in and out of his lungs. Iliana's striking blue eyes became the focal point of the world as it began to spin. Her eyes grew darker until they became a deep, piercing blue in the center of the whirlpool. Like a drowning man he sought the only solid object in this malleable reality: her eyes. And then her mind opened up to him and he could see everything.

The thoughts were formless but crashed against him in waves and he understood. She felt ashamed that Cole had to see her like this; that he had had to see a client in the throes of withdrawal. And beneath that Iliana was angry with him for making her do this, for not being man enough to accept her services himself. Because they were friends, because that was what the ceremony was meant to be, to learn more about one another, to bring two people closer together. Cole's continuous denial of himself shamed her even further. Iliana had never been so disgusted with him and with herself.

And still Cole fell deeper, to a place inhabited by her emotions and Iliana was a jumble. Anger, shame, frustration held court and yet weaving through it all, like a luminescent fish through a tangle of seaweed, intense waves of pleasure.

Cole felt his heart pounding so fast he thought that it would burst. And then he realized that it was her heart, not his, that raced with such ferocity. It was her mouth that clamped, that sucked, her arms like steel around her client. Cole realized at once that he was not feeling Father Matteo's reaction to the kiss, as he had with the other clients. He was feeling Iliana's. The whirlpool spun faster. He tried and failed to remain lucid. His knees buckled and he heard them hit the hard-packed earth but felt nothing. Only the unwavering irises of Iliana's eyes kept him upright. He felt that to break that contact, to lose that connection, would be to die.

And there it was: the urge to die, to have it end in bliss so sweet, in light and pleasure so intense that his body ached for release. At the same time Cole recognized that it was Iliana's body that ached, not his, and she didn't want to die. She wanted to kill.

At that moment she wanted to drink more, to relieve Father Matteo of his life, his urges, his sins. She wanted to kill him and he would let her. Father Matteo would let her do as she wished even though he had not asked for it. And right then Cole knew he would have followed, willing and blind, simply because she would lead him and that was all that mattered.

Like the flare of a match Cole suddenly felt envy so complete it destroyed what was left of rational thought. He wanted Iliana's touch, her lips. He wanted to break Father Matteo, to smash his body into a thousand pieces just because Father Matteo received that kiss and he, Cole, did not. He tried to stand, to act on this urge, but he couldn't. He balled his hands into fists until his unkempt nails bit into his palms but still felt nothing but seething jealousy.

Lost in Iliana's eyes, reacting to her impulses as if they were his own, Cole felt her respond. He felt her push deeper into Father Matteo, drawing upon his life and his soul until the pleasure became a sharp, sweet pain. Cole felt himself smiling. Yes. This was what he wanted.

Then, just as fast as it had arrived, the sadistic impulse faded. Cole could not let Iliana kill this man. He did not want that taint on Iliana's soul. He did not want this. No. Cole said that word, a mere whisper but Iliana heard him and obliged.

All at once she closed her eyes and released Father Matteo. When the connection broke Cole felt as though he had just been yanked out of a warm, soothing ocean and slung into a wall of frigid air and the sensation knocked him backward. He couldn't move. He lay in the mud, wondering what had happened. He didn't understand anything. He didn't know if he was somehow injured or even if he was still alive.

A plethora of colors danced in the air above his open eyes like faeries, just out of his reach. His palms burned. His head was full of pressure and a dull throbbing that echoed the beat of his heart. But throughout his body the warm afterglow of bliss continued to smolder. He had never felt anything like it and more than anything, more than he wanted his vision to clear and his head to cease throbbing, he wanted that bliss to continue.

Somewhere along the edges of consciousness, Cole heard footsteps, sure and light. A shadow crossed his face like a cloud covering the sun and hovered just above him. The face was hazy but the voice when it spoke carved into his pliant mind.

"You should have listened to me. I told you I didn't want to do it. Meditate on it. And the next time you want to feel this, at least have the guts to ask for it yourself."

The shadow passed as Iliana walked out of the alleyway. Cole could neither move to follow her nor form words to refute her statement. And as he lay there, as burgeoning daylight finally made its way into the alley, he knew she was right. He had wanted her to take him and in a roundabout way he had asked for it. He felt ashamed. Not because his evil desire was a sin against the Church but because he had sinned against their friendship.

A few minutes later he heard more movement, a shuffling sound, coming toward him. Another shadow crossed his sightless eyes and Cole felt the cold footsteps of panic racing up his spine. Should Father Matteo choose to confront him now Cole would be unable to defend himself. He felt weak and dizzy and he couldn't see much more than vague shadows. There was no way he would be able to fight.

But as Cole cringed, waiting for the blows to begin, Father Matteo leaned over him and slurred, "You can have her. She's been tainted. She can rot like the rest of them when the judgment comes." Father Matteo shuffled off without a fight but Cole remained tense with thoughts of the coming genocide.

After a quarter of an hour alone with his thoughts he felt

ready to stand. Using the rough brick wall for support he pulled himself to his knees, then his feet and wavered there for a moment until he felt steady enough to walk. Then he left the alley, a solitary figure in a sunbathed street with guilt in his heart and the aftertaste of pleasure on his tongue.

42 The following evening all the members of the Council who were gathered in Drake's Hall stared at Governor Drake in silence as he prepared to speak. There were so many people in the large room that some of them had had to stand against the walls, as every member, close to one hundred active, inactive, retired and normally absent, had been called to this special meeting.

Drake was an exposed nerve as he perused the papers spread before him. Beneath that lay a copy of the book On Transformations in the original Native tongue. Drake was reading it when the members came in, poring over the words that had long since stopped making any sense to him. The book gave up no new secrets, just made his muddled mind more anxious.

Sweat already dampened his stiff collar and the room seemed too hot and cramped to breathe. Drake forced the humid air deep into his lungs, willed his hands to stop shaking, willed his voice to remain steady and began.

"Thank you for coming. This meeting is to inform you of our plan to thwart the threat the Colonists pose. We want you to be well-informed of what is in store this Festival. But be forewarned: this information does not leave this room. Before we begin I must have your agreement. The audience in the chamber nodded almost in unison, some looking fearful of the news they were about to receive, some excited.

"Very well," Drake said. "Let us begin. You are already aware of the threat the Church poses to our civilization. Our spies have discovered that the Colonists have decided to move forward with a plan to destroy us. They have engineered a virus that they will release during the Festival of Semiveh." He paused as some of the Council members fidgeted. This news was not new to any of them but that didn't make it any less disturbing to hear it spoken aloud. Drake had lived with the knowledge for a long time and yet it still felt strange to say the words, as if he were speaking in a dream. But this was a not a dream. They were going to die unless they took action.

Drake began again, "As most of you know, Iliana, daughter of Gabriella, has been chosen to undergo the Transformation. Three days before the Festival Adam, Katla, Mario and Magna will collect Iliana from wherever she happens to be and take her to her cell."

All eyes swiveled to Drake's right, where Adam and his three soldiers stood at attention. Mario was a captain in the City's Guard and had more muscles than body to hold them, giving him the look of a barrel on legs. Katla was a wisp of a woman. She was tall and thin with skin the color of the rich clay unearthed during the violent desert storms. She was older than the others, three hundred come the next Festival, and her eyes held the determination of stone, of one who has had to fight for everything she had, of one who would never give up. She was a member of the Council's Special Guard, an elite spy, and so could adapt to any task that was required of her. Magna was small, shorter than all of the others and dark as ancient, varnished wood. But his stature was not an indication of his prowess as a soldier, for he was as strong as a man twice his size and quick on his feet.

Adam smiled and nodded toward the Council. Drake was proud of his son and he knew that after what had just happened between him and Sigrid no one would challenge Adam's right to lead this party.

Drake continued. "In her cell two of our guards will keep watch until she is taken to the unnamed room where the Transformation will occur. Let me say it again so that you all understand: no one is to speak to her about what is to come. Am I clear?" The Council members nodded, all except Sigrid, who sat staring at her hands.

"Good. After escorting Iliana to her cell Adam will lead a band of approximately 50 selected guards to Afet's Wall. At the end of the day, before the members retire for the evening, they will break into the Congress hall and take captive everyone within the room."

Drake watched fear spread like a virus across the faces of several people. Before they could dispute this plan he added, "They will not fight back. No weapons are allowed inside the Capitol building and our attack will be unexpected so the Church elders will be too surprised to respond.

"Adam will bring these people back and hide them in the Palace dungeon, where they will await Iliana's judgment."

"If all goes well this will not change the normal course of the festivities during Semiveh. On day one of the Festival we will announce the matches we have made, as usual. After the announcements, Iliana will be led into the room and the Transformation will take place. Ezekiel and his helpers will preside over that event, as he has for the past three Festivals."

Ezekiel, who stood in the corner behind Drake's right shoulder, gave a slight nod but refused to meet the questioning gazes of the members as they turned to look at him. He was odd-looking and fidgety, and it was obvious that he was uncomfortable being the center of attention. At the age of 600, his black hair had turned gray at the temples and his skin appeared thin and dry as parchment. He was tall and had a protruding stomach that was out of proportion with his wiry arms and legs.

Ezekiel was the City's High Priest, though the Natives had no organized religion to speak of. It was his duty to perform the rites for the dead and to preside over the Transformation. He did not consider the day-to-day running of the city important and tended to stay out of sight, to everyone's relief. Drake agreed with the general consensus that Ezekiel was odd and Drake dreaded when he had to meet with him and tried never to do so alone.

"Ezekiel, the Transformation should take a little more than a day... Is that correct?"

Ezekiel nodded, "In theory." His voice was as abrasive as sandpaper.

"Thank you, Ezekiel," said Governor Drake. He turned his attention back to the task at hand. "On day two the books say that Iliana will adjust to her new awareness and abilities. On day three we will lead the Church Elders to her and she will offer them the same choice they gave us once upon a time: to become one of us, or die."

The Council shifted in their seats, uncertainty written on their faces, but only Nero could find the voice to speak above the mounting tension. "What if they fight back?" he asked.

"Without the Church Elders no one will harm us, for only the Congress knows the details of how their plan was to be carried out. And by the time the Colonists figure it out they will know that we have the Elders and they will back down. They will not risk killing their God-given leaders.

"Day three marks the end of the Festival but the beginning of our newfound freedom. Now, do you have any questions?" He was asking for support, not opening the topic for debate, and every last member knew that they could not change the course that had just been laid out for them.

When no one said anything, Drake added, "I realize that this plan is rash—"

Another member of the Council cut him off in a bitter, trembling voice. "It is rash," she said, "And such rashness has led to death in the past, when Natives from the Outer Circles would plan kidnappings and murders outside of Adara Vega. They never got very far and never achieved their goals. What makes you think this time it will work?"

The others looked back to Drake for a rebuttal. Drake licked his lips. They could not sway his mind but he still wanted their support.

"The plan is solid. I have to believe it is better than anything thought up by anyone outside of the Palace, anyway. And if we do not at least attempt this we may as well just lie in the streets and wait for the end."

Adam's voice filled the silence, saying what most of them were too nervous to even hope. "I think it will work."

Another member spoke up, one of the retired men. "Aren't you concerned about getting caught? I hate the idea of our young people venturing outside the city alone."

"If you want to go and supervise them, then by all means go," Drake said in irritation. "But if we don't do this they will kill us. Their plan is going to happen whether we sit here and do nothing or we fight back. At least this way we have a chance."

"And we won't be alone," Adam chimed in. "We have recruited some of the Colonists who live within the city to bring us to Afet's Wall, hidden from view."

"And how do you plan to get out of the city? No doubt the Church will have some force guarding the only road out, making sure we don't leave."

"I would rather not disclose the particulars of the plan at this time but believe me it will work. As for the Church, they may place guards at our gates but not until the Festival begins, as usual. We should have no problem getting out so early and if we have a problem getting back in, well… we are nothing if not resourceful. We will have the most powerful men in the Church in our possession. We could do anything. We will do anything."

In Adam's voice Drake heard the dreamy quality that belied Adam's cocky image. He knew that Adam lived for moments like this. He wanted to shine, to be a hero. And if all went as planned then he would be. But while Adam claimed his glory Iliana would be losing her soul to an ancient ceremony that could very well kill her. Drake didn't want to think about it but images of Gabriella kept flashing in his mind. He shook his head and moved forward because he had no other choice.

"Now," Drake said, "For the vote. Those in favor of the plan please stand and be counted."

The Council stood. The older members climbed to their feet, working through their aching joints. Others jumped to their feet as if their seats were on fire. No count was necessary. The vast majority of the people were standing

"Thank you," Drake said with a sigh.

As the others took their seats Sigrid stood and addressed Governor Drake. "I oppose this plan. Even though I know I will be overruled I must say my piece. I think that it is dangerous and frivolous to send our young men and women out of the city during our time of need. This is a foolish plan, Governor, and I will not be to blame when it goes wrong." She paused to look at the faces around her. No one came to her defense, no one stood in solidarity against the Governor's plan.

When she found no support she added, "I just wanted to voice my objections," and returned to her seat.

Despite Sigrid's negativity Drake felt that it was a good plan, the best they could hope for in their present situation. He thought it would work. No, he knew it would work, because it had to. Failure was not an option.

"Thank you for your input, Sigrid, but you are overruled. And thank you to all of you. I believe we have come to a decision. We have five days until the plan is set in motion."

Sigrid stood again, her chest puffed out like an angry bird. "You may have reached a decision but we have not yet had a chance to see for ourselves."

"What does that mean?"

"It means that you have not yet allowed us to interview her like you promised."

"The arrangements have been made. I offered her a position on the Council with the stipulation that she submit to be interviewed by the High Council first. I have only one rule: you must not mention the true purpose of the interview."

"Why is that?"

"Because if she knows she will run," Adam offered.

Sigrid scoffed. "That doesn't sound like the kind of leader I want."

"Do you take issue with my decision, Sigrid?" Governor Drake demanded. He didn't want to have a power play in front of the Council but if she wanted a fight he would give her one. In response to her sneer he let the anger he felt at her disloyalty smolder in his eyes, the only part of his face not obscured by the blue paint. After several moments of silence Sigrid looked away. It was a small victory.

He lowered his voice. "Let's not argue, Sigrid. Interview her. Ask her what you will. And then I challenge you to come to me and say that I was unwise in choosing her."

Sigrid offered him a shallow nod. The Council, sensing that

the discussion was over, began to leave.

As the Council filed out of the room under a veil of quiet chatter, Drake turned to Adam and said, "Begin recruiting but be discreet. I trust your judgment. Within three days I expect to have a list of every member of your party. Once that is done we can start on the specifics."

"As you wish," Adam answered with a serious face. "What about Iliana?"

Drake addressed Adam's soldiers. "Katla, find Iliana and follow her, but stay out of sight." Katla nodded and slipped out of the doors just as the last member exited. She never made a sound.

"Mario, Iliana knows of your friendship with Adam so I cannot use you in this venture. Instead you can help Adam gather soldiers for the party that will go to Afet's Wall. And Magna, I need you to seek out the Colonist named Father Cole with whom Iliana has formed a friendship. Follow him and inform us when he leaves the city for good."

He paused and took a deep breath. He felt as if he had just pronounced a sentence of death upon Iliana's head and it chilled him to his soul. More to himself than to anyone else, Drake muttered, "There is nothing she can do now."

Adam seemed to be on the verge of saying something but hesitated. Drake asked, "Something wrong?"

"Are we doing the right thing?" Adam asked.

When Adam raised his eyes from the table in front of him Drake saw the conflict flit across his features. He was concerned and with good reason. Drake felt no better about the circumstances but since it was his duty to appear strong he patted his son on the shoulder and answered, "We do what we must to survive."

"Of course," Adam said. He left without another word and the two remaining soldiers followed him out.

Drake turned to look up at the cherubic paintings on the ceiling and sighed. He did not want to do any of this but he had no choice. As he gathered up his paperwork and left the meeting hall he prayed that the Transformation would be easy for Iliana even though he knew it would not.

43 Cole spent one day and night in his hotel room, his head full of clouds and confusion. When he wasn't sleeping he stared at the walls and berated himself for what had happened. He waited for Iliana to turn up, thinking that she would not be able to resist an opportunity to argue with him, but she never came.

When she still hadn't appeared by sunset of the second day he spent the entire night searching for her every place he could think of, aside from the Palace. Though Iliana had assured him that the Governor now sanctioned their friendship Cole remained wary and did not want to press his luck. But Iliana was not at any of her regular venues.

He even went so far as to peek into Father Matteo's church but the church was empty save Father Matteo, who was reading in his office by candlelight. The altar stood empty and the walls were bare of all decoration. Boxes were stacked three high along the back wall. Curious, Cole peeked into the closest one and found tattered hymnals. In the large crate beside it were the tapestries from the walls, folded and stacked in neat piles.

It seemed Father Matteo was packed and ready to go when the time came. Cole was disgusted. After all of his talk about the means of communicating with the divine the craven priest was not willing to stay and fight for what he believed. It was a disgrace.

Cole crept out of the church to avoid an unnecessary confrontation. He didn't want to be face to face with him and risk punching Father Matteo in his self-serving, cowardly jaw.

Near midnight he ate in the café he and Iliana had come to several times and glanced more than once at the lace curtain he had hidden behind during their first meeting. He traced the scratches in the table with his fingertips. They were still meaningless.

He missed her.

44

In the garden Adam stood alone. Clouds hovered low over the tops of the buildings and the absence of moonlight made his bronze skin seem darker, unreal. His face showed the faintest traces of the bruises from his recent beating. The pain had faded but a faint darkness still ringed his eyes like spectacles and traced along his jawline like dark kisses. Even bruised he was beautiful and he knew it.

The small garden was over-planted and overcrowded and the leafy stalks of some of the plants rose up to Adam's hips. He caressed the nearby leaves with deft fingers, like he would caress a lover's skin. He imagined himself as one of the unusual plants here, growing tall and straight, nourished by moonlight, waiting to be plucked out of the mud and given a purpose.

Situated between the back wall of the chapel and the high sandstone wall that surrounded the compound, the garden made the perfect place for Adam to wait. For the last two nights Adam had come at sunset to meet Yourian and lingered all night. This was where Adam had first taken Yourian and made him an ally, an act that had happened quite on accident.

That night Adam had scaled the wall around the compound to hide from the jealous husband of one of his clients. And as he crouched in the waist-high weeds Yourian had appeared to gather some herbs that could only be picked after sunset if one hoped to retain their potency. Since then he and Yourian had often made use of this little hideaway to complete their trysts and so Adam had thought this the perfect place to see Yourian again. But for two days Yourian had not come. Adam was tired of waiting.

So he gave up. He was hungry and bored and positive that after just standing by and watching his brutal beating Yourian would not want to continue their relationship. He wanted to be angry but he wasn't. Yourian had proved useful but now that the plan was in place there was nothing more he had to offer. In a way he felt relieved.

Adam found a handhold in the stone wall and hoisted himself up. As he searched for the next indentation he heard a gasp. He paused, unsure whether he should continue to climb or turn and face the source of the noise. As it tended to do, curiosity won out over survival and Adam turned around to see Yourian, dressed in his standard brown robe, carrying a basket in one hand and a pair of gardening shears in the other.

"Adam," Yourian breathed. Adam felt that one word like a caress and knew at once of Yourian's concern for Adam's life, along with his guilt at being impotent to help Adam during his assault. That, along with regret and anticipation and lust, all salty on Adam's tongue. One beat later Yourian dropped his basket and waded towards Adam through the sea of plants. He fell to his knees and clutched Adam's legs, murmuring a soft prayer.

"Oh thank God. I thought they had killed you I thought I would never see you again and I'm sorry. I am so sorry I didn't help you I just couldn't. I'm so sorry…"

Adam looked down at the pathetic creature groveling in the foliage before him and decided to have some fun before releasing Yourian from his service. He widened his eyes until the sting of night air touched them and they began to tear. He slumped his shoulders, pulled his lips into a frown and said, "I knew you would forsake me."

Yourian stopped babbling. His head snapped up.

"No," said Yourian, "I would never—"

Adam cut him off, savoring the desperation in the young man's moist eyes. "I do not blame you. You have a life to think of and I am a doomed man. You must separate yourself from me. And you have already begun. You kept secrets about your people's plans for our destruction and then you let your brothers try to beat me to death as you watched."

"No…" the tears finally evidenced themselves in his voice, choking him.

Adam sensed that Yourian's tears were less about remorse and more about the fear of punishment. He kept his voice level, almost eerie in its calmness in contrast to Yourian's mounting distress. "Is this a game?"

"No."

"Did you enjoy watching me? Perhaps you achieved some satisfaction from it. Perhaps you have replayed the scene a thousand times since then and fallen asleep with a smile on your face."

"No, stop it. You don't understand," cried Yourian, releasing Adam's legs and sitting back on his haunches. Plants rustled, stalks broke.

"Don't I? I think your kind will always sacrifice love for the sake of survival, if only to eke one more pointless day out of your petty and insignificant lives."

"Please." Yourian's face crumpled. "Stop saying these things. That's not how it is. To see you so helpless was to die a little. And I have died a little more each day when you did not return. I thought my heart would burst for love of you."

"You lie even now."

"No. I have always been truthful to you. I have worshipped you without thought or regret. What can I do to prove myself?"

Adam restrained a smile at the thought of what he could do, the example he could make of this pathetic creature. "What are you offering?" he asked, intrigued.

"I have nothing to give but myself."

"Your body?"

"My blood. It's yours…"

"You are asking to die," Adam said, his voice emotionless. He had hoped that Yourian would come up with something a little more entertaining. Instead the young man's eagerness bored him.

Yourian crouched at Adam's feet once more like a supplicant begging favor from his lord. "When you drink only a little you give me the greatest pleasure. I cannot begin to imagine the heights you could show me before death."

A dreamy smile played on Yourian's face, moving upward until it lit up his glassy, vacant eyes. Adam had always known that Yourian's sole motivation was pleasure, not love. Yourian was attracted to Adam, true, but he would have donated to anyone for just a fraction of the pleasure such a tryst brought.

"Is there anything else you've learned about the plot to destroy the city?" he asked, keeping his voice as hard as flint, his cruelty revived.

"Nothing further," Yourian admitted and Adam gauged he was telling the truth.

"Thank you. And goodbye then, Yourian." Adam's voice was soft, yet threatening.

Yourian's resolve turned to fear and he muttered a quick, "Wait," before Adam was upon him and choked off the rest of the words.

Adam took no pains to be gentle as he sliced at Yourian's throat with this metal-tipped thumb, opening a deep gash into his surprised flesh. Yourian's voice stopped as the blood began to flow and Adam's tongue flicked against the wound to keep it open. Without that movement, his saliva would have closed the wound in a matter of minutes, which was the normal procedure. But not this time.

Adam went deeper into Yourian than he had ever gone. He forced his consciousness in through the wound and through his blood relived Yourian's memories. As a child Yourian had often hidden in his sister's closet and watched her undress. In chapel at school he experienced a rich sexual fantasy life during boring sermons. Throughout adolescence he had visited the Palace several times, once even stealing money to pay for an escort. And then he relived his first meeting with Yourian, but what Adam had viewed as a simple seduction, Yourian remembered as a twisted, frightening montage of blood and sex. Yourian loved Adam in his own way but he loved more this hedonistic pleasure.

The memories faltered and still Adam pulled at the throat, even when Yourian's heart stuttered, even when Yourian's body, which had been arching against him in pleasure, went limp in his arms. He felt the pressure building inside Yourian's body and

knew that the young cleric now existed solely within that pleasure, within the rush and pull of blood, within the sweat and
painful longing.

Yourian longed to die. Adam felt it and recognized it even
though the ecstasy that sang throughout Yourian's body had enveloped him as well. And though he wanted to be rid of this
man, though knew that the world would not miss him, Adam
just couldn't bring himself to give Yourian what he wanted.

Against everything in his nature he released Yourian. It took
all of his faculties not to stumble into the plants like a drunk as
the sensations enveloped him. Yourian slid to his knees and then
onto his back, crushing the foliage beneath him, drunk on pleasure. He was teetering on the edge of the abyss. Adam could taste
death, acrid and cold on his tongue like dirty ice. His own head
was a jumble of dizzying images and emotions as he knelt beside
his victim, just out of reach.

Yourian's glazed eyes grew wide and looked up at Adam,
no doubt surprised that he was still alive. The gash in his throat
had already stopped spurting blood and now just oozed over the
torn skin. Adam pulled a handkerchief from his pocket, wiped it
across his lips then tossed it away.

"This is for failing to help me when I was attacked and almost killed. You will never get another chance."

Yourian blinked but could not speak. Adam stood, still
dizzy but getting better with each passing moment. He scaled
the wall with as much ease as he would a ladder and was gone.
Behind him, lying on the ground, oozing blood and unable to
move, Yourian began to cry.

45 Iliana woke up unhappy. She had also gone to sleep unhappy and for two days had been unable to shake herself out of this funk. She felt capable of doing two things: roaming about the Palace and frowning at everyone she passed, or staying locked in her cell. She didn't even care about the quota she was once again neglecting to fulfill.

Cole had disappointed her. And then she had disappointed herself by letting him have such an uncensored peek into her psyche. He was unprepared for what she had to show him, for the intensity of the experience. He couldn't have known that when one is used to the kiss and goes without, the sensations are heightened. The madness that comes from the addiction is matched by the madness that the kiss brings, drawing the entire experience into one of sublime sensory overload. But she had known. And she had let him have it all just because he had hurt her feelings. So she hid in the Palace, now more because she was ashamed of her behavior than because she was angry with Cole.

The third evening came on fast like a blanket had been thrown over the city. Iliana sat on the divan in her cell and watched the small rectangles of sky through her windows darken until the stars shone through and she was sure that most of the escorts had left the Palace. Then she left her cell, hoping to cross paths with no one and pleased with the empty elevator when it came for her.

She stopped the carriage on random floors on the way down and stepped out. The hallways, to her pleasure, were empty, and she wandered between those gilded walls and saw nothing. She inhaled, she exhaled. She counted the number of footsteps from door to door, from mirror to mirror. Once or twice she glanced at her reflection but averted her eyes. Her face angered her, for it was the face of frustration and she didn't need to be reminded.

On and on she went until she reached the ground floor but when the doors opened and she saw the throng of glittering bodies flushed with excitement and waiting to board her elevator, she pressed the button to close the doors. The surprise on those eager faces was the first thing to make her smile in days.

Since she had already traveled the upper floors the only place to go now was down. The Palace basement had several levels but one elevator stop because the subterranean floors were not in high demand. She had been in the basement a few times, most of which involved playing out some scheme of Adam's. It wasn't that the area was off limits or creepy, it just wasn't that interesting. Fun and pleasure and laughter all lived above ground so why would anyone want to venture below?

The doors opened, the bell dinged to signal her arrival and she stepped out into the basement. Like all of the other floors, this one was arranged as a hallway with closed doors leading off of it. But whereas in the other floors the hallway was circular, always bringing you back to the elevator bank, in the basement the floor sloped downward off to her right, creating a descending ring of rooms and doors until it ended almost four stories beneath the ground. A few feet to her left the hallway ascended, turning right and leading up to a set of doors that would take her to the first floor lobby. From that direction she could hear the soft murmur of so many voices mingling in the air. Everything within her recoiled from that sound, so she turned and went to the right, deeper into the basement.

Here the walls and the floor were made of ruddy brown stone blocks. Electric lights, a newer addition, were recessed into the ceiling every few feet. She had no idea what the Church had used the basement for but the Natives used this place for storage and for the behind the scenes running of the Native trade.

She knew that the basement contained several massive storage rooms and two huge laundries. Iliana had never had a reason to enter either because the man who ran the laundry excelled at his job. She had seen Neek a few times. As Natives went he looked plain, almost like a Colonist, and she supposed that was why he did the escorts' laundry instead of being an escort himself. But that was just a guess because she had never spoken more than pleasantries to him. He worked during the day while most of the Palace slept.

She passed dozens of unmarked doors on both sides and did not stop because she already knew what was in there. Besides the personal favorites kept in the escorts' cells all of the clothing the escorts wore came from these storage rooms. All of the escorts had sizable collections of costumes for any possible occasion and at the beginning of every month they would request the specific costumes they wanted for the next 36 days. In just a few days the new clothing would be cleaned and hung up in the cells as the escorts slept. Iliana didn't need to see these rooms.

She kept walking. She went deeper into the basement than she had ever gone before. As she turned a corner the pleasant aromas of flowers and soap wafted toward her. She had found the laundries. The air here was warm and moist, almost heavy against her skin. A faint mechanical hum could be heard as she passed the double doors marked "Laundry" on either side of the hallway, but that noise faded when she turned another corner.

The farther she walked from the laundry the lighter and cooler she expected the air to get. But instead the air grew more and more oppressive until, as she passed into a corridor that dead-ended a hundred paces ahead, she smelled the unmistakable, metallic scent of blood. She stopped. One lone door broke the otherwise flawless lines of the wall and it stood closed on the right-hand side.

She approached it with caution, but when nothing jumped out at her she placed her hand on it. The smooth, battered metal warmed to her touch in an instant, as if it had been waiting for the contact. Iliana knocked twice and the lack of an echo told her how thick the metal was. The handle was a simple metal bar and she tried it. The door was locked but the bloody aroma continued to pervade the hallway, intriguing her, confusing her.

She stood and stared at the door for a long time, wondering

what lay behind it, wondering if one of the keys she had copied would open it. Her first thought was to get Cole to come back here with her to try her set of stolen keys. And there he was, filling up her mind almost like second nature and she realized how foolish she was being, how childish and cruel. On the heels of that thought she became worried, for she had left him sprawled in the alley, unable to see or speak, helpless and confused.

She scowled at her self-absorption, shook off the remainder of her remorse and began the ascent back to the main floor. She had wasted most of the night with her wanderings but felt sure she would be able to find Cole before sunrise.

Eager feet carried her to the surface and as she turned the final corner into the elevator hallway she collided with Governor Drake. Iliana stepped back and noted his brushed silver hair, his pristine gray jacket and slacks. He was dressed as if for a special occasion but Iliana could think of no reason for it. The blue paint on his face seemed fresh and glistened a little in the sparse electric lights. He smiled and looked pleased to see her and Iliana knew that his sudden appearance was not a coincidence.

"Good evening, Governor," she said. She was curious what motives could make him seek her out in the basement but wiped the shadow of her thoughts from her face and regained her composure. She offered him an easy smile while her heart raced in her chest. A short time ago she would have been ecstatic to spend an evening with Governor Drake because it would have meant a surprise for her, a gift or a special outing. Now she couldn't help but be wary of him and it made her feel disloyal.

Governor Drake's smile widened. He rested his hands on her shoulders and kissed her cheek. His mouth was dry, his skin cold.

"You have a cold nose," she said. "Are you ill?" And even she was surprised at how congenial she sounded.

Drake stepped back and brought his hand to his nose. "Sorry. It's cold out tonight."

They shared the passing silence sizing each other up. Drake was nervous. Even with his arms hanging at his sides Iliana could feel it, as if the very air around him trembled with it. She thought that she had made herself clear but just in case he asked her to bear a child again she made up her mind to punch him in his chilly nose. Just a tap, she told herself, because she didn't want to hurt him, just remind him that she was her own person.

"I am through playing games, Governor. You know where I stand so if you're here to try to talk me into something, don't waste your breath."

Drake feigned innocence very well, though not well enough to fool Iliana. Her words had cut him. "I'm not here to play games, Iliana." His voice was low and concerned, like a parent trying to guide his child. "And I will not mention my wishes again. I know well how you feel."

She sighed. "Then why have you followed me? Am I still in trouble? Has Adam whispered more lies into your ears? Am I to be punished?" The anger she felt surprised her but she embraced it, took power from it.

Drake scowled at her, finally showing some true emotion. "Iliana, you are acting as if your life is your own—"

"It is my own!" she screamed and turned to walk away but Drake grabbed her arm and pulled her back.

"No, it isn't. Our lives are not our own. The Church has seen to that. Our lives belong to each other. We live and we work for each other, always."

She jerked her arm out of his hand and he let her go. She rode the surge of anger until it broke within her body, all chaos and white noise, and through that she found her voice. "I've heard the propaganda, Governor. I even believe the propaganda. But it doesn't mean I have to fit the mold they've created for me. That you've created for me. I'm not a child. I don't want to do things this way. And if you came here to tell me I have to then I will leave."

Iliana stopped then and took a breath as the echo of her threat hung between them in the empty hallway. She waited to feel guilty, waited for the apology to form on her tongue. But in the moments that followed she felt nothing except the cold satisfaction that follows the release of angry words.

Instead of arguing Drake shook his head. "I'm afraid we got

off to a bad start. I told you I was not here about my wishes for you. I am here about yours."

"What does that mean?"

"The Council has agreed to a time for your interview, Iliana, or have you already forgotten about your request?"

"Go on," she said. His face was earnest enough, his voice level. He wasn't lying. But she still wasn't sure she could trust him.

"I told them what you told me. That you would rather fight with us than be included with the other women. I told them that you would be better served as an apprentice to the Council than as a mother-to-be. I also told them of your connection to the Church, through your friend."

Iliana stared at Drake in silence for a moment and wondered if it was true. All of her life Iliana had rebelled against the whims and strictures of the Council and now, it seemed, it was paying off. This was her chance to rise above, to become something more, to bring about change. But then again, it also meant becoming a part of the intrigue she despised, all of the games and manipulations.

She looked up at Drake's smiling face. A cool wind blew in from the foyer of the Palace just a hundred feet ahead and it ruffled Governor Drake's hair. The strands glittered in the overhead lights like spun silver.

"What will this cost you?" she asked, her voice sudden in the tomblike calm of the hallway.

Drake once again rested his hands on her shoulders and his eyes gave up the secret of how he cared for her even before he spoke. "I want you to be happy. I want my people to be happy. And I believe that you could help us fight the Church better were you not with child for the first few weeks as a member of the Council. I can think of no greater way for you to serve your people."

Again, Iliana felt that he spoke the truth. Filled with joy, she flung her arms around his neck and squeezed. He returned the hug and when they released each other Iliana said, "Thank you."

"You'll make a wonderful Council member, Iliana. Just be honest during the interview and you will have no problems. And please, try not to make me look bad," he chuckled.

Iliana smiled. "When is it?"

"You will meet them tomorrow, at sunset, in my meeting hall."

"Will you be there?"

"I'm afraid not. The old member who recommends the incoming member may not attend the interview. They're afraid I'd be too subjective." He brushed a lock of stray hair from his face but it fell right back out of place. "Which I would be, of course."

Drake cleared his throat, glanced up the hall to where the noises of the escorts and their clients had grown louder. "I must go now." He took a few hobbling steps, as if the walking pained him.

"Are you alright?' she asked.

He waved away her concern. "Oh yes, I'm fine. Just these old bones don't like these cool nights." And then, "Would you care to join me?"

He offered his arm to her, but she shook her head. "No thank you. I need to find Cole. I owe him an apology."

Governor Drake returned to her side and said, "Why is that?"

Iliana looked at her feet, ashamed at her behavior. "The last time we spoke I was childish. I need to go apologize."

"Did you have an argument?" Governor Drake asked. He was trying hard not to give anything away but the slight lift in the tone of his voice belied his curiosity.

"We had a disagreement. I was in the wrong. I need to apologize. So if you would excuse me…" Iliana started to move past Governor Drake but he took her arm and guided her to a stop.

"It would be better if you did not leave the Palace until after the interview. You will need to explain your friendship with this priest to the Council so perhaps your evening would be better spent in reflection on the nature of your relationship."

Iliana pouted, upset at being thwarted but unable to express what this meant to her. "But I haven't seen him in over two days. And the last time I saw him… I didn't treat him well at all. I need to see him."

Governor Drake smiled and said, "Let me talk to him."

"What?" Iliana asked, incredulous. "I'm not sure that's such a good idea."

"Why not? I would like to meet this young man who might save us all."

Iliana hesitated. She wasn't sure what Cole would think if he opened his door and saw Governor Drake standing in the hallway. He might panic. He might try to run. Or he might be the man she had come to care for and invite the Governor inside and pick his mind like he had picked hers ever since they met.

But what would Governor Drake do? Send the guards as soon as she revealed Cole's location? Capture him? Torture him? Kill him?

She couldn't make up her mind. "What good would it do for you to meet him face to face?" she asked to stall for time.

"It would satisfy my curiosity."

Not sure how to answer, Iliana blurted out, "I don't know if I can trust you not to harm him." She added, "Please don't be offended."

"I'm not offended. I understand. After what we have put you through, and what your brother has threatened to do, I cannot blame you for keeping me at arm's length. But since I cannot allow you to leave the Palace until after the interview, perhaps you'll let me redeem myself in your eyes. Let me talk to him, Iliana."

Iliana studied his face, the wrinkles hidden beneath the blue paint, the bushy eyebrows, and his bright and intelligent eyes. She felt that he was telling the truth. "Can I trust you?" she asked more to herself than to him.

"Let me prove that you can."

"Fine. But understand that if you hurt him or mistreat him in any way I will disappear and you will never be able to find me."

"The threat is understood," said Drake.

"He is staying in the Palace Green Hotel. Room 27," Iliana said in a rush. She felt uncomfortable revealing that information but couldn't think of a reason to withhold it. The Governor was giving her everything she wanted. She was going to be able to help her people and not have to bear a child. He trusted her to be a part of the Council so she felt she needed to respond in kind and trust him with her friendship.

"I will go there now," said Governor Drake. "No sense in keeping the boy waiting. Goodnight, Iliana, and good luck." And he turned away and headed toward the noise.

Iliana stood in the hallway, quite aware of the commotion happening just around the corner, and for the first time in her life she felt like this was her city. These were her walls, her buildings and her towers. It was her Palace and these were her people. She would finally have the chance to connect with her world. Pride warmed her from the inside even as the excitement faded and the cold hallway air closed around her body like a clammy fist.

She smiled to herself and pressed the button to call the elevator. Cole's memory floated like a ghost beside her as she focused on mental preparations for the interview. When she entered the empty elevator carriage she hummed a song she had learned as a child and the industrial music that pierced the night outside carried on without her notice.

46

Drake rounded the corner then peeked back to see Iliana step into the elevator. When he noticed her smile he felt about two inches tall. He hadn't wanted to lie to her again but it was a necessary evil. He hoped Sigrid and the Council were cautious when they spoke with Iliana. He hoped they gave nothing away.

Drake pulled a royal blue handkerchief from his breast pocket and dabbed at his forehead. His hands shook so much it took him two tries to get the handkerchief back in its place. Then he sighed and turned toward the small alcove opposite. A lanky shape stood in the shadows there. It made a noise as it shifted, the scuff of a shoe against tile, and Drake made no show of surprise at its presence.

Without so much as glancing at the figure, Drake mumbled, "Find Adam and the others. Tell them to locate Father Cole and to tell him whatever they need to tell him to get him to leave the city now. It will be easier for Iliana if Cole is already gone when the Council is finished with her. Afterwards you can return to your post outside Iliana's cell. She will not try to leave before the meeting, I am sure."

"Of course," Katla said but never stepped out of the shadows. Drake turned and walked toward the rectangle of golden light streaming in from the lobby.

47

By the third night without Iliana Cole's hope began to deflate. The worst part was that he didn't know if her absence was because she was still angry with him, or because she was somehow imprisoned in the Palace to keep her from fraternizing with the perceived enemy. Frustration made him anxious, for there was nothing he could do about it short of walking into the Palace and demanding to see her, which would be foolish considering Adam had twice threatened his life. He had snuck in before but that had been before they got caught in Governor Drake's office and he doubted that he would be as lucky again.

Cole spent the night loitering outside the Palace gate because he didn't know what else to do. He stood in the shadows between two lights and searched through the metal bars of the fence for any sign of Iliana but he couldn't find any trace of her in the chaos of the courtyard. Still he watched, scanned faces and gestures, desperate for a whisper of her name, a sign that she was at least still alive.

"Are you here to meet someone?"

Cole looked to his right. From the other side of the fence a Palace Guard fixed his striking blue eyes on Cole from beneath a brow as steep as a mountain slope. He was a head shorter than Cole but more than made up for his height by being wrapped in layers upon layers of muscles beneath the plain, gray guard uniform. Cole shook his head. He hadn't spoken with anyone in days and it took him a moment to remember that he was supposed to answer.

"What?" he asked. The word sounded raspy and foreign in his ears.

"What's your business here, sir?"

Should he lie? Should he avoid saying Iliana's name just in case Adam had gotten his way and she was in trouble? But if he did that and she never came back he'd never know what happened to her.

"I'm looking for Iliana," he said.

"She is working with the Council, sir, and cannot be bothered. Would you be interested in another escort?"

"No, thank you," he said. He hadn't even entertained the thought that she would be working side by side with the same people who were trying to destroy her. It made no sense and so he wasn't sure that he believed it. "I'd rather wait."

He could feel the guard's eyes on him but refused to look. Instead he focused his eyes on the countless, tiny windows in the tower and wondered which floor she was on, and with whom was she spending her time?

The guard cleared his throat. "I'm sorry, sir, but you cannot stand here."

"Why not? I'm not bothering anyone."

"It is not allowed. Please leave."

Cole's fingers tightened around the bars until the knuckles turned white. "I'm going to wait for Iliana," he said in a harsh voice.

In response the guard withdrew a knife and pressed it into Cole's ribs. Cole jumped and released the bars but the guard reached through the bars and grabbed his arm to yank him back into place. The point of the knife felt dull through Cole's coat but he knew that the fabric alone wouldn't stop it if the guard decided to punctuate their conversation with violence.

The guard's voice dropped in pitch and became menacing. "You need to leave, sir, or I will use force. This is your final warning."

Cole considered letting the guard gut him right there but then pushed the thought away. He would be no good to Iliana or the Natives if he died. And he couldn't even blame the guard because the man was just doing his job. So he blamed himself.

"You win." He sighed and the guard loosened his grip just

enough for Cole to take a step back. "I'll go."

Cole didn't even try to watch the courtyard from another, less conspicuous spot. He was tired of this fruitless search, tired of waiting. He found an empty seat in a nearby bar and filled it.

At first he didn't want to drink, he just didn't want to be alone. But in the crush of bodies laughing and talking, joining and separating, he felt more isolated than ever. At least the noise dulled his frenzied thoughts somewhat and so he stayed. And he drank. It was only a little, he told himself. It didn't mean anything.

As sunrise brightened the sky he started back toward his hotel and wondered if this was his punishment for disobeying his Church: to wander forever unfulfilled, unable to return to what he was but also unable to move forward or grow. He tried to squash such thoughts, knowing that they led to madness, but his mind always turned back and the ideas began to mutate into even more poisonous thoughts.

Alcohol ignited the darkest parts of his mind that had been dormant during his sobriety. In no time at all he had convinced himself that Iliana had played him. She had prayed upon his weakness and used him for her own twisted amusement. And now that she had turned his mind, made him unfit to return to his previous life, she had lost interest. She would never come back.

Passing by the Palace on the way back to his hotel, Cole narrowed his eyes to try to see even father into the yard but failed to make out any new details. The courtyard was full of bodies fleeing from the light, heading indoors now that the night was over. None of them looked like Iliana. None of them would do. But even as the anger burned hot within his chest it was tempered by sadness. He had so wanted all of this to be true. He had so wanted to be important to someone, to do something meaningful, to believe in something again.

Now he was just one man, cold and alone and unimportant, standing in the burgeoning sunlight on the wrong side of an insurmountable fence in the shadow of lost companionship.

48 For her interview Iliana chose a simple, black velvet dress with a modest neckline and a hemline that just brushed her toes. Over that she wore a cropped charcoal jacket that hit just below her ribs. She swept her hair up into a complicated tangle of curls that she thought made her look focused, more serious. A set of low-heeled black boots and understated makeup completed the outfit.

She rode the elevator alone to the second floor. As she walked down the mirrored hallway the black of her dress made her pale skin glow like moonlight and she took a moment to admire the effect before turning to face the enormous double doors of Drake's Hall. White foliage and scrollwork were painted around the edges of the doors and twined through the center on a field of royal blue. She took a deep breath to steady herself and then knocked three times.

"Enter," said a muffled voice from the other side of the door. She went in and the door swished shut behind her.

The high windows revealed small squares of indigo sky but the meeting hall was filled with the soft yellow glow of dozens of candles. The room was large and loud, just like the Governor himself. Draperies of bright blue, red and rich green decorated the walls and between those swaths of fabric hung paintings of forests and rivers, parts of the world that Iliana had never seen before but longed for.

All twelve members of the High Council along with some of their aides were present at this hearing. Most of them wore the blue paint on their faces from throat to hairline. Their true faces streamed along behind the false ones, making it seem like there were twice as many people in the room than there actually were. Even with the paint Iliana recognized them all but she knew only a handful of them personally.

She nodded and smiled as she passed them on the way to the empty seat at the head of the table. Iliana was almost afraid to breathe, lest she fill the pressing, almost tactile silence with uncomfortable noise. She felt eyes on her back but resisted the urge to look over her shoulder.

When she reached the high-backed chair Adam's friend Mario stepped forward and pulled it out for her. She recognized him and met his sky blue eyes long enough to see warmth within them. Then the right corner of his mouth twisted up in the barest of smiles. That tiny gesture gave her courage, because even if the rest of the room was cold at least she had Mario on her side. She moved in front of the chair and he pushed it in beneath her. Then she felt him move away.

Iliana met the stern faces with pride. She sat erect in her seat, her forearms resting on the carved wooden arms of the chair, and a slight smile playing upon her lips to hide her nervousness. She wanted them to know that she knew she belonged here even though on the inside she felt like a child playing dress-up. But she was prepared for that. She had, after all, made a living out of playing dress up, out of pretending to be what people wanted. Now they wanted her to be a Council member so that was what she would give them.

Sigrid stood at the other end of the long table and acknowledged Iliana and the assembled Council with a deep nod. Iliana didn't know Sigrid well but even so she could see the heat of anger cocooning her. Iliana thought that perhaps Sigrid didn't want her on the Council, which, she realized, just made her job that much harder.

"My fellow Councilmen and women. This child has come before us to be questioned. It is our duty to determine her worth." Everyone nodded in understanding without looking back at Iliana. Sigrid regained her seat and said, "You may begin."

The interview consisted of each member asking Iliana a question. They started out with simple questions that everyone present already knew the answers to, such as, "What is your name?" and, "What is your age?"

When they asked the name of Iliana's parents she said, "Gabriella."

A moment passed in silence and then the same man asked, "And your father?"

Iliana met his eyes and said, "I do not know who my father is." She thought this would be common knowledge, especially among the Council members, but a couple of people blinked in surprise. Others looked away. Maybe the question was a test of some kind, she thought. Maybe she had just failed.

"What do you think of yourself?"

"I don't understand the question," Iliana said.

"Are you happy? Do you consider yourself a part of our society?"

"I am as happy as my present situation allows."

"Do you have many friends?"

Here she hesitated. Though she was angry with Adam at the moment he was the only friend she had ever had. Drake was more of a father than a friend. And what about Cole? She felt certain that it couldn't hurt her chances to be on good terms with a Colonist, especially someone in such a powerful position.

"My brother, Adam," she said. A moment later she added, "And Cole."

This got them talking, wondering out loud.

"Cole?"

"Who is Cole?"

"Is he an escort?"

"I don't recall that name."

Iliana interrupted their speculation. "He's not an escort. He's a Colonist." The revelation was followed by gasps of surprise sharp enough to shred her confidence but she held herself together.

Sigrid narrowed her pointed eyes. "Iliana, we are not friends with the Colonists. They use us. They do not consider us equals."

"Father Cole does. And he has a Church in Afet's Wall. And when he leaves Adara Vega he will become Father Deven's third in command. He has powerful friends and he believes that we should be left alone to govern ourselves. He believes that we have souls and the Church has abused us for too long."

More gasps. "Are you sure?" asked someone on the left side of the table. Iliana didn't know who had spoken so she addressed her answer to everyone.

"Yes. He wants to help us."

Some of the members seemed concerned by her revelation. Some seemed intrigued. But Sigrid changed the subject and even though there still seemed to be some unspoken questions among them none of the members were willing to challenge her.

Sigrid asked, "Have you ever taken a life on accident?"

"No," Iliana said, startled by the question.

"Have you ever considered taking a life when it has not been given freely?"

Iliana thought about Father Matteo and the urge she'd had to end his life in that dusty alley but she pushed him to the back of her mind. "Never. I consider my job sacred and as glib as I may be sometimes I would not endanger the trust of my clients, nor would I bring such a danger upon our people."

"Do you have any special gifts or abilities?"

Iliana shook her head. "I don't understand."

Another member took up the questioning. "Your mother had the ability to see inside people's minds even without drinking from them. And when she took a client she could share the feeling with anyone she touched."

"Share?"

"Make someone else feel what her client was experiencing."

"Oh." Iliana thought about what Cole had asked her, how could she make him feel what Father Matteo felt? She took this to be a good sign. Perhaps all of the members of the Council were special in some way. "I have shared the experience with someone else. I didn't even need to touch him."

Some members exchanged surprised glances. The secretary made some quick notes. Even Sigrid widened her eyes a bit before burying all emotion beneath her stony mask. After a few moments of silence and exchanged glances that included everyone but Iliana, Sigrid stood and the room fell silent. She turned her piercing gaze on Iliana.

"Have you answered all of our questions with the truth as you understand it?"

"Yes."

"Do you have any questions for us?"

Iliana thought for a moment and then looked at the faces down the table. Some of them avoided her gaze and still others watched her with fear in their eyes. She wanted to ask why they suddenly seemed afraid of her, what she had said to cause this reaction, but she held her tongue.

"No," she said.

"This interview is over. Iliana, you are forbidden to tell another soul of what has transpired here. Do you understand?"

"Yes."

"The penalty for lying or betraying our confidence is severe."

"I know," Iliana answered, irritated that she had just sat through an interrogation for adulthood only to be treated like a child now that it was over. It took all of her concentration to keep from showing that irritation on her face.

"Very well. You are dismissed but you are not to leave the Palace grounds until we send for you."

Iliana rose, bowed her head in deference to the Council and left the room. She felt their eyes the entire time just as she had when she'd come in and she couldn't wait to get out of there. Those eyes judged her, picked at her. She still didn't want to be a part of that, to become but another pair of judgmental eyes, but neither did she want to conceive a child with someone she did not know, or worse, did not like.

The door clicked shut. The only noises in the hall were her footsteps but her head was too full of worries to hear them.

49 Iliana waited in her cell all night for the summons that never came. By morning she was exhausted and annoyed and stir-crazy. She needed to get out of the Palace and stretch her legs. She also needed to see Cole, to find out what Governor Drake had told him, to apologize in person.

She changed into a comfortable, cream-colored dress and covered it with her floor-length, red velvet cloak. She buttoned up the cloak and eased the hood over her elaborate hairstyle. Several of the escorts had cloaks just like it so she felt confident that she would be able to get out of the Palace courtyard without being recognized.

Iliana hurried out of the Palace and ran across the courtyard. She was so eager to see Cole again that just the thought of him made her heart flutter in her chest. She couldn't wait to share the news that she might be joining the Council. Now they could both work to bring peace to their opposing sides.

As she walked through the gates, happy and anonymous, not one of the stragglers spoke to her or even glanced her way. But when she was close to Cole's hotel she heard someone fall into step beside her. The hood destroyed her peripheral vision but she didn't dare remove it. Something about the stranger's silence bothered her but she assumed it was just a meaningless coincidence. After a while, however, the person was still there.

When she reached Cole's hotel and the person still hadn't moved from her side she decided to pass by the hotel without stopping, preferring not to take any danger, real or imagined, to Cole's doorstep. She dared not turn to face the stalker, afraid that if she were recognized she would be dragged back to the Palace and locked in her cell to await the Council's decision.

She took alleys and meandering roads to circle back towards Cole's hotel in hopes of losing her own personal echo but he was persistent. A moment later the stranger cleared his throat and Iliana knew who it was. She stopped, feeling foolish for her dry mouth and overactive mind. A slow turn of her head revealed Adam in all his glory, beaming at her like a cat would smile at a cornered mouse if cats could smile. No more bruises or cuts marred his face. He was perfect once more, a living doll.

"What do you want, Adam?" she sighed.

"Just wanted to see what my little sister was up to." He touched her shoulder and kissed her cheek. His lips were warm, his nose cold.

"I am meeting someone," she answered. The last thing she wanted right now was to be waylaid by her brother's endless schemes.

"Your priest?" he asked, and his grin faltered. He glanced away from her for a moment, long enough for her to know that he was about to reveal something very unpleasant.

She got the feeling that Adam already knew where she was heading, so she didn't bother to make something up. "As a matter of fact, I am going to meet Cole. What business is it of yours?"

Adam's grin returned, but his perfect face was shadowed by something, perhaps sadness, perhaps regret.

"What have you done?" Iliana asked, though she wasn't sure she wanted to know the answer.

The smile dropped from Adam's face in an instant and he just looked exhausted. His eyes were cold. "If you want to see him don't bother going to his hotel."

She looked at him in confusion, hoping for an explanation. He answered by gesturing to a squat, run-down pub across the street from Cole's hotel. Iliana's heart sped up again. Adam's demeanor alone told her that Cole wasn't just sitting at the bar and sipping water.

"What is he doing in there?"

Adam laughed but it was forced, containing the faintest

echo of his earlier derision. His voice was full of spite. "Your glorious saint, your supposed savior, is in that bar drinking himself into a stupor and he can't say enough about you."

"What do you mean?"

"He caught my eye when I came in and asked me where you were. I told him you were helping the Council plan their attack on his people."

"You did not." Iliana's mouth went dry and her breath caught in her throat.

"Oh, yes I did. And since he was already quite drunk this little piece of information set him off. He wanted me to tell you that you are a self-serving demon of a woman. He said he would make good on his promise to help us because he believes that what the Church is doing is wrong. But he never wants to see you again."

Iliana felt the tears rising and fought them back with anger. She slapped Adam's face as hard as she could, hissing, "How could you say something like that?"

Adam pulled Iliana into his arms. One hand went up to stroke her hair while the other stayed on the small of her back. He spoke into her hair and Iliana was so caught off guard by the motion that she did not fight. His voice was soothing, his words were anything but.

"He needs to leave the city as soon as possible to argue our case against the Church and I needed to tell him whatever I could to get him to go. You were supposed to stay in the Palace until he was long gone."

"Supposed to? Did the Council put you up to this?"

Adam hesitated and then said, "No. Drake told me to take care of it. I would have done this sooner but the man is quite difficult to find when he's not pouting in his hotel room."

"Drake?" Iliana gasped. "But he told me he wanted to speak with Cole. He couldn't have meant for you to do this."

"He never had any plans to speak to your precious priest."

Iliana couldn't wrap her mind around the fact that Drake had lied to her. So she challenged Adam because he was the one standing in front of her. Her fury with Drake would have to wait. "How could you say those things? How could you lie like that?"

"Oh, but dear sister I did not lie." She tried to pull away but he held her fast, trapping her hands against his chest, useless. "I heard about your interview. You impressed them just like Drake knew you would. You are the one."

"I don't understand," she said, praying the tears in her eyes didn't fall even as the world around her did.

"The Council has chosen you as our secret weapon. We are going to do to you what we did to your mother and this time it will work. You will be our sword, our vengeance, our savior."

He spoke like a lover into her ear, his hands and body touching her in a too familiar way. Iliana was stunned. The truth blew around her, scattering the mists of denial that had shrouded her until she felt naked and vulnerable.

"Bastard," she spat. And at that moment he released her, pushed her away so hard that she stumbled and almost fell. Her scuffling feet kicked up a cloud of dust that hung suspended in the stillness of the morning.

"We will fight and we will win and you will be our weapon," he said matter-of-factly.

"You lie."

"It's pretty to think so." Adam approached her again and she stood her ground and stared at his haunted eyes, his taut lips and knew that as much as they both wished that he was lying he had never been more truthful. "It's nice to think that the Governor would put the life of his pretend daughter above the lives of his people. Right now you are less than nothing, just another body to line the streets when they come to kill us all. But soon you will be everything." He paused and when he spoke once more his voice had become dark. "And then we will have our revenge."

"We?" Iliana asked, her mind and body full of icy numbness.

"You and I. King and Queen of the new world." His voice held a world of regret as he added, "This is how it must be."

She met his eyes with defiance as he leaned in like he was going to kiss her but his lips stopped just short. He breathed the words into her mouth and his breath was sweet with wine.

"I promise you that we will take them down. We will win. And when we do we will rule them all."

Iliana said nothing and after a time he lowered his hand from her face and backed away. "See you soon, little sister," he said, then turned and left her standing in the street in the shadows of the dilapidated buildings. On the other side of the street Cole's hotel was warmed by burgeoning sunlight.

Iliana blinked the tears from her eyes. She looked at that innocuous building with its dingy white walls and thought that at least the windows were clean. It was four stories tall and Cole's room faced the street. She estimated where she thought Cole's room would be and found the beige curtains pulled tight across the window as if to keep the daylight out. She wanted to see him and explain away everything that Adam had told him but she knew that if he were as drunk as Adam said her words would just slide off of him like water.

She stood in the middle of the street in indecision. Before it had even begun her life for her people was over. Now she had no choice. She had to leave the city. She could never think of the Palace as her home and she would never look at Governor Drake the same way again.

Iliana pulled the hood back over her head, grateful for the early hour and the deserted street. As she started walking back toward the Palace she felt the panic rising and fought it with logic. In a way she was a figurehead and most of the people who lived in Adara Vega knew her on sight. But in spite of her privileged status she had no true friends among the Natives and no one to confide in besides a man who would probably spit on her now as soon as help her.

But she had to ask. Cole would be leaving the city soon and so would she. First she would return to her room, pack a few things and paint herself with the ageless potion that would allow her to appear as someone else. She wouldn't let herself believe that it wouldn't work because she had no other choice. If Cole wouldn't listen to her, if he refused to help her, then she would leave on her own. She found no comfort in the plan as she returned to her cell alone.

50

"Mankind is weak; let us give you strength. Mankind is divided from within; let us mend you. Mankind is devoid of spirit; let us fill you."

"Oh no," Cole mumbled and placed his forehead on the cool, sticky bar in front of him. He put his hands over his ears but it didn't muffle the pretentious sound of his own voice booming out of the radio behind the bar.

"There are those wish to lead you away from the path of righteousness with temptations of pleasure and excess."

"Liars!" he shouted. His ears popped beneath his palms.

"Do not pay them notice for they will crumble to dust and fade away. Come to the Universal Truth. We will show you the way."

Cole uncovered his ears as the music returned but the world still sounded muffled. He stumbled from his barstool and steadied himself with a hand on the bar. He had no idea how much time had passed since he had watched Adam's lithe form retreating through the open door. Could have been seconds, minutes, hours. No, probably not hours, he thought as he turned to the door and saw the sunlight still faint in the street. Faint, but growing brighter by the second. He wanted his hotel, his bed, sleep.

Being drunk never led to happiness but it had never felt as bad as this. His head tried to wrap around the room as it spun and for the most part succeeded, not in stopping it but at least in slowing it down. He wiped his greasy hands on his pants and took a step. Another step. And another, placing one clumsy foot in front of the other until at last he made it to the door.

He rested there a moment and held onto the doorframe, felt the hot pain as a splinter pierced his palm, didn't care. His eyes squinted into the sunlight until they refocused. The world remained fuzzy around the edges but at least it eventually stood still long enough for him to walk through it.

His shoes crunched on the loose gravel of the street like percussion, multiplied and amplified. Cole heard hushed voices and turned his head to see a couple embracing in the street. He kept shuffling across the street to his hotel but something kept his eyes trained on the man and woman. There was something familiar and frightening about the two of them together. It made him feel uncomfortable. This uneasiness rippled through him, stopping him mid-stride. It kept him anchored in the sunlight, ten steps from the safety of his hotel.

When the embrace ended Cole recognized Adam's face, hard in the morning light. Then Adam stepped back and revealed Iliana. Cole steeled himself against the flood of emotion he always felt upon seeing her but nothing came, not relief that she was alright and alive, not even anger that she had disappeared for four days without a word. No fear, no pity, no insane desire to save her soul. Nothing.

Cole made it the last ten steps to the door of his hotel without even realizing he was moving. He watched Adam touch Iliana's cheek and lean in like a lover about to bestow a kiss. Cole's stomach turned and hatred surged forward to fill the emptiness within him. He fled into the building before the kiss was completed, disgusted by the audacity of their sins and so full of rage he thought his head might burst, steam spew from his ears and fire lick off his tongue. They were disgusting and vile and shameless, the both of them.

He fell once on the stairs, his drunken muscles refusing to obey the commands of his muddled mind, but he made it up the flight on all fours. As he unlocked the door he saw the embrace. As he used the bathroom, swaying over the toilet, he saw Iliana's hard eyes and tight lips. And as he passed out the last thing he saw was Adam leaning into Iliana for that sinful kiss.

51

Cole opened his eyes and groaned. He felt like he had been turned inside out while he slept but the drunken fluff inside his head remained stuck in place. He smacked his parched lips and ran a thick tongue over his fuzzy teeth. He wanted a shower, a shave and a new head. But none of these things would be forthcoming unless he hauled his uncooperative body out of bed. He inhaled to yawn and gagged at the smell of his own breath, like rotten fruit.

He sat up and clamped his eyes shut against the tidal wave of dizziness that made him wish he was still asleep. And when he opened them again he saw the last person he ever expected to see.

Iliana watched him, her wide blue eyes were cautious and glazed with tears. A crust of blue face paint was visible around her hairline and chin.

"Get out," Cole murmured. The words lacked conviction. His voice was hoarse and lifeless.

Iliana did not move except to breathe. And after one long exhalation a single tear escaped her eye and slid down her cheek. "What have you done?"

Anger gave him the strength to throw off the blankets and plant his feet on the floor. "Don't you dare cry for me."

"Can I open a window?" Iliana asked as she wiped the tear away and sniffed. Cole just glared at her. Without waiting for a reply she stood and cracked open the one window, peeked around the curtains and then snapped them shut once more.

"I need your help," she said as she turned to Cole and took a seat on the foot of the bed. Her face was a mask of professional distance, the same one she had worn in the beginning of their relationship. God, how he hated that mask.

Cole shook his head but stopped when the room shook with him. She was sitting too close to him. Despite her now impassive face Cole could tell from the tiny, fluttering movements of her hands and her constant glances to the door that she was afraid but he didn't have the desire to comfort her. He would not allow himself to be moved. Her fears meant nothing to him anymore.

"You disgust me. Get out."

"Cole, you don't understand—"

"I said get out!" Cole roared and then moaned with regret as the pressure in his head doubled. He swayed on his feet and clutched his head as if he could squeeze out the pain. It was unfair of her to confront him like this when he was not at his best. Willpower kept him from collapsing right then.

Iliana just stared up at him and refused to move. Cole sighed, sat down on the bed and put his head in his hands. He couldn't look at her anymore.

"I told your brother that I would help your people but I did not want to ever see you again. And yet here you are, haunting me. I do not enjoy being played and I do not appreciate being lied to." His voice rose in pitch and volume as he spoke until the momentum of his words drove him to standing again. He glared at her with all the vehemence he could muster. "Your brother told me how you used me for information."

"Since when do you take my brother's word as gospel?" she asked, her voice no longer fearful or concerned, but biting.

"I was killing time for you."

"Oh, stop with the self-pity, Cole. It never did suit you."

"No. Your brother told me everything. You used me and you lied to me. You are no better than they are, playing at compassion while planning to kill us all."

"Cole, stop!" she screamed and for a moment Cole's ears rang with the shrill echo of her voice. And for the first time since waking up he looked at her and actually saw the woman now sitting on his bed.

She wore no jewelry, no makeup. Glossy black ringlets that used to be buoyant instead hung limp around her shoulders and the natural glow in her skin had faded, leaving her stark and sallow. Eyes that used to be bright were rimmed red from crying and Cole knew it couldn't all have been over his sorry state. She had changed over the past four days and though no wrinkles marred her perfect face he felt her age like a hot wind gusting through him from those haunted eyes. Against his will Cole felt the rage dissipate. He sighed but he couldn't let it go.

"I was worried about you." His voice became gentle as the fight drained out of him. "I stood outside the Palace for three nights hoping to catch sight of you. Everyone I spoke with hadn't seen you."

"I was angry with you at first and so I did stay away. Then when I was ready to see you again and apologize they kept me inside."

"One guard told me you were with the Council and when I refused to leave he pressed a knife into my side."

"I told you. They wouldn't let me leave…"

Cole ignored her and continued. He felt like he had been keeping these thoughts inside for so long that now he had to speak or he would explode. "When your brother tracked me down I was already a little drunk. And after our talk I was a lot drunk. And then I saw the two of you in the street."

Iliana's eyes went wide. "You saw us…" It was a statement, not a question.

"Kissing like lovers," he finished for her. He winced and shut his eyes as if he could erase the image from his mind but it remained in the darkness. "It's disgusting. I can't be a part of it."

"He knew you were there." The scowl disappeared as realization struck her. "He did that for your benefit. He knew that you would see."

Cole scoffed. "I wish I had missed the show."

Iliana patted the bed beside her. "Cole, please, sit down. I'm in trouble and I need help."

Cole felt that she was telling the truth as she believed it but he didn't know whom to believe anymore. Still, he sat. The fight was over. He'd had his say but felt no satisfaction. Instead he just felt deflated. Cole couldn't even look at her anymore. He just stared at the wall behind her as she spoke because he couldn't stand the desperation on her face.

Her voice was soft but urgent, pleading for understanding. "Adam did this on purpose. He wanted you to fight with me, cast me out and leave me alone. He told you what he thought would make you leave the city before they released me from the Palace. But you're smarter than that. And even if you don't believe me, please keep your promise to help us because even if I hate them right now they don't deserve to die.

"I was on my way to see you when Drake told me that I was to attend an interview for a seat on the Council. But it was more a personality quiz than any sort of competency assessment. They didn't want me on the Council."

Her voice changed then, a thin undertone of panic coloring her words. "Cole, look at me."

When Cole looked up and saw the conviction on Iliana's face he knew right then that no matter what she told him he would believe her. And if she asked him, he would help her.

"They are going to do to me what they did to my mother. That's what Adam said when you saw us together. He was trying as much to unnerve me as to upset you."

"I don't understand."

"They are going to turn me into something. Adam called me the savior, their vengeance. But I don't want to kill anyone. I don't want to be anyone's savior."

"But how?" Cole had trouble wrapping his mind around the idea of Iliana as a weapon. It seemed to go against her nature.

"I don't know how and I don't know when. But I gave your name in the interview and so I'll bet you'll be watched until you leave. And when you do I want to go with you."

Cole blinked hard and studied her face. "I don't know."

"If you say no I will find my own way out."

"But—

"If I don't go they'll kill me, or worse."

The terror in her voice stopped him. He had seen fear before in the faces of his congregation as he preached, in the faces of those who believed they had done something unforgivable.

But never like this. The room was thick with it almost like it was a perfume, without smell but with texture. All color had drained from her face.

Cole looked away from those imploring eyes and stared at his empty hands, so pale against the black and red tones of the room. He didn't know how to go about smuggling Iliana out of the city. Everyone knew her because of her connection to the Governor and there was no way she could pass for a Colonist. Plus the guards at the entrances searched your belongings before letting you pass out of the city.

He told her as much but Iliana already had a plan. "We can leave through the western gate. As you are searched I will sneak past the guard."

"That's ridiculous," Cole said.

"Not if you've done it before." Cole's head snapped up and Iliana replied, "We did it as kids. As a dare, I guess."

"I see." In another place, under less duress, he might have laughed. So much happened here that the Colonists were un-aware of.

"And we'll have this on our side." She pulled a small glass vial filled with electric blue cream out of her black handbag.

"What's that?"

"Our special anti-aging cream. The older Natives wear it when they still want to work as escorts."

Cole took the jar, opened it and smelled inside. It didn't smell like anything but the cream wavered and sparkled as if under sway of an invisible current. "What does it do?"

"It makes the wearer look different. Sometimes it will make you look like a younger version of yourself. Sometimes it makes you look like someone else."

Cole shook his head. "How? That doesn't make sense."

"It doesn't matter. It works. And the only time you can see through the magic is when you already know it's being used. The guards at the gates always expect it so we can't use it when we leave. But if we change clothes and wear this on our faces we should be able to pass about unnoticed until it's time to escape the city."

"Why not just leave now?"

"It will be easier to slip out in the rush of people leaving the city right before the Festival."

Cole sat for a moment in silence and Iliana plucked the jar from his hand and dropped it back into her purse. "Do we have a deal?" she asked after giving him a moment to consider her offer.

He took a swig of water from the glass beside the bed. "What will you do when we get to Afet's Wall? You can't go out in public. Everyone will know what you are."

"I'll hide until the threat of mutual destruction has passed. Without me my people cannot wage war against the Church and so your city would be safer for me than here."

Cole took it all in. The plan was ridiculous. He didn't think it would work. He raised his head to tell her this but the hope in her eyes stole his argument. She was supposed to be the savior of her people but now he had become her savior. Everything rested on him. Could he handle it? Could he take her hope and make it a reality? Through all of his doubts he thought that if she trusted him he had to trust himself.

"Okay," he said. The tension in the room broke. Exhaustion flowed into him and he wanted nothing more than to return to bed and sleep for weeks.

Iliana's sadness turned at once to jubilation and then to solemnity in a matter of moments. When she looked at him her eyes were filled with tears. "Thank you."

Cole swallowed all of his doubts, stood, pulled her to her feet and embraced her. She stiffened at first but then relaxed and clung to him as if Cole was the last piece of land in a heaving sea.

"We can switch hotels tonight," Cole said, releasing her. "That way we can blend into the crowd."

"Okay." She wrinkled up her nose and looked away.

"What's wrong?"

"You stink," she said and took a step back.

"Ah… Sorry." He stood up and walked into the bathroom and shut the door behind him.

Under the piercing stream of scalding water he marveled at how easy it was to forgive when he ignored dogma and obeyed instinct. He was about to do something illegal and yet his only concerns were for Iliana. The Church could put him to death if they found out but he didn't care what happened to him. The most important thing now was that he got a chance to plead his case before the Congress. If they were caught then it would all be for nothing and Iliana would become one of the starving souls beneath the old Capitol building, languishing in filth and maltreatment. And if that happened the Natives would die with no chance to fight back because he had helped Iliana escape. Depending on how this played out he would either be their savior or their executioner.

He turned off the water. With a towel around his waist he emerged from the bathroom. Steam rose from his skin and followed him into the room. At first he did not see Iliana and worried that he had dreamed the whole thing, but then he saw her lying in the bed with her back to him. She was under the blankets, sound asleep.

Cole dressed and then climbed into bed beside her, not touching her, just close. It was comforting to have her by his side again but his mind kept replaying scenarios of what would happen if things went wrong. They could both die, or worse.

But what could happen if it worked? He tried to hold onto that lone positive thought as exhaustion overtook him and sucked him under once more.

52 Cole had one suitcase. Iliana had a small travel case. In tense silence they changed clothes, packed and then took turns painting each other's faces. Iliana smeared the blue paint all over Cole's face, over his lips, rubbed it into his eyebrows, and even into his ears and down into the collar of his shirt. As he did the same to her she told him not to lick his lips or move his face in any way while the paint dried or it would crack and shatter the magic. When they were both coated and dry Iliana allowed him to look into the mirror.

They stood side by side and looked at the strange reflections that stared out at them. Cole's nose was a little wider, his cheeks and lips thinner than usual. His eyes had a deeper set below a more prominent brow. And beneath all that, like a ghost image he could see his real face, tinted blue and looking confused. Iliana's new face looked more mature. She had higher eyebrows, wider set eyes, fuller lips and a jaw more square than soft. She was used to the effect of the paint and could look past it to see herself without difficulty but Cole seemed to be having problems.

"Why am I so ugly?" he asked, frowning at his reflection.

Iliana smiled, "The magic chooses the form for you, a different one every time you use it. And you're not ugly, just different."

"Differently ugly," he said and turned away from the mirror. "Staring at myself and seeing two faces is giving me a headache."

"If you can see two faces, then everyone else will only see one. That means it's working. So it's time to go."

They picked up their bags and left the hotel hand in hand. Iliana squeezed his hand as they stepped out into the crowd. This was for show, just in case any of the Governor's spies were watching, which they both knew was the case.

They took to the streets. The crowd making its way to and from the Palace and the main street of clubs and parties swallowed them. Twice the flow of revelers threatened to separate them but Iliana and Cole clung to each other's hands and the danger passed. Her eyes searched the faces for Adam, for Drake, for anyone she recognized as they maneuvered the streets, weaving around couples and groups, nimble as dancers. She looked for any sign that they were being watched but saw nothing suspicious. Still, she knew they were out there. She wouldn't let herself believe that their move had gone unnoticed.

They entered a hotel, the most expensive on this street, and stepped up to the counter. Iliana placed one hand against the cool, polished stone and wished she could place her cheek against it as well. She wanted to rest and to stop worrying about what they were attempting to do, but knew that she could not close her eyes and quiet her mind at the same time.

A plain-looking Native in a crimson coat came through a doorway behind the counter and asked, "May I help you?"

"We'd like a room, please," Cole said in a nonchalant voice. Iliana was surprised at how calm he appeared to be. But she knew the truth. The hand that squeezed hers had a pulse that pounded like a miniature hammer against her skin.

"Do you have any preferences, sir?"

"A private room on the ground floor," said Cole. "One facing the alley, if possible."

The clerk raised his thick eyebrows at the strange request but said nothing. If nothing else the Natives knew how to keep a secret. Their lives depended upon it.

"How many nights?"

"One."

"Payment?"

Cole paused then said, "You can bill my church. The Second Star of Universal Truth in Afet's Wall."

"As you wish." The clerk wrote down Cole's information onto a sheet and Cole signed at the bottom.

"Here you are, sir," the clerk said while handing Cole a gold key with a square black tag dangling from it. He gestured to the glass double doors to Cole's left. "Your room is right through those doors. Enjoy your stay."

"Thank you." Cole took the key and walked away. Iliana caught up with him and took his hand once more. His touch kept her grounded.

Once they were beyond the glass doors she whispered, "Nice touch, billing your church."

He grinned back at her. "They're already displeased with me, so why not?"

They went into their room and locked the three locks behind them. The room was the opposite of what his first room had been. Whereas his other room had been all hulking, dark furniture and screaming red walls that grated on one's nerves, this one was delicate and light and soothing. It was decorated in soft yellows and browns to reflect the desert landscape. The bed looked so plush, the pillows soft and inviting, that Iliana wished they could stay here for their final night in the city but that wasn't part of the plan. They had to keep moving. They hoped that if someone had recognized them they'd think that Iliana and Cole had checked into this hotel. This small diversion should give them enough time to escape.

Iliana led Cole to the window, opened it and crawled out into the alley. She watched the openings to the alley as Cole lumbered out of the window behind her and eased it shut. As they picked their way between the dumpsters of the back alley Iliana blushed, thinking of what Cole had witnessed between her and Father Matteo. But that was the past and could not be changed so she shook it off and focused on the task at hand: hiding in plain sight.

Since the night was young they encountered a few people lingering in the alley, escorts waiting for clients to happen by. Upon seeing Cole and Iliana together the others passed out of the alley, leaving them alone, a courtesy common in the business. They worked their way back to the hotel they had just checked out of and entered through the back door to avoid any unnecessary contact with others.

Cole led them up the stairs to the fourth floor, which was

under renovation and there they had their choice of rooms. The hallway smelled of new paint and sawdust and it made Iliana's nose itch, her eyes water.

Cole stopped in front of the first room to the right of the stairwell and Iliana stopped behind him.

"Just in case we need to make a quick exit," Cole said. Then he knelt down and worked two thin, metal pins into the lock.

"What are you doing?" Iliana whispered.

"Picking the lock. How else did you think we were going to get into the room?" He wiggled the pins, twisted them and within moments the lock popped. He looked back at Iliana's questioning glance and said, "I told you I used to be quite delinquent."

"I see," Iliana said, not without some admiration.

"Let's get inside."

The room they entered was sterile and smelled of fresh paint. At least it was complete, with bone-colored walls and crisp, neutral furnishings. Iliana peeked out of the window once then pinched the drapes closed, shutting out the night. She sat on the bed and the new comforter crinkled beneath her.

"How long before they figure out what we've done?" she asked as she flipped on the bedside lamp. She was more than a little worried that their plan hadn't worked and it showed in her trembling voice.

Cole set his suitcase beside the door and looked around the room. For a moment they shared Iliana's concerns in silence but then Cole said, "If anyone did recognize us they'll think we checked in to the other hotel, so there will be no need for them to go see if we're in there until they become desperate to find you. By then we should be gone."

Iliana wanted to believe him. She wanted to believe that this would all work but it took too much energy to remain positive. She started to pace the length of the room. Nervous energy was building inside of her, mounting an attack on her senses and making her want to scream. At any moment she expected to hear a knock on the door that would signal the end of her life as she knew it.

Cole watched her for a little while in silence and then as she passed by him yet again he grabbed her arm and pulled her to a stop. "Calm down. You can rest now. You're safe."

Iliana tried to smile but couldn't keep her lips from trembling and so scowled instead. "Safe? I'm not safe. We're not safe as long as we're in this city. And I won't be safe in Afet's Wall."

Cole rolled his eyes. "Okay, so we're as safe as we can be at the moment."

"I just can't believe they would do this to me," she said and hugged herself as if to stave off a chill. "I trusted them with everything. I trusted them with my life. And they found a way to use my trust, to twist it for their own purposes, to turn me into something else. A monster. And I went along with it like a fool because I wanted to believe that I could make a difference and end this without a war, to believe that one person can change things."

"But look what we're doing. We are changing things. Our relationship has changed things." Cole touched her arm, trying to reassure her that everything was going to be okay. "It's changed me, at least."

"How do you know?" she asked. Once again she was desperate to believe but her mind was overflowing with doubts. "How do you know that the Church will even listen to you? They've never listened to anyone before. What makes you think you're the one?"

Cole's voice wavered as if he was trying to convince himself as well as her. "Because I have to believe. Without hope there's no point and I might as well stay here and drink myself to death. But you have given me hope and now I don't want to do that. So even though it may be foolish and misguided I have to believe."

Iliana looked at him, saw the sympathy in his eyes and the anger faded. "We're in the same boat, aren't we?" Cole nodded. She sat on the end of the bed and looked down at her hands clenched in her lap. "I'm scared. But I'm not angry with you. I'm just terrified that they'll find us and they'll take me and change me into a monster."

Cole just shook his head. "I'm not going to argue with you just to blow off steam. You know how I feel. You have a soul. All of your people have souls. You have changed me, one of the most pig-headed, indoctrinated men in the Church. Have a little faith in that, at least." When she didn't say anything he added, "We can change them. We can change it all."

Iliana wanted to crush the look of wonder on his face. It was petty and she knew it but the urge remained. Instead of acting on her selfish, self-destructive impulses she moved to the window and once more peeked through the slimmest opening between the drapes.

"Aren't you nervous?" she asked after a moment of silence so great even the monotonous music outside couldn't fill it.

"Of course I am. But I see no point in lashing out or becoming defensive. I choose to trust that things will go well."

"Since when were you the stoic?"

"Iliana, come here."

She turned around to see Cole watching her from his seat on the bed. She wanted to be angry at his attempt to comfort her but couldn't muster the rage. So instead she left her post at the window and sat on the bed facing him. His hands were warm as he gathered hers from her lap and gave them a squeeze.

"I understand your concern. You stand to lose so much more than I do. I may die, but everyone dies, and at least I will go to my grave knowing that I tried to make a difference. You however, face an uncertain future."

"I'm so glad you get it," she said.

Cole continued as if she hadn't spoken at all. "The Church teaches that we have been put on this world for a reason. That each life has a purpose and a direction it must take to fulfill this purpose. I always thought my way was clear. I would excel in my parish and join the Congress. But you helped me to see that my purpose exists beyond that."

"And?"

"Instead of playing that part they want me to play I will bring about change. I will guide the Church into adopting a more tolerant doctrine."

Iliana looked away, terrified and disgusted by the bright hope in his eyes. "I'm glad you've found your true calling but after we leave tomorrow it will get worse for me before it gets better… If it gets better." She stood and started to pace again.

"I can't believe this is happening. If I stay they'll try to change me and I'll either become a monster and wage war against your people, or lose my mind, or die. If I go, I'm nothing more than a prisoner, for if I leave your house I'll be seen and captured and it will destroy both of our lives. What kind of life is that? How am I supposed to live in a cage? I can't bear to be boxed in like that, hidden away. Cole," she turned back to look at him and saw peace reflecting in his eyes. "I don't think I can do this."

Cole rose and came toward her. Iliana's heart raced. She recognized the resolute look on his face from some of her other clients and thought that he might try to kiss her. It had never been comfortable with the others and she wasn't sure how she felt about it now, even though it was Cole.

As he stood in front of her and grasped her arms she held her breath. Instead of attempting to kiss her on the mouth he pressed his dry, soft lips to her forehead. Peace radiated from him and Iliana felt herself relax a little. Her eyes slipped closed for a moment and when she opened them again it was to see Cole's sad smile. Iliana could see why the Church valued him. Now that he was focused he had the unusual ability to make things easier just by being present.

"Give it a night. If you wake tomorrow morning and you still feel this way then I will return to Afet's Wall alone. I will not force you to make the trip. It will be difficult and maybe even unbearable for a lot of the time. And you, who have never had to temper your desires, may not be able to live the way you must."

Iliana nodded, so Cole stepped back and asked, "Would you like some food? I can go out for something."

"I'm not hungry."

"Okay."

Though they were in this together and Cole was just a few feet away, Iliana felt so distant from everything, detached. So she sat on the bed and patted the pale yellow comforter beside her for Cole to sit. Once they were settled, once the warmth from his body began to thaw her fear, she started asking questions. About his home, his city, his life. And somewhere in all of the babble she made a decision. In the middle of a fascinating tale about his youthful indiscretions with a girl named Abigail, Iliana asked him the question she had wanted to ask him for a long time.

"Cole, why have you never asked for my services?"

He pursed his lips and looked away. She watched his cheeks flush and felt her own redden as well. But before she lost the nerve she added, "Because I would be willing, if you wanted to. Then you wouldn't have to tell me all of these stories. You could show me"

Iliana placed a hand on his knee. His body stiffened at the contact and drew away from her a little so she took back her hand, feeling foolish. She looked at everything in the room but his face, at a loss for what to do. No one had ever reacted to her that way.

"I'm sorry, Cole. I shouldn't have said that. Forget it." She finally looked at him but after a moment she had to look away again. There was such pain in his eyes, such loneliness waiting to be quenched.

"It's a personal choice."

"I understand," Iliana said, even though she didn't. When he didn't continue his story right away she grasped his hand. "Please, don't stop. I want to hear about your life. I want to hear your voice. Will you finish your story?"

After a moment's hesitation he said, "Okay," and picked up the story of his night of recklessness with Abigail, though his telling was not a spirited as before. As one story merged into the next Iliana felt her eyes close and before she could say anything she fell asleep.

53 Cole noticed when Iliana's eyelids fluttered and fell. He let his voice trail off and watched as her breathing slowed, as sleep overtook her, and was awed. He covered her with the white blanket that had been folded across the foot of the bed and then sat in the hard wooden chair by the window with his elbows on the small table in front of him. Outside he could feel the urgency of the crowd in the street in their futile search for satisfaction and understanding. He was no longer saddened or disgusted by the mass desire to be comforted, loved and touched, even if only for a moment. His time with Iliana had shown him that he had been cut off from his emotions.

For years now he had tried to pretend that he existed as separate from his desires, had pretended that that part of him had died when he entered the Church. But now, with Iliana's friendship, with the promise of an end to his self-imposed seclusion he felt years of denied desire rush through him at once, charging his skin with the beat of his heart, warming his body and sharpening his mind.

And then he realized that he had let Iliana down. She had offered her services and just maybe, he thought, the sharing worked both ways. Perhaps she craved the same comfort sought by her clients and through the act of drinking she could absorb something of them. The Natives must need that moment of closeness like everyone else and if he had said yes perhaps she could have found some peace from her own troubles.

At that moment, full of desire and curiosity, he stopped caring about rules or dogma. He didn't think about the consequences or what people might say. He thought about how good it felt when he touched Iliana's hand, when he kissed her forehead. He thought about how strange and wonderful it had been to share her clients' sensations. At that moment all he wanted was to touch and to be touched, to be comforted, to feel again.

He stood and crossed the room, his mind resolute. Iliana lay on her side with her back to him. He sat on the bed and just watched her for a moment. Her hair rippled like black satin across the cheap, scratchy hotel pillowcase. He caressed the strands, let it run through his fingers and allowed himself to feel the texture, to enjoy it. He lifted a handful to his face and inhaled, savoring the aroma of Iliana's curls, memorizing it, like flower-scented rain, like some sweet and nameless candy from his childhood.

And still she slept on, unmoved by his ministrations. One of her arms lay on top of the blanket and he brushed his fingertips across the back of her hand, then her wrist and forearm. By the time he reached her elbow his palm rested flat against her arm, his skin so dark against hers.

She stirred.

Cole leaned over her and whispered, "Iliana." She sighed in her sleep and he answered with her name, louder this time and sharp with need. "Iliana."

She rolled onto her back, opened her eyes and gave him a drowsy smile. She opened her mouth but before she made a sound the door swung open. They swiveled their heads in unison to see Adam standing in the doorway.

Cole froze, still hovering over Iliana, his face flushed at being discovered in such a compromising position.

"I found you," Adam said. He grinned at Iliana, then at Cole, a wicked gesture devoid of warmth. "Finally decided to partake of the pleasures we have to offer? I'm sorry, Iliana is unavailable at this time but if you're still in the mood once she's been delivered I would be more than happy to initiate you."

Iliana pushed Cole away and sat up. "So you found me. So what?" Her voice was steady as a rock but sitting so close to her Cole could almost hear her heart's frantic pace echoing in each shaky breath.

"So what? So this." Adam stepped into the room. Behind him followed three of the Palace Guard, two men and one woman clad in steel gray, the Governor's crest blooming scarlet over their hearts like a wound. Their faces showed no emotion as they came forward to take Iliana.

"Mario?" Cole heard Iliana say as he grabbed her around the waist and pulled her over him as he rolled off the bed. He had intended to put the bed between them and their assailants but he was a man of God and not used to combat. He just wasn't fast enough. As Cole hit the floor Iliana was pulled out of his arms.

He sat up to see Iliana as she was dragged back across the bed. One of the guards had a hand clamped around her ankle. Cole grabbed her wrist and she looked up at him, her eyes wide and terrified. That small contact seemed to ignite the fire of self-preservation within her once more. She gripped his arm, drew her lips into a tight line and kicked at the guard holding onto her ankle. Her blows first caught him in the chest and the legs. But it was the blow to the face that made him release her.

But as she started the crawl toward Cole two things happened at once. While one guard held onto his face and stumbled backward the lone female guard grabbed Iliana around the waist, threw her onto her back on the bed and landed a vicious blow to the side of her head. Iliana's body went limp at the same time the last guard rounded the bed and punched Cole in the stomach, then the chin. Cole toppled over like a stack of paper, his thoughts sent fluttering.

Cole gasped, tried to breathe, couldn't. He caught a brief glimpse of Iliana's flaccid body being hoisted over a guard's shoulder before the other male guard blocked his view of the door. Cole coughed and tried to call out to Iliana and in response got punched twice in rapid succession in the face. His head flew back and hit the table leg with a sharp crack and he wondered if it was his head or the table he had broken. He shut his eyes against the bright pain singing through his body and knew it was over. Involuntary tears filled his eyes.

After a few moments the pain was replaced by a sort of pressurized numbness, like his head had been filled with stuffing.

He felt his assailant step away and cool air touched his face. He licked his lips and tasted blood. A quick peek through swelling eyes showed one man carrying Iliana out of the door, her hair swaying like black reeds caught in an invisible current. The other two guards followed.

And then Cole was alone with Adam and he couldn't even be afraid. He raised his eyes to see Adam standing above him, frowning as if he couldn't understand why Cole had done what he had, risked what he had for Iliana. Cole tried to speak, coughed, then tried again but the blow to his gut as well as the lump in his throat at having failed Iliana prevented the words from forming. Instead he just clutched at his chest and lay useless on the floor.

Adam was far enough away that Cole couldn't reach him but close enough to speak in a conversational tone. He knelt and said, "Don't try to find her. You have been a companion for her and for that I am grateful. You are a better man than I gave you credit for. But you can't win. Leave the city. I am warning you, not as a friend but because Iliana would want me to, if you value your life do not return to Afet's Wall." Then he stood, smoothed the wrinkles in his leather pants and left, closing the door behind him.

Once he was alone Cole found the voice to scream. He let loose a wordless, mindless shout that propelled him up off the floor and onto his feet. He used the table, then the dresser to keep himself upright on the way to the mirror.

The unkind glass showed his face just beginning to swell along his left cheekbone and brow and he thanked God that it was still numb. The flesh was already deep red turning to purple and his left eye was half swollen shut. Cuts on his cheek and his lips oozed blood.

He leaned on the dresser and looked down at his hands. Iliana was gone. He felt her loss like he would feel the loss of a limb. Instead of feeling sorry for himself as he would have just a couple of weeks ago, he moved into action. It wasn't over, not yet. He still had a chance to get to Afet's Wall and change things before it was too late. It was a slim chance, he knew, but he seized upon it and drew strength from it.

In the bathroom he splashed cold water on his face and

slicked back his hair. He didn't bother with disguises since Adam had all but given him his blessing as long as he left the city at once. His bag was already packed. He had three days before the Festival of Semiveh began. From what Iliana had told him the Transformation they had planned for her couldn't take place until then. That gave him two days to get to Afet's Wall and convince the Church to stop its plan.

He ignored the doubting voices in his head, the ones that told him it was fruitless, that he was doing nothing but delaying the inevitable. He ignored them because he had found his faith and nothing was going to stop him from doing what he felt was right.

It took him two hours on foot to reach the western gate of the city. As he waited for the attendant to return with his vehicle he tried to prepare himself for the marathon trek through the desert. What had taken two lazy days to get him there he now hoped to traverse in less than one.

By the time he climbed into his vehicle and took off on the dusty road around the city he had a handful of ideas for the case he would present to the Church. And to keep him going as he set out on the main highway connecting Adara Vega to Afet's Wall he pictured Iliana's face, the look in her eyes when she had clutched his hand before she was taken away. He had seen hope reflected there. It was hope tainted by fear, but hope nonetheless.

He pressed the accelerator forward as far as it would go, speeding down the empty road toward the future. On the other side of the road traffic was backed up for miles as people tried to make it into the city for one final tryst on this last night before the pleasures of Adara Vega were gone forever.

54 Consciousness came to Iliana by degrees. First she noticed that her head seemed to have developed its own unnatural heartbeat that pulsed just beneath her left temple. Her second thought was of Cole. She hoped that he had gotten away and was safe. She opened her eyes by degreed, afraid to see what had become of her. A quick glance showed her bedroom bathed in bright, golden afternoon sunlight and that calmed her a little, for she had expected to be somewhere much, much worse.

The relief was short-lived when she turned her head to see Adam sitting beside her bed in a chair he had pulled from the outer cell. His elbows were propped on his knees and his back was hunched, a position he did not often affect because it made him look less regal. He stared unfocused at the tiny windows near the ceiling. He hadn't noticed she was awake yet.

"What did you do to Cole?" she whispered. The answer might have frightened her but not knowing would be worse. She had to know. She had to know how much she would hate Adam for the rest of her life. She and Cole had both disobeyed the Governor's orders and if Adam was willing to let his own sister be beaten… She cringed, unable to follow the thought through to the end.

Adam transferred his gaze to her, ran his long, delicate fingers through his black hair and sighed. He gave her a tired half-smile. "I let him go. I warned him not to go back to Afet's Wall and I let him go."

Iliana released the breath she had been holding and a tear fell. When she closed her eyes another tear chased the first down her cheek. "Thank you."

"He was a good friend to you," Adam allowed.

"Yes, he was." For a time the siblings just watched one another like strangers sizing each other up. Iliana didn't entertain thoughts of fighting her way out. She knew she could not go hand to hand against him and hope to win. They both fell silent for a time, until Iliana couldn't take it any longer. She needed to know what was coming.

"Am I to be trapped here until it's time to die?" she asked as she sat up. Movement made the pounding in her head worsen. Her voice was hoarse but there was no water in sight and she was too proud to ask for it.

"We are not trying to kill you."

"Oh, because the Transformation has worked so well in the past."

"It will work this time." He stood and came toward her and Iliana could see he was torn. All of the things he had told her in the street, his callous words and cocky smile were gone, replaced by a somber demeanor tinged with something akin to regret, a foreign emotion for him.

He sat on the bed beside her and Iliana drew her feet up to her body and hugged her knees. "Iliana, you don't understand what an honor this is. You have been chosen to lead our people. Aren't you the least bit excited?"

"I don't want to die. And I don't want to kill anyone."

"This is the only way. Bowing to their rules made us weak and diplomacy got us nowhere. This is the end, the last strike, the one thing we have left."

Iliana could sense his yearning for some bright, utopian future as if it were a tangible thing. And the feel of it was familiar because it was what they all wanted. But she had never had designs on greatness, had never wanted to be a leader. She just wanted to live as she wished. But if the price of this freedom was war and blood on her hands she wasn't sure it was worth it.

"You do it, then," she said. "You are a born leader and I am not meant for this. You know it and I know it. So you should take my place."

"It has to be a woman," he muttered. "It has to be you. If I could I would and nothing would make me happier. But there is no way I can take your place." He hesitated and then added, "I know because I already asked."

He leaned toward her, touched her cheek with soft fingers and placed a gentle kiss on her forehead. Iliana closed her eyes. His breath tickled her hair.

"I am sorry about your face," Adam said. "She wasn't supposed to hit you." His fingers traced the edge of the bruise along her temple.

Iliana slapped him as hard as she could. Adam closed his eyes. Beneath his skin the muscles in his jaw tensed and his hands clench into fists on her bed but he did not retaliate. When he looked at her again Iliana hoped that her eyes conveyed the depth of her rage and she was pleased when he looked away a moment later.

Adam stood. "I'm leaving for a few days," he said, as if she hadn't just slapped him in the face. "We have some special guests coming to the Festival. I'm going to fetch them."

Iliana uncurled on the bed and slid to the edge. "And what am I supposed to do?"

"You will be held here. If you try to leave they have orders to put you in restraints."

"And who ordered that?"

Adam ignored the question and she didn't press the issue. It didn't matter whether it was Adam or Drake who had betrayed her, all the mattered was that she had been betrayed.

He continued, "You will have use of your cell but there will be guards outside at all times. The windows are too high to climb out of and the door will be locked."

"I guess you've thought of everything then."

"I'll be back soon."

Iliana heard voices when he opened the door to leave but they were cut off when the door closed. She was alone. Tears sprang to her eyes but this time Cole wasn't there to allay her fears. She did not rage, she did not scream, she did not even move. She put her head down and wept. She had lost the battle and soon she would lose the war. Her one consolation was that Cole had left the city and she held on to the hope that he would remain safe from the monster she was to become.

55 Adam and Katla waited in an oppressive room where they felt as if the walls were closing in on them. This apartment, where the teams had been preparing ever since receiving their orders, was not large enough to hold the entire party of fifty soldiers plus the four generals. Instead they had worked in shifts and even then it had been too crowded, even stifling at times. Now even though the space was empty Adam was eager to get out. He needed fresh air on his face even if that air was the dry and dusty air of the desert.

"Is it time?" Adam asked and licked his lips with a tongue had had suddenly gone dry. Now that the moment was here his nerves faded beneath the rush of excitement that made his fingertips tingle. He felt as if his body were made of pure sensation, his awareness sharpened by anticipation. His eyes picked out new details in his companion, Katla's, face: an old scar just above her top lip, a series of fine lines in her forehead, flecks of gold in the deep blue of her eyes.

Katla crossed her arms over her flat chest and said, "Of course. The soldiers are in place and our allies should be at the gate by now. Everything should be set."

Adam pulled his hood up over his head. "Good. Let's go."

Adam and Katla drew their hoods over their heads as well and pulled their cloaks tight around their bodies so that they would blend in with the travelers. They went out into the street where night fell thick and black in the First Circle without the beacon of the Palace to light the darkness. And with night came the crowds, the customers too poor to afford a Palace escort and the Natives not perfect enough to become one. Life pulsed through streets littered with debris like blood through a body.

Here in the First Circle the dilapidated apartments and businesses overshadowed the dusty streets, looking as though only hope and habit kept them standing year after year. People wandered with hopeless faces and vacant eyes. The exhausted, the depressed and the addicted all found fleeting peace in the arms of whatever Native they could afford.

As Adam and Katla strode through the streets he tried to avoid the Colonists but they seemed to sense what he was even though his face was covered. On accident he met one woman's pale brown, hopeless eyes and her weathered face became reverent. Then came the whispers, the prying hands, more eyes peering into his hood and trying to discern the face beneath. Once upon a time he might have basked in the adoration, might have used it for his own gratification. But he couldn't be troubled with them now. More than once as he passed groups of people he had to swat at hands that reached out to touch some part of him.

"They know what you are and they seem to love you," said Katla with a smirk.

"They'd love anyone who would pay them attention." Adam's tense voice did not invite further conversation and so Katla said nothing more.

She led him through the crowds until they reached the East Gate, which was overcrowded with Colonists trying to leave the city before the Church's deadline. Down in the melee the reek of sweat and dust and death filled his nostrils. These were the smells of the Colonists, the scents of oppression. Adam tried not to breathe through his nose as he sought out the Colonist who had coordinated with the resistance. It didn't take long. The woman stood a head taller than the crowd and toward the back, affecting an air of discontent as she half-hid behind a stiff curtain of thick, matted brown hair.

Adam locked eyes with the solemn woman and they exchanged the barest of nods. Then Adam and Katla turned around and let themselves into a house that stood to the left of the Gate. There in the sitting room stood about twenty of their recruits. When Adam and Katla entered Magna called out an order and they all snapped to attention. These hand-picked members of the Palace Guard were all dressed in drab browns and grays like Colonists, and each had a cloak with a hood to hide their faces.

"Where is everyone else?" Adam asked.

"Some are upstairs. Some are in the basement," answered Magna in his usual succinct style.

"Is everything set, then?"

"Yes."

Adam turned to Katla. "Gather those upstairs and lead them down. You take the rear." As she took off up the creaking stairs Adam asked, "Where is Mario?"

"In the basement."

"Good. He can take lead. I'll follow with my people. Then you lead your troops. Then Katla with hers. Wait here for her to return with the men and come down to the basement."

Adam turned and climbed down the splintered wooden ladder that jutted out of a square hole in the kitchen floor. Once his feet were on the ground again it took a moment for his vision to shift so that he could see in the gloom. The basement was lit every so often by small lanterns and filled with the hulking, shadowy forms of soldiers. No one spoke out loud but the air carried currents of murmured conversation. The soldiers were both nervous and excited and Adam echoed their sentiments. He could feel each heartbeat in his throat, pounding against the collar of his jacket. This was the moment they had been waiting for.

Adam found Mario standing like a guard dog in front of the tunnel that would lead them beneath the wall. Alternating crews of Native soldiers had started digging this tunnel twenty years ago but the finishing touches, like the lighting, were recent. It was large enough to allow for the width of six men standing shoulder to shoulder and the ceiling was just high enough that almost any Native could stand upright. Lit by lanterns at even intervals and buttressed by thick wooden beams, it was a marvel that no one would ever know about if everything went as planned. The tunnel ended just around the curve of the outer wall and out of the line of sight of the East Gate. The trapdoor opened in the desert several hundred feet from the wall, alongside the road that went around the city. The plan was for the Colonists leaving the city to pick the soldiers up on their way to the main road to Afet's Wall.

And this was the part of the plan that was whispered between soldiers in furtive voices. This was the cause of the nervousness that was almost tangible in the dark, stuffy room. They had to depend on Colonists for the plan to work.

"Is this going to work?" Mario asked. His voice was no louder than the others.

"Of course," Adam replied. He didn't want to get into speculation because then he would start to doubt himself. He needed to focus on the here and now. And when they got out of the city he would focus on the caravan, and after that, the Church, and so on.

Mario still looked doubtful and so Adam said, "It will work," in a voice that did not leave room for argument.

"How long do we wait?"

"We don't. On the way in I saw one of the resistance. And if one of them was there then the others were there as well. She'll make sure they all get out at once."

"How shall we move?"

"You will go first with your twelve men. Then I will follow with mine. Then Magna and then Katla with her group of thirteen."

"Sounds good," Mario said and he turned to the room full of soldiers, most of them much taller than him. "All right then, listen up," he barked. The room grew quiet by degrees but Mario did not speak until he had their full attention.

"My soldiers fall in line. We will take the lead. Once we reach the trapdoor we will check the horizon to ensure we can exit without being seen. Be prepared to wait if our caravan has not already arrived. Let's go."

Mario took off down the tunnel and twelve soldiers followed after him, their faces serious and their thoughts turned inward. None of them knew what they were heading into, so they simply hoped for the best and feared the worst.

As Adam arranged his men Katla and Magna came down the ladder, followed by the remainders of their teams. Adam nodded to the other two commanders and then motioned for his team to follow him into the tunnel.

Once he was inside he could hear nothing but the sound of feet tramping hard-packed dirt. The tunnel smelled like mud and sweat, rain and mold. The lanterns swayed from side to side from the passage of so many bodies. Adam counted the buttresses and tried not to think about what could happen at the end of this journey on the other side of the tunnel. He tried not to think about Iliana, alone and frightened in her cell. He told himself it couldn't be helped but it didn't make him feel any better. The guilt stayed with him, ephemeral as a shadow, until he turned a corner and almost collided with the Mario's team.

"What's wrong?" he asked.

The soldier in front of him turned around and said in a hushed voice, "The Church has placed guards on the road."

Adam's blood ran cold. This could not be happening. He would not let this be happening. "How many?"

"Two."

"What are they doing?"

"Just sitting, for now. But they have large packs as if they intend to stay. And they've inspected the two vehicles that have gone past since we stopped here."

"I see."

Adam looked away, his mind whirling with possibilities. If there were guards here then perhaps there were guards at the intersection with the main road, and then farther along the road, and then at the entrance to Afet's Wall. No, he told himself, one problem at a time.

"Let me through," he said and the soldiers parted so that he had a path straight up the stairwell to where Mario sat on the top step and peeked through the gap between the trapdoor and the desert floor.

"What are they doing?"

"They just checked their third vehicle and they were thorough. They'll see that the caravan vehicles are empty and wonder why. And we can't leave the tunnel without them noticing."

"Let me see." Adam switched places with Mario and looked

out. Thirty paces away stood two men in the middle of the road. On both sides of the road there were waist-deep gullies, which left little room for anything but the vehicles. It made it more difficult for bandits to attack travelers.

The men appeared to be deep in conversation. They wore the Church's standard black uniform with a fat, diagonal gold band across the chest. At their feet sat two bags stuffed with goods. Adam saw no weapons but he doubted the Church would send them there unarmed.

"What are your orders?" Mario asked.

"I heard that there were people outside," said Katla as she came through the press of bodies. Magna followed her, silent and grim. "What should we do?"

Adam bit his lip. This was unexpected but he thrived on the unexpected and they had gone too far to turn back now. "Back down the stairs," he said to the others and they obeyed, moving away from him, their eyes unsure.

"Adam, what are you going to do?" asked Katla.

"Give me your dagger, Magna." Magna did as he was told and Adam tucked the blade in its sheath into his belt and then pulled his shirt out over it. "Wait here. No need for us to reveal ourselves just yet. If they have reinforcements we'll know soon and then we can fight. If not..." he left the rest unsaid.

With a grunt he pressed against the trapdoor as he stood and it fell open with a bang. Both of the Church Guards snapped their heads in his direction. As Adam walked toward them they couldn't hide the surprise on their faces that someone had just emerged from a hole in the ground.

"Hello, gentlemen," Adam called out in his most genial voice. He forced himself to smile. His eyes ticked to the nearby dunes and desert caves but he saw no waiting forces, no other soldiers on the horizon. These men were alone. Adam let the smile bleed into his eyes.

One guard found his voice and asked, "Who are you? What are you doing out here? This is a restricted area."

"I'm just out for a walk, much like you."

"We are here on official Church business." Adam got close

enough that they could see what he was. As soon as they realized that he was a Native their demeanor transformed from confusion to outrage.

"You've made a mistake," one of them said.

"A big mistake," said the other.

The possibility of violence hung heavy in the air between them. But Adam didn't want violence. He had to be quick. "No need to get upset, gentlemen. I was just out for a walk."

"You people aren't allowed out of the city. You know that."

"Oh dear, I knew I was forgetting something…"

One guard approached Adam and grasped his collar in both hands. "Where did you come from just now?"

"Over there," Adam gestured in the general direction of the trapdoor. "You saw me." He hoped that the others who were watching wouldn't surge out of the trapdoor to save him. He needed to get this under control, and fast. He touched the hand of the guard holding him and met his bloodshot eyes.

"Perhaps we can make a deal," Adam whispered.

The guard loosened his grip a little. "What are you saying?"

"You know what I am."

"Yes," said the guard, confused.

"Then you know what I'm capable of." He couldn't believe that they were being so daft. He wanted to knock their heads together but he stayed the course and prayed that no vehicles came along.

"Yes, we know what you're capable of and we're not interested," said the other guard and with those words the one holding Adam released him.

"We're not?" he asked, incredulous.

"Your friend seems surprised? Have you never had a Native before?" asked Adam. He took a step toward the angry guard, his frame taut and ready for an attack. But none came. When he stood toe to toe with the man he asked, "Have you never felt it?"

"I don't want to. It's a sin." So, he was a true believer. He hated Adam for no other reason than that he was a Native and would just as soon kill Adam as look at him. But beneath the bravado of faith Adam smelled fear. Adam breathed it in and continued.

"That's a shame," Adam muttered, his own fear evaporating in the hot sun.

"Why is that?"

"Because I could have led you out of this life with a smile and a sigh. It could have felt good to die."

Realization bloomed on his face like a flower as the guard registered the threat too late. "You're the one who is going to die," he said and reached for something in his pocket. Adam didn't wait to see what it was. He withdrew Magna's dagger and slashed at the guard's throat in one fluid movement. Blood spattered the burnt yellow sand at their feet. The guards' hands flew to his throat to stem the flow but the wound was too large. It yawned in his throat like a second, bloody mouth.

As he fell gasping to his knees the other guard tackled Adam from behind. Adam dropped Magna's dagger as both men pitched forward and slammed against the ground. The struggle rolled them away from the dying man and the gurgling sound of each breath faded beneath their ragged grunts, the sound of fists connecting, the noise of the struggle.

Adam thrust out a leg to stop the roll and as he sat atop the other man he punched him twice in the face, the attack too fast for retaliation. Then Adam pinned the guard's hands beneath his knees and waited for him to regain his senses. The guard's nose was crooked and leaked a sheet of blood down the front of his face. The blood trickled down his cheeks and filled in the lines around his lips, between his teeth. He licked his lips, gagged and opened his eyes. Pain and fear made his gaze sharp. He knew what was coming.

"Why are you here?" Adam asked. The guard closed his eyes and grimaced. "Answer me," Adam hissed.

"What's the point?" the guard answered, his words slurred over swollen lips. "You're just going to kill me anyway."

"So it doesn't matter to you how you die?"

He opened his eyes and looked right through Adam as he understood the gist of Adam's words. He swallowed hard and said, "I knew you'd fight back someday."

"Then why would you come here?"

"I volunteered for this duty. I just wanted one more taste before we massacred you."

Adam's cheeks flared as the anger turned his blood to fire. He grabbed the man's uniform in both hands and twisted them to lift him off the ground. Their faces almost touching he said, "You mean that you wanted to use us one last time."

"Yes," the guard answered. He averted his eyes as if he couldn't bear to see the demon that had sprung to life in Adam's eyes. When he blinked tears rolled down his temples and into his hairline. He was so young.

"I'm sorry," he said.

"It's too late."

Adam pulled his own dagger from the sheath in his boot and slit the guard's throat. Blood sprayed like a fountain and spattered Adam's clothing. He watched the blood drain from the body and pool into their footprints. He watched life fade from the plain brown eyes at his feet and felt nothing, not even satisfaction, when the man's twitching subsided.

Adam sat back on his heels and looked at the face of the guard. The Colonists looked so alike you could swap one for another and no one would notice. They were worker bees. They were expendable. Adam didn't regret these deaths because they were inevitable. And they were the first of many, he was sure. War was coming.

As the thrill of the fight leeched the tension from his muscles like ice melting in the sun, Adam heard someone say his name. He turned to see Mario and Katla standing beside him. He didn't know how long he had sat there staring at the dead man's face but the blood was already congealing.

"A caravan is coming," said Katla. Adam looked toward the city and could just make out a shape through the rippling heat.

"We have to get the bodies away from the road," Katla said.

"Fine," Adam said and stood up. "Help me with this one. Mario, get that one and we'll hide them just under the ridge. We can cover them with sand and take their belongings with us."

With a loud grunt Mario heaved the first dead guard over his shoulder and carried him to the side of the road. Without ceremony he dumped the body and it landed with a dull thud and a spray of sand. Adam grabbed the hands and Katla the feet of the other man and together they brought him to the edge and dumped him over. The sand was deep enough and the wind high enough that they did not need to cover them. Nature would hide the evidence for them.

The caravan became clearer with every moment. It was a big one but Adam couldn't be certain it was the one for them. "Head down," he said. "I'll follow."

As Mario and Katla returned to the tunnel without a word, Adam gathered the guards' two heavy bags and started back. He glanced over his shoulder. He could almost make out the approaching vehicles and the trail of dust they spewed into the air behind them but almost wasn't close enough.

He jumped down from the road and ran to the tunnel, slipping into it and closing the hatch just as the first vehicle came into view. He watched its progress through a thin gap and within moments Adam knew it was one of theirs.

"It's ours."

"Let's go," said Katla.

"Wait," Adam said and held up a hand. "They could have taken it, overpowered our drivers. It could be a trap."

But as the huge vehicles roared to a stop and the door opened, Adam's doubts turned to excitement. It was their people. They had gotten out. They had done it. But it wasn't over yet.

"Hurry," Adam urged.

56

"Father Cole? You have returned to us. Welcome home. But you have come to us at the end of our session and so you will have to wait until morning for a proper welcome."

"No," Cole panted. He shook his arm and the guard that had been holding onto it let go, placated by Father Deven calling Cole by name. The guard stayed close by, just in case, and Cole wasn't going to argue as long as no one touched him.

He took a deep breath to give himself a moment to arrange his thoughts. He had sped all the way there, with rust colored dunes streaking past him in blazing sunlight, and then through a night darker than he could remember. He had arrived just as the Congress session was ending for the day and had raced past the guards, who were now standing on either side of him, unimpressed. Sunset pressed against this windowless chamber and he could feel the Congress's irritation at being held up just as they were about to leave for the night. But Cole knew that if he did not speak now he would not get another chance.

On Father Deven's right side Father Piotr wrinkled his nose at Cole's disheveled appearance but his eyes were kind as he touched Father Deven's shoulder. "Let him speak, Father. Can you not see that he has been through the fire to reach us this evening?"

Father Deven nodded and settled into his seat once more. The sound of rustling papers and clothing filled the chamber as the other priests followed suit, none of them looking pleased with Cole and some of them grumbling at having to stay longer.

Father Piotr asked, "Who has harmed you, my son?"

Cole shook his head, mindful of the pressure in his throbbing, swollen face. "That's not important, Father. I come here on a matter of great urgency."

"Are you ready to take your place beside me?" Father Deven asked.

Cole took a deep breath, forced the trembling out of his voice and said, "You have to call off your plans to destroy Adara Vega."

At that the great hall filled with gasps of indignation and remained unsettled even after Father Deven stood and motioned for silence.

"My child, what are you talking about? You have traveled far and it is clear that you have been through many tribulations. You are tired and imagining things." His face was beneficent but Cole knew that the heart inside was black.

"I know of the plot to destroy the Natives. I spent my leave there and I wish to plead for mercy on behalf of the city."

Father Deven laughed then and after a moment the others joined in until the laughter echoed around Cole's head like a halo. And above that sound he heard Father Deven saying, "Just because you found relief for your stress in that wicked place does not mean that you understand the politics governing our decision."

Cole blurted out, "I did not make use of an escort while I was there. But you have…" he turned in a circle to take in all of the faces that had become silent and solemn. "You all have, at some time or another." Some of the priests met his eyes with defiance but most looked away in shame. "You have all benefited from the pleasures available in Adara Vega. You have all used the Natives to satisfy your needs. And you know that beneath those shimmering skins and seductive glances there are hearts that beat and minds that comprehend your derision. They have souls."

"Hold your tongue, Cole," Father Piotr admonished. Cole saw fear deepen the wrinkles in the old man's face but Cole wasn't finished yet. What could the Church do to him that would be worse than what would happen if they don't call off their insane plans for genocide?

"I cannot remain silent any longer. Before I left Father Serrano showed me the atrocity that lies beneath our feet and it almost destroyed me to realize that my Church could sanction such acts against other living beings."

"It is all in the name of God," Father Serrano quipped but no one was listening.

"I don't care whose name it is in. What matters is that you let those people go and that you send them home and that you stop trying to destroy them."

Father Deven scoffed. "Don't be ridiculous. You are so full of hot air and liquor that you do not even know what you are saying. A few days home will soften your zeal."

"You don't understand!" Cole shouted, frustrated at the lack of cooperation in his peers. He turned in a circle, imploring those angry faces to believe him. Most remained stern and unhappy but in some he thought he could see disapproval of the Church's plan. And it was to these people that he appealed, hoping that even one of them would speak out. "The Natives know what you have planned and they are going to fight back. They are not stupid and they will not just lie down and die."

"You are serious?" asked Father Deven, incredulous. "You are trying my patience, Father Cole. If you persist in this you will lose your position in this Congress and in your Church. You will lose everything."

Cole looked up at the man upon whom he had modeled his life and saw nothing but hatred, jealousy and anger. In a clear voice that echoed throughout the chamber Cole announced, "I reject your offer. I reject your Church. And I reject you."

As the last of his words faded into stunned silence Cole saw movement out of the corner of his eye. It was just a flash of color amid the black shirts of the priests but his heart fell. He was too late.

Father Deven spoke down to Cole in a tight, deep voice that exposed his fury. "You are nothing." Then to the guards, "Get rid of him." And then he stood to go.

"Wait!" he cried, wanting to warn them, wanting to help them in spite of everything. But at that moment the room filled with an echoing 'bang' as all of the exit doors slammed shut as one. And following that a familiar, jovial voice said, "Don't leave yet. We haven't said our peace."

Silence settled over the room. Cole searched the crowd of priests for the owner of the voice and found Adam at the back of the room behind the lesser priests. The men leaned away from him as he sauntered through the crowd toward the front row and threw off the black hooded robe that had hidden him. He wore black leather pants and a blue shirt as bright as the evening sky. And whereas Cole looked and felt like he had driven all night, Adam looked like he had just stepped out of the house after a perfect night of sleep. He was a colorful flower among blades of dead grass. He was beauty in a plain world and it was once again apparent to Cole why the Natives' company was so sought after.

"We have come to pay our respects to this fine governing body," Adam said. At his words several more men came forward, uncovering their heads and blocking the doors. Each man held a weapon, some had guns and some had knives, and Cole did not want to know how much damage they were willing to do.

Adam didn't bother to look down to where Cole stood in the middle of the floor in the open; he seemed to only have eyes for Father Deven. And so Cole crept into the shadows by the wall. From there he hoped to watch the scene unfold and avoid a confrontation between himself and Adam.

Father Deven met Adam's blazing eyes with indignation. "Who are you and what do you think you're doing?"

Adam smiled in an easy way and let his gaze slide over the other Congress members in a wide circle before coming back to rest on Father Deven. "My name is Adam. This envoy was sent here with a message from Governor Drake of Adara Vega. He would like for you to accompany us back to our city where we will detain you until you call off the plan to destroy us."

Fear raced across the faces of all in attendance like fire and Cole felt the panic building within him as well. Already a plan had taken shape in his head. If he could just get out and follow the envoy back to Adara Vega perhaps he could work on the Natives to stop it from their side.

"We will do nothing of the sort. We will not enter that heathen city on our own and you cannot expect to carry us out of here in chains and have no retaliation…"

Adam laughed. "You'll see that you do not have a choice. The Capitol is closed. Most of your guards have gone home and those that remained are now unconscious in a locked room on another floor." Father Deven blanched as Adam continued. "But don't worry about Adara Vega being destroyed during your visit. Each guard has a note pinned to his jacket explaining the situation. We have all of you in custody, and if the city goes, you go as well. Is this clear?"

Some members nodded in fear, others began to whimper and still some remained impassive, as if in denial that this could be happening.

"The only way for you to live through this is to come with us. If you fight you will die and we would much rather present all of you to our Governor than some."

"Why? What is the purpose of this?" Father Deven stammered. Cole couldn't tell whether the old man was stalling or just trying to smooth over the situation with forced civility.

"Governor Drake requests an audience with you on his own terms, on his own turf."

"For what purpose?"

"To convince you not to kill our people."

"This is ridiculous."

Adam clucked his tongue. "Pity. That's what we were thinking about you."

And that was all it took for pandemonium to break out. Cole caught a glimpse of a grinning Adam surveying the chaos before bodies blocked his view.

As the guards behind him turned to assist the priests more Natives surged through the only unblocked exit and overcame them. Cole stayed against the wall, clung to it to avoid being torn into the center of the room, and inched toward the door. Above him Cole watched his fellow priests struggling with Natives hand to hand. Some of the Natives used the guns as clubs but none ever fired, which led Cole to believe that Adam's orders were to take the Congress alive.

There was nothing Cole could do for them now. He tried to distance his emotions from the sight of so many of his brethren being beaten down as he inched along the wall, feeling for the doorjamb with his fingers. One priest, then several, decided to jump into the lower level where Cole was. As soon as they hit the floor the Natives surrounded them. Cole couldn't see what became of Father Deven and Father Piotr, for he was suddenly enveloped by nameless faces frozen in terror and the angry surge of Native bodies pressing against them, like fingers pressing against a wound to keep it from bleeding.

And then he was there. Cole felt the edge of the doorframe but refused to give in to the relief that flooded through his system at the touch. He waited until a group of Natives wrestling with two young priests blocked his view of the room and prepared to slip out of the doorway. But before he could he felt a hand on his wrist and turned to see its owner.

Adam stared hard at him, his gaze questioning as if he couldn't understand why Cole was there. He tugged Cole closer and shouted to be heard over the din, "I warned you not to come back here, for Iliana's sake. But this time I can't let you go. The others wouldn't understand."

"But Iliana—" Cole started but Adam cut him off.

"It's too late to change anything." After a moment he added, "I'm sorry."

Cole saw the blow coming in slow motion but didn't have time to get out of the way. Adam's weapon cracked against the side of Cole's head and he careened off to the right. He felt no pain, just tremendous pressure and then the brightness of stars filled his skull until he could see nothing. Still, he wanted to say something, anything, to stop this massacre. He had bitten his tongue as he fell and now it swelled to fill his mouth, immobile and stupid. The sound of the brawl became louder until it overwhelmed him and roared in his ears. And then he passed out.

57 "My people, today you have come here to meet your partner for the Festival of Semiveh. It is your duty as members of our society to keep our civilization strong and independent, to produce children every 100 years." Governor Drake paused for the obligatory applause and the speakers strewn throughout the Palace courtyard scratched out high-pitched feedback. He stepped back from the microphone and waited for the noise to die down.

He cast his eyes over the Natives, his people, and saw that even though the numbers had dwindled over the centuries the old divisions still remained. There had always been three classes of Natives in the city and the passing centuries had not changed that. Closest to the stage and Governor Drake stood the Palace escorts, all glamour and affectation. Behind them stood those who worked behind the scenes in the Final Circle: the bartenders, the cooks and the hotel clerks. They were here because it was their duty and they took it seriously. And behind them came the gaudy, sometimes dirty, maybe even criminal Natives of the outer circles. They stood apart from the other two groups as if afraid that something might rub off on them. Governor Drake couldn't guess what that might be.

Once the ever-present strains of music surged like a wave to fill in the silence he came forward again. "Each of you has been assigned a companion based on the questionnaires you submitted several months ago, as well as on the opinion of the Council as to whom would be your best match. We hope that you are pleased with the choices we have made for you." Again he held for applause.

Governor Drake looked over his shoulder at Adam, who stood just behind him and was dressed in the Palace guard's charcoal gray uniform with the red crest. Adam nodded at Governor Drake though nothing was said. They had decided, along with the rest of the Council, that it would be unwise to mention the Transformation or the possible destruction of the city during these announcements. Now that he stood before them, however, Drake felt uneasy leaving so much unsaid. It felt wrong to let his people believe that everything was fine when they could all be dead in a matter of hours.

Governor Drake returned his gaze to the crowd and began to read the names of the matches. Even though the heat had sucked all moisture from the air the faces swam before him, changing shape and direction, ever shifting. In his addled state this was more disorienting than usual. His mind overflowed already with images of Iliana and those memories had worn him down. He had started to question himself, after all, though at the same time he knew he had taken the only option available. He dabbed his forehead with a white handkerchief then stuffed it back into his pocket. He smiled at the crowd and wondered whether, from that distance, in the wavering air, they could tell that it was a forced gesture.

"Let the Festival of Semiveh begin. Return here in two days' time for the closing celebration. Until then, may Semiveh bless you. May you have luck with your partner and find joy in each other's arms."

The crowd murmured in rising waves that lapped against the façade of the Palace as people began to drift off in pairs. Governor Drake watched them go, jealous of their ignorance. Most of the Natives did not know about the failed Transformations in the past. The Council was the keeper of that information and the members did not live in the private sector. Once you were Council, you were Council for life and Council business was never discussed outside of the offices and meeting rooms.

He stepped back from the microphone and rewarded those who stayed behind to applaud with a gracious smile and a bow. Then he turned around and marched into the Palace, dreading every step, his guilty thoughts like weights accumulating on his body, dragging him down, pulling him back. He took the elevator to the second floor and shuffled toward his office, unable to keep Iliana out of his head. He had read the accounts. He knew what she would soon experience and could not shake the terrible guilt that smothered him whenever he thought of her, of her mother.

"Governor!" Adam shouted.

Drake turned his head and looked back at Adam as if surprised he was there. He hadn't heard any footsteps but his own. "Yes, Adam?" he asked. He kept walking, afraid that if he paused in any way the weight of his thoughts would drag him down, keep him from moving ever again.

"It is time now?" Adam asked. "Should I go get her?"

They had reached Drake's office and went in. Drake hung up his ceremonial blue velvet jacket on a hook on the wall. Then he sighed and looked out the window at the clear afternoon sky, at the distant mountains streaked with color and felt no joy, just trepidation about the future.

"Are we doing the right thing?" he asked Adam.

Adam came to stand beside Governor Drake and looked out the window as well. "I don't know," he said. "I don't want her to get hurt but if we let the Church Congress go with just a promise to change we both know that they'll come back and kill us all."

Drake tore his eyes from the serene landscape and looked over at his son. Adam wore the gravity of his emotions all over his face. His lips were pressed together into a thin, straight line. His eyes were moist and surrounded by the finest lines that hadn't been there only a few years ago. Adam seemed to have grown up in the last few weeks and now, instead of cracking jokes and bursting with exuberance, he seemed to understand the consequences of their actions. He was losing his sister and he and Drake were the ones handing her over to the ancient power that had killed before and might kill again.

"Go to Drake's Hall and notify the Council," Drake said, "Those who wish to attend can meet us outside the room, though

I doubt any of them will come. Then round up a host of guards and go with them to fetch Iliana. I expect she'll put up a fight so be prepared. I will see you downstairs."

"As you wish," Adam said and started to leave but Drake called him back. "Yes?" he asked.

"Please, be gentle with her."

"Of course."

Once Drake was alone his already unpleasant thoughts grew darker with each passing breath. He allowed himself a few moments of despair, time to mourn for the girl he had always considered his daughter. Then he shook off the stupor and moved into action. There would be time for mourning later.

Drake stood and pressed the hidden button on the wall and the bookcase popped open. In an instant the magic swarmed around him. It felt along his body with sharp, painful barbs of power. It seemed excited, as if it knew that its time had come.

He didn't want to touch the box, didn't even want to be in the same room with it, because even with the lid down it leaked a constant stream of power. But he could stall no longer. The back room was full of prickling energy and as he picked up the box the magic flowed up his arms as though searching for a home. His heart raced. He left the room and set the box down on his desk long enough to ease the secret panel back into place.

He picked up the box, shivered as the magic raced up his arms once more and left his office for the depths of the Palace, a place he had tried to avoid ever since Gabriella's failed Transformation, a place that had scarred him far more than anything the Church had ever done.

58

"Wake up, little sister. It's time."

Iliana felt the hand brush against her arm. Her eyes popped open and she bolted from that familiar touch before she was even awake. With movement came realization as her fear flared to life.

She eyed the six guards who now stood around her bed and realized that she was outnumbered. She recognized Adam's friend, Mario, and the other two guards who had stolen her from Cole's room. Mario smiled as if to ease the tension but Iliana was not feeling friendly at the moment. Her body was rigid against her headboard and she hugged her legs to her chest as she weighed her options. She would lose in a fight, she was sure, but she could not go to her fate without at least trying to escape.

Adam held out his hand and offered her a grim smile. His dark eyes were full of sadness. "They are waiting." He twitched his fingers a bit as if to entice her to take hold of them.

Iliana's mind raced for a distraction. "Why hurry?" she asked. "We could wait a few days. The Church may change its mind still."

The nameless guards laughed then and their sardonic braying refused to be confined to her bedroom. It echoed up and up until it found the small, high windows and escaped. Adam and Mario did not join in the laughter. Instead Adam held up a hand and threw them an evil look until they stopped.

"There is no doubt that they will change their minds," Adam said. "But our plan cannot be altered now that it has been set into motion. You have to come now."

Though she hadn't planned on it, Iliana's self-preservation flared to life and in the next moment she smacked Adam's hand away and jumped off of the bed. The guards seemed unprepared for such defiance and hesitated, which allowed Iliana to push through them without a fight. But as she ran from her room her heart sank. The broad shoulders and hard faces of another six guards blocked the only exit out of her cell.

She hesitated just long enough for Adam and his entourage to surround her once more and her brief flash of hope faded like a falling star. She had no choice. Adam put his arm around her shoulders and whispered into her ear.

"Please don't fight it, Iliana. There is no way out of this. They will drag you kicking and screaming if they have to but that kind of display is beneath you. Please, go with dignity." He whispered close to her ear, "Perhaps if you are willing it will hurt less."

At once Iliana shook her arm free and stared with defiance at the amused faces of the guards blocking the door, then at Adam and his team. She knew that Adam was trying to be comforting but she was beyond comfort, she was furious. "How would you know about the pain?" she spat as she looked each of the guards in the eyes. "No woman has ever survived to speak of it and no man is strong enough to endure the process."

At that all of the guards stopped smiling and looked as though they might want to knock her unconscious. Only Adam seemed unfazed by her angry words. He linked his arm with hers as though escorting her to supper instead of to her possible death. Iliana's mouth went dry at the thought. This was the end. And as much as she hated to admit it Adam was right. In the end the only thing she had left was her pride. So though her legs threatened to buckle and her eyes swam with tears she held her chin high.

Her voice trembled only a little when she said, "Lead the way."

Adam started to move with somber grace. The usual smugness disappeared as his features softened, his eyes became round and his lips frowned. His movements were slow and smooth, almost like a choreographed dance. Now that the time was upon them Adam worried about her. Iliana could feel it, could smell it in his sweat like stale air from a room that had been closed up for too long.

As they entered the deserted corridor with six guards in front, six behind with her and Adam in the middle, she could smell fear in the other men as well, heady and contagious. Her heart sped up to accommodate the terror that swelled within her chest.

They rode the elevator in silence even though Iliana was screaming inside her head. As they passed through the lobby and into the hallway that led into the Palace underworld Iliana felt the curious glances of onlookers who had not yet gone to bed with their mates. She focused her eyes on the neck of the guard in front of her, concentrated on the way it bulged above his collar and focused her will on projecting nothing but inner fortitude. She could not meet anyone's eyes, afraid that if she let her gaze slide out of that small patch of stubbled reality on the guard's neck then she would lose control of her emotions. She knew now that there would be no eleventh-hour savior. No one was coming to her rescue and so she was determined not to show how frightened she really was.

As the passageway led deeper into the bottom levels of the basement, plunging into a tunnel with smooth sandstone walls, Iliana found it more difficult to keep her composure. She thought of Cole, tried not to worry about him and failed. She told herself that at least if she worried about Cole there wasn't room enough in her heart to worry about herself. And if she were to die tonight she wanted Cole to live and spread their message. She hoped he would forgive her for what she was about to become and knew without doubt that he would. She also hoped that he had taken Adam's advice and left the city for parts unknown but she knew better than that. She knew he would have gone straight to Afet's Wall in a last attempt to save all of their lives. He was so foolish that way.

Iliana was not as selfless. She would not welcome death now any more than she would have welcomed it before she knew any of this. As they led her deeper still she began to imagine that Governor Drake would be there at the end of this journey to congratulate her on passing the final test to become a Council member. She imagined her fear evaporating in the glow of smiles like a puddle beneath the midday sun.

Hope flared again even in the airless vacuum within her soul. She hoped even as she knew it was hopeless, even as the cold air leeched into her bones and the stone slapped her bare feet. And then at the end of all these thoughts she hoped that death would be kind.

When they turned that last corner the air started to hum against her skin and Iliana saw Governor Drake. He was there but not with a smile and a hug. She looked through the gap between the shoulders of the guards in front of her and saw that his face was dour and beneath the blue paint he looked ill and unhappy, like the old man that he was. He stood at the forefront of a group of huddled Council members and two high priests, one of which Iliana recognized but whose name she couldn't remember. No other women were present and Iliana felt a superfluous twinge of anger that no women would come to support her.

Drake offered Iliana a pale smile in greeting but said nothing. Iliana's entourage stopped just short of an open metal door. Iliana recognized it. It had confused her before, with its sweet and metallic pervasive odor of blood. Stronger now that the two-inch-thick door stood open, the smell of blood permeated the air around them and the source was whatever lay in the darkness within that room.

The guards backed away and Iliana listened to their footsteps fade as they turned the corner. Though they were out of sight she doubted that they would go very far just in case she got free and tried to run. Adam seemed to sense her thoughts and so tightened his grip on her arm. For once she was glad for it because she had begun to tremble so much that she didn't trust her legs.

"Iliana, daughter of Gabriella, who gave her life for her people, we welcome you," the tall, pale priest said with solemnity. The shorter priest came forward and anointed Iliana's forehead with some sweet smelling oil from a red glass bowl he held in his other hand. Though she could see no source of heat nearby the oil was hot on her skin and continued to sting even after the initial burning had subsided.

"May your journey be peaceful. May you see behind men's minds."

The priest anointed her lips and the smell of the oil turned her stomach. Sweet and spicy, it burned in her nostrils and made her eyes water. Then for a moment she felt light-headed and calm but that sensation passed as well and she was back to blinding fear.

"May you speak the truth."

The priest gestured for her hands and when she hesitated Adam took both of her wrists and held them out. The priest anointed the centers of both palms.

"And may you be mighty in justice and deliverance."

When it appeared the ritual was finished and the small priest withdrew Iliana yanked her hands back, startling Adam and drawing gasps from the throats of those assembled.

A moment of silence passed before Governor Drake stepped forward. Without touching her at all he leaned in and kissed the air beside her left cheek, then her right. When he straightened up he held her gaze and Iliana read the apology in his eyes. It angered her that he would dare expect forgiveness after his deceit. Looking into the pained face of the man she had always viewed as her father she still couldn't comprehend why he had misled her. So instead of granting him the forgiveness he was desperate for Iliana spat in his face.

Again the people gasped but Drake just looked sad, beaten, hurt and resigned. Iliana was glad she had hurt him. Drake wiped off his face with his handkerchief and returned to stand with the Council members without speaking. There was nothing he could say to make things right and she was grateful that he didn't try.

Iliana looked toward the open door and the darkness within. She didn't need to see what was inside because the darkness alone terrified her. She looked at Drake, then at Adam and took what pleasure she could from the sadness and fear in their eyes. Their pain satisfied her, made their betrayal the tiniest bit easier to endure.

The tall priest began some incantation about focal points of power or some such nonsense. Iliana stopped paying attention as her head filled with regret and she began to shake again, worse than the first time. She felt Adam come up behind her but she stepped away. If anyone touched her, made any gesture of kindness, she would break. She didn't want to break. She didn't want to give them the satisfaction. She took a deep breath and blinked hard. Her vision was blurred with unshed tears and she witnessed the proceedings without comprehending a thing.

The priest droned on for so long that hate bubbled up from inside her and dried the tears and then regret filled her eyes again. She lost track of how many times she volleyed between these two emotions before someone took her arm with cold, dry fingers. The short priest. And then the tall priest took her other arm. Their hands guided her toward the open door and the shadows beyond. Her body stiffened and all she could think about was getting away. She wanted to hit, to run, to bite, scratch and claw her way out of those offending hands and out of that oppressive tunnel. But as she moved the oil on her lips stirred and once she smelled it peace settled over her, brought her mind into sharp focus. The momentary calm passed in an instant but it left a mark. She promised herself that if she had to die she would die with dignity.

She lifted her chin and forced her legs into motion just as she forced her heart and her mind into a place of numbness. She remained numb as the two priests led her into the room and torches on the opposite wall burst into flame though no one was there to light them. She was numb when they led her to a wall of tacky, black rock and made her stand against it. She didn't want to think about it, about what the tacky substance could be or why it hadn't dried in the past one hundred years.

She felt nothing, not even embarrassment, as they unfastened the back of her dress and pulled it over her head. Naked, she stood erect and let them capture her wrists in manacles attached by long chains to the wall. The manacles stuck to her skin and her mind tried not to recognize the blood that coated them like paint that had not yet dried.

As one priest checked the strength of the manacles the other left the room. He returned moments later carrying something draped in a dark purple cloth. He set the object on the floor across from Iliana and removed the cloth. As soon as the box was uncovered the power hit Iliana's naked skin like a warm breeze, concentrated in her forehead, lips and palms. Her body recognized it, responded to it. She swooned, fell against the wall and pulled away at once. Some of the old blood stuck to her skin.

The power infiltrated her mind and amplified her anger. Rage surged through her limbs and she suddenly felt as if she could snap the chains that bound her to the wall and that she could brush aside the priests and the guards without any effort at all and flee from the Palace forever.

But when she moved her arms to test the theory the voice from the box whispered inside her head. *Wait. Let them go. You do not need them. Your strength lies here.*

Iliana's arms relaxed at the suggestion. She ignored the blood, ignored the men who moved around her, ignored the fear and focused on the box. It was black with designs carved into the wood but in the dull light her eyes could not pick out any more detail. The short priest flipped a tiny latch on the front of the box and Iliana closed her eyes against the flood of power that washed over her. She didn't see the priests leave but she heard the door close and that sharp noise jolted her out of her trance. She was alone.

59 For a time Iliana did not move except to blink at the stone room around her, lit only by the flickering torches. Every muscle in her body was taut, prepared for flight even though she was chained in place. But nothing happened. The breath of power continued to trickle across her skin, no more or less than before, though now that the door was closed the very air seemed to vibrate.

It hit her then. This was the end. She could not fight or struggle for there was nothing against which to struggle. The stoic mask she had cultivated began to crumble and the tears she had suppressed so well rolled down her cheeks.

The longer she stood there while nothing happened the worse it all became until with a cry of rage and futility she sank to her knees on the stone floor and wept. She covered her face with her hands even though there was no one there to see her face contorted by emotion. She wept because she had lost, because she was terrified of what was going to happen, because she was alone now in a room with a box and some torches and she wished that whatever was going to happen would just happen and end this terrifying anticipation.

"Why are you crying?" a small, inquisitive voice asked.

Iliana's head jerked up. Her heart stuttered when she noticed the lid to the box stood open. The level of power that prickled her skin had intensified and the anointed parts of her body burned. She was no longer alone.

A little girl of about eight Colonist years stood beside the box as if she had just stepped out of it, though there was no way she could have fit. She wore a tattered dress that may have been white once but had faded to a dingy brown. Her long, glistening hair was the color of sunlight and floated around her face and shoulders in half-formed curls and waves. Her skin had the velvety smooth texture and rich color of the sand dunes at dusk. She did not smile or pout. She just watched Iliana with eyes so dark they seemed to swallow the torchlight.

Iliana forced a breath in past her racing heart. She had expected monsters or ghosts. This was something else. She wiped at her face with both hands and cleared her throat. "Where did you come from?"

The little girl answered in that same strange voice but the words were a riddle. "I came from the land, from your land."

"Just now?" Iliana asked, not in the mood for riddles.

"No. Just now I came from there." The little girl pointed to the open box.

"I don't understand." Iliana looked around. To her right the featureless door was still closed tight. In front of her stood the little girl and the box. To her left and further into the room a small pool of water reflected the torchlight on its placid surface. She wondered at its purpose. It couldn't have been for her benefit because the chains on her wrists weren't that long. Her mind was eager to conjure up the type of monster that could rise from that glassy water and she shivered and turned away from the pool.

The little girl watched Iliana with detached curiosity. Iliana felt the little girl's gaze moving down her body and as it went the power in the room spiked once more. Iliana felt as if insects were crawling just underneath her skin. She wiped at her bare arms but the sensation would not pass.

"Look at me," the little girl said. Her voice was non-committal, as if it didn't matter whether Iliana obeyed or not.

But Iliana looked. She was compelled to obey that tiny voice and the moment their eyes met her mind softened like melting butter. She could feel her thoughts flowing within her head and the oil on her forehead began to burn. She thought of her anger with Drake, Adam's regret and Cole, her last sight of him, of the pain in his eyes as she was taken away from him. The tears returned. She didn't want to be a monster. She didn't want to become her mother. She didn't want to die.

After a moment the burning receded and Iliana could focus her thoughts again, but the memories felt as though they had been dampened somehow.

"I know you," said the little girl.

"I don't think so." The words rose in her mind like bubbles in a vat of syrup.

She narrowed her little black eyes in concentration. "I know your mother. You share blood with one of my children."

"And my father?" Iliana asked. It seemed to take her forever to form thoughts into words, words into sentences.

"I am your father. And your mother."

"No, my mother was…" Iliana began but she couldn't finish the thought. She couldn't remember who her mother was supposed to be, though the name was right on the tip of her tongue.

"The others could not handle the change. It is painful and difficult. But you have some power already. It will be easier for you if you do not resist."

That's what Adam had said. The thought of Adam snapped Iliana out of her trance. She blinked at the little girl and began to tremble as the fear she thought she had set aside washed through her. She tugged on the manacles to test their strength but they were well made.

"Sit up on your knees," the girl ordered.

Iliana wanted to say no but the power wouldn't let her. It made her move, forced her into position as if she were a doll. Fear made her body cold and caused her heart to thrash inside her chest.

"I can't do this," Iliana whimpered.

"Of course you can. It is what you were made for."

"What's going to happen?"

"I will live through you. And we will bring justice."

"We?"

"You."

Iliana hesitated, then asked, "But will I still be here? Will I still be me?"

"Do you want to be?" asked the little girl.

Iliana hesitated. Was it worse to be aware of the atrocities she would commit or to be unaware? It was happening too fast and with the power humming around her she couldn't focus long enough to think it through.

The power was impatient. The little girl said, "Place your arms at your sides, palms facing me."

Iliana's body obeyed even as her mind rebelled. "Wait. Please," she whispered.

"It is too late."

The little girl disappeared in an instant and the power swelled to fill the room. It seared Iliana's throat, burned her chest as if she were inhaling smoke and exhaling ashes. It built upon itself, multiplied until the air was thick. It toyed with the torch flames and made them sputter and then blow out. Iliana gasped, locked her gaze onto one of the dying embers and used it to ground herself. She could see nothing but those glowing orange spots in darkness that had thickened like congealing blood.

And when the power crested and broke it crashed into her body like a sandstorm, the smooth, velvet air sprouting teeth, and she felt it take pieces of flesh at it passed. Her lips burned as if they had been torn off. Her palms and forehead felt like they had been impaled by white-hot metal spikes.

She screamed against the pain with a tongue that refused to work. And just when she thought it had reached a crescendo the power crashed into her again and she screamed until her throat was dry and ragged as it pulled blood, tears, sweat, every possible excretion out of her body through any means that it could. She vomited but could not move so the bile ran down her chin to puddle in her lap. Her eyes cried tears scalding as lava as the pressure within her body mounted until she thought she would explode, until blood sprayed from her pores like a crimson fountain. The air became thick with the aroma. The power wrung the mortality from her flesh like water from a sponge and Iliana lost herself within the agony.

And then it stopped. With the magic no longer supporting her she fell onto her side like a broken doll. She wanted nothing more than to die. The heartbeat in her chest slowed until each single beat echoed throughout her body as if she were hollow. She could feel it in her skin, still warm and slick, in her fingertips that still gripped the stone floor with her last bit of strength. Some residual part of her understood that she was dying but she had no energy left for fear.

She heard no movement, saw nothing in the darkness, but the little girl's voice echoed through the room. "All that remains is the kiss and I will be a part of you."

Without warning Iiana felt the little girl come closer but she couldn't move away. She lay supine and defenseless, waiting for pain, waiting for the agony to begin anew. Instead she felt soft, tiny lips pressed against her right palm, then her left, and the places that the child kissed grew cold. The coldness traveled up her arms to bind her chest in ice. Then the lips touched her forehead and Iliana's mind became clear, the events of the last few minutes erased.

By the time those lips found hers Iliana was willing, she wanted nothing but that power to wash through her and finish the job, clear out all traces of her previous self. Something within her surged up to meet the girl's kiss and at contact the vibrations shivered across her skin and through her body, filling the emptiness.

She welcomed the frigid skin that enveloped her, embraced the power and opened her mind to it so that it could quench the last embers of agony still burning deep within her. The wind whispered secrets to her, caressed her. And in that stillness Iliana found peace. She slept.

60 The cell was filled with the murmurs of quiet, speculative conversations. No one wanted to give voice to the possibility that they could die. The Church Congress members, bruised and bloodied by battle, huddled around Father Deven, waiting for him to speak, to comfort them, to save them.

Instead the great man prayed. The hands of those closest to him clutched at his robes and the touching radiated outward so that all of the members were connected in some way. Few, however, were silent enough to hear Father Deven's monotone chant. The rest just whispered together in fear or wondered in silence whether faith alone would be enough to save them.

At the other end of the large cage Cole sat in a corner alone, watching the scene with disgust. His head pounded as if the devil himself was hammering away inside his skull and Father Deven's self-righteous babbling was the last thing he wanted to listen to. Part of Cole hoped that they all got what they deserved but the rest of him just tried to think of a way out of this mess without bloodshed. So far he had come up with nothing but a worsening headache and a disposition that grew darker with each passing second.

Across from Cole sat the only other person not even pretending to buy Father Deven's sermon. Yourian, the brother who had not participated in Adam's brutal beating, sat in a miserable heap about as far from everyone else as he could get. Cole had already tried to talk to him but Yourian had just shot him a dejected look and turned his back. Since they had thrown him in the cell some time while Cole slept he had no idea why the boy was in there or why he hadn't left the city with his brothers.

When he got sick of listening to the same repetitive, holy nonsense, Cole shouted, "Enough!" To his relief the prayer stopped short and all eyes turned toward him.

Father Deven raged, "How dare you interrupt our prayer!"

"How dare you continue to preach to these men who are going to die because of your greed and intolerance?"

Father Deven's face grew red and he opened his mouth as if to speak but Cole cut him off. "You sit here and preach about evil and about monsters and sin and you still refuse to grasp the most basic of facts. The Natives are people with souls and personalities just trying to live in the world you've confined them to. Do you think they enjoy it?"

"Of course they do. They live drunk on hedonistic pleasures…"

"They are what you have made of them. They have come to define themselves by your narrow definition of them. And this is all because of you and your selfish interpretations of God's law."

Father Deven stared at Cole with buglike eyes. His bottom lip trembled with rage. From behind Father Deven's right shoulder Father Piotr shook his head to tell Cole to back off.

The following silence was broken by slow, echoing applause. All eyes turned toward the door where Adam stood clapping, the grin gone from his face. All arguments ceased at his appearance and for the moment at least they were all united against a common foe.

"What a wonderful speech, Father Cole. Be honest, you knew I was there, right?"

"No," Cole answered. He stood up, bracing himself against the wall as his vision swam with darkness. He wanted to speak but the frail, twitchy Brother Yourian reached Adam first, stumbling over his own feet in his excitement.

"Oh, Adam, thank God it's you. They put me in here with these people," he paused to sneer at the assembled Congress members. "But I don't belong in here. Please let me out so we can be together like you promised. It's our time now. Let me out."

Adam looked deep into Yourian's face and something he saw there seemed to upset him. He narrowed his eyes. "You have served your purpose, Yourian. You should have left when you had the chance."

Yourian's eyes filled with tears, which overflowed and traced clean lines down his filthy face. "How can you say that?"

"Because it's the truth."

"But I love you."

Adam rolled his eyes. "I almost killed you in the garden and still you haunt me. What is wrong with you?"

Yourian was sobbing hard and sniffled between words. "I gave you everything. Why are you being so hurtful?"

Before Adam could respond Cole stepped forward. "He's in a cage now, Adam. There is no need to be cruel."

Adam turned his eyes on Cole and they filled with rage. For a moment Cole felt burned by the heat of the gaze but then his eyes softened. "You are right, Father." Then he looked back to Yourian. "Come, Yourian, let me help you."

Yourian's tears evaporated and Cole had enough time to call out, "Don't," before Yourian leaned toward Adam through the bars as if for an embrace. In a move too fast for Cole to stop it Adam reached through the bars, grabbed Yourian's head, yanked it and twisted it hard to the side. The crack as Yourian's neck snapped raised the already tangible tension in the cell. Adam left the boy where he fell crumpled against the bars.

He turned to Cole, ignoring the whimpering of the other priests in the corner. "See how merciful I am? I let him die now rather than face Iliana."

At the mention of her name Cole started. He ran forward and clutched the bars and didn't care that Adam was inches away and could snap his neck, too, if he so chose. "Where is she? If you've hurt her, I'll—"

"You'll what?" Adam asked. Cole had expected a laugh or at the very least a mocking grin but the old pleasure Adam once took in being cruel seemed to be gone. In its place was some emotion that Cole couldn't name.

Cole could think of nothing to say but he was rescued from having to respond when a woman's scream filled the room and cleaved the silence like an intangible hatchet. Everyone looked around for the source of the noise but Cole found it first. It came from a vent high up on the far wall. Another scream followed a moment later and then nothing but echoes bounced around the room. Cole looked at Adam, whose face had grown pale and frightened, and he knew at once to whom the scream belonged.

"That's her, isn't it?" he asked.

Adam's eyes shifted to look at Cole and they were haunted. He nodded and looked away once more as if he was ashamed.

It's over, Cole thought. No more fighting, no more deception, no more railing against the injustice of it all. Iliana had undergone the Transformation and whether it changed her or whether it killed her it was all the same. She was lost to him now. They were all doomed. He expected to be furious, to be inconsolable but instead he felt all emotion run out of him like water out of a busted pipe. He loosened his hold on the bars and rested his forehead against them.

"You didn't want to do this," he told Adam. It wasn't a question.

Adam swallowed hard. "Sometimes you have to make a choice between two vile things. The life of one for the lives of all."

Cole nodded and closed his eyes. "I understand."

"I am sorry that it had to be this way."

"As am I."

Adam turned and left without another word and Cole became aware by degrees that everyone was looking at him. He didn't think he owed them anything so he turned his back on those imploring faces and went back to his corner. There he sat and wrapped his arms around his knees and hid his face in the bend of his elbow.

"Cole?" asked Father Deven. "Who is Iliana?"

"She is their salvation and our destruction," he answered without answering.

Father Deven scowled, puzzled by Cole's riddling speech. "But you know her?"

"I knew her. I do not know the thing she has become."

"Can't you just appeal to her as a friend? She won't kill a friend."

Cole leveled his eyes at Father Deven and the older priest flinched as if struck. "Won't she?" Then he turned away from them and ignored all other pleas for information. It was petty, he knew, but he wanted them to be scared, terrified even. But as he sat alone he prayed over and over again, not to God, but to Iliana, the woman he used to know, to please be merciful.

61 Drake stood alone in his office, having dismissed his guards as soon as Iliana was locked away. They would not know until they opened the door tomorrow evening whether or not the Transformation had worked. Drake was dreading that moment more than anything. More, even, than when he had opened the door on what was left of Gabriella. Gabriella had been willing to go into that room and he had said his goodbyes. She had even smiled at him before they closed the door.

In contrast the hatred in Iliana's eyes before they put her into that room had shredded his heart and his will. He had never seen such loathing before and never would have believed Iliana capable of it. Worse, he knew that he deserved it.

Drake looked out of his office window and into the empty streets, knowing that the rest of the city would look much like this. The lack of movement in the city during the first two days of the Festival had always unnerved him. It felt like everyone had disappeared, just like they had so many years ago when the Colonists who had built this city evaporated beneath the fiery desert sun. Or at least that's what the Colonists thought had happened. They believed that all of their people had just vanished one day, a mystery destined never to be solved.

At least, that's the story that most people knew. But Drake and a few others knew the truth. Back then the power in the box hadn't needed a body upon which to bestow its magic. It was ancient and alive and it craved freedom. So the Natives had chosen one of the Colonist's finest cities and loosed the magic upon it. Its hunger had been so great that it took everything: body, bone, and blood. It had left behind a clean, haunted city.

The truth of what had happened wasn't taught in lessons anymore in fear that it might be leaked to the Colonists. Now those who knew the truth were dying out and the teachers sugarcoated the Natives' past to generate a hatred of the Colonists in the young. The truth was that they were all varying degrees of wrong and they all deserved what they got.

Except Iliana. She had been innocent. Drake had always watched over her, protected her from the dirty politics. He had spent the last century knowing that she was meant to be his daughter, hating that she wasn't but loving her just the same. Every so often when he looked out at the men surrounding him he would try to find in any of those faces a hint of Iliana. But for 100 years now the perpetrator had kept his secret and those who did know had either died or would never tell. The truth was that Iliana resembled Gabriella too much for Drake to make any true comparisons between the daughter and her anonymous father.

At the thought of Iliana as his daughter, as anyone's daughter, tears stung his eyes. Unable to stop them and since no one was present to see them anyway he let them fall. After a time they had carved pale lines through the thin layer of blue paint.

As night claimed the empty city Drake knew that his tenure as Governor had ended. Whether this Transformation worked or not he wanted out. He felt far too weary to be making such painful decisions. He didn't want to think about anything anymore. For 700 years he had lived his life according to the needs of his people and now he was almost too old to live for himself.

He suddenly felt ancient and decrepit. He moved over to his chair and sank into it. As darkness overtook the daylight, so did it leech into his bones, his muscles and his mind. It filled him with shadows that no lamp could dispel until he felt like nothing more than an echo of the man he had been.

The next day was day two of the Festival of Semiveh. If they were still alive in a few hours they would know that the Church was taking them seriously. For the first time in his life Governor Drake wasn't sure which way he wanted this to end.

311

62 She opened her eyes and sat up. There were no lights in this room but her vision was clear. She lifted her arms and the chains that held her to the wall snapped as if they were made of paper. Her hands and the manacles that wringed her wrists were sticky and brown, covered with dirt and congealing blood.

Hunger rumbled in her gut, new and raw. As a test she licked the back of her hand. Her tongue was rough against her skin. The blood tasted sweet and made the hunger flare up until it consumed her. She dropped onto all fours and began to lap the blood from where it had pooled into crevices in the rock. It was cold but satisfying and she stayed at her task until the only blood left had soaked into the dirt and congealed on the rock and her tongue was crusted with mud.

She stood, wiped the mess from her lips with the back of her hand and sniffed at the air that still tingled with remnants of power. She took a few tentative steps and her feet stuck to the floor. A glance showed her body painted with drying blood and other fluids. She disliked being sticky. Her eyes scanned the room until they found the small pool in the back. Without hesitation she walked into it. Her mind registered that it was cold but her skin was far colder. The water tingled, connected with her.

When the water touched her skin she understood, without quite knowing how, that the pool had been there for a long time. Within the currents she felt the subtle fluctuations of power that had taken place in this room over the centuries. The stronger ripples pressed against her, washed the muck from her skin. She bent her knees and submerged herself.

As she worked her fingers through the matted tangles of her

hair she opened her eyes and saw black rock broken by shadows and crevices. Nothing special here except the currents, which felt like little pinching fingers as they picked at her. She stood again and looked down. Her skin was clean and seemed to glow with a soft, white light.

As she left the pool her eyes trailed upwards. There was a metal grate sunk high up into the opposite wall. When she stood beneath it she heard murmuring voices. She couldn't make out what was being said but the words were of no interest to her. Flowing from that vent was the intoxicating, musky scent of fear.

She breathed it in. She stayed beneath the grate, swaying as the hunger paced like a starving animal in her stomach. And beneath the wondrous scents and the cacophony of emotions flowing through that grate she heard a voice in her head, soft but growing stronger, pleading for mercy, over and over and over.

63 Adam waited in the empty lounge, which was the part of the Palace that had once served as the nave of the church. He had hidden himself there after hearing that agonizing scream down in the cells and he had not moved since. Now he waited. At first he waited for the virus to come and his thoughts ran so dark and riddled with guilt that at times he would have welcomed it. When sunrise marked the second day of the Festival he started to let himself hope. Then midday came and went and nothing at all happened and he knew that they had succeeded. They had survived. Their plan had worked.

Mere survival could not lessen his tension. Instead it turned his thoughts to Iliana. He was not known for his patience and he had already counted the tiny golden stars on the ceiling, estimating where the colors were obscured by centuries of smoke. It reminded him of Iliana. As a child she used to spend much of her time staring at this ceiling with wide blue eyes, her lips mumbling the numbers as she counted. He would sometimes find her in the morning, splayed across a couch or on the floor behind the furniture, sound asleep. She never did count them all.

Lying on his back on one of the many plush couches, he turned his eyes upward and tilted his head back to see the enormous statue of the three phases of man, its arms stretched outward, beckoning to him. Adam snorted as he wondered which phase the Colonists would be entering once Iliana spoke with them. Then he wondered if Iliana would be able to speak at all.

He thought about the scream. He thought about what could have happened to make her scream like that. And then he couldn't get it out of his head. He closed his eyes and tried to concentrate on anything else and at long last exhaustion overtook him.

"Adam!"

He sat up. He had fallen asleep but it seemed like only a moment had passed. He looked up to see the two priests coming toward him through the sea of brightly colored divans.

"Adam," the tall one said once they reached him. They were both out of breath. "It is time."

"Time for what?" he asked.

"Time for you to go and collect Iliana from the room."

Adam shook his head, thinking that perhaps he was delirious. "What? It can't be time yet."

"It is evening. It is time."

Adam rubbed his face to wake it up. He had slept for longer than he thought. "I didn't realize…"

"You must go retrieve her."

"Why me?" he asked as fear gripped his heart with icy fingers. There was nothing he wanted to do less than to be the first person to open that door. "You should go get her. You're the high priests."

"We can't," she shorter one said.

"Yes, you can. You're just afraid," Adam said. And when they didn't contradict him he became angry. "What if it didn't work? What if she's dead? What if she's mad? She is my sister. I don't want to see her like that."

"All the more reason for you to be the one. She knows you. She trusts you."

"Not anymore," he said, thinking of the way she looked at him when she was cornered in her room before the ceremony.

"It won't matter."

"What do you know about it?"

"The rituals are quite clear on this. The first face she sees should be a familiar one. It makes the transition easier."

"Then why not the Governor?"

"Governor Drake is in his office with the doors locked. He does not respond to any attempts to get in. We cannot wait for him."

Adam looked back and forth between to two priests. Their eyes were so full of fear that Adam almost laughed. At another time, perhaps, he would have taken pleasure in their outright terror but not now. Not when he knew that the same anxiety reflected in his eyes as well.

"Fine," he said. "What do I need to bring?"

The short priest handed Adam a small key, a thick, dark blue blanket and a small flashlight as the tall one explained. "Here's the key. The magic extinguishes the torches in the room so you'll need some light to find her. She'll be naked and probably covered in gore." Adam flinched. "You can cover her with this blanket until you can get her upstairs and into a bath."

"Am I to bathe her as well?"

The tall priest nodded. "Those who survived the Transformation in the past needed help. We just want you to be prepared."

"What if she didn't survive?"

"Then leave her be and come to us."

"Anything else?"

"That is all."

"Tell the Governor that I am going to collect her and take her to her room. Once she is settled I will come and get him, so tell him to be ready. Yell it through his door if you have to."

"We will. Thank you," the small priest said and they both hurried out of the room as if they were afraid that he might change his mind and make them go along. But if Adam had to do this he didn't want an audience just in case things went wrong. Just in case.

He took the supplies and started down the sloped hallway into the basement. The closer he got to that room the harder he had to work to keep his breathing steady, keep his legs from buckling. As he walked he chastised himself for giving in to emotion. He had been waiting for this for so long and now he was afraid to see the outcome of a century of planning. He told himself it made no sense. He should be excited. Instead he was terrified.

When he reached the door he placed the key into the lock and then paused as reality caught up with him. What would he see? Would Iliana even be recognizable? Would he have to break the news of Iliana's death to the Governor? He had given up his mother, then his sister to this ancient magic and if it hadn't worked, if Iliana were dead in that room, Adam didn't know what he would do. Although if that was the case he entertained thoughts of tearing apart every member of the Church Congress by hand and sending them back to Afet's Wall in pieces.

Adam shook his head to dislodge the bloody thoughts, took a deep breath and turned the key. The lock slid back with a muffled click and Adam worked the heavy door open. He flicked on the flashlight in preparation for darkness but it was unnecessary. All four torches burned in their sconces, just as they had when the door was first closed.

Confused, Adam stepped into the room. To his right lay the box. The lid was down and it felt dead and empty and cold. Remnants of power that had been confined there coasted on the air currents and pinched and poked his cheeks as if tasting him. To the left, where Iliana had been, the chains and manacles were broken and lay in a tangled heap against the wall. The floor was sticky beneath his shoes and he noticed some dark blood glistening in crevices on the floor and on the walls, but most of it had congealed into the layers beneath it.

The thick aroma of blood unnerved him. It clung to his face, clogged his nose and coated the inside of his mouth. He would have gagged but the chill in the air kept the stench from being overwhelming. He hugged himself and couldn't decide whether to be worried or pleased about Iliana's disappearance. He found himself wondering if she had somehow escaped and was surprised at the pleasure he took from that thought, just the smallest fire of hope springing out of the dead embers in his soul.

Adam ventured farther into the room. He passed the blood and saw the pool like a black mirror reflecting the torchlight. Iliana was not there, either. He turned around, prepared to run from the room and deliver this disturbing news to the Governor, and then froze.

Iliana stood with her back to him, naked, her skin shimmering in the firelight as if it was wet. At the sight of her he realized that the power that pierced his body like frozen arrows belonged to her.

His foot shuffled against the floor and though she didn't move, not even to breathe, he knew she had heard him. The frigid power caressed him, enveloped his body like a winter wind and then released him. His head buzzed and his lips went numb.

"We can hear them," she said without looking at him. Her voice filled the room and seemed to be made of several, harmonious voices at once. It filled his head with clouds and his mind with images of blood. It made him crave his own death at her hands. He shivered at the unwelcome thoughts and shook his head to dislodge them. Some of the clouds parted and he found his voice.

"Iliana?" he asked. He wondered at her use of the word "we" when he could not hear anything coming from the grate. It unnerved him.

"Is that our name?" she asked. Adam felt that she was not asking him so he did not answer. "Yes," she said after a moment. "We are Iliana." She looked back at the grate. "And someone in there is asking us to be merciful."

She turned then and when she set her eyes on Adam the power surged forward to engulf him and he stumbled backwards and landed hard on the uneven floor, his fingertips brushing the icy water of the pool. Without makeup, without the exotic hairstyles, without the exquisite gowns, she was magnificent. Her lips were the perfect color of pale pink rose petals. Her eyes had become vast black lakes deep enough to drown in, without irises, without whites. The black of her hair caught and reflected the firelight like a thousand tiny torches framing her face.

Adam stumbled to his feet and dried his hand on his pants. "Iliana," he said. Then he remembered why he was there. "We have to go."

She blinked twice over those blank, alien eyes. "Who are you?"

"I'm your brother, Adam."

She frowned and appeared deep in thought. "You belong to her."

318

"What?" asked Adam. He feared for a moment that madness had taken her but she didn't appear insane and he had a duty to do.

He unfolded the blanket, approached Iliana and placed it across her shoulders. His hand brushed bare shoulder and at once he felt her body relax as if he had flipped a switch. Something flowed back into her, filled her up. when that happened the power ebbed and Adam took a deep breath for the first time since entering the room.

"Adam?" she asked. She blinked up at him as if waking from a trance. She took his hand.

The coldness had left her voice, but this close Adam could see that her teeth seemed sharper than before and the hand that grasped his had nails like knives that bit into his skin almost hard enough to draw blood. Right then all he knew was that he didn't want to bleed there, alone with her. The coldness still seemed too close to the surface, the animal he saw caged in her eyes waited for freedom. Though he hated to admit it, she scared him a little.

"Yes?" he asked.

"Take me out of here."

"Of course," Adam replied and sighed in relief. As he led her toward the door she leaned on him as though her legs did not want to work. "I'll take you to your cell. Drake will want to see you." Her hand brushed the back of his neck and it was ice cold. Adam shivered and led her out of the room. He pretended not to see the wistful glance she threw over her shoulder toward the grate and whatever sounds she had heard coming out of it.

The walk back to her cell was uneventful. Most of the city's residents lay spent in each other's arms. That night marked the end of the formal parts of the Festival of Semiveh and the beginning of the after-party. None of them knew that the world they would be emerging into had changed overnight. But he did. And now that he knew Iliana was all right, at least on the surface, he felt some of the old excitement returning.

Everything had gone according to plan and he couldn't wait to share the information with Drake. It was time for the next stage but here they had to be careful once again because none of them knew how it would turn out. No one had ever made it this far before.

Adam thought of the Colonists in the cell below them and dreaded the moment when Iliana met Cole once more face to face. He wanted to warn her, to prepare her so that she could steel herself against any emotion that might rear its head. He did not know how she would react and they could not afford to show weakness in front of the prisoners.

He started to say something but when he looked at her blank face and saw no warmth, no reflection of his sister, he just sighed and continued to walk in silence beside this woman who felt like a stranger in his arms.

64

Adam took her to her cell and instructed her to get dressed because Governor Drake would be in to see her soon. Then he left without saying goodbye. He seemed distracted. She could sense that she made him nervous. When they had passed the guards in the hallway they had seemed at times transfixed by her and at others afraid to look at her. Those posted outside her cell even now exchanged fearful glances and whispers. She could hear their hushed voices through the doors.

Her room felt alien. She couldn't imagine that she had ever lived there and felt as though she was visiting a place she had only seen in pictures. When Adam came to get her she had sensed what he wanted. He wanted his sister. So she took her cues from him and tried to become the sister. But now that she was alone with no role to play she was once again a blank slate, an empty vessel. It was unsettling, at best, though she didn't understand why.

She walked into the outer cell and saw it with new eyes. The painting of the nude woman on the ceiling appeared flawless but Iliana could see cracks in the plaster, crossing her body, her face, marring the perfection of the figure. There were no lights in her cell but the moonlight that seeped in through the high windows showed the furniture, the cushions in the pit, the tapestries along the walls. Everything seemed foreign and wrong, threadbare and dirty. Even the air tasted strange, stale and dry.

The sense that she had lost something that she couldn't name drove her back into the bedroom but found no comfort there. Her new eyes picked out the cobwebs. Her new nose rebelled against the mingling scents of stale perfume, sweat and dust. And just standing amid the pillows and baubles that were supposed to mean something to her but didn't, filled her with rage.

She let the blanket fall from her shoulders and swept the bottles and trinkets from the dresser with both hands. The glass shattering on the floor satisfied some deep urge inside of her and she paused to study the carnage. The cracked and broken crystal lay in a heap, glistening like shards of bloody bone poking out of a body.

A moment later the aroma of her spilled perfumes and scented oils mingled and assaulted her nostrils. The combined stench was much worse fresh than it had been stale. So she stopped breathing. For several minutes she stood in the middle of the room and didn't breathe. And she did not grow weak or faint or lightheaded. Her body no longer needed that function. Her lungs now moved air out of habit alone.

Her mind rebelled against this new reality. This was not possible. If she wasn't breathing then she must be dead. And if she were dead then how was she standing in this foreign room that was supposed to be hers?

She was filled with the sudden need to connect with something. She needed to destroy and hurt, needed to feel real. She used a candlestick to smash the mirror above the dresser and as the glass fell to the floor she stepped on it and cut open her bare feet but she didn't feel it. She attacked the bed, ripping the curtains from the frame and tossing them aside. The pillows she tore apart at the seams until tiny brown feathers spilled across the floor like dirty snowfall and floated about her, unmelting snowflakes to rest in her eyelashes, caress her cheeks. With bare hands she split the mattress wide open and then tipped the chest of drawers onto its side.

She stopped. The room was ruined. Blankets and bottles lay everywhere and her razor-like fingernails had scarred the furniture with deep grooves. She had torn through the room like a force of nature but she wasn't even out of breath. She stood at the center of the storm, calm amid the chaos, and surveyed the devastation, wondering what had happened to her.

As she looked at the shattered possessions of her former

life her memory snapped back into place. Her head exploded in agony, splintering her vision. She crumpled to the floor as an echo of the agony she had felt at the hands of the little girl passed through her. In response her new power flared to life. It caused the candles in the outer cell to burst into flame. It disturbed the mess she had made and picked up some of the spilled feathers and floated them around the room. The power cresting within her lessened the pain and she let it spill uncontrolled out of her skin until the walls began to vibrate.

The strange reflection in the shattered mirror caught her attention. Her skin shimmered in waves moved by unseen currents and her black eyes appeared fathomless. Like a distant memory seen through foggy glass she could remember what she had looked like in her previous life and now she was both mesmerized and appalled by the creature she had become.

Tears filled her eyes and traced crimson lines down her cheeks as her body was consumed by emotions she didn't understand. She wanted to sob, to cry out, but she didn't need to breathe to do so and that frightened her into silence. Turning away from the hateful mirror, she slunk to the far corner of the room. She slid down the wall and hugged her knees, her eyes shut tight as if by blocking out the room she could make it all go away.

Time passed. She didn't know how much. And then she heard a soft knock and a familiar voice.

"Iliana?" Drake's voice was uncertain.

She peeked through the curtain of her tangled black hair to see the Governor standing in the doorway. She watched as his eyes left her huddled form to take in the destruction.

"What happened?" he asked.

At the sound of his voice she felt the power spike once more within her rebellious body, overwhelming her senses with breathtaking speed. Drake must have felt it, too, because he shivered and turned his attention back to her.

Standing as he did, watching her with terrified eyes, he looked like nothing more than a feeble old man. She couldn't believe that she had once depended upon him so for so long. She watched his face brighten as he realized that she was the source of the prickling energy that filled the room like frigid wind.

"Iliana, what happened?" he asked again. "Adam told me that it had worked but now… You've destroyed everything." She looked up at him and as the hair slid from her face he gasped.

"You're magnificent," he breathed.

"I'm dead," she answered. Her monotone voice once again sounded like many voices in harmony. Drake seemed taken aback at first and struggled to get himself back under control.

"Of course you're not dead, my dear," he reasoned. "You're talking. You can move. You're not dead, just confused."

"I'm not dead?" she asked. His patronizing tone disgusted her and she wanted him to know just how much.

He hesitated then answered, "Of course not."

"Then why am I so cold?" She shivered a little and clutched her legs, all the while keeping her wide eyes trained on him. She could smell his fear. She could see his age and exhaustion like a muddy gray aura surrounding his body, preceding his every movement. He was wondering whether or not he should leave and if he did, should he run? Beneath that she felt the pangs in his chest as he recalled Gabriella after the change. She felt his concern for her but she was not moved. It was too late for that.

"You must cover up then." He withdrew a thick blanket from the mess, shook it free of debris and held it out to her.

"Can you help me?" she asked, her voice feeble. "I'm just too cold to move." Her teeth began to chatter.

Drake hesitated and she knew he was weighing his options, trying to decide if she was dangerous. But in the end fatherly instinct overcame fear and he came forward and draped the blanket over her shoulders. When he pulled away she grabbed his wrist and held it fast. As confusion danced across his wrinkled face she stared hard into his eyes.

Her head was full of voices vying for supremacy. Finally one of them came out in a hiss. "See what you have made us."

Drake tried to get his hand out of her grasp but she was stronger. He began to tremble. She pushed her magic into him through the place where their skin touched and he whimpered.

He looked into her eyes and a moment later his knees buckled and hit the floor with a loud crack. She didn't flinch at the sound, not even when his eyes swam with tears and begged for mercy. She could not grant him that.

With their eyes locked Iliana found Drake's mind pliable, ready to give up its secrets. She knew that he was going to retire after this affair with the Church and she knew it was because of her. She also knew that this was his fault, knew that he had orchestrated this from the moment of her birth. He had told her a lifetime of lies but none of that mattered anymore. She knew what she had to do.

The magic rode her anger and she injected more and more of it into Drake through their connected hands. He struggled. His eyes were wide, his lips parted and mute but he could not move to save himself. She felt his heart racing and nearing collapse as he sat on his knees before her, unable to look away, captured and drowning in her eyes like black whirlpools.

Hunger rose on the waves of power. She whispered, "Feel how cold you have made us." Drake trembled so much she felt the tremors moving up her arm. "Feel how you have killed us."

With those words she let him see the emptiness yawning within her, the confusion of being a walking corpse. His heart stuttered under the vision and undid him. There was a sudden tension in her top jaw, followed by release. She ran her tongue over her teeth and discovered that they had become like fangs. Instinct drove her to lift Drake's wrist to her open mouth and bite. She had no need for the metal tipped thumb now.

Her fingernails sliced ribbons of blood into his forearms as she held him still. He winced and she sighed as blood, sweet as candy and more satisfying than anything she had ever known, filled her mouth. As she suckled from his arm her eyes drank in his face. She saw the light fade from his eyes just before they fluttered and closed. And when his heart made its final, shuddering beat hers began to beat anew.

With a jolt she released Drake's wrist and fell backward against the wall. Her spine arched, her limbs stiffened and her muscles twitched beneath her skin. Her hands clenched at the air, grasping in vain for something to hold on to as a tide of agony pulled her under once again. Her eyes were blinded by the pain, her mind erased. It seemed as though it would never end. She wished to die. And then it stopped.

Something had changed.

She waited, not breathing, still, until the last echoes of pain receded. When her chest began to burn she drew a tremulous breath. Then another. And another. She felt the blood pumping in her veins like never before, her heartbeat at the tip of each finger like her own personal percussion. Drake's blood had reanimated her body and his memories had given her a purpose. She existed to bring the reign of the Church to an end, to destroy the tyrannous Congress and usher in a new era. Drake's memories flashed in her mind and she felt anger and hatred well up from within, warming her almost as well as the blood, flushing her pale skin.

She stood up and glanced at Drake's body. His face looked peaceful, or perhaps resigned, and she felt no guilt over his death. She strode to the closet naked, no longer cold, and chose an ornate, sleeveless white gown. As she dressed she caught another glimpse of herself in the broken mirror and saw what the blood and the power had done to her physical body. Her bottomless eyes now pulsed with alternating flecks of red and violet. Her lips were full and scarlet. Her skin had become translucent and she could see the network of veins crossing beneath her flesh like a roadmap. It was no longer frightening or disorienting. She was home within this body, no longer Iliana but at least something close. She finished dressing and left the bedroom just as Adam entered.

His face transformed from concern to terror as he looked at the thing she had become. She just blinked at him. She recognized him as her brother and she knew of his part in the plot that had changed her. She waited for the rage to take control of her again, waited to desire his death as she had Drake's but nothing happened. She watched his face fall as his eyes moved from her face to the floor behind her where Drake lay on his back amid the debris of her former life.

Without a word he pushed past her in the doorway and knelt beside Drake. He grazed the ragged wound in the old man's wrist with his fingertips. She saw this and felt nothing except pleasure at the fear that radiated from Adam like a lullaby.

Adam took a shuddering breath, turned toward her and asked, "Iliana, what have you done?" Tears were poised on his eyelashes and his face was hard as stone, as if an artist had made a sculpture of the concepts of Rage and Pain and set it atop Adam's body.

"He killed us. We killed him." Then she ran her tongue over the four new, sharp teeth in her top jaw and watched Adam shudder, felt his fear rise. She knew she should feel sad. She knew that Drake's death should be painful for her. She knew that she should be angry with Adam for his part in her abduction and Transformation. She should be afraid of herself, of her actions. But she felt nothing. Pain and fear and guilt could not touch her anymore. She watched Adam weigh his options in silence and then saw his face fall when he realized that he could not fight her and hope to win.

As that realization hit his face she said, "You cannot harm me anymore. You wanted to be king and queen of this new world and here is your chance. Now you are Governor."

Adam stood up and she could almost see the connections forming in his head. She had just given him the thing he had always wanted. Never mind that he would have been given the title anyway since Drake had planned to retire soon after this was over. She did not tell this to Adam. He didn't need to know.

"Come," she said and held out her hand. Adam hesitated but then accepted it. At the moment of contact she saw in her mind a windowless room with bars, packed with bodies praying, crying, arguing and stewing in their own fear.

She smiled as Adam's knowledge washed over her. "We want to see them."

Adam spoke over the lump in his throat. "I'm to escort you to the first ballroom."

He led her out of the room. When they passed the guards in the hallway the men all pressed their backs against the wall as if they were afraid to touch her in any way. She met no one's eyes but did nothing to disguise the cold void gaping within her, or the trickle of power seeping from her skin. The guards fell into step behind them like shadows but she felt their distress like a prickling energy that flowed ahead of them and buoyed her down the hallway.

65

"Come on now. It's time to go."

Cole raised his head at this new voice. For four days he had lived with the droning voices murmuring prayers and pleas and the thick odor of unwashed flesh and he had managed to tune it all out. The time had been broken by Adam's visit and by the guards who came to claim Yourian's body, mercifully before it began to stink.

And now this.

Cole used the wall to push himself to his feet and fought the wave of dizziness that threatened to send him back to the floor. He hadn't eaten since his trip back to Afet's Wall and too much movement caused his head to swim. Looking around he saw that his fellow prisoners were also standing up, fear bright on their dirty faces.

Several guards stood around the cage and each one carried a dagger or a club. Not one weapon was pointed at the prisoners but all were at the ready. One of the guards, a stocky man with more gold badges on his chest then the others, came forward and unlocked the door. No one moved. No one spoke. They stayed that way for so long that Cole grew tired of waiting.

He approached the door and asked, "Where are we going?"

The guard studied his face and for a moment Cole worried that he would be struck down for daring to speak. After several tense moments the guard answered. "We are to take you to Drake's Hall to be sentenced." A whimper went up behind him but Cole ignored it as the guard continued. "But first, to the showers. You all reek and I assure you, you do not want to offend the judge. Now, move."

Cole led the way and the others soon followed. No one

had to be hurt or forced to follow and for that Cole was grateful. The guards led them into a hallway that sloped upward and then turned left into a room that smelled of old sweat and harsh detergent. There they were forced to strip naked and bathe in an underground lake that took up the entire back end of the cavernous room. Once again Cole led the way. He took off his clothes and entered the water without hesitation. Modesty had no purpose here, considering that they had been reduced to nothing more than cattle waiting to be slaughtered.

The waist-high water was frigid and his skin recoiled. He kept thinking that it would get warmer but it seemed the longer he stayed the colder it got. He dunked his head and resurfaced, biting his cheek to keep his teeth from chattering as he slicked back his hair and rubbed at his face. He kept his back to the others to discourage conversation and so was surprised when someone tapped him on the shoulder.

"Don't turn around," Father Deven said.

Cole glanced up to see the guards standing around the rim of the lake. The exit was blocked by three of the largest men so no one was paying much attention to the prisoners. In fact they seemed rather bored with their duty.

"What?" Cole asked and then splashed some water on his face for show. He was shivering already and not feeling up to having a conversation.

"You're the only one who can help us now, Cole."

"And how am I supposed to do that?" Their words were hidden beneath the sounds of bathing and Cole fought the urge to raise his voice.

"You know them by name. You can fight for us. You can argue for diplomacy. You can—"

"I can do nothing." Cole thought of Iliana alone and scared and suppressed the thought of whatever could have made her scream. He had failed her. Now he couldn't make himself care about anything else.

The voice behind him turned angry. "But you have to save us, Cole. You're one of us." Deven's desperation tugged at Cole's sympathy but it wasn't enough to make him act.

"I don't have to do anything," he said. "Leave me alone."

Cole felt Deven move away and finished rubbing the filth from his body. He emerged from the water first and was handed a pair of loose black pants and a black shirt. He dressed in silence, staring at the floor, but as blank as he tried to make his mind and his face his hands shook when he fastened the buttons on the shirt.

The others emerged from the pool one by one, unable to draw out their bathing any longer and likely suffering from mild hypothermia. Cole stood to one side with his hands clasped before him, staring at his feet. No one tried to speak to him again. Cole continued to watch his feet as the guards led them up a long tunnel into the main floor of the Palace. He noticed when the sandstone floor became gray slate and knew that they had entered the foyer of the Palace. When the tile became plain, polished black stone Cole knew they had passed into a hallway.

A door opened and they were herded into a room with floors of white marble. He had decided to remain mute and stoic throughout the ordeal no matter what happened but when the priests around him gasped he forgot his own rules and looked up. The walls were white with gold embellishments and several beveled mirrors worked into the plaster. The vaulted ceiling was painted the brilliant blue of the morning sky just after dawn, flanked by clouds painted pink and gold. Brilliant light came from two enormous electric chandeliers that dripped with heavy crystal and several hidden sconces along the walls that offered up their light in distinct cones toward the ceiling. Guards dressed in slate gray stood at even intervals along the walls and a group of about 13 Natives sat behind a short partition along the wall opposite.

"Bring them to us."

66 Cole's head snapped toward the front of the room to see Iliana perched like a queen on a plush, black chair. Cole blinked hard and then stared. Since hearing Iliana's scream he had imagined how she would look the next time he saw her a thousand times but he had never imagined this. She radiated light. Her hair seemed like liquid night pouring over her shoulders, a stark contrast against her sleeveless white gown. Her skin had always been flawless, her face had always been striking, but now she seemed to glow with her own light. She had always been beautiful, now she was exquisite. Cole was entranced and he allowed himself to feel relief that she was alive and, as far as he could see, well.

Adam stood at Iliana's right shoulder. He wore a guard's formal uniform but with gold buttons and accents. His left hand rested on the back of Iliana's throne. He looked like he belonged there but for the first time since Cole met him Adam was not the one with all the power.

Iliana stood and walked down the steps toward them, so graceful that she seemed to float just above the floor. As she came closer Cole's relief started to fade. She looked like Iliana but she was not the same.

"You are to be judged," she said and Cole shivered. Her voice sounded like four or five voices speaking in harmony. He looked around and saw some of the others squirm with discomfort but not one of them looked away from her monstrous beauty.

Father Deven came forward to stand beside Cole, shot him a dirty look and said, "We can be judged only by our God. Who are you to think you can judge us?"

Iliana came to a stop in front of Father Deven. She was shorter than him but that didn't seem to matter for she was by far the more intimidating of the two, a fact which everyone but Father Deven seemed to understand. Her eyes sucked light from the room like black holes and even though she wasn't looking at him Cole felt himself falling into them. He couldn't imagine what Father Deven, who stood face to face with her, must have been feeling. Iliana reached out and touched the old priest's hand and he did not pull away as Cole had expected. If anything he seemed pleased by the contact, as if he viewed it as a precursor to something more pleasurable.

After a moment her crimson lips parted in a smile, revealing white teeth with four sharp fangs that hadn't been there before. When she spoke her voice fluttered in Cole's thoughts like a thousand wings beating inside his head, "I am Alpha and Omega, the beginning and the end."

Father Deven yanked his hand back as if she had burned it and backed away. The other priests followed suit, some of them shaking their heads as if her voice had filled their minds with unspeakable images. To a man they looked confused and terrified.

Iliana looked over the men with an expression of hunger, as if she were perusing a selection of the choicest desserts and wondering where to start. Then her eyes fell upon Cole and he met her vacant, hungry gaze with his own. They stared at each other in silence for a long time. When he saw no spark of her former self the emptiness within him yawned as wide as ever. She was gone.

A moment later recognition sprinted across her face, enlivening those bottomless eyes. "We know you," she said. Her face was curious but detached, the fangs hidden behind pursed lips.

"I knew you," he answered.

She smiled and reached up to touch him. He offered his hand, desperate to see anything on her face besides this strange, vacant curiosity. She ignored his hand and touched his cheek instead. When their skin touched he felt the invisible wall separating them evaporate like so much smoke.

"Father Cole," she said and he nodded. But even though

333

she knew his name there was no familiarity or warmth present in her face. She was like an immaculate copy of the woman he had known, an exact replica of a work of art devoid of the soul that had created it, without life. To see her like this broke his heart.

Cole's eyes grew moist as his hope died. Iliana was right in front of him and yet she was gone and that was something worth shedding a tear over. "Oh, Iliana," he sighed. "What have they done to you?"

"Let us show you." She cupped his face in her hands and he closed his eyes. She filled his mind with darkness. The memory of her pain wracked Cole's body until he was empty and hollow, then death came and filled him back up. Then he felt boundless hunger that tore his mind in two. But it wasn't his mind, it was hers.

He opened his eyes and took back his hand. When the contact broke he thought he saw a momentary flicker of sadness on her face but it soon faded beneath the cold façade of this new creature.

Cole wiped at his forehead where sweat had beaded. His mouth felt as though he had swallowed the desert, his stomach felt twisted. "I am so sorry," he said. He apologized not only for his inability to protect her, but also for the wrongs his people had perpetrated against the Natives and for her lost soul. She was dead.

Iliana did not acknowledge the apology. She took a step back to address all of the prisoners at once. "You have been brought here to make a decision."

Once again her voice contained such power the prisoners just stared, rapt and blank-faced. All except for Cole, who refused to let that voice draw him in. Still, he could feel it, could feel how his body wanted to respond, wanted to be seduced, so he dug his fingernails into his palms and focused on the pain. By the time she continued the voice was less soothing, her power less overwhelming.

"For too long you have expanded unchecked, killed our people without mercy and bled us dry. That will not happen again. Now it is you who must bleed.

"Here is the choice: you may choose to die here by my

hand. It can be done now, and with mercy, though you have shown none to my people. Or you can join us, let me drink from you and fill you with my power, and we will let you return to your precious Church where you will implement a new policy with regards to our people. You will declare us equals and you will no longer practice the systematic bleeding using my people for your pleasure."

Father Deven spoke up, blubbering with sudden, sickening enthusiasm for this plan. "Well, I believe I speak for all of us when I say that we choose to live and return home." A slight murmur went through the assembled priests.

But Iliana had shown Cole what the Transformation meant, injected the visions into his mind where he couldn't ignore them. He knew that it meant pain and blood and that the end result was a worthless half-life. He couldn't hold his tongue and watch them waddle blindly towards extinction.

"Father Deven, I don't think that you can speak for everyone. They don't understand what it means to agree." He turned to Iliana, who watched him with amused eyes, the way a cat would watch a mouse trying to escape. "Tell them what will happen. Tell them the truth."

"Your transformations will not be the same as mine, and you will not have the power that I now wield. But it is painful. It is beyond pain. It is agony such that you will be begging for death but afterward you will find peace. I can wash your mind and body clean of all toxic thoughts and bestow upon you a semblance of eternal life, for as long as I live so you, too, will thrive. Isn't that worth dying for?"

Again the murmurs and again Cole couldn't take it. These were men of God and at least some of them, Cole assumed, still had faith in the basic tenets of the Church. And those men were now being asked to give it all up. He wondered how many would rather die than become that which they hated.

"Wait," Cole said and all eyes turned toward him. "May I bargain with you?"

"Cole, what are you doing?" Father Deven said. He touched Cole's arm but Cole shrugged him off.

"Stop it, Cole," said Father Piotr. "It's not funny."

"What do you propose?" Iliana asked and the others fell silent.

"Their lives for mine. If you let them go I will undergo the Transformation and I will return to Afet's Wall as a liaison between the Church and the Natives."

Iliana blinked, still amused, as if she knew something Cole didn't. "You would do this?"

"Wait a minute," interrupted Father Serrano, who pushed himself toward the front of the crowd. "Don't bargain for our lives." Some of the others echoed his sentiment.

Cole turned to the crowd, incredulous. "What?"

"She is offering immortality, Cole, or something close enough." said Father Serrano. "Some of us are old men and, blasphemous as it may seem, the thought of our approaching deaths is not so appealing."

"Don't do us any favors," said Father Piotr.

Father Deven held up a hand and the arguments stopped. "You're not being as noble as you think you are. You're selfish, keeping this boon for yourself and leaving us to die."

Cole stared in shock at the men to whom he had devoted so much of his life. They hated the Natives almost as much as they loved their God. They had taught him to hate the Natives. And now they were willing to throw away their God for just a taste of immortality.

"We can make the decisions for ourselves and for our people. It is what they entrusted us to do."

"Do you understand what this means?" Cole asked.

"Of course we do," said Father Serrano. "A near-eternal life. How can that be bad?"

Cole sighed as the last bit of his illusions slipped away. Nothing in the Church was sacred anymore. Iliana had broken him of his belief in the purity of the Church and now he saw just how deep the corruption ran.

"Do what you want," Cole said. "I will not stop you."

"So, have you decided?" asked Iliana in that same powerful monotone.

Father Deven puffed out his chest and announced, "We have. We, the members of the Congress of the Church of Universal Truth, accept your offer of eternal life in exchange for a reversal of our policies regarding Native/Colonist relations."

"Very well." Iliana turned toward the waiting Council members, the guards and Adam, who remained standing beside Iliana's chair like a page, and announced, "They have accepted our offer. Should they go back on their word we will hunt them down and destroy them all."

At this some of the prisoners balked and started asking questions: "What will happen?" "Will we survive?" "How much will it hurt?" "Who goes first?"

Iliana held up her hand and an uneasy silence settled over them. "We have long known of your experiments on our people. And we knew of your plan to destroy us with a lethal virus. Know now that if your designs are deception you will die. For once you undergo the Transformation you will carry a fraction of my power within you and this will make you similar enough to us that should you release your virus it will kill you as well."

"What do you mean we will have a fraction of your power?" asked Father Deven. "Won't we be just like you? Or if not like you, then at least like the other Natives?"

"No. You will be something in-between, neither Colonist nor Native, and under my control." She did not give them time to process this information before announcing, "The bargain has been struck."

And then her voice became soft once more and she said, "Father Cole, come to me."

Cole looked up to find her still monstrously beautiful and his heart ached at the sight of her. He stepped forward and the guards stood aside to let him pass. He walked on unsteady legs out to the center of the room where Iliana waited. He felt uncomfortable speaking with her in front of all these witnesses. The forum was too public for the things he wanted to say.

Cole, she said without even a twitch of her scarlet lips. It took him a minute to realize that she was speaking in his mind.

He whispered, "What?"

You were a good friend to us. We are sorry that it has come to this.

Then stop it, he thought back at her. Let them go.

We can't do that. You know they would destroy us as soon as they went back. This is the only way.

But you said you didn't want to kill anyone. Her use of the multiple pronouns bothered him. He saw only one person looking out of her eyes at him and that person was a stranger.

The magic changed us, made us more, made us powerful. It is our duty to use that power for the greater good. Saving our people is the greater good.

But what of my people? Cole asked in anger. His hands balled into fists but his arms hung impotent at his sides. He could not lift a hand against her.

There are some who will fight against any edict that declares my people to be equals with yours. We are prepared for the coming rebellion. Your people will get what they deserve until we find a balance.

You don't have to do this.

It is judgment day. Your peers chose the Transformation to death but we sense reluctance in you. And since you have been a good friend we are offering you the choice alone. We cannot let you go because it would be a show of weakness that we cannot afford. So you have to decide on your own. Will you join us or are you ready to die for your cause?

Cole looked at Iliana and thought he saw the faintest hint of sadness there, though he could have been seeing his own reflection in her blank stare. Still, he swore that for a moment her face seemed softer and became the face Cole knew, the face he cared for. Even her voice in his head had changed. It was no longer a chorus and he allowed himself a moment to imagine living on as her companion. The thought was not unsatisfying.

Then he turned to look at the prisoners behind him. Father Deven and his favorites smiled and looked pleased with themselves while the rest of the priests wore their terror like masks. He imagined living forever with these men. He imagined the world with the same select few people in power for centuries and he knew that this was not a world he could live in.

He turned back to Iliana to find her face still riding that edge between aloofness and melancholy. But beneath that veneer of sadness he saw very little of the woman he had known. He felt no humanity within her. And that was because she had become the soulless creature he had been warned against. She was a walking corpse and should he choose to go with her he would be the same. To live forever without a soul, to be damned to an in-between existence, was too big a price to pay. Even though he railed against the Church's dogma he still believed in the fundamental teachings of his religion and this Transformation had broken several.

"I am so sorry," he said aloud, feeling the futility of words to convey what he felt, which was desolation. The weight of his decision hunched his shoulders as if he were holding up the world. "I can't do this."

Iliana's rigid face faltered as if she hadn't expected this decision but she recovered fast enough that he doubted anyone else would have noticed. She rested her cold hands on his upper arms. Then she leaned in, stood on tiptoe and kissed his forehead. Her lips were cool and her breath smelled of blood, tart and metallic. He wondered whose life she had already taken.

Iliana turned him around to face the prisoners. Cole felt numb. He saw nothing as Iliana pressed her body into his back and wrapped her left arm around his waist. Her hold on him was so tight that he couldn't have pulled away even if he'd wanted to.

With her right hand she reached around and curled her fingers in his hair, pulling his head to one side, opening him. He trembled as fear mounted and he started to question whether he had made the right decision. Iliana's breath tickled his throat and a blanket of goose bumps unfurled down his body. He noticed the other priests watching him with hungry eyes and so closed his against the sensation, embarrassed, terrified and excited. He was finally going to experience what everyone else already knew.

She pressed her lips to his throat with slow, languid kisses and Cole's body reacted like any man's. In the moment before she struck she leaned in and whispered in the voice Cole knew all too well. "I'm sorry, too, Cole."

And then she bit him and Cole cried out at the sudden, sharp pain. At first he felt only the sting and the burn of being entered by force and the pain toppled his reality. He leaned into Iliana as dizziness overtook him and she was strong enough to hold him up.

After a moment the pain faded, followed by a period of intense sensation. Cole surrendered to it. He felt her lips, the suction of her mouth and the flick of her tongue against the wound working to keep it open. He felt his blood as it raced through his veins, speeding toward her hungry mouth as if eager to go. His fingers started to tingle. His legs became weak and useless.

With his right hand Cole touched the arm that bound his waist and it burned against his skin. With his left hand he touched Iliana's face. Beneath his fingers he felt her jaw working. His body had never felt so alive, so full of energy and unbridled sensation. Every organ seemed a tactile organ. He forgot where he was as he lost himself within her. And once he did his mind's eye began to see things.

He saw Father Tanaka, younger and thinner, teaching a toddling Cole to ride a bicycle. He relived his first communion and the dreams he had thought were divine visions as a child. Then came the cigarettes and the drinking, the teenage years, the girls, his hands roving over soft flesh, his mouth kissing a new pair of lips almost every night. Then came the night of his second calling, when he swore the statues had spoken to him and his terrified date had bolted naked from the altar. Then the forlorn faces in the cell below the Capitol. Then his breakdown.

His first meeting with Iliana was one of the brightest memories, followed by the fierce happiness he had felt when Iliana came to him after being caught in the library. He learned from her, taught her and befriended her. And then the last time he had seen her, when he had come so close to having what he had always been curious about. Then this.

Everything started slowing down in his body as it flowed toward some strange, ephemeral endpoint. He had the dizzying sensation of being in two places at once. Part of him felt this incredible euphoria and peace that filled him until he thought he would explode. The rest of him knew that he was dying in Iliana's arms.

And still she drank until even this duplicity faded and death crashed into his body like a wave of darkness against the shore of his excited flesh. The darkness spilled over him and through him. The euphoria remained like an echo but now Cole saw another side of the experience. The darkness in his mind began to rise and in that void he felt the thing that Iliana had become. Just as she had shuffled through his thoughts he could now see inside of her and what he saw terrified him.

At first Cole fought against that terrible nothingness by pushing himself further into Iliana, as if to press the emptiness out of existence with his own life. But because the void had injected itself into him he had nowhere to hide. So he gave up and embraced it, gathered it within himself and held onto it.

Cole tried to move, tried to pull away from Iliana but his limbs just twitched like a broken doll. His heart felt like it was racing so fast it would burn a hole through his chest but he knew that it was beating slowly, too slowly to sustain him.

And the infinite space between two heartbeats Cole changed his mind. Then the void yawned before his sightless eyes he felt Iliana's mouth release him. A shudder of pleasure tore through his body and brought him back from the brink but the reprieve was short-lived. Blood continued to seep from the wound on his throat, tickling his skin as it ran into his collar, burning as it went. He felt so cold, so full of Iliana's darkness that he started to cry, and he mourned her with his death. As the tears escaped his eyes he felt Iliana wipe them away, her fingers like the brush of a summer wind. He had become the cold one and she was the fire against which he wished he could warm himself.

From far away he heard her telling him not to fight it, telling him to relax, to let go. The timbre and cadence of her voice soothed him and his consciousness slipped. It was only for a moment but it was enough. He tumbled into the void with her name on his lips and peace in his heart.

67 Iliana lowered Cole's body to the floor, cradling his head all the way down. She looked at his face, so pale and peaceful, and tried to come to terms with him never opening his eyes again. She brushed still damp hair from his forehead, touched his cheek and realized that she didn't want him to die. She felt as though there were two very distinct people within her: one was the creature of cold and darkness and the other was filled with light and warmth and wanted nothing more than to hear Cole's voice again. It was not as drastic as the first Transformation but something had changed within her.

Moments earlier she had only wanted him to make a choice. Then she had only wanted to give him the pleasure he had denied himself in her arms. As he fought to live she had wanted only to give him a peaceful death. And now he was dead and she would have given anything for him to be alive.

That desire alone brought knowledge to the surface and she knew in an instant how to bring him back. The power rose to her lips unbidden until she felt her head would catch fire. She gathered his hands and pressed her lips to them, breathing the power into each of his palms. Then she leaned over him and pressed her lips to his forehead and she felt something deep within him respond, wake up.

She brought her lips lower for the final step to bring him back to her but before she could consummate the reanimation with a kiss she felt a hand on her shoulder and it startled her back to reality. Her concentration shattered and she looked up to see Adam standing beside her, shaking his head. The air surged with power so thick she could almost see it.

"What are you doing?" Adam asked. His voice was so low she doubted anyone else could hear.

"I'm bringing him back."

"You cannot do this."

He was right. She looked back at Cole and had to fight the wave of emotion that swept through her at the thought of him dead. This was something she hadn't anticipated. Emotions were supposed to be a thing of the past, a trivial piece of her previous life. But at that moment she felt a pain that defied words.

"But I want him back," she whispered.

"If he chose this then you must honor his decision."

"But…"

"Iliana, it was his choice to make."

Iliana sat back on her heels and closed her eyes. She knew Adam was right. She knew she shouldn't bring him back but along with his blood Cole had given her something else: his life, his warmth, his humanity. She doubted he had done it on purpose but now she had desires that went far deeper than those for blood and power and she didn't know what to do with them. She wanted his friendship back. She wanted his voice and his laugh, even his derision. She felt tears rising and didn't know how to fight the grief that swelled within her chest as if her heart was about to explode.

Adam knelt beside her and blocked her crumbling face from the curious eyes of those assembled. He took her hands and said, "There will be time for grief later, I promise you. I do not know what he did to you, how he brought you back, but you have to set it aside because you have a group of enemies watching your every move and a Council that will be searching for any sign of weakness, for any excuse not to follow your lead. You must be strong. You must not give them any reason to doubt you or this is all for nothing."

The darkness she had felt after the Transformation was nothing compared to the despair she felt at Cole's death but Adam was right. She could not let it get in the way. Iliana nodded and swallowed hard against the lump in her throat. Adam cupped her face in his hands and made a show of kissing her forehead while with his thumbs he wiped the tears from her cheeks.

When she looked presentable once more he took her hand and helped her to her feet. She turned toward the waiting priests, most of who were no longer filled with excitement. The eyes that looked back at her were wide, the faces confused and frightened. They all seemed to be waiting for her to speak but when she opened her mouth her voice couldn't get past the grief.

Adam sensed this and took the reins. He gestured to Cole, his body a dark stain against the pale marble floor. "Your colleague chose a quick death to eternal life. When this is all said and done you might wish you had done the same."

The prisoners shuffled their feet and as Iliana looked at them she recovered enough to continue. She found strength in anger. Anger made it so simple. She blamed the priests for Cole's demise and she wanted them to suffer for it. She held her head high, took in the entire group and arranged her face into a blank mask.

In anger she found the power, embraced it and forced it from her lungs in that strange, multiple voice, "Let the war begin."

About the Author

Like most independent authors, Selena Jones has a nine-to-five job. She just works hers from 6am to 5pm. This gives her Mondays off, which may or may not make her a better person, since everyone knows that working on Mondays is evil.

She spends Mondays and other slivers of free time with her family, usually in a Star Wars-related activity. She also plays ukulele, bakes delicious treats (to the delight of her extended family), practices yoga and runs the occasional half-marathon. Oh, and she writes, too. She sometimes even finds time to tweet at @ThatSelenaJones and invites readers to visit her website at www.selenawrotethis.com.

She also hates writing bios and talking about herself in third person so she outsourced this to some friends.

Other works by Selena Jones include the novel *Every Day is Like Doomsday*, and the novellas *A Creation* and *A Garden*.

www.ingramcontent.com/pod-product-compliance
Lightning Source LLC
Chambersburg PA
CBHW021529250626
47154CB00006BA/2039